FREESTYLE

ACADEMY OF STARDOM - BOOK ONE

BEA PAIGE

For the dancer in all of us and for the kids who dare to dream.
This one's for you.

Bea Paige
xoxo

"We are all in the gutter, but some of us are looking at the stars."
— **Oscar Wilde.**

NOTE TO READERS

Dear Readers,

Whilst this book is most definitely about dance, it's also about friendship, hardship, gang culture and the darker side of life. For Pen, dance is her escape, her outlet. It's also mine too, though I won't profess to being the greatest dancer, just appreciative of it. I love art in all its forms and three of my series include artists in one form or another.

I'm also British. There are words throughout this book that are spelled differently to what you might be used to, and some slang you might be confused by. Hopefully you'll enjoy those differences and learn some Brit slang too!

Lastly, I hope you enjoy this book. As Martha Graham once said: *"Nobody cares if you can't dance well. Just get up and dance. Great dancers are great because of their passion."*

Be passionate about what you love. That's a motto I live by and most definitely apply to my writing.

Much love, Bea x

PLAYLIST

The theme song for this book has to be **_Gangsta_** by **Kehlani**. I love a book playlist, and had loads of fun finding songs for this book.

Other favourites are:
Boys by Lizzo
Da Rockwilder by Method Man
X Gon' Give to Ya by DMX
Yummy by Justin Bieber
Work Song by Hozier
In Da Club by 50 Cent
Listen to the full _Freestyle_ playlist on Spotify.

PROLOGUE

Zayn

WE'RE THE BREAKERS.

We're friends. A crew. A fucking team.

Me, York, Xeno, Dax.

Inseparable.

We all loved the same girl.

See a Penny, pick it up, all day long you'll have good luck.

She was ours. Our Pen. Our shiny gold coin, and aside from dance, the only other bright thing in the pile of stinking shit that was our lives.

She was our first, our last, our everything.

Not anymore.

It's been three years. Three years since we've seen her, talked to her, laughed with her, danced with her, fucking touched her.

Now we're back.

Forgiveness is a luxury we can't afford.

Too much has happened.

She believes we betrayed *her*. The truth is it was Pen who betrayed *us*.

We can't let that go.

We won't.

CHAPTER ONE

Present Day

"I CAN DO THIS. I can do this. I *can* fucking do this," I repeat under my breath, over and over again as I enter the main lobby of the Academy.

The air is thick with nervous excitement as I stand in the long queue leading to the harassed looking receptionist. Around me chatter and laughter lifts into the air and floats up high into the glass domed roof. There are girls in leotards and expensive dance gear talking in groups with boys who are just as well turned out. They all look like they've walked out of an Abercrombie and Fitch ad, but I refuse to feel inferior. Just because they look the part doesn't mean they can actually dance. I glance down at my beat-up Nike trainers, baggy sweatpants, and thin black t-shirt that I've tied up around my waist and blow out a steady breath.

You can do this, Pen.

A group to my left starts laughing loudly and my body flushes with heat under their scrutiny.

"I didn't realise the academy was opening the doors to the local chavs," one particular snooty bitch remarks. I meet her disgusted gaze with a steely one of my own.

"Chav?" I bark out a laugh. "*Bitch,* I'm a street kid and we learnt from a young age that words have zero power. My fists, however, *they* pack a punch," I retort through a gritted smile. Her pretty mouth drops open and her cheeks flush a crimson red. I don't suppose she expected me to respond.

Well, fuck her.

In my world, bitches get stitches. She's lucky I'm here to make a good impression or her pretty white teeth would be scattered across the parquet flooring by now. I refuse to let anyone make me feel small. I deserve to be here. This is my last chance to get a dance scholarship. It's a one-year, intensive course that should I be lucky enough to win, would open more doors for me than hoping to get spotted dancing at nightclubs. I'm twenty and fully aware that the older I get the harder it will be for me to have a career in dance.

"Ignore her, she's an arsehole," the girl in front says as she turns to face me. She gives me a lopsided smile then swipes a strand of curly, orange hair off her face before holding her hand out for me to shake. I look at it hovering between us. "I'm Clancy," she explains.

"Clancy?"

"That's right, it means *red-headed warrior.*"

"Because of the hair?" I ask, ignoring her hand, which she drops back to her side.

"No, because my mum once loved the Clancy Brothers..."

"Who the fuck are the Clancy Brothers?"

She snorts with laughter, and shakes her head. "Never mind. *Yes*, because of the hair."

"Got it," I note.

"Aren't you going to tell me your name?" She cocks her head and gives me an amused look, not put off by my scowl.

"I'm Pen," I answer after too long a silence.

"Nice to meet you, Pen. Is this a call-back or your first audition?"

"My first audition."

"Me too." She glances across the room to the stuck-up, haughty cow who dared to belittle me, and pulls a face. "That's Tiffany. First class bitch of epic proportions."

"You know her?" I ask as we move forward, the queue slowly moving up. I'm eight places from the front and getting more and more nervous with every passing minute, though I do a good job of hiding it. I just want to grab my registration documents and get to the audition.

"Know her? Yeah, I know her. That's my sister. She's auditioning here today as well. Specialises in ballet, tap *and* modern," Clancy explains, puffing out a breath and rolling her eyes for good measure.

"She's your *sister?*" I look between them both. They're nothing alike. In fact they're complete opposites. Clancy is petite like me, with pale skin and bright red, curly hair, freckles, and pale green eyes. Pretty. Quirky. Tiffany, however, is classically beautiful, modelesque. She's tall, slim, with dark hair and olive skin. She's got no tits to speak of, but is beautiful in a cat-like way. Though I'm betting she'd sooner scratch your eyes out than rub against your leg, and has the attitude that only the privileged carry around with them like an expensive Louis Vuitton bag. You know the kind of people I'm talking about, right? The ones that shop at Fortnum and Mason, who drive the latest Audi, wear Givenchy and drip with jewels. Money keeps people like Tiffany on a pedestal, except for days like today, when raw talent counts for something and money can't always buy happiness or a future in dance. Well, that's what I tell myself anyway.

"That bitch is your sister?" I repeat, trying to correlate the two.

"My *step*sister," Clancy clarifies.

I pull a face. "Shit outta luck there. What a piece of work."

"Don't worry, we hate each other. You can call her all the names you like. I really don't care. She's made my life hell for the last five years since her mum married my dad. You're currently looking at Cinder-fucking-rella. I kid you not, she more than makes up for the lack of a second ugly stepsister, the least she deserves is a bit of her own medicine."

"Fuck, that sucks."

"Yeah, it really, *really* does." Clancy grins and I give her a begrudging smile. She seems alright and nowhere near as stuck up as her catty stepsister.

"Is she already a student?" I ask.

"No, she's auditioning as well today for a scholarship."

"A scholarship?" I scrunch up my nose. "Then why is Tiffany acting like she's one of the rich kids that go here."

"Because she *was* a rich kid before her mum left her dad and married mine for love. Her dad was an abusive twat and cut them off in spite, so Tiffany has to rely on my father to support her. We're not poor, but he can't afford the fees for the two of us. So here we are."

I nod, making a mental note. There's nothing worse than a stuck-up posh nob than an ex stuck-up posh nob pretending they're still rich. We fall back into silence mainly because I'm not great at making friends. Actually, that's not strictly true. Once upon a time I made four best friends, but then it all went to shit.

Pushing thoughts of the *Breakers* firmly out of my head, I focus on the receptionist in front of me now that I've finally reached the front of the queue. Out of the corner of my eye I see Clancy hovering by the end of the desk. She's chewing on a nail and when I glance at her she gives me a rueful smile.

"Thought I'd wait for you," she shrugs, unperturbed by my lack of social skills and standoffishness.

"Whatever you want," I mutter.

"Name," the woman behind the desk snaps, raising her perfectly plucked eyebrows.

"Pen Scott."

"Pen Scott?" the woman repeats, running her finger over the long list in front of her. She looks up at me with her murky brown eyes. "Not on the list. Move aside," she snaps.

"Wait, what?!" I look at her in shock whilst the boy who's standing behind me tries to elbow me out of the way. "Back the fuck off!" I growl at him under my breath before addressing the receptionist once more. "I received an invitation to audition. Check again."

"Listen, you're not on the list. If you're not on the list there's no audition, got it?"

"Got it?" the boy repeats, staring down his nose at me and

giving me the same shitty look as everyone else in this goddamn place. Everyone bar Clancy, who's currently looking at me with pity.

"This is bullshit. I've got a letter of invitation! Here," I growl, pulling out the crumpled audition letter and slamming it on the counter.

The receptionist sighs, taking it from me. "So you do. But you're not on the list and I have very strict instructions from the principal not to let anyone audition unless they're on the list..."

I'm close to throwing a fit right here in the middle of the prestigious Stardom Academy atrium when Clancy steps up beside me and rests her hand on my arm.

"There must be a clerical error. Pen has the letter of invitation to audition. I'm sure Madam Tuillard would hate it if a potential student was turned away because someone hadn't done their job properly."

Clancy gives my arm a squeeze and I get the feeling she's willing me not to go apeshit. I take a deep breath and in the calmest voice possible, ask the receptionist to check again.

She looks down her list of names one last time. "Oh, wait," she eventually says, "There's a Penelope *Sott* right here on the list..."

"That's it. Must've been a typo." Clancy smiles sweetly at the receptionist who nods her head and gives me a tight smile.

"Yes, must be. Studio 14, second floor, third door on the right." With that she dismisses us both without an apology. Fucking old hag.

"YOU'RE ALL HERE today to audition for a scholarship at Stardom Academy. We have just thirty places open and over two hundred dancers auditioning today. You lucky few have myself and my business partner as judges. Make this count, because another opportunity like this won't come around again," a tall, elegant looking woman announces to the room. There must be about thirty dancers in here, though I'm not paying much attention to them, honestly. I need to focus.

"Who's that?" I ask under my breath.

"You're kidding, right?"

I pull a face. "Should I know her?"

Clancy shakes her head, eyeing the graceful ballerina who is currently talking to a guy who looks like a cross between Ne-Yo and Usher. He's hot and vaguely familiar, though I can't seem to place why. The pair together are polar opposites. Elegance and grace versus edgy and street. I like that.

"She's Madame Tuillard, founder of the academy and the principal."

"I thought Madame Tuillard was ancient?"

"Nope, not exactly ancient, she's forty. Set this place up five years ago. She was a prima ballerina for some of the most famous ballet companies in the world. Danced with the greatest. Have you ever heard of Luka Petrin, he stopped dancing when his wife committed suicide? Rumour has it that she killed herself because he was such a manwhore. Madame Tuillard danced with him too, perhaps they shagged..."

"Awesome," I cut in, not particularly interested in ballet and even less so in some famous dancers' sex lives. Don't get me wrong, I do appreciate ballet and its place in the world of dance, but it's just so... *controlled*. Every step has to be perfectly executed. A ballet dancer has to have perfect toes, perfect hands, perfect legs, perfect posture, perfect face, perfect body, perfect *everything*.

Perfect, perfect, perfect.

I like to move my body in a different way. I like the imperfection of hip-hop, of break dance, even contemporary allows for it. I like the freedom those dances allow me, and the fact I can improvise in those dances without pissing off someone like Madame Tuillard who epitomises perfection with her willowy figure and coiffed hair. I like the way I can express myself through those dances.

"And the guy?"

"Ah, that's Duncan Neath, or D-Neath to the dance world at large."

"*He's* D-Neath? Fuck!" I glance back over at the guy and a thread of nervous energy lashes through my stomach. That explains why he's vaguely familiar. I can't believe I'm about to audition in front of *the* D-Neath.

"You've heard of him then?"

"Heard of him? He's a bit of a legend where I come from. He grew up not far from where I live. The guy's known in all the illegal underground dance clubs. Believe me, his reputation precedes him, and it isn't all about dance either."

"So I've heard..."

"You have?"

"Yup. My dad's a lawyer in a big law firm in London. They represented him. Got his sentence down from fourteen years to just five for drug racketeering."

"How come he's here then?"

"He was released a year ago. Apparently they're fucking..."

Clancy explains, her eyes widening with glee as she looks between D-Neath and Tuillard.

"Shut-up! Those two?"

"Opposites attract and all that..." Clancy's voice trails off as Madame Tuillard coughs, her pretty grey eyes falling on us both. She arches a brow and we both shift uncomfortably under her stare.

"Let's get started, shall we?" she says, glaring down her nose at both of us.

Nervous energy ripples beneath my skin as she picks up a clipboard and runs her fingers over the list of names before her. Around us, the chatter dies down and everyone holds a collective breath as they wait to be called.

"First up is *Zayn Bernard*," she says, looking up from her clipboard and towards the back of the studio.

"What the *fuck*?" I whisper-shout, my whole body going rigid. Next to me Clancy flinches, my abject horror startling her.

No.

Fucking.

Way.

"What is it?" she hisses, but I can't answer her. All I can do is shift my gaze to where Madame Tuillard is staring.

"Why? How?" I grind out, my mouth drying up as I watch the boy I once loved unfurling from his spot in the furthest corner of the room. I hadn't noticed him when I entered, too distracted with my residual anger at the receptionist and that stuck up bitch Tiffany, but by the look on his face, he sure as fuck noticed me. He's scowling, a sneer pulling up his lip as he stares directly at me and unzips his black hoodie. Shaking it off, it falls to the studio floor at his feet, and all I can do is stare open-mouthed at his muscled physique and tight black t-shirt. Both his arms are covered in multicoloured tattoos that work their way up from the crook of his elbows to his shoulders, disappearing beneath the material. The last time I'd seen him he didn't have any tattoos. None. He wasn't as broad or as tall either. He was a boy on the cusp of manhood. All four of them were.

Zayn, Xeno, Dax and York were my Breakers, and I was their girl.

Was being the operative word.

Now Zayn's a man. A man who's looking at me like I'm an enemy, not a long-lost friend.

A shiver tracks down my spine as my stomach curdles with anxiety and long held pain.

"Do you know him?" Clancy presses.

Out of the corner of my eye, I can see her check him out. In fact, every damn female in the room is unable to take their eyes off him, Madame Tuillard included. He knows it too. He's always had this kind of magnetism, and he oozes confidence. I'd admired that once. Now I can barely look at him without wanting to sprint from the studio and throw away my chance of a future in dance. It takes every ounce of strength to remain seated.

"Yeah. We've met before," I say vaguely, not willing to elaborate further. I can't. It hurts too much. Looking at him hurts. His hair is the same shade of dark brown, his eyes still a deep black and his mouth just as plump and as kissable as it was three years ago when I last saw him and the others...

Stop it.

"He's *hot*," she states, matter-of-factly. "But can he *dance*?"

"He can dance," I confirm with a whisper, wrapping my arms around my legs and hugging myself tightly as I watch him move out into the empty space. "He can most definitely dance..."

As if he heard me, Zayn meets my gaze and winks, reminding me of the first time we met six years ago. Except this time his wink isn't followed by a warm smile and the possibility of friendship.

Now there's nothing but hate in his eyes.

CHAPTER TWO

Six Years Ago

"YO! WHAT YA DOIN'?"

I turn around, my arms dropping to my side, my body stilling as I look at the boy standing behind me. He's tall, like a foot bigger than I am, maybe even as tall as my older brother, David, who's eighteen and towers over my Mum now. Apparently, I don't have the tall gene. We'll see.

Crossing my arms over my chest and breathing in deep, I look at the boy with dark hair and dark, dark eyes. They're like the sky at night without any stars. If it weren't for his amused smile that makes his lips pull up into a crooked grin, I might have been more wary of him.

"What's it look like I'm doing? I'm dancing." I retort, rolling my eyes.

Obviously.

A bead of sweat slides down my forehead and I swipe at it with the back of my hand. I wonder how long this kid has been standing there watching me. My skin heats. I don't dance in front of anyone, and the only reason I'm here in this playground is because no one on my estate uses it. The place is a fucking dump.

"Yeah?" he winks, sitting down on the rusty swing in front of me, that smile getting broader. He has really white, straight teeth, except for one which has a chip in it. There's a little piece of his front tooth missing, and I find myself wondering how he did it.

"I haven't seen you around here before," I state, giving him a once over as I cock my hip, planting my hand there. He's wearing beat-up, black Nike trainers and grey baggy joggers with his boxer short strap showing above the waistband, and a white t-shirt rolled up at the arms making his skin look tan against it. He's kinda cute, but I'm not really interested in boys. Especially not ones who spend their time hanging out on street corners and causing trouble for the rest of the people living on the estate. Boys like my brother, David, who wears a cross around his neck like he's one of God's disciples even though he belongs to the fucking Devil himself. I've never understood it. My mum's a church going, religious nut, and pretends she's holier than though when really she's worse than those nuns you hear about beating the shit out of kids in orphanages.

"That's because I just moved here a couple weeks ago. Just scoping the place out..." he looks around the playground, unimpressed. "So, this is *shit*."

The curse word rolls off his tongue with ease. I mean, I'm not shocked or anything. Everyone swears around here. I swear too, but mostly under my breath or in my head because my mum would give me a slap if she caught me. Not that she needs an excuse to hit me, she does it often enough without reason.

"Like *really* shit," he emphasises.

"Yep," I agree, popping the p.

He's right, this playground *is* shit. There's one swing, which he's sitting on, a rusty see-saw and a slide that's seen better days. The frame is covered in graffiti that isn't proper graffiti, just a bunch of cuss words and images of dicks and tits. Totally unoriginal and nothing like the graffiti by Bling and Asia that's dotted around Hackney. Those are *real* works of art.

"Did someone set a moped on fire?" he asks, jerking his chin towards the pile of rubble just over the other side of the iron fence surrounding the playground.

"Couple weekends ago. Stolen." *By my brother.* Though I don't say that part out loud. What's worse than someone who snitches? Someone who's blood and snitches. I keep my mouth shut. Telling on David would be a death sentence. A literal one. I have no doubt that my older brother is a certifiable psychopath.

"Figures." He rolls his eyes, jaded by the environment just as much as I am.

"None of the kids who live on this estate ever come here," I explain, untying my long brown hair and shaking it out a little. I'm not sure why I decide to take it down, maybe it's because Mum says it's my best asset with a face as plain as mine. It's the only backhanded compliment she's ever given me. She doesn't think I'm pretty. *I* don't think I'm pretty. I push that thought away. "Most of them hang out on street corners, smoking weed."

"Yeah, noticed that. So you come here to practice your

dance moves?" He gives me a once over and I feel suddenly shy at his ogling. I don't think he's being creepy, just interested. I checked him out, he's checking me out. I guess we're even now.

"Where else am I supposed to dance?" It's not like we've got any room at home. I share a bedroom with my little sister, Lena. She's eight, annoying, and takes up all the room with her dolls.

"I know somewhere... Want me to show you?"

I bark out a laugh, almost doubling over. "You gonna offer me a sweet next in exchange for a blowjob?"

"*What*?! Fuck no!" he splutters, dragging his heels over the ground so that he's no longer swaying, but still.

"So you're not some weirdo, preying on young girls then?" I ask, folding my arms across my chest and trying to look all badass when inside I'm giggling like a freak because I made him so uncomfortable. He's not a weirdo, I can tell.

"No. I *swear*..." he scrapes a hand through his thick, dark hair and grins when I burst out laughing. "I'm just making friends, and I dance like you. Thought we could hang out." He shrugs.

"Show me..." I challenge him. I wasn't born yesterday. He might not be a pedo, but he still might have an ulterior motive. I've not met one person around here who hasn't. "Prove to me you're not a pedo."

"Fuck, man. I'm *not* a pedo. I'm fifteen. Besides, you're not really my type."

"I don't hook up with boys," I say haughtily. Thou shalt not covet dangerous boys with chipped teeth and black, black eyes. Nope, definitely not.

"Fair enough. How old are you anyway?" he asks, getting to his feet. I have to look up to meet his gaze. This kid is tall for

fifteen, and broad. By the looks of his arm muscles, he can probably throw a wicked punch too. He's not quite as filled out as my
brother, David, or as scrawny as some of the guys on this estate,
he's kinda in between. His face is the same... in between. Like,
he's not really a kid but not really an adult either.

"Fourteen," I answer.

"And your name?"

"Pen."

"You're called *Pen?*" He grins again, snorting with mirth.

"Short for Penelope. I hate it. So call me Pen, *got it?*" I scowl
a little, hating the fact he finds my name so amusing. I like Pen. I
don't like Penelope.

"Yeah, got it," he retorts, holding his hands up in mock
defence, watching me with his night-time eyes.

"Good." No one's gonna make me feel small. Besides, I'm
used to kids throwing their weight around. It's kinda what we do
here on my estate. You either show the bullies that you're a
badass or you let them walk all over you. Despite my lack of
height, I'm not a victim. Never will be. Besides, I've had plenty
of practice dealing with shitty people, my brother's the biggest
bully on the estate and he takes great pleasure pushing me
around. Blood might be thicker than water, but it means jackshit
in my house. I hate him.

"Are you gonna tell me your name then?" I raise my
eyebrows, waiting.

"It's Zayn."

"Zayn?" I snort with laughter, immediately thinking up
rhyming words. "Zayn, the pain... in my *arse.*"

Zayn scowls. "I could be a *real* big pain in your arse if you
say that again." He steps forward, puffing out his chest and

staring down at me, the smile gone. For a moment, his black eyes don't look so friendly. Now it's me who's backing off, though I don't think he'd actually hit me like some of the arsehole's my brother hangs around with would.

"Whoa, just kidding. Chill, man."

"I *am* chill..." He seems to shake himself. "Just don't take the piss, and we'll be good. Yeah?"

"Yeah."

He makes a funny grunting sound that only makes me bite back another laugh. "So, *Zayn*, you were gonna prove to me you're not some weirdo coming onto me, and can actually dance..." I say, standing back and folding my arms across my chest.

"What, right now?"

"Yeah, right now. It's only fair."

"There's no music..."

"And?" I question. "You don't see me wearing fancy head-phones, do ya? I can remember a beat well enough. I got all the music I need up here," I shrug, tapping a finger against my head.

To prove my point I start tapping my foot, swaying my body in time to the rhythm in my head. *Filthy* by Justin Timberlake starts to sound in my mind. When the first beat drops I lift my arms up and slide my foot across the floor, folding my body over as I turn my head to face Zayn. Giving him a quirk of my eyebrow, I make quick, jerking movements, keeping my hips still and torso stiff whilst moving the rest of my body robotically. Occasionally, I'll intersperse my jerking movements with a smoother flow, my head rolling on my shoulders, my arms floating in the air as I spin on the ball of my feet. This is a dance I'm perfecting. A mash-up between contemporary and hip-hop,

I guess. Well, at least I think it is given I only have YouTube to go by. Zayn watches me, a sudden light flashing in his eyes as he bops his head in time to my movements.

"Sick moves," he says appreciatively.

"Thanks," I respond, grinning back. Apart from my little sister, no one has ever complimented my dancing. Mum thinks it's a waste of time and my non-existent father doesn't even know my name; let alone the fact I love to dance. My brother, David, he just mocks me any chance he gets, all the while holding onto his fucking cross as though that absolves him of all his sins. Urgh. "Come on then, start moving…"

Zayn swaggers towards me. "Alright, *Pen*. Demanding, ain't ya?"

I stand my ground as he lifts onto the balls of his feet then shifts back onto his heels as he moves from side-to-side. He smirks then flicks his right arm out to the side in a wave that undulates back up his arm across his shoulders and to his left arm, his body following the movement.

"That's all you got?" I question. It's customary to provoke another dancer, and something about the arrogance he's showing makes me want to do just that. I can already tell by this one simple movement that he's a good dancer, he has rhythm. I just ain't gonna let him know that.

"I got it all, Pen. I got it all," he responds, taking the bait.

Zayn crosses his legs and spins on his feet, working his shoulders and snapping his wrists in time to a beat only he can hear. When he holds his arms out wide then smirks, I know he's about to throw an impressive move. I wait, holding my breath. My skin prickles as he flips forward onto his hands and lifts his legs up in the air, scissor-kicking before flipping over and landing before me, kicking up dust and tiny grains of stone as he moves. He straightens up, panting, then crosses his arms over his chest and gives me this cute little smirk like he knows he's the shit.

He *is* the shit. This boy *can* dance.

"Believe me now?" he asks, meeting my gaze.

"Yeah, I believe you."

We stare at each other for a moment. My lip twitches as I try not to grin stupidly. I feel like I've made a friend. That doesn't happen too often for me. I like my own company, mostly. Trust isn't something I give very easily, and you have to trust someone enough to be friends with them.

"So, do you wanna know where you can dance without needing a tetanus jab, Pen?" Zayn asks, tipping his head to the side as he stares at me. I like the way he says my name.

"Sure..." I mutter, gnawing on my lip. My heart pounds at the thought of having a place to dance without fear of being caught by one of the arsehole kids on my estate and having to defend my passion. "Where?"

"You know the boarded-up house on Jackson Street?"

"Yeah. I know it, that's where the drug dealers hang out." Zayn shuffles on his feet and gives me a look that I don't like. Shit, that's where he dances? I step back, shaking my head. "No way, I ain't going there."

"It's not a big deal, Pen. We got the basement to use as we like... We're there most nights, hanging out."

"We?"

"Me and my dance crew."

"You have a dance crew?"

"Yeah, we've been looking for a fifth member. Interested?"

I am interested, but there's no way I'm getting involved with that shit. My brother's well known by the crims running the place on Jackson Street. "No."

"I swear, we ain't involved in any of that gang shit. We just use the space to dance. That's it."

He looks sincere enough, but I know how things go around here. Whatever Zayn's connection to that place is, it will bite him on the arse one day even if he's not involved with them right now.

"Look, I ain't stupid. Whatever agreement you have with the *Skins*, I don't want no part of it."

Zayn sighs. "I'll lay it out for ya. Jeb is my uncle. He promised my mum he'd look out for me. That's what he's doing."

"Jeb, the *leader* of Skins is your uncle. Like hell-to-the-fuck, no." I start walking away, all hopes of a new friendship and somewhere safe to dance disappearing with every step. Jeb is well known around here, not because he's a good guy with good intentions, but because he's an arsehole who fucks people over and sells drugs to kids.

"Wait!"

Stupidly, I do just that.

"I swear. We just use the place to dance..."

"And?"

"And that's it."

"Yeah, right."

"It ain't like that. Jeb's blood."

"Won't stop him from being an arsehole." *I should know.*

"Maybe not to the general population, but he's cool with me. I swear."

Shaking my head and rolling my eyes I give Zayn a long hard look. "For now, maybe."

"So you won't come?"

"No. Not now, not ever."

Except, a month later I find myself at number fifteen Jackson Street, eating my words.

CHAPTER THREE

Present Day

"HOW DO YOU KNOW HIM?" Clancy asks me, her voice rising with interest. "He's *amazing.*"

"We grew up on the same estate... he moved away. I haven't seen him in three years. We barely know each other," I lie, trying to make my voice sound light, unaffected. "I doubt he even remembers me."

"Oh, I think he remembers you alright. He keeps looking over at you every chance he gets... *Whoa!*" she suddenly blurts out as Zayn backflips from a standing position then drops to the floor, spinning on his back, only to jerk back upwards on his forearm before flipping to his feet again. A smug look drags across his face as he regards the room, he's barely breaking a sweat. His gaze meets mine and I see the fire there, and the anger.

He always danced best when he was angry.

Well, fuck him. I'm angry too. I've been angry for three fucking years.

"Holy shit on a stick!" Clancy exclaims excitedly. She's not the only one whose mouth has popped open. There isn't one person in the room not impressed by Zayn's moves, his ability. Yeah, he's still shit-hot.

Zayn was the frontman of our crew even if he wasn't the leader. Confident, arrogant and the best dancer of us all. At least back when we were friends anyway. York came in a close second. Me and Dax were on an equal footing and Xeno was the best allrounder and also the leader. What he said went, no matter what.

"Did you just see that?"

I don't respond. Of course, I did. I'm not fucking blind. Though, right now I would gouge my own eyes out with a wooden spoon if I had one to hand so I wouldn't have to look at the boy I once loved dance with such fury and fire. With such *passion*. My stomach rolls over. If I wasn't in the mood for small talk earlier, I'm even less so now. I can't believe he's here. The consequences of him being back will be catastrophic for me... I force that thought away. I have to get through this audition.

He continues to dance, throwing in his signature moves. Hip-hop was always his speciality and Zayn was never afraid to innovate. He knows all the steps: popping, locking, tutting, gliding, robotting. He can do them all. The key with Zayn is that he takes a classic hip-hop dance move and makes them his own. I've lost count of the amount of times I've seen him do a windmill then rise up on his arms and literally launch himself into the air into some crazy arse move no one has ever seen before.

He's a genius.

Right now he's freestyling. Just moving to the music, anticipating the next beat to drop, and delivering every time. I can tell that he hasn't practiced this routine over and over to get it perfect like the rest of us have done. This is Zayn dancing from his soul. That was always something he was so proud of, being able to cut up a dance floor and wipe the floor with his opponents in a battle from sheer ability and musical rhythm. He's still amazing. In fact he's better than amazing. He's outstanding.

That only makes this so much harder.

I groan internally. There's no way he won't be given a spot at the academy after this. When he finishes up with a well-placed freeze, his hands flat on the floor, the side of his head pressed against the wooden floorboards and his torso lifted off the ground with his legs bent, the room roars with appreciation. Clancy is clapping her hands like a kid on Christmas morning, but all I can do is sit with a stiff back and cold dread trying not to look at his six pack on show.

"*Why?*" I whisper, my question lost beneath the noise. Why has he come back now? Why is he here of all places? Why is he looking at me like I'm the one who fucked everything up? Why does my stupid heart hurt so damn much? Why? Why? Why?

As if hearing my silent questions, Zayn stands and locks eyes with me, jerking his chin. He's offering me out, just like he would an opponent in a battle. Unlike a battle, this challenge won't end once the music stops.

No. I recognise that look. It's the one he saves just for his enemies.

Looks like that's me.

"Thank you, Zayn. Take a seat," Madame Tuillard says,

holding her hands up to quieten the room. He gives her a nod, then flicks his gaze to D-Neath who gives him a sly wink that no one else seems to notice given they're all looking directly at Miss Prim-and-Proper.

I smell a rat.

"He is mag-nif-i-cent," Clancy says, drawing out the word like she's praying to a new god. I look at her and notice the lust in her eyes and roll my own. I refuse to acknowledge the pang in my chest. He was always a babe magnet. That seems to have intensified over the years.

"Sure," I mutter, forcing myself to look at Madame Tuillard and not track Zayn's every move back to his spot in the corner of the room.

I refuse to give him the satisfaction.

For the next half an hour, ten more dancers, including Clancy, get up and audition. Of them all, Clancy was by far the best. Tap is her specialism and she knocks it out the park with quick footwork, musicality, and incredible expression. If York were here, he'd be impressed. The guy loved Fred Astaire and Sammy Davis Junior, imitating their moves from the old movies he used to watch on repeat. All self-taught. I used to love that about him, his exuberance and fascination with all the old black and white movies. Whilst the others messed about and played table football, we would huddle up on a beat-up sofa together in the basement of Jackson Street and watch all the old films. I was his Ginger Rogers once upon a time...

Fuck. Stop it!

Seeing Zayn has opened up old wounds and painful memories that I've long since buried. I can't afford to think about him, about *any* of them. I just need to get through this audition and figure out what to do after. Shaking my head, I grit my teeth and wait my turn, choosing instead to go mentally through my dance steps.

"Who's next?" Madame Tuillard muses, consulting her list before she glances over at D-Neath. He looks down at his clipboard, taking his time to decide. I tap my finger against my leg, barely holding onto my nerves. I need to audition so I can get out of here and away from Zayn and everything he represents.

"Penelope Scott."

My head whips around as I focus on D-Neath who is looking at the room expectantly. Relief at finally being called and a deep, gut-wrenching nausea simultaneously fills me. Clancy nudges me in the side when I don't get up immediately, a sudden rush of terror keeping me still.

"You're up, Pen. Knock 'em dead," she grins, and I grimace, not used to getting any support let alone encouragement, particularly as she has no idea if I can dance or not.

"Fuck," I mutter, unfurling myself.

Standing, I dig deep. I know I'm a good dancer, even if having Zayn here is fucking with my head. Forcing my nerves away, I refuse to let his appearance ruin my one and only opportunity to prove my worth. I'm *not* a hopeless dreamer like my mum accuses me of being on a daily basis. I'm *not* worthless for wanting more from life than working in a bar every weekend serving guys who just see a girl they want to fuck or an opponent they want to beat in a battle for kudos.

I'm Pen. I'm more than what people perceive me to be. I *can* dance. I *am* worth something.

Funnelling that energy and the righteous anger I feel whenever I think of my mum and her cutting barbs and endless disappointment, I take up my spot in the middle of the dance floor. The assistant, who's been loading music into the surround-sound for every auditionee before me, looks at me with a question on his face. "There doesn't appear to be any request for music?"

"I'm not dancing to music," I tell him.

He gives me a surprised look. "What?"

"I'm not dancing to music," I repeat, my jaw gritting at the familiar scoff I hear. Fucking Zayn.

The guy shrugs and I hear him mutter 'it's your funeral' under his breath. Arsehole.

"When you're ready then..." Madame Tuillard comments. She's perched on the edge of the desk looking at me with interest. Breathing in deeply, I refuse to look at Zayn though I can feel his stare. It fucking burns my skin.

Well, fuck him. FUCK HIM.

Dropping my head, I count for five seconds before I look up. My chest is heaving as I stare directly at Zayn and jerk my chin. You want a battle, you've got one. He's careful to hide his reaction, but I know him well enough. The hard line of his lips, the muscle ticking in his jaw and the tautness of his shoulders tell me what I want to know. I'm affecting him as much as he's affecting me.

Good.

Spinning on the ball of my left foot, I fold over at my hips and kick my right leg out, pivoting in an imperfectly perfect circle then launch my body forward into a front flip. I land gently, the firmness of the wooden boards creaking slightly beneath my feet.

The room descends into quiet, and I know I have them all in

the palm of my hand. I'm not arrogant, not by a long shot. Deep within I'm fucking trembling with anxiety, with my mother's words telling me I'm not good enough. But dance has always been freeing to me. Whatever shit is going on in my life, it falls away the minute I move my body. Over the years I've perfected my mash-up between hip-hop and contemporary, combining the two disciplines. I'm strong, precise with every step. But more importantly, I dance with every single cell in my body, with every last part of me.

This isn't the time for holding back. I need this spot at the academy. I need this so fucking bad.

Dropping to my knees, I lean forward onto my hands and lift my whole weight off the floor, acing the *turtle* with ease. Back when I was friends with the Breakers I was never able to pull this move off. I've been practising. When I flip back upwards, I catch Zayn's gaze. He's scowling and I almost laugh. If I didn't have a routine to finish, I would have laughed in his fucking face. Shutting him out, I let go of the rigidity of hip-hop and switch into the free-flowing movements of contemporary. Loosening up my rib cage and limbs, I twist and turn my body in time with the beat only I can hear inside my head.

Then I lose myself to the dance.

It takes over.

Filling me up.

When I dance, I'm *free*.

Free from expectation. Free from responsibility. Free from my past. Free from my mother's hate. Free from the drudgery of a life with no prospects. I'm even free from my own feelings. The Breakers can't touch me when I dance.

I'm untouchable.

I move with passion and purpose, my feet barely touching the floor. I'm flying over the wooden boards, lost in the magic that always seems to burn in my veins when I dance. I don't look at anyone. Not Madame Tuillard, not D-Neath, not Clancy or any of the other dancers watching my every move.

Not even Zayn.

Especially not Zayn.

I twist and turn, gliding over the floor. I use every single part of my body to express myself, from the tips of my toes to the top of my head. Flipping forward in a tumble I land purposely on my arse with my legs straight out in front of me. Sweat dribbles down between my breasts as I flip onto my stomach, then crawl on my hands and knees, swaying my hips seductively. A deep cough has my eyes snapping up and as I curve my back forcing my arse and head upwards, I lock gazes with Zayn. His eyes spark dangerously, giving me pause. Once upon a time I would've seen stars in his night-time eyes, laughter, kindness, friendship and belonging. Now I see nothing but an endless darkness that makes me wonder what he's been involved in over the last three years. For some reason that I can't quite fathom, I wink at him and smile slowly.

Anger flashes in his gaze, but beneath that I sense something more. Ignoring the scorching heat burning beneath my skin, I slide into the splits before bringing my legs together and flipping backwards into an arch. I'm light as a feather, as sharp as a knife.

I'm *me*.

Dancing has always been a personal experience. Even when I was part of the Breakers, I was always a single unit within the whole. Yes, we danced together. We perfected our moves, synchronised our routine, but we rarely got close enough to really dance with each other like partners might in ballroom or Latin... or bachata.

Bachata.

God that dance. So fucking sensual, so sexy.

So, *Xeno*....

By complete chance, I found out one afternoon just how much he adored bachata. About two years after I was first introduced to the crew, I walked in on Xeno dancing with a girl in the basement of Jackson Street. It was a rainy day, and the rest of the guys were late to arrive. Neither Xeno nor the girl had heard me entering the room. He had no idea I was watching his every move. I'd stood in the doorway transfixed as he practically fucked the girl with his dance moves. They might have been wearing clothes, but the way they undulated against each other had made my cheeks burn, my heart pound, and an intense kind of jealousy writhe in my stomach like a pile of hissing snakes.

I'd only ever seen him dance hip-hop, nothing else. But the way he moved. The sway of his hips, the sensual slide of his feet over the ground and the gentle but possessive way he held this girl threw me into a tailspin. It was the sexiest thing I'd ever seen. Before that point, I hadn't fancied any of the boys. They were my friends, that was it. But that day, that day I fell hard for Xeno.

Zayn might have been my first friend crush, but Xeno had been my first real boy crush. Hormones had well and truly kicked in at that point. Over the coming months I found myself falling for each of them one by one...

Until I'd loved them wholly and completely.

Forcing those painful memories away, I catch a glimpse of

myself in the wall to ceiling mirror as sweat pours from my alabaster skin, plastering my hair against my head and brightening my cheeks with red spots as I move. I'm not sure how long I've been dancing for, but eventually, finally, my dance comes to a natural end. Panting, I finish off with a gentle sway of my body then stop, dropping my head and hunching my shoulders as my chest heaves with exertion.

I can hear nothing over the rush of blood pumping through my veins. When my racing heart finally settles enough, the room is silent. There's no clapping. There are no cheers like Zayn had experienced.

Just pin-dropping silence.

My heart fucking sinks. Have I just thrown away my one chance at a future in dance? Did I just royally fuck up? Should I have stuck to contemporary on its own? Perhaps I was foolish breaking up my routine with hip-hop moves. Were they too stark amongst the fluidity of contemporary?

Shit.

I look up slowly, my throat tightening with anxiety, and find myself locking eyes with Zayn once more. Why, in my most vulnerable moment, do I seek him out?

Because he was your rock once, that's why.

And yet, all I see when I look into his eyes is malice. It's cold, vicious, and bordering on maniacal. I'm sure if he could cackle like some fucked-up psychopath in one of those Marvel movies he used to love watching and get away with it, I bet he fucking would.

My heart sinks.

No, it plummets.

Sighing heavily I move towards my spot amongst the other

dancers, wanting the fucking floor to swallow me up. Except, somebody starts clapping, stopping me dead in my tracks. I look over at Madame Tuillard who is watching me with interest.

"Bravo," she says, her hands coming together over and over again in time with the crazy pounding of my heart. "Don't look so surprised, that was quite extraordinary."

"*Extraordinary?*" I chirrup, like some psycho parrot. My skin is flushed with heat, burning under her scrutiny. I realise the whole room is staring at me. Some of the dancers look at me with respect, but a hell of a lot more with barely veiled envy. It brims in their eyes.

"Yes, extraordinary," she says to me before turning her attention to the rest of the dancers. "Despite my specialism, and the assumptions that come with dancing ballet, I appreciate passion over perfection, grit over cowardice, innovation over stagnation. The rest of you who are yet to dance, take note. To be able to follow dance steps is one thing, to be a true dancer who cannot live without movement, quite another."

I'm too gobsmacked to speak let alone move, so I simply stand like a moron whilst Madame Tuillard looks me up and down. She's not being rude, simply curious, like she's trying to work me out. I swallow hard, studying her as much as she studies me.

"Please sit, Penelope," Madame Tuillard says after a moment. She gives me a warm smile that she hasn't shared with any other dancer until now. Even after Zayn's impressive routine, she'd remained neutral.

"It's Pen," I blurt out.

For a fraction of a second I look over at Zayn and am reminded of the connection we once shared. A connection born from a love of dance, a crappy upbringing, and a loyalty to one another that, once upon a time, every single one of the Breakers would've died to protect. Apparently, that connection has well and truly been severed.

"Well, Pen, please take a seat whilst the remaining dancers audition."

I nod tightly and do as she asks, sitting back down next to Clancy.

"Oh. My. God. You were fucking *amazing!*" Clancy exclaims, wrapping her arm around my shoulder and drawing me into her side. I'm too spaced out to shake her off. I'm not used to such overt appreciation. Instead of thanking her, I kind of just grunt and wrap my arms back around my legs, watching Madam Tuillard as she takes a seat next to D-Neath and whispers something in his ear. He nods, his gaze flicking over to the corner of the room, to the spot where Zayn is sitting. Whipping my head around, my spine stiffens as a look passes between the two.

Another hour later, the final dancer completes her audition and Madame Tuillard dismisses us all. "Thank you for coming today. If any of you are lucky enough to be offered a place, you will be called by Friday and expected to start on Monday when induction week starts. Unsuccessful candidates will receive a letter in the post."

With that she glides out of the room, D-Neath following her with a smirk. I watch him as he leaves and notice that, yet again, he meets Zayn's gaze, a silent conversation happening between them. Goddamn it. They're up to something, but it's not as if I can ask. I'd rather cut out my tongue than have a conversation with Zayn right now.

The room empties, but I take my time gathering my stuff hoping Zayn will leave and I don't have to face him. It's one thing to exchange glances, however heated they might be, quite another to actually have a conversation. It's been a long time since I've been in his company.

I should've fucking known he wouldn't let me off that easy.

"Sweet moves, Cherry. I like your style," he says, completely blanking me as he congratulates Clancy. I stiffen at his closeness, gritting my jaw. Still, I refuse to look at him. Instead, I concentrate on Clancy whose cheeks are flaming under his compliment.

"It's Clancy... and thanks," she mutters. She glances between me and Zayn, understanding that there's a connection, sensing the animosity and wondering why neither of us are acknowledging it.

"I know, but you sure do seem like a *Cherry*. Sweet, curvy and something I'd sure like a taste of. Me and my crew will be at Rocks Friday night. *Come*," he says, making sure to smile around the innuendo when my head snaps around to look at him.

Hell-to-the-fuck-no.

Clancy splutters, her mouth popping open and closed like a damn fish out of water. He's fucking coming on to her. My gut churns.

I shouldn't care. I *don't* fucking care.

"Over my dead body," I say through gritted teeth. I might not know Clancy all that well yet, but she seems like a good person and I refuse to let her be used by Zayn. He was always a ladies' man, at least until I revealed my feelings towards him. Then it was different.

Leaning in close, Zayn chuckles evilly. "That's what I'm counting on, *Pen*."

With that, he twists on his feet and walks away.

"What was that all about?" Clancy asks, her eyes widening. "Did he just ask me to Rocks on Friday night?"

"Clancy, I don't think that's a..."

She pulls a face. "Girl, I'm not a complete moron. I know he wasn't asking because he wanted *me* there. He was doing that to make you jealous or some shit. Want to tell me what the hell is going on?"

I shake my head. "That's not a conversation I want to have today. If ever," I add.

"Fair enough. Look, I'm going to be straight with you. He's fit and all that, but it's always chicks before dicks for me. I'm guessing he's off limits?"

My silence is answer enough.

"Well then, I won't touch him with a bargepole. Okay?"

I nod tightly. "Okay."

"But..."

"But?"

"That shouldn't stop us from going to Rocks. I've always wanted to check it out. It'll either be a night to celebrate, or commiserate, or both. What do you say?"

"Sure. I finish my shift there at midnight anyway."

"Wait? *What*? You work at Rocks? Why didn't you say so?"

"I just did," I shrug.

Looks like Friday night's going to be interesting.

CHAPTER FOUR

Present Day

FRIDAY MORNING, I'm sitting in my bedroom when my phone vibrates. I snatch it up. It's the academy. Fuck.

FUCK.

Drawing in a deep breath, I bite out an answer, my nerves getting the better of me. "Hello?"

"Is this Pen Scott?" a familiar voice asks. My throat dries out at the posh accent of Madame Tuillard and the deep rumble of laughter that is D-Neath in the background.

"Yes," I squeak, my heart nearly busting out of my chest.

"Congratulations, Pen. You start at the academy on Monday."

"Shit," I blurt out, tears springing into my eyes. I blink them away.

"Is that a thank you?" Madame Tuillard laughs, not in the

least bit perturbed by my rude arse response to being offered a place at her school.

"Fuck, *yes*. It's a yes. I'm sorry. *Thank you*," I ramble.

She laughs again, and I realise that it isn't me who's causing her so much glee, but D-Neath. I swear I can hear kissing noises now. Her laughter is more of a giggle and completely inappropriate for our conversation. She coughs, clearing her throat.

"You may or may not know that we have live-in accommodations at the academy. There are a finite number of rooms available, but for my most promising students..."

"That's okay. I only live an hour away. I'll just get the train," I interrupt lamely, not sure what she's getting at.

"Pen, *you* are one of my most promising students," she clarifies.

I am? *Fuck!* "Thank you..." I stammer.

"So, I'd like you to move in, that way you'll get extra time to practice your techniques in the dance studios before and after your daily classes. You will also get extra training in whatever specialism you choose."

"You're actually saying that you want *me* to stay at the academy, in my own flat?" I'm glad we're not having this conversation face-to-face because she might be regretting her decision given I look like a complete fucking moron with my mouth wide open and tears brimming in my eyes. This is unreal.

"Yes, that's exactly what I'm offering."

"Will there be others too?"

"There will be other students staying. All of them have been handpicked by me. You can move in immediately."

A thread of worry rushes through my veins. As much as I want to jump at the offer, I can't afford to pay for my own studio flat. "I would love to, but I can't really afford it..." My voice trails off and I feel like a fucking loser. Working at the club barely covers the cost of living with Mum, let alone a place of my own.

"There's no charge for living in the annex, Pen. All you need to do is buy your own food. That's it. Call it the perks of being a gifted dancer."

"You're kidding?"

"No, I'm perfectly serious." Though she does let out another giggle before her voice is muffled by her hand covering the receiver. "Apologies about that, I have a very demanding colleague who wants... my attention."

Yeah, I bet. D-Neath is well known for his womanising ways. Apparently he's hung like a horse and had his knob tattooed whilst erect to prove what a badass he is. I've no issues with a tattooed dick either way, but I'd rather not have this conversation whilst they're getting up to God knows what. Pushing all thoughts of D-Neath's cock out of my head, I thank Madame Tuillard.

"You won't regret your decision. I'll work harder than anyone. I'll do whatever it takes. I won't let you down," I respond in a rush, trying to drown out the sound of D-Neath making grunting noises. Is he *fucking* her whilst she's on the phone? Gross.

"Good. See you Monday," she replies, before the line goes dead.

My hands are shaking so much that I drop my mobile phone onto my lap and stare at the wall opposite my bed. *"I'm in,"* I whisper, not quite believing it. "I did it!"

"Did what?" my sister, Lena, asks as she enters the room with a cup of tea and a packet of Salt and Vinegar crisps dangling from her fingertips. I stare at her, unable to respond. She cocks her head to the side and squints her eyes at me. "You on something?"

"No!" I laugh a little hysterically which only causes her to raise her brows at me and give me her signature *'yeah, right'* look.

"I swear it..."

"Hmm," she responds, haughty little minx.

Sweet Jesus, at fourteen she's twenty times worse than she was at ten in terms of attitude, and don't get me started on her tidiness, or lack of it. Instead of dolls and toys littering the space, it's make-up and clothes. She's got *a lot* of stuff. Too much actually. It's particularly suspicious especially since she's still at school, doesn't have a weekend job and no money to buy all this shit. Our mum barely gets paid enough in her job as a mobile hairdresser to cover the rent money, bills, and her addiction to wine, which is bordering on alcoholic, let alone my sister's addiction to making herself look pretty. Either Lena has a sugar daddy, is running around with the Skins or is stealing it all. I'm hoping for the latter because the other two options don't bear thinking about.

"Then what's up with you, Pen? You look pale as fuck." She places her mug and crisps on the dresser beside her bed and sits down next to me. "Have you thrown up again?" she asks, putting the back of her hand against my forehead to feel for a temperature. She might be a pain in my arse most of the time, but underneath it all she's a good kid.

"No, I haven't puked..." Well, at least not today anyway.

Over the past two days nerves have got the better of me, add to top it all off, the shock at seeing Zayn again after such a long time meant my stomach has taken the brunt of it. To make matters worse, where Zayn is, so too are the rest of my Breakers. *My* Breakers? Fuck. They're not mine anymore. Inside, my heart squeezes painfully and nausea rises up my throat despite the good news.

"What is it then?" Lena persists.

Turning to face her, I push down every other thought and concentrate on the one thing that I've been working towards all my life. I can't control what the Breakers do any more than I can control the actions of other criminals who run this estate. Whatever happens, happens. I'm not part of their crew anymore. Gripping her hand, I squeeze tightly and force myself to smile.

"I got into Stardom. I'm in, Lena. *I'm in.*"

For a moment Lena just stares at me, then she squeals loudly and throws herself into my arms. The sound is loud enough to make my mum come running.

"What the hell is going on?" she shouts, her gloved hands covered in peroxide mixture as she stands in the doorway. In the front room, Karen, our neighbour, and mum's friend, is having her roots dyed.

"Mum, Pen got a place at the academy. She got in!"

I can't help but smile at Lena's enthusiasm, but my grin disappears the second my mum's gaze lands on mine. Here we go.

"Just perfect. Now who's going to help me pay the bills, huh? Did you think of that before you went swanning off to audition after I strictly forbade it?"

"Mum!" Lena snaps, but I reach for her arm, squeezing gently.

"I'm an *adult*. You can't stop me from doing anything."

"Need I remind you that you live under *my* roof, so you follow *my* rules. Call them back and tell them you're not taking the spot." She glares at me and I wonder, not for the first time, why she hates me so fucking much.

"No."

"No?!" she spits, her face turning pink with anger. "Do as you're damn well told or find yourself somewhere else to live."

I get up, my body vibrating with anger as a huge well of sadness opens up inside my chest. "I'm moving out. I've been given a studio flat to stay at in the academy," I say tightly, flicking my gaze to Lena who bites her lip. I hate leaving her, but what else can I do?

"You selfish little bitch!" Mum hisses, her nostrils flaring as she flicks her gaze down the hall. On the surface Mum's a nice, regular, church going woman who's brought her kids up without a husband but under the watchful eye of God. Yet, no one has any idea just how fucking evil she really is beneath the bullshit façade.

"Me, selfish?" I splutter, unable to hide the hurt I feel. "David chose a life of crime. He barely checks in with you from one month to the next and you're telling me *I'm* selfish when all I've done is hold this family together and work my arse off so that you can feed your forty a day cigarette habit and get pissed every other night at the local pub? David has only ever cared about himself. He's incapable of giving a shit about anyone else given he's a fucking maniac!"

"Shut the hell up, Penelope," she snarls through gritted teeth, peering nervously down the hall.

Oh, yeah, I forgot that we can't talk about the fact that David is high up in the drug trafficking set-up the Skins have got going and is a fucking psycho to boot. I'm glad he's not living here anymore and has fucked off to Mexico. At least Lena's safe from harm. That's all that matters.

"What's wrong Mum? Afraid the neighbours will learn your son doesn't work undercover for the goddamn Met Police like you keep telling them and is in fact the prick everyone thinks he is?"

"I'm warning you, Penelope. Shut your mouth!" she hisses.

"Mum, Pen's right. David's no good..." Lena says, attempting to back me up. Mum rounds on her, her eyes narrowing.

"David does his bit. He sends money home. At least he has a future."

"A future? Are you fucking kidding me? Do you actually live in cloud-fucking-cuckoo-land? The *only* future David has is an empty cell waiting for him at Her Majesty's pleasure, because sooner or later he's gonna be locked up, Mum, and I'll be dancing all over Hackney when that day comes!"

"Enough!" she snaps. "They won't ever be able to catch him because he's not stupid enough to come home. Now, grab your crap and get the hell out of my flat. Do not expect to come crawling back here when all your plans go to shit and whoever offered you a place realises their mistake."

"Mum, *please*..." Lena begs, her eyes welling.

I look at my sister and shake my head. "It's okay. This was always gonna happen."

Mum scoffs, then stabs me in the heart with her words. "I should've aborted you when I had the chance."

"Tell *that* to your God," I bite back, pointing to the silver cross that hangs around her throat, identical to the one David wears. "I'm sure *He'd* have something to say about it! Then again He hasn't helped me all those times you've beaten me over the years, so I don't suppose he would've given a fuck if you'd aborted me like you wish you had."

"Get out of my house," she repeats, before turning on her feet and leaving me bleeding out on the floor.

Lena's hand flies to her mouth, tears pricking her eyes, but I refuse to cry. Not this time. Not anymore. "I can't believe she just said that."

"It's not the first time," I admit. Mum has always been so careful not to say those hateful words in front of Lena or any of her friends. Not today. She's dug the knife in and twisted.

"I hate her."

"You don't. She loves *you*," I heave a sigh, beyond jealous. For a long time I was envious of my sister because Mum doted on her so much. Even David tolerated Lena, never once laying a hand on her, mainly because Mum wouldn't let him, and he had me to lay into whenever he felt the need. I can't begrudge Lena Mum's love. I wouldn't wish this feeling of worthlessness on anyone, especially not my little sister. Aside from my friendship with the Breakers, she's been the only bright thing in my life. At least I still have her.

"I don't care. As soon as I'm eighteen I'm getting out of here, Pen. I can't stand her."

"If I could take you with me, I would. You know that, right?"

She nods her head. "Yeah, I know..."

I open my arms and she walks right into them, holding me close as she buries her head in the crook of my neck. "I'm proud of you, Pen, even if Mum isn't. I don't understand what her problem is..."

"I don't know either, Lena."

The truth is mum has always hated me. As far back as I can remember she's looked at me like I'm nothing but a disappointment. Maybe it's because she had us so young. Getting pregnant at fourteen with David, then at eighteen with me, must've been hard, especially when our father walked out on us a few weeks after my birth. But I've always tried to be a good kid. I went to school, I worked hard, and I stayed out of trouble. It's why I took up dance instead of following in my brother's footsteps. Despite that, she still dotes on him even though she hates me. At least she loves Lena. I don't think I would've been able to leave her alone with mum if she treated her the same way as she's treated me over the years.

"Make sure you call me every night, yeah?" Lena asks, sniffling. She pulls back, rubbing at her pretty blue eyes. They're such a lovely shade of light blue, the complete opposite to my murky brown ones.

"Every night. I promise."

"Are you going now?"

"Yeah. I don't think I have a choice."

Lena smiles sadly. "At least this time you're not running away, and I'll be able to see you when I want, right?"

I gulp down the sudden ball of anxiety in my throat as my hands begin to shake. "You remember that time?"

"Of course I remember. I cried the whole week you were gone."

"You never said anything at the time... or after."

"I didn't want to bring it up. I thought you'd run away again if I did. So I pretended that I believed the story Mum made up about you going to stay with your dad for a week. We all knew that wanker fucked-off and started a new life somewhere else not long after you were born."

"Fuck, I'm sorry."

Lena gives me a brave smile and a brief hug. "It's okay, I understand why you ran. Mum's always so mean to you. Honestly, I've often wondered over the years why you didn't do it again."

I breathe out slowly, willing myself to keep hold of the secret about what really happened the night I ran away. Plastering on a fake smile, I grin at my sister and make light of the situation. "Yeah, I've often wondered why too. Perhaps it's Mum's amazing Sunday roasts that stopped me," I joke.

Lena rolls her eyes. "Let's face it, her cooking is enough to send *anyone* running."

We both burst out laughing, and whilst on the outside I'm smiling, on the inside I'm dying a little. That night changed everything for me, in more ways than one.

CHAPTER FIVE

Six Years Ago

WET through and with my backpack slung over my shoulder, I stand on the pavement on the opposite side of the road and look up at the front door of number fifteen Jackson Street. Rain pours over my skin, plastering my hair to my head and my clothes to my body. My jaw chatters uncontrollably and without looking in a mirror, I know that my lips are blue. It's taken me thirty minutes to walk here in the pouring rain. Most of that time I spent avoiding any of the hotspots in our estate and kept to the shadows. I'm not a complete idiot. A girl my age out on her own at one in the morning is a prime target for arseholes and predators.

Running away without a plan isn't easy, or sensible, but I had no choice.

Music pumps out between the gaps in the wooden boards

covering every window of the building. Light filters through those same gaps and despite its derelict appearance, there's plenty of life inside. The Skins don't bother trying to hide the fact that this is their headquarters. As far as they're concerned they're above the law. No one around here fucks with them. Not even the posh nobs who live down the same street. I bet they hate having the Skins as neighbours. Two million-pound houses sit either side, huge iron fences and electric gates a pathetic attempt at blocking the Skins out.

It won't work.

Rumour has it that Jeb has several of these rich pricks, and the local police chief, in his pocket anyway. If anyone dares to complain about the noise, they're quickly silenced with violence or the threat of it. Neighbourhood Watch ain't gonna work around here.

Which really makes me question why, of all places, I've found myself here tonight? Maybe I *should* try the homeless shelter in central Hackney. It might be another thirty-minute walk in this shitty weather, but it's got to be better than a squat filled with criminals. Then again, a fourteen-year old kid turning up with two black eyes and bruises on her body is going to raise alarm bells, so perhaps not. Lena and I don't need social services knocking on our door and digging too deep.

I hate my mum and my brother, but I can't risk being separated from my sister. Sometimes it's better the devil you know. I'll just give it a few days to let the dust settle and then I'll go back home. Mum won't send anyone looking for me anyway, and she loves Lena, so there won't be any issues there.

It's not like she'll let anyone hurt her...

Pushing down my rage and ignoring the pang inside my

chest at the injustice of it all, I sniff loudly and wipe my nose on the sleeve of my soggy jumper.

I'm strong. I can do this.

But instead of heading over to the house, I lean against the trunk of a large Oak tree and study the building under the cover of its huge branches and thick canopy of leaves that protect me from the rain. Shame it can't do the same about the cold, though. I'm freezing.

Apart from the boarded-up windows and thick metal door designed to keep squatters out, the house itself is a huge three-story Victorian townhouse with half a dozen steps that lead up to the front door. It's run down, with tiles missing on the roof, and weeds growing up through the cracks in the driveway, but I can see how beautiful it must have been once. A little love and care, and the place could be as stunning as the other houses on the road. Even in its dilapidated state, you can still see its beauty. I kind of like that. Not everything that glitters is gold, and not everything broken is worthless or without beauty. I don't know when I got so deep, and I laugh a little at myself.

"Are you just gonna stand there all night, or are you going in?"

I almost jump out of my skin as a guy steps out of the shadowy archway of an alleyway that I hadn't noticed before now. Fuck, my street smarts are outta whack tonight. Rookie mistake. Though it's not surprising given what I've just been through.

Curling my fist around the strap of my rucksack, I narrow my eyes, ready to swing my bag at him if the need arises. He notices but instead of approaching me like I expect him to do, he pulls back his hoodie and gives me a once over. White blond hair springs out in all directions and he appears ghostly in the bright streetlight that illuminates his skin. Actually he looks like he could've stepped out of one of those Twilight movies. I swear his eyes are the lightest blue I've ever seen. Even in the dark, they're shockingly bright.

Definitely a vampire.

I hug myself tighter. He could totally suck me dry and no one would come to my rescue.

"Who did that to you?" he asks, pointing to my black eyes.

"None of your business," I retort through the chattering of my teeth.

"Was it someone in there?" He points to the house across the road and frowns.

"No." I shake my head violently, then wince as my eye sockets start to ache.

"Okay. So are you waiting on someone? Shouldn't a little girl like you be in bed?"

This time he steps closer and I pull my rucksack off my shoulder, readying myself.

"You fucking touch me, and I'll swing for you!" I warn, gritting my teeth. He might be a good foot taller than me, but I will fight back despite the bruises I wear and the pain in my side when I breathe.

"Hey, I ain't gonna hurt you. I was just about to head over to the house and noticed you standing here like a drowned rat.... No offence," he adds hastily.

"That's a new one," I retort dryly at the insult.

"I didn't mean it like that, but there's no denying you look like shit."

"Thanks." I can't seem to hold back the sarcasm. I'm so over tonight already.

"Look, why don't you come in. My friends all hang out in the basement. They're cool. Jeb leaves us alone for the most part, so you've nothing to fear from him or the *Skins*." He seems to spit the word out like it's poison. "We keep out of his way."

"So you know Zayn then?"

The kid smiles, because he's definitely a boy and not a man despite his height and build. "Yeah, I know Zayn well. I'm one of the Breakers," he says proudly.

"The Breakers?" I ask, swinging my bag back over my shoulder and wincing with the pain.

"We're the Breakers crew. Me, Zayn, Dax and Xeno."

"You're one of Zayn's crew?" I ask stupidly, given he's already told me that.

"Well, strictly speaking it's Xeno's crew. Zayn's just a cocky bastard and talks shit because he's the best dancer. Xeno humours him."

"Oh," I respond, not really knowing what else to say.

He grins, holding his hand out. I stare at it hovering between us. "My name's York and I don't know about you, but it's fucking freezing and I could use a drink. Coming?" he asks, stepping forward, still offering his hand.

For some reason only known to the old man in the sky, I throw caution to the wind and slide my trembling hand into his, totally under his spell. He squeezes my fingers and pulls me gently across the road towards number fifteen Jackson Street.

&

LAUGHTER SOUNDS as we enter the basement through a side door rather than the front one. It opens onto a darkened hallway that makes me squeak with fear. York grins, pointing to the stairs that descend into more darkness. "Don't be scared. I swear no one here will hurt you. Just watch your step."

I don't know why I trust him, but I do. Perhaps the double punch to my face has knocked the sense out of me? "You don't want to drink my blood then?" I mumble between full on body shakes as I allow him to lead me downwards, my free hand running along the wall to keep me steady. It feels cold to the touch and gritty, like plaster is coming away in fine grains all over my fingers.

York barks out a laugh, and if it wasn't the middle of the night and pitch black in this poxy staircase I'd bet he'd start sparkling like Edward fucking Cullen. "You're kind of weird, do you know that?"

"And you look like a bloodsucking vampire," I retort.

He chuckles and guides me down the stairs. "Yo, dickheads! I'm here. The party can begin," York says as he releases my hand and pushes open a door before looping his arm over my shoulder. I yelp when his hand lands on a bruise on my upper arm, drawing the attention of the three boys inside the room.

"*Pen?*" Zayn shoots to his feet, his eyes wide with shock. His gaze flicks from me to York and back again. "What the fuck happened to you?"

"I..."

"York?" Zayn accuses, getting the wrong end of the stick completely.

"Fuck you, man, don't look at me like that! I don't hit girls. I just found her outside. She said she knew you, so I invited her in."

Zayn turns his attention back to me. "Why are you here?"

I swallow hard, forcing my body to stop shaking whilst simultaneously trying really hard not to lean into the warmth of York's body. I've no idea how he's stayed so dry. Must be his vampiric skills, dashing through the raindrops or some shit.

"You invited me, remember?" I say quietly, suddenly feeling like a first-class tit.

Zayn puffs out his cheeks, swiping a hand through his hair. Okay, so maybe he was full of shit that day in the playground. My stomach plummets. He's about to say something more when a scowly looking kid pipes up. He's got brown curly hair, and the greenest eyes I've ever seen, they're the same shade as the grass covering Hackney Common. His skin is a few shades darker than Zayn's olive tone, hinting at an inter-racial heritage and offsetting the tone of his eyes beautifully.

"Who's this?" he asks, looking me up and down. That scowl turns to a sneer, making him a little less attractive. He's friendly... *not*.

Urgh. I don't like him. "Who are *you*?" I retort back, unable to help myself and feeling way too prickly. It's been a long night and I could do without his unkindness. Folding my arms across my chest and ignoring York's surprised laugh and Zayn's grimace, I give him my best haughty look, which isn't all that easy when my face hurts so bloody much. The curly haired arsehole is about to respond when he's beaten to the punch by Zayn, who's clearly on damage control.

"This is the girl I was telling you about, remember?" he

explains, as York guides me into the room and kicks the door shut behind me.

"Want a drink?" York asks, ignoring everyone but me as he gives me a gentle smile. I'm not sure why he's being so nice, given we've just met, but I appreciate it anyway, even though the last thing I want is alcohol. I took a swig of Mum's cheap wine once, it was disgusting.

"I don't drink."

"I don't mean alcohol, you're like ten or something.

"Fourteen actually. I'm just small for my age."

"Fourteen then. What's your poison? Cola, Pepsi?"

"Cola is fine."

"Sure thing, Titch," he says, leaving me to stand awkwardly in front of his friends. Great, I've known him for five minutes and he's already calling me names. I groan internally feeling way out of my comfort zone as Zayn and the douchebag with curly hair have a whispered argument, and another kid looks up at me from beneath the rim of his baseball cap. His grey hoodie is pulled up over his cap, casting his face in shadow. All I can see are his lips and chin. He has a pretty mouth.

"Hi," I manage to say.

He doesn't respond. He doesn't even smile. He just looks at me for far longer than is comfortable, before turning his attention back to the arguing boys.

"I can go..." I say, but they don't seem to hear me. "I'll go," I repeat, a little louder this time.

"Sit!" the guy with the curly hair suddenly snaps. He points to the spot on the sofa next to the quiet dude, a scowl on his face. He might be pretty, but he's an arsehole. Figures.

"It's fine. This was a mistake..." My gaze flicks to Zayn who is gritting his jaw in anger and looking at me with an apology in his eyes.

"Not so fast, Titch," York says, jogging towards me. He pulls my rucksack off my shoulder before I can stop him and hands me a warm can of Cola.

"Thanks," I mutter, shifting from foot to foot. This isn't awkward.

"You should probably sit. Xeno can be an arsehole if you ignore his orders," York says with a grin. So that's Mr Scowly's name. Xeno.

"Fuck off, York. It's one o'clock in the fucking morning. Who turns up at that time looking like that?" Xeno growls, folding his arms over his chest.

"Someone who's desperate and needs help?" Zayn says, hitting the nail on the head. My skin flushes crimson and Xeno gives pause, looking at me. I notice a shift in his gaze, like he's suddenly realised he's being an arsehole. Just when I think he's about to redeem himself, he looks at York and snarls.

"Actually, why the fuck are *you* so late? You were supposed to be here at eleven."

"Shit to do," York responds with a shrug.

"So you decide to rock up late and bring *Tiny* with you."

Great, another goddamn nickname. I wish they'd pick something other than my height to focus on. Jesus, I'm not *that* small.

"She's just a *kid*... Leave her alone," Mr Face-In-Shadow comments. He has a deep voice, deeper than the others. He's built too. He can't be the same age as the rest of them.

"I'm not a kid. I'll be fifteen in a few months."

He laughs, shaking his head. "Sit down, Kid."

"Dax you're only fifteen yourself," York comments, rolling

his eyes. "Titch here ain't no harm. Just get over yourselves, alright?" He turns to face me. "Go sit, make yourself comfortable, yeah?"

My cheeks warm. I like York, even if he does look like a bloody vampire. "I'm soaked. Is there anywhere I can change?" I ask, looking between the boys. Even if I'm not staying, I need to get out of these wet clothes. I'm smart enough to know that much. When they stay silent, I continue. "I have a change of clothes in my bag..." My voice trails off when I realise that I've basically just fessed up to running away.

"Here," York says, handing me back my rucksack.

Zayn sighs, then motions for me to follow him. When we reach the corner of the room, he pulls me into a closet that's tucked away there. It's dark and smells of mould. Stepping close, Zayn reaches for something behind me. I can feel his warm breath on my skin as a dim light turns on overhead, illuminating the small space that is empty apart from a wall of shelves with nothing on them.

"Fuck, someone did a number on you, didn't they?"

I grit my teeth and nod.

"Want to talk about it?" he asks. There's a gentleness to his voice that makes my eyes well with unwelcome tears.

"No."

"Okay, well, if you ever do. I'm a good listener." He steps back, giving me a bit of space.

I let out a long whoosh of breath. I don't feel like talking about what happened to me. I don't think I'll ever want to talk about it. "I'm sorry if I've got you into trouble. I didn't have anywhere else to go."

"I'm not in any trouble. Xeno's just a little bit..."

"Of an arsehole?" I fill in for him.

"No, protective of what we have here. He was just caught off-guard. When you get to know him, you'll understand that he's a good guy under it all."

"Okay."

"I'll let you get changed then," he says, backing out of the door and shutting it gently behind him.

It's only then that the tears come, hot and heavy. I stuff my jumper in my mouth and sob, choking on them as they wrack my body. By the time I emerge from the cupboard ten minutes later in dry clothes, my red-rimmed eyes are wiped free from tears and the boys are talking quietly. If they'd heard me crying, they don't mention it. Instead, Mr Face-In-Shadows makes room for me on the sofa between him and Zayn. I sit down, clutching my hands together in my lap. Feeling ten times warmer and fifty times more awkward.

"You good?" Zayn asks.

"I'm good."

"You can stay here as long as you need. Jeb never comes down here, so you don't need to worry about him. Besides, one of us will be here with you at all times, just in case."

"You don't have to do that..."

"We're doing that." I look up at Xeno who is now watching me intently from the armchair opposite. He meets my gaze with a glare. "We're doing that," he repeats.

York grins, his weird sparkly eyes, shining. "Bagsy first."

"What are you, fucking five?" Xeno snaps.

York laughs, shaking his head with mirth.

"Don't you have school to go to?" I ask.

"Don't you?" Xeno retorts.

"Not this week..."

"Then neither do we."

We fall silent for a while and I know that I've upset the balance between this group of friends, but I can't even seem to find the energy to feel guilty about it. Right now, I need to sleep as a sudden bone-weary tiredness washes over me. My eyelids start to droop and before I realise what I'm doing, my head drops to the side, falling onto a bony shoulder. I jerk awake, my head snapping up.

"Sorry," I mumble.

"S'alright. Do what you need. I'm Dax by the way," Mr Face-In-Shadow says, pulling back his hoodie and removing his cap. He has a shorn head, a wide jaw and strange coloured eyes that are a mixture between grey, green and blue.

"I'm Pen."

"See a penny pick up, all day long you'll have good luck," he mutters back, before cupping my head gently and resting it back on his shoulder.

From that day on I became their Pen, and they became my Breakers.

CHAPTER SIX

Present Day

HAULING my bags up the fourth flight of stairs, I finally reach the level where all the studio flats are situated. They're at the top of the main building through a secure door that can only be opened with a code. Luckily for me I'm pretty fit and I've barely broken a sweat, but a lift would've been nice. I can't afford to pull a muscle just before I start at the Academy.

Grasping my bags, and with the key fob to my flat gripped between my teeth, I search for the door with the number four on it. It's right at the end of the corridor, opposite flat number seven. Dropping my bags, I slip the key into the lock and open the door to my new home for the next year. Flipping on the light switch, and hauling my bags inside, I step inside the room. So far I haven't seen any of the other students who'll be my neighbours. I doubt any of them needed to get out of their family homes as quickly as I did. I don't really mind being on my own though. It gives me time to settle in.

Besides, it was fun to collect the key from that bitch receptionist who very nearly ruined my chance at being a dancer with the stunt she pulled the other day. Her surprise at seeing me was priceless. Well, fuck her.

I'd given her a toothy grin, snatched the key fob from her hand and practically run up the stairs, peering through the door to each floor with interest. As much as I wanted to explore every level whilst the academy was quiet, I wanted to see my new studio flat more.

"I can't believe this is mine," I say out loud, laughing at the fact that I'm actually talking to myself now. This is insane. Getting into Stardom Academy is one thing, but being given a flat, all expenses paid, was something else altogether. I feel lucky. Privileged.

Directly to my left is another door that leads into a bathroom. A shower sits over one of those half-sized bathtubs. There's a sink with a mirror above it and a toilet. It's all white, basic, but it's clean and mine. I don't have to share with a shitty mother who pukes her guts up after drinking too much night after night, or a little sister who spends hours preening herself no matter how much I love her.

I grin, letting out a squeal of delight. It's not often I'm this happy and for once I'm going to enjoy my good fortune. I refuse to let thoughts of my mum or the Breakers ruin it.

Twirling on the balls of my feet, I spin down the noticeably short hallway that has a built-in mirrored wardrobe on one side, and enter the main body of my flat. There's a kitchenette built into an alcove with an oven and electric hob, a sink, an under the counter fridge and a few cabinets. More than adequate for my needs. When I open the drawers and cupboards, I find that they're fully stocked with all the kitchen utensils and pans I could ever need. Relief floods through me, I literally have fifty pounds to my name and that's got to cover my food costs for another three weeks until I get paid again. Working at Rocks is a double-edged sword. I love the music, the dancing, and the regular wage, but I don't love the gangs or the drug dealing that happens in the dark corners of the club, or the reason why I'm stuck working there still, for that matter. Zayn's uncle Jeb owns the club, but he's rarely seen there, thank God. He returns periodically to check in on the businesses he owns. Regardless, it's going to be even harder working there now that the Breakers are back.

Fuck, I really wish I could find another job.

Shaking out the nerves I feel at the possibility of seeing the Breakers tonight, I walk around my new flat. The ceilings are high, and there's a large window that forms an arch at the top letting in the last rays of sunlight from a warm September afternoon. A set of pale blue blackout curtains hang from the ceiling, brushing across the wooden floor. They're thick, and very obviously expensive. In the corner of the room sits a single armchair, and a colourful rug covers the middle of the floor. It's only then I realise that there isn't a bed.

"Fuck, what am I supposed to sleep on?"

"The bed folds out from the wall, you donut," a familiar voice says behind me.

I whip around, a grin spreading across my face despite myself. "Clancy! You're here!" I realise how excited I sound, and tone it down. I'm not one of those squealy girly girls.

"Girl, you're looking at one of the most *promising* students," she replies, finger quoting the air. "I'm in flat seven opposite you."

I almost run towards Clancy and throw my arms around her, but I come to my senses and realise that that kind of behaviour isn't becoming of a street kid. We fist and shoulder bump. Rarely do we hug. "When did you get the call?" I ask instead.

"This morning. Dad wanted to drop us off today so we could use the weekend to settle in."

"We?"

Clancy pulls a face. "Yep, the ugly stepsister got a place too. Looks like I can't get away from her."

"Well that's just a stinking pile of shit," I say with a smirk. Sod's law that bitch got in too.

"No kidding. Though I can't wait to see her face when she finds out you're here. She didn't believe me when I said what a fricking awesome dancer you are."

"Bitch."

"Yep, first-class one at that. Anyway," Clancy says, waving her hands in the air and wrinkling her nose. "We really don't need to give her any more air-time. Do you know who else got a spot?"

"No clue," I shrug, refusing to think the worst.

"Do you think Zayn got in...?"

"I don't know. He was good enough," I admit. I might feel sick at the possibility of having him so close by, but at least I can admit that he was good enough to be here. There's no denying his skill as a dancer.

"Well, so far it's just us three. Girl, you and I are going to be besties," she exclaims, breaking out into another wide grin. I can't help but think she's right, and a little bit of the anxiety I've been feeling all afternoon vanishes.

"So, wanna show me how I get the bed down?"

Clancy rolls her eyes and saunters over to a set of shelves on the wall. She reaches up onto her tiptoes and grabs a small leather strap that I hadn't noticed until now and gives it a yank. As it lowers, the shelves slide out and somehow become the base. I make a mental note not to put anything on them.

"There, a perfectly comfortable bed," she says, sitting on the mattress and bouncing up and down. "There is a duvet and some pillows in that cupboard."

I move around the bed and open the cupboard built into the wall recess that she's pointing at and find the items. There aren't any pillowcases, sheets or covers. My heart sinks a little. Shit. I don't have enough money to buy any either. I literally have my clothes and a couple of towels, and some toiletries Lena gave me, that's it.

"What's up?" Clancy asks, noticing the look on my face.

"It's nothing." I plaster on a smile and shake my head.

"Pen, spill it. If we're going to be friends you need to trust me. I know we've only known each other five minutes, but I swear I'm not an arsehole like my sister. I actually have a heart."

"I can see that," I respond with a weak smile. "I don't have any covers or anything for the mattress and duvet. Mum wouldn't let me take anything other than my clothes. I even had to steal a couple of towels when she wasn't looking."

"I'm guessing that you don't get on with your mum?"

"That's the understatement of the year. She basically chucked me out for accepting my spot here."

"Wow!" Clancy looks at me with pity, and I puff out a breath of air.

"It is what it is. I'm glad to get out of the flat if I'm honest. I'll miss my little sister, Lena, but that's it."

"Okay, well, screw your mum. I've got a spare duvet cover set. You can have them."

"No, I can't."

Clancy rolls her eyes. "Seriously, it's no big deal. I only need one set. There's a launderette at the end of the hall. It's not as if you won't keep them laundered."

"You sure?"

"Of course I am. I'm gonna go unpack and get settled in. I'll bring them to you a bit later. You still working at Rocks tonight?"

"Yep. My shift starts at eight o'clock. I get off at midnight, usually spend the last couple hours dancing until the club closes. Helps me to let off steam."

"Excellent, I'll swing by at six with takeaway pizza. You can tell me all about your little sister. Then we can get ready together and I'll come to the club with you. Keep you company until you get off at twelve, then we can rip up the dance floor. How about that?"

"You don't have to do that. The pizza and stuff..." What I want to say is that I can't afford take-out pizza and was planning on eating some plain noodles for my dinner.

"I know, but I want to. We're friends now, got it?"

"Sure." I'm about to explain about my lack of funds when Clancy reaches the door and calls over her shoulder.

"Oh, and the takeout is on me as a thank you for not being a bitch like my sister. I'm glad to have a friend here."

"Me too," I reply, but she's already gone.

⚡

THE CLUB IS PACKED with Friday night revellers and I've been rushed off my feet all night, barely having a chance to chat with Clancy who, true to her word, has sat at the end of the bar the whole evening, chatting to me when she can and fending off admirers the rest of the time. We got ready together in my flat, scoffing down pepperoni pizza whilst Clancy tried on different outfits. She ended up settling on a pair of cut-off black denim shorts and a cute green t-shirt that has *I love Fred Astaire* written in bold lettering across it. Admittedly, that had reminded me of York, and I'd felt a pang inside my chest that I shoved deep inside, refusing to acknowledge it. After much debate, I ended up wearing my usual tight black t-shirt, baggy black cargo pants that are cropped just below the knee, and my trusty Nike trainers. I don't need to impress anyone, and therefore, I don't really give a shit what I put on. Besides, the last time I actually made an effort, I ended up sleeping with some wannabe gangster arsehole who'd immediately regretted getting mixed up with me, but that's a whole other thought for another night.

Tonight, Clancy's had her fair share of admirers. She's a new face and really cute. It's no surprise then that she's attracted a stream of guys, and some girls. Right now she's having a conversation with a guy I recognise from the hip-hop scene back in the day. He comes to Rocks fairly regularly, though I've not seen him for a while. Leo's a few years older than me, in his mid-twenties and a pretty safe guy. As far as I'm aware he's not into heavy drugs or a member of any of the gangs that hang out here on a regular basis. He just likes to dance and comes to the club when he can afford to.

"Hey, Pen," Clancy calls, waving me over when she notices the group around the bar has eased off.

"Just a sec!" I reply, removing the empty glasses from the bar and stacking them in the wire tray ready to be picked up by the cleaning staff.

Boys by Lizzo starts playing, and the crowd on the dance floor roars. It's one of my favourites. I start bopping to the music, eager for my shift to end so I can release some of this pent-up energy I feel. I've been on edge the whole night expecting to see Zayn or one of the other Breakers. So far they haven't shown. I doubt they will now, there's only a few hours until the club shuts, the relief I feel knowing that is immense. Holding both hands up to Clancy, I indicate I've still got ten minutes left of my shift, but when Jess, another barmaid, ducks down and grabs a bottle of beer from the fridge and passes it to me with a wink, I know she's giving me the okay to get off early.

"Thanks, J," I say, gulping down the whole bottle in one go before sliding out from behind the bar.

"Is it time to dance?" Clancy asks me, a huge grin spreading across her face.

"Sure as fuck is," I respond.

"Leo this is Pen. Pen this is Leo," Clancy introduces us, even though we know each other.

"Alright?" I ask him.

"Yep. I'm good. You?"

"Better now I've clocked off. I haven't seen you around for a while."

"Oh, you know each other already. I'm such a tool!" Clancy exclaims, her cheeks flushing.

"Pen is pretty well-known around these parts," Leo explains, giving me a look.

"She is?"

"No more than anyone else who works here," I interrupt before Leo can drop me in it. He's a regular, or at least he was until a couple weeks ago. I'm fairly sure he was there the night my world imploded, but that's a conversation I don't want to have right now. Leo seems to catch my hint and drops the subject. Definitely a good guy then.

"What have you been doing lately?" I ask him, forcing the conversation into safer territory.

"Keeping my head down mainly. I haven't got as much time for dancing with my nine-to-five job."

"Sorry to hear that," I say. He's a good dancer, but that means shit when you've got responsibilities. I'm fairly sure his mum's disabled and his dad ran off with a younger model.

He shrugs. "Ain't got time to dwell. I'm happy enough. So, Clancy tells me you both got into Stardom Academy. That's pretty fucking impressive," he says.

"We did, and thanks..." My gaze flicks to the dance floor. I'm over the small talk.

"Come on, let's dance," Leo says, sensing my reluctance.

We don't need to be told twice.

Just like every night at Rocks, the dance floor is heaving, and the place is lit. I've been working here most weekends since I was seventeen and sneaking into the club for a few years before that as well. This place holds a lot of memories. Good and bad ones.

Boys is still pumping through the speakers and its funky atmosphere has everyone grinning and letting loose. The air is a heady mixture of booze, sweat and perfume. There's an interesting kind of energy here tonight. It's a fun vibe, but with an edge of something else, like everyone's waiting for shit to go down. Or maybe that's just me who's feeling on edge. Whatever.

If the Breakers turn up, then they turn up. There's nothing I can do about that. I'll just have to deal with the fallout.

"This place is insane!" Clancy shouts over the pounding music and the appreciation of the crowd who are throwing their hands in the air and busting moves left, right and centre.

The best time is when the battles start, usually between one and two am, just before the club shuts down at three. I've entered many battles over the years with the Breakers, but only accepted one-on-one challenges in the last six months. More often than not someone offers me out whenever I'm on shift. It's no skin off my nose, I like to dance, I love to battle, and I never lose.

Tonight though, I'm going to give it a miss. It's been way too much of an emotional day, and I'm drained. I'll dance for an hour, then head off home before the battles start because I will be challenged. There's always someone who wants to take the crown. Tonight they can have it. I'm fully aware that if you forfeit a challenge you have to start at the bottom again. Prior to getting into Stardom Academy I would've done anything to hold onto first place, now I feel differently about it. It doesn't seem so important somehow.

Clancy follows Leo into the centre of the dance floor, pulling me along behind her. By the way they're eyeing each other up, it looks like they'll be getting their freak on tonight. The crowd parts, and I get a few nods of acknowledgment from various regulars and fist bumps from others.

"Are you some kind of star here?" Clancy asks, as people move back to give us room to dance.

"Not really..."

"Don't listen to her, Clancy. She's the reigning champion. No one's beaten her in a dance battle since she took on the first challenge six months ago."

Clancy grins, bumping my shoulder with her fist. "You go girl!"

"It's no big deal," I grin.

"Sure, it's not."

Clancy starts dancing, grooving to the beat. Her specialism might be tap, but she's got rhythm, and perfect timing. Madame Tuillard was right to choose her as one of the most promising students because the girl can move. When she starts a complicated series of tap steps, interspersing them with shit-hot street moves, Leo's mouth drops open and I swear I can see little love hearts floating out of his eyes.

"Girlllll, damn! You. Are. Fire!" he shouts out over the music.

She grins at him, then winks at me. Pretty soon they've only got eyes for each other. I don't mind, I'm here to dance and not act as a wing-girl. Not that she needs my help in the slightest. Leo is all over her like a hot rash.

Another hour later, sweaty and feeling much better for dancing all the restless energy away, I hear the sound of the club's MC, Little Dynamite, shouting out his signature 'braaap, braaap' over the mic. Everyone who comes here regularly knows what that sound means, and those who don't quickly move off the dance floor when it empties out around them.

Clancy drags Leo behind her as she rushes to catch up with me. I'm heading towards the bar to grab my coat and bag that's stashed behind it, swerving through the growing crowd of revellers.

"Hey, Pen, where are you going?"

"Home," I say, loving that I can call my new studio flat back at the academy home. Well, for the next year at least. After that, I'll have to figure out what to do. "I'm whacked, it's been a long day. You stay, I'll be fine getting back on my own. Leo's a good guy, he'll take care of you," I say as the crowd around us thickens.

Leo grins. "I'll make sure she gets back safe."

"Aren't you gonna stick around for the battles. I'd love to see you rip up the dance floor especially since I'm told you're the queen bee around here."

"Nope. I'm out tonight."

"Yo, yo, yo!" Little Dynamite begins, interrupting us and grabbing the attention of the crowd. "It's battle time, homies! Get ready for the best of the best!" The crowd roars and I back away, disappearing into the thickening crowd. Clancy turns, searching for me and I wave.

"I'm going!" I shout over the din. She nods, giving me a thumbs-up. Then I lose sight of her as people jostle to get closer to the dance floor. Ducking my head, I twist on my feet and weave through the crowd, then smack straight into a wall of hard muscle. Two large hands grip my upper arms.

"Not so fast, *Tiny*."

CHAPTER SEVEN

Five Years Ago

"NOT SO FAST, TINY," Xeno says, grabbing hold of my hoodie and yanking me backwards so my arms cartwheel in the air. I have to shuffle my feet quickly in order to stop myself falling onto my arse.

"Hey, dickhead, you could've choked me to death!" I shout, twirling on my feet and punching him on the arm. "I'm done with your crap today." He's been snarky all morning and I'm over it. He lets me go and laughs.

"Don't be such a girl!" he accuses, enraging me further. Of all the Breakers, Xeno is the one who pushes my buttons the most. He's always challenging me one way or the other, but today I'm not in the mood for his games.

"Go fuck off and die, Xeno." I sidestep him, ducking beneath his arm when he holds it out to stop me.

"Woah, Tiny, you on your period?"

Low blow, arsehole. I'd been waiting for my period to start for ages, then last month it had, and what a shit show that was. I had to rely on Zayn to get me some sanitary towels because I came on here in the damn basement. Sod's law. I was mortified, but at the time all the guys were really cool about it. Zayn even bought me chocolate. Now, Xeno has switched and seems intent on rubbing my face in being a woman, which is like a red rag to a bull with me. Narrowing my eyes, I turn to face him, folding my arms across my chest.

"You know I'd like to meet your mum," I say.

"Yeah, why's that?" He smirks and folds his arms across his chest, jerking his chin. I see the flash of challenge in his eyes. Yeah, that's right, motherfucker. I might be tiny, but I'm not a pushover.

"Because I'd ask her whether she still likes Mother Nature despite what it did to you."

"Burrrnnnnnnnnnnn!" York holds his closed fist up to his mouth and starts laughing. Dax smiles and Zayn chuckles, watching us both. They know what's coming next. This verbal sparring is becoming a regular occurrence between me and Xeno. Since we became friends almost a year ago, Xeno has spent a great deal of time trying to get me to fall in line. I won't. No one's the boss of me. Besides, despite appearances, I quite like the verbal sparring. It's fun.

Xeno smiles evilly. He holds his hands up as though he's shading his eyes then makes a show of looking for something. Eventually, he lowers his head and stares directly at me. I puff out my chest and straighten my spine, but I still only reach his chest. He's as tall as I am short. Arsehole. I know what's coming.

"I promise not to make fun of your height, I would never stoop to that. Might put my back out."

Zayn, Dax, and York all chuckle. Out of the corner of my eye I can see them talking under their breaths. When we get going like this they make bets as to which one of us is going to win. The winner is always the one with the best cuss. If I can make Xeno belly laugh before he can do the same to me, then I win. Today, I'm winning.

I bark out a laugh and make a point of running my gaze up from Xeno's feet over his low-slung denim jeans and white t-shirt, all the way to the top of his very curly-haired head. "I'm glad you're tall, it gives me more of you to dislike."

Xeno's eyes spark with mirth, but his mouth is a hard line. I know he's holding back a laugh. "I could eat a bowl of alphabet soup and shit out a better line than that."

The Breakers lose it and start rolling around the floor holding their stomachs. Arseholes.

Xeno smirks, thinking he's won this battle. Stepping closer, he uses his height and size to try and intimidate me. He should know by now that there's nothing about him, or any of the Breakers that intimidate me. I like them all way too much. Right now I'm desperately holding onto a laugh.

"Ha! Nice one, Xeno, but do you know what?"

"What?"

"You should save your breath because you'll need it to blow up your girlfriend later."

"Whaaaaaaaa!" Zayn calls out, thumping Dax hard on the back because he seems to have turned blue from laughing so hard and not getting enough oxygen. York has tears rolling down his face. I look back at Xeno with a straight face, whilst his lip twitches and his eyes flash with amusement. His shoulders start to bounce and a moment later laughter bursts free from his lips. Pretty soon he's doubled over.

"Take that, arsewipe!" I grin.

"Tiny, you fucking kill me. You know that, right?"

"I make it my life's work to keep your ego a decent size."

"Come on. Let's get back to it," he says, before wrapping his arm around my shoulder and rubbing his knuckles over the top of my head, successfully messing my hair up.

"Lay off," I grouse, pushing at his hand, but not pulling away from his hold. I feel safe there.

Strange, but true.

If I'm being honest, I feel safe with all my Breakers. Some days I worry about how much I've come to rely on them in such a short time. The only other person in this world I care about just as much as them is Lena, but she's too young to understand me like they do. Plus, I need to shield her as much as possible from the shit that goes on in my life, so it's not as if I can confide in her like that. She's too little. With his arm still slung around my shoulder, Xeno motions for the guys to get up.

"Right dickheads, you need to move your lazy arses because we've got a routine to finish."

"Ah, man, I was having fun watching you two. Best laugh I've had all week..." Dax's voice trails off and we all know that his home life has been rough lately. The darkening bruise on his chin tells us as much even though he hasn't said a thing. His dad is as much of a bully as my mum.

Giving Xeno a gentle nudge, I duck out of his hold and move towards Dax. "Come on, Dax, let's dance those arseholes out of our system," I say.

We lock gazes, understanding passing between us. "Alright, kid, anything for you," he says.

I roll my eyes at his nickname for me. Dax is exactly six months and two days older than me, but apparently that's enough of an age gap for him to be able to call me a kid. Maybe I should start calling him Daddy... Okay, no, that would be weird.

Half an hour later after repeating the same set of steps over and over again to *It's Like That* by Run DMC we all flop onto the sofa's panting and sweating.

"I think we got it down," Zayn comments, a pleased look on his face. He should be pleased, it's pretty much all his choreography. The guy's a genius.

"I agree. Good job. We could probably win the battle at Rocks Friday night," Dax says, casually.

"That's a nightclub for the over eighteen," I point out.

"Yep, an *illegal* nightclub run by my uncle that doesn't give a shit about underage kids so long as they can fucking dance. We're tight, we could win," Zayn points out.

Xeno frowns, looking between us before his gaze lands on me. "No. Not yet."

"But..." Zayn interrupts.

"I said not yet."

And just like that the conversation ends.

York, sensing the tension, does his mother hen thing and grabs us all a drink from the mini fridge that Zayn took from a skip a week ago. One of the posh knobs down the street is getting their house refurbished and was throwing away all sorts of good shit. Jeb had taken most of it, but Zayn managed to nab the fridge before anyone else could.

"Here we go, ladies," York grins, chucking us a can of Cola

each and successfully curbing the argument between Xeno and Zayn.

Of the group, York is the most light-hearted, and thoughtful. The dude would make someone a great wife. Also, I'm fairly sure he's Mother Theresa reincarnated. I chuckle to myself at the thought of him wearing a nun's habit.

"What's tickled your pickle, Titch?" he asks, flopping down on the sofa next to me. He throws his arm around the back of the seat and I get a whiff of his aftershave and the musky smell of sweat that should be gross but isn't. I have to stop myself from wrapping my arm around his waist and breathing in deep. The guys are always flinging their arms around me in a friendly, best friend kind of way and whilst I'm cool with that, I'm not so great at returning the favour physically.

"You, York, you tickle my pickle. I like it," I respond instead.

Zayn flashes me a look at the exact same time as Cola fires out of his nostrils. What the actual fuck? I start giggling uncontrollably as he wipes at his face. He's such a plum. Dax slams him on the back and Xeno watches us all with amusement from the armchair opposite. But when I look at York, his face is a bright red, and he looks more like a tomato than Edward-sparkling-Cullen.

"What did I say?" I ask, genuinely miffed.

York is always coming up with random sayings. I was just doing what I always do and taking part in the fun. York shakes his head and grins, the colour fading from his cheeks.

"Nothing, it's nothing. You're just funny, that's all."

But I'm not to be put off. I want to know what all the looks are for. Even Dax seems to have sunk lower into the sofa and has pulled up his hoodie to hide the expression on his face. Even though he's not making a sound, I know he's laughing. His shoulders are moving up and down with mirth.

"What?!" I repeat.

Xeno opens his mouth then slams it shut again when York gives him the stink-eye. It's Zayn that finally caves. He's the one who always caves first. The guy can't keep anything from me. I like his honesty and I like the fact he trusts me enough with it.

"Your clit, Titch. When York refers to 'your pickle', he's talking about your clit."

Beside me York groans. "It's just a phrase, I didn't mean anything by it."

"My clit? What the fuck are you all going on about?" I ask, genuinely confused. *What's a damn clit?*

"Oh, fuck no! I'm out of this one," Xeno exclaims, getting up and striding over to the bathroom. He slams the door and I jump.

"Would someone mind telling me what the hell is going on?"

Dax makes a kind of whooshing noise with his mouth, and sinks further down into the sofa like he wants it to swallow him up. Beside me, York is once again bright red.

"Sorry man, I gotta go. Shit to do," York blurts out, rushing to his feet. Dax grunts, gives me a wave and mumbles under his breath something about helping York with the shit he's got to do, leaving right behind him.

"Motherfuckers," Zayn exclaims, swiping a hand through his hair.

I look at Zayn helplessly. "What did I say now?" I'm baffled.

Zayn puffs out his cheeks and looks up at me from beneath the flop of black hair. His night-time eyes sparkling with something I don't understand. His cheeks flush pink a little, and he kind of winces.

"Zayn, I swear to God, if you don't tell me what the big bloody deal is, I'm going to lose it."

"Okay, okay," he says, lifting off the couch he's sitting on and plonking himself down next to me.

"So, erm, you're seriously telling me you don't know what a clit is?" He looks at me like I've grown a second head, and I immediately feel defensive.

"No, I don't. I'm not a know-it-all like you. Just spit it out!"

"You do know how babies are made, right?" He asks me slowly, like I'm dense.

"Of course I do. I'm not a complete fucking idiot..."

"Thank fuck. I'm not doing that talk as well."

"That talk... Wait, where's this going?" I suddenly realise that perhaps this isn't a conversation I should be having with Zayn, but curiosity has got the better of me now, and for better or worse I need to know what they're going on about. It's not as if I can talk to my mum or Lena about anything like this.

"You do have Biology lessons at school, right? And Sex Ed?"

"Well, yes, but Biology doesn't really cover much more than cells and things like that. In Sex Ed I kind of switch-off."

"Then from now on perhaps you should pay a bit more attention..."

"The clit, Zayn. Just tell me what the fuck it is so Xeno can come out of the bathroom and the guys can finish the *'shit they got to do'* and come back," I say, rolling my eyes.

Zayn squares me a look then grits his jaw. "You know guys have dicks..."

"Yes, I'm aware guys have dicks, Zayn." For fuck's sake.

"Well, girls have a pussy," he coughs, then chokes a little, then shakes his head. "I mean they have a vagina."

We both stare at each other for far too long. This isn't good. Why in all that is fucking holy did I pursue this? "Yep," I squeak, trying not to die a little.

"So, when York was referring to your 'pickle' it was his roundabout way of describing the clit..."

"I'm not sure I want to hear this..." My voice trails off when Zayn continues, determined to fucking embarrass me.

"And the clit is a part of the female genitalia. It sits at the top of your va-jay-jay, where the, erm, lips meet..."

Female genitalia? V-jay-jay?

He catches my gaze and I look down, wanting to be invisible right about now. I want to stick my fingers in my ears and say 'la, la, la,' like a five-year-old, but I can't seem to do anything other than sit glued to the sofa. It's horrifying. Zayn takes that as a cue to keep bloody talking.

I want to die.

"The clit is the Holy fucking Grail and is extremely sensitive. It gives pleasure to a woman when someone touches it. Wait," he muses, "That's not strictly true, the G-spot is actually the Holy Grail."

G-Spot? Holy Grail? Oh my God, kill me now! "York wants to touch my clit?" I screech, wishing I'd just shut the hell up. Now I'm the one flushing a deep crimson. I feel heat spread out beneath my skin. Through the closed bathroom door, I can hear Xeno cursing loudly.

"No! No, it's just a saying... and actually, it was you who said that he *'tickles your pickle'* and that you *'like it'*, remember..."

"Oh fuck, no! He doesn't, I swear it. I would never. I don't even..." *I don't even know where the clit is.* I mean I know now that it's a part of my lady bits thanks to Zayn, but I've never explored down there. Like EVER. What's grossing me out even more is that it's been described as a goddamn pickle. I mean, even the small ones are like a mini penis. That can't be right, can it? I do not have a dick. I almost put my hand over my crotch to check. Almost.

"We know that. It's just a saying." He chuckles, giving me a playful shove. Urgh, this is not the conversation I wanted to have with anyone, let alone Zayn. I've never wanted the floor to open up and swallow me more than I do right this second. They all must think I'm a complete loser not knowing about this shit. Oh god. This is embarrassing.

"So that's about it. Any more questions?" Zayn asks.

"Hell no!" I stand, ready to bolt. Honestly though, as much as this is cringeworthy, I actually do have more questions.

So. Many. Questions.

But I don't ask them. I keep my mouth fucking shut.

"Well, if you ever need to know more, you know where to come."

"Yup." Like that is never *ever* going to happen.

"You can come out now, Xeno," Zayn shouts, grinning at me.

When he emerges Xeno can't look me in the eye, which is just as well because I really couldn't feel anymore embarrassed than I do right now, and I can't face him either. Making my excuses, I leave, practically sprinting out of the basement just like York and Dax had earlier. Behind me I can hear Zayn laughing and Xeno tell him to shut the fuck up.

Later that night at home, I look up 'the clit' on the internet and spend the next three hours finding out all about sex and pleasure. My world opens up in ways I *never* imagined, and despite my embarrassment at how the whole subject came up, I can't help but feel grateful for Zayn's explanation and the fact a clit looks nothing like a goddamn pickle, because eww. One thing I do know for sure is that from now on in I will be avoiding offering up my *pickle to be tickled* by any fucking one, *especially* the Breakers.

CHAPTER EIGHT

Present Day

MY EYES LAND on Zayn first who jerks his chin and gives me a dangerous smile beneath the shade of his cap. Beside him, propping up the bar is York looking less like Edward Cullen and more like Eric from True Blood. He's wearing a black leather jacket and boots, with distressed blue jeans. York meets my gaze, and my heart stutters. This time there's no warm smile, no genuine affection in his icy-blue gaze. There's nothing but a blank mask. He raises his shot glass to me then knocks back the dark liquid in one go. Xeno's grip tightens on my upper arm as he shifts me back around.

"Where's Dax?" I murmur, my pulse racing.

I don't know why I ask. I don't care. I shouldn't care. Yet, I do.

"Fuck, Tiny, you always were a little dense. I thought you

might grow out of your naivety by now though. Looks like nothing's changed." He lets me go roughly, and wipes his hands down his jeans as though I've dirtied him up somehow.

I'm too shocked to think up a cutting response. By the time my brain kicks into gear and I'm ready to verbally spar with Xeno like the good old days, a familiar song starts to play out over the speaker system, and I'm rendered speechless.

No! No, fucking way. A cruel smile carves across Xeno's face and I grow cold.

"We have our first challenge!" Little Dynamite calls out. The crowd roars, but my heart sinks.

"No," I whisper. He just laughs, looking down the length of his nose at me. His gaze cutting into mine.

He's haughty. Beautiful. *Angry*.

"The infamous Breakers are back and guess what...?" Little Dynamite continues as Xeno crosses his arms over his chest. Beside him, Zayn and York appear. All three of them glare at me. I swallow hard, my throat closing over with pain.

"What?" the crowd roars back, getting into a frenzy.

"Tonight, *Teardrop Dax* is challenging... PEN!"

The crowd erupts. My stomach bottoms out.

"No!" I respond, shaking my head. "No. I'm leaving." I move to walk away, trying to push past the three of them, but Xeno grips my wrist.

"The fuck you are, Tiny. You ain't walking away from us again," he snarls into my ear, then proceeds to drag me towards the dance floor. The crowd parts like the fucking ocean did for Moses, allowing us a clear path through. I fall in step beside him, trying to regain some of my dignity. There are too many people here who will talk. Spread rumours, tell lies. I can't afford for my brother to hear any of them. So I grit my teeth and try to stem the raging emotion I feel at seeing them all again after so long. Truth be known I want to throw myself into their arms, hold them close. I want to get back what we had before we ruined it all so spectacularly.

I want to hate Xeno. I want to hate York and Zayn, Dax. Part of me does, and yet...

Hate is often at its most powerful when it's formed on the back of love. Sometimes the two emotions are so thinly separated that tiny droplets filter from one into the other, discolouring the truth, blending it until you don't even know how to feel anymore.

"*Pen?*" Clancy begins, looking between me and Xeno as we pass her by. She moves towards me, but Leo holds her back.

"Leave it, Clancy. I'll be fine," I call out over my shoulder.

I don't get to hear her response, because Xeno is intent on humiliating me as he manhandles me onto the dance floor. Right now it's clear that he doesn't give a shit about the show he's putting on. He certainly doesn't give a shit that I'm going to be left with a bruise from the tight grasp of his fingers, triggering me in the worst possible way.

Motherfucker.

Hate blooms, darkening that deep-seated love, making it murky and unclear. This isn't the boy I loved. This man before me is a stranger. I need to remember that. When we reach the centre of the dance floor, I yank my arm free, then turn on Xeno and punch him as hard as I can on the arm. I would've punched his face if he wasn't so damn tall and my reach wasn't so fucking short. The crowd sucks in a collective breath, but I'm too mad to worry about the consequences or the throbbing of my hand.

Little Dynamite makes some more 'braaaap, braaap' sounds over the mic, shaping his fingers into guns indicating that this is a battle both on and off the dance floor. Dick.

"That was a mistake, Tiny," Xeno growls, leaning over me.

"Get fucked, Xeno."

His eyes flash with rage, but I know him and he'd never, ever, hit a woman. Yet, when his eyes darken and that grass-green I used to adore so much deepens to an almost black, I realise that I no longer know him at all. Maybe I never did.

"The only person getting fucked is you, Pen," he snarls, before wrapping his tattooed hand around the back of my head and yanking me against his body. Before I can even try to fight him off, his hot, angry mouth is pressed against mine in a kiss that simultaneously obliterates all my defences and riles me up like nothing else. The kiss is savage, brutal and when his tongue pierces my lips and swoops in like he owns me, I have to shove down all the righteous emotions he conjures so nobody sees just how affected I am by his words and his actions. With an angry hand clutching the back of my head and our bodies thrust together, Xeno steals a kiss I wasn't prepared to give him.

Hard.

Taut.

Vicious.

He ravages my mouth, bruises my lips, batters my defences. He doesn't soothe *me*. He doesn't heal *us*. He doesn't answer any of the questions I've harboured for the last three fucking years. This kiss maims. This kiss tears, shreds, and stings. This kiss *hurts*.

And the worse thing of all, this kiss is our *first*.

Letting me go with a shove, Xeno leaves me panting as he

stalks off the dance floor without a backward glance. Anger and betrayal rips at my skin, threatening to shred me to pieces.

I want to scream. I want to fucking rip out my hair. I want to pummel my fists against his retreating back, but worse than all of that, I want him to kiss me again.

Instead, I force myself to be still, to stop shaking. I force myself to internalise every last emotion, shutting them down one by one and forming a thicker, more impenetrable defence.

"Well, well, well. Looks like there's trouble in paradise," Little Dynamite taunts.

I catch his eye and sneer. He knows just as well as I do that the Breakers and I haven't been friends for three fucking years, that it's an impossibility. Little Dynamite is just some prick who'll be nice one minute and a wanker the next. He loves the drama, gives him and the rest of the revellers at Rocks something to gossip about. If I wasn't forced to work here, I would've left a long time ago.

"Just fucking get on with it!" I shout out over the cawing of the crowd.

There's no backing out now. If I want to keep my pride in place and my reputation intact, I have to battle. If it were anyone else, I wouldn't give a shit, but the Breakers know exactly which buttons to push. What they fail to realise is I'm not the same girl I was three years ago. This woman fights her own damn battles. I learnt the hard way that you can't rely on anyone but yourself. The Breakers were the last ones to break my heart.

Never again.

Jerking my chin and folding my arms, I wait for my opponent. Little Dynamite holds his hands up to silence the crowd who look like they're about to witness a dirty brawl in an underground fight club and not a battle on a dance floor. Though, to be fair, both can be just as dangerous, especially when you're battling against a member of a gang and not just someone from a dance crew like I am tonight.

"Hurry the fuck up," I add, glaring at the MC.

"Feisty, Pen. I like it," Little Dynamite retorts, winking.

I flip him the finger.

It's not hard to see whose side he's on tonight. Raising his arm, he indicates for the music to be turned up. The bass vibrates up through the floor as *In Da Club* by 50 Cent pounds out through the speakers. A song that has so many layers of meaning for me and the Breakers. I close my eyes and let the music fill me up, long buried memories forcing themselves to the forefront of my mind.

CHAPTER NINE

Four Years Ago

"KID, YOU FUCKING ACED THAT!" Dax laughs, picking me up and spinning me around, not caring that the whole club is watching. My legs lift off the floor as we both enjoy our moment of success as the crowd cheers and hollers around us. Beating Trey and Nazeen in the doubles battle is something we've been working towards for months now. All that hard work and hours of practicing together has finally paid off. *In Da Club* by 50 Cent was the song picked at random to battle too, an oldie but it still packs a punch even now.

"Give it up for Pen and Dax!" Little Dynamite roars over the mic one last time.

The club erupts once again as people cheer and hoot at our success. Dax settles me back onto my feet as Zayn, Xeno and York push through the crowd barrelling into us both.

"You fucking did it!" Zayn explodes with happiness.

"What the fuck man, that was insane shit right there!" York fist bumps Dax and pulls me into a tight hug.

"Best of the best. That was a tough crowd to please," Xeno says, grinning widely.

"I'm so fucking pumped right now!"

I've never seen Dax so happy. Yes, this might be Rocks, an illegal club that turns a blind eye to the underage kids that come here and sells booze and harder drugs to anyone who can afford it, but we've never come here for that. This has always been about the dance. Winning tonight means everything to us, because even though Dax and I claimed the title, it belongs to all of the Breakers.

"Well, I reckon we all deserve a drink to celebrate. I'll grab 'em. You guys sit," York says, before jogging over to the bar.

Dax puts his arm around my shoulder, and we head to a quieter area of the club to relax and regroup. The place is packed tonight, and the atmosphere's pumping. All night long the guys have had a stream of girls chatting them up. For a while Xeno disappeared with one particularly good looking blonde, and Zayn was side-tracked by a girl who had insanely long legs and curvy tits and arse. Even York had his head turned by a petite brunette, though I didn't stick around long enough to see if he took her up on her offer. Dax was the only one tonight who remained by my side, and I'm betting that was more to do with the fact we were battling together, and he didn't want to jeopardise that in any way. It's not as if he didn't have a long line of girls ready and willing to climb up his... *pole, stick, lollipop, banana?*

Well, if they can call a clit a pickle then I sure as fuck can call their dicks a generic term too, right? I swallow my smile at the thought, my skin flushing. I've been thinking about their dicks a lot lately. Well, not strictly just their dicks, though I am intrigued. I've been thinking about *them*. All of them. Feelings have crept in. Feelings that I can't and don't want to control. Feelings that go way beyond friendship into an unknown, scary-as-fuck, zone.

Thankfully, for now, they all seem content enough to be by my side and I try not to let their womanising ways get to me. It's not easy, but tonight I'm going to think happy thoughts and not ones where I'm tit-punching the next girl who comes onto one of *my* Breakers.

"Next up is the group battles, and this time there's prize money to be had," Xeno says with a sly grin as York rests a tray of drinks on the table. He hands them out to each of us. A bottle of light beer for Zayn, brandy over ice for Xeno, Bailey's for York, whiskey for Dax and a Malibu and cola for me.

"Yeah? That's new," York muses.

Xeno sips on his drink, grinning. "It's an easy win. We're better than all of the crews here."

"How much is the prize money?" Dax asks, leaning forward in his seat. His thick, muscular thigh presses against the side of mine. My cheeks heat at the touch. This time, I don't shift my leg away like I normally would. Instead, I press my thigh firmly against his, feeling brave even though my heart is thundering. He pauses, glancing over his shoulder at me, and I can't help but smile behind the rim of my glass.

"Five thousand," Xeno responds. "We could all do with the money, right?"

Dax whistles. "I ain't gonna lie. A thousand pounds would come in handy."

"Then it's a no brainer. We enter the competition," York says with a shrug.

"Fuck, yeah. I've already got shitloads of ideas." Zayn's grin widens, and I can see the cogs whirring as he goes into choreographer mode. Generally, battles aren't choreographed and happen spontaneously. However, as this is a competition with winnings, choreography will be expected, which means we can get as creative as we want.

"That's settled then. Bring it fucking on!" Xeno exclaims. He raises his glass, and we all do the same, chinking them against one another. A surge of happiness rushes through me as I look around the table at my Breakers. *My* Breakers.

A familiar beat drops as *Da Rockwilder* by Method Man blasts out over the speakers.

"Tuuunnnneeee!" we all chorus, jumping up as the excitement of our win and the upcoming battle scorches like fire in our veins. I feel high on life, on the adrenaline of the win and tonight, loving these boys in secret.

Xeno and Zayn are on the dance floor first, barging their way through the crowd and not giving a fuck who they knock out of the way. York follows, his feet tapping like lightning over the hardwood floor as he mashes up street with tap dance. The effect is insane and pride swells. Just yesterday we'd watched Singing in the Rain together, and after a few tries, York had perfected one of the more difficult sequences in the movie. I recognise some of those steps now. I'm forever in awe of his talent. He's so fucking gifted when it comes to tap.

Dax and I follow, my hand gripped within his. Happiness

makes my heart beat wildly. I'm pumped up by the music, our recent win, and the fact that Dax hasn't let my hand go even though we're in the middle of the dance floor surrounded by the rest of the Breakers.

The air is charged, electric. Booze, happiness and the recent high of our win fuelling us. The surrounding dancers move back, giving us room, sensing we're about to give them one hell of a show. Dax grips my hand tight and pulls me against his chest, laughing freely at the surprise on my face. He leans over and presses his mouth against my ear.

"Dancing with you, Kid, is *better* than sex."

I let out a nervous laugh. Since when has sex and me ever been mentioned in the same sentence? I'll tell you when, *never*. When I look up at Dax, my heart trip-traps in my chest like a billy goat crossing a bridge just waiting for an ogre to come along and ruin its happiness. That thought seems all too perfectly timed with Dax's scowl as his gaze snaps up.

"Hey, Pen, fancy pairing up with me?" Frederico, leader of Dante's Crew and an arsehole of the highest magnitude asks as he yanks me out of Dax's hold. Before I can even push him away, he's grasping my arse like he owns it, rocking me against his half-mast cock.

"Get off me!" I shout, pushing at his chest and slamming my clenched fist into his chin for good measure. The pain in my knuckles is overshadowed by my anger and Dax's roar.

"You fucking cunt!" His rage drawing the attention of the other Breakers and sending the surrounding dancers scattering. Zayn, York and Xeno step up. This isn't the first time they've had to fight for my honour, and it isn't the first time I've been mauled by some opportunist prick either, but so openly and brazenly in front of the Breakers, never. Frederico must be that high, or plain stupid. Either way, he doesn't get a chance to touch me again because right now Dax has him by the throat in a death grip.

"Motherfucking cunt. Do not touch *our* girl!" Dax spits.

Realisation dawns on Frederico's face and through the haze of alcohol and cocaine, he begins to understand the error of his ways. Pity then that Dax has his throat gripped so tightly, he can't actually speak.

"Dax, it's cool. He's fucking high," I say, pushing the flat of my hand against his heaving chest. I can see the remnants of white powder dusting Frederico's nose. He's our age, and something close to sympathy overtakes my anger. I reach up, trying to pry Dax's hand from around his throat. "This is the drug talking, Dax. No one needs to get hurt tonight. I doubt he'll even remember what he said come morning."

My stomach coils at the look of cold disgust on Dax's face aimed squarely at Frederico. He won't let this go. He won't let him go. Shit.

"Dax, it's not worth it." I stand before him, trying to ease him back but I recognise that look in Dax's eyes. I've seen it before. He's going to erupt, and when he does, it won't be pretty.

"Please," I cajole, cupping his face. Dax flicks his gaze to mine, then releases Frederico who gasps for air.

"Come near her again and you're dead," Dax promises, before wrapping his arm around my shoulder and attempting to walk away.

"Ah, come on, man. Just a little taste. I promise I'll get her ready for you boys. Sharing is caring, right?" Frederico pushes, too fucking high to see sense after all. I stiffen, ready to put myself between Dax and the fucking imbecile when York lunges for me, wraps an arm around my waist and yanks me backwards out of harm's way.

"No way, Titch. He had his chance to walk away. This dude fucking deserves all he gets," he murmurs into my ear.

I watch with sick fascination as Dax launches himself at Frederico, laying into him with a punch that launches him backward into the baying crowd who push his stumbling body back towards Dax. Blood pours from Frederico's nose, the combination of regular cocaine use and the power of Dax's punch most likely breaking his nose. The kid's so out of it that he doesn't even register the pain or the heavy bleeding.

"What? We all know that you're all fucking her. Sharing ain't a problem with you lot, is it?" he argues back, blood leaking into his mouth and staining his white teeth, red.

York tenses around me, out of the corner of my eye I can see Zayn's expression change from derision to explosive anger, but it's Xeno's calm control that scares me the most.

"Do it," he snarls.

Dax looks between me and Xeno, and nods once. There is no hesitancy in Dax's attack, just a resolute kind of rage as he runs at Frederico like a cyclone about to destroy everything in its path, and by destroy I mean *kill*.

"Stop!" I shout, struggling to get out of York's hold and pull Dax off of Frederico now that he's straddling Frederico's chest, pummelling him with vicious blows. No one seems to care that he's turning into a bloody mess aside from me, and whilst I hate the cocksucker for what he just said, I don't want this to go any further for Dax's sake.

"Fucking stop!" I yell again, elbowing York's chest so he loosens his hold enough to let me go. I fly towards Dax, yanking at his arm. When he gets like this, I fear for him. You don't live with abuse and have it not affect you in some way. Dax is used as a punching bag on the daily, and this is the result: an unstoppable, uncontrollable rage. If I know him like I think I do, he's imagining his dad's face beneath his fist right now, because when the rage takes over all you see are the people who hurt you the most.

"Enough!" I pull at him as hard as I can, and somehow manage to yank him off Frederico. We end up in a heap, sprawled out on the floor. The kid's a mess, his face swollen and bloody, but he's still breathing, *just*.

I don't think, I act.

"We need to get out of here," I shout, rushing to my feet. I pull Dax up with me, catching the violence in his eyes that has my heart racing and my blood pumping. "We have to go!"

Tugging on his arm, we push through the crowd. I don't look back. The Breakers know what to do. They'll run too, and this mess will be cleared up by Jeb.

It's not the first time a fight has broken out in Rocks and it won't be the last. This place runs on dance, music, drugs, alcohol, and violence. There's an unspoken rule that if someone gets fucked-up in this place, then there's never any repercussions with the law. No police. Ever. Not unless you want to live. That's something to be grateful for at least, though I'm not foolish enough to believe that Dax will get away with this. He'll owe Jeb a debt now, and Dante's Crew will be gunning for our blood.

Yanking on Dax's hand, we run. The crowd parts and I head

towards the exit at the back of the club not wanting to leave by the front in case we get jumped. Pushing through the fire exit, we step out into the night. Fear lodges in my throat as I pull Dax down the darkened alleyway, my foggy breaths wispy in the cold night air. When I realise that no one is following us, I stop to catch my breath.

"Dax, are you okay?" I ask, pulling him into a darkened recess and pushing him up against a locked door there. He stares at me with an absent kind of violence, locked inside a moment in time that has nothing to do with Frederico and everything to do with the abuse he endures at the hands of his dad. "Dax...?"

He raises his hand, his fingertips shaking as he blinks away whatever memory he's trapped within. I capture his fingers in mine, not caring that they're covered in Frederico's blood, only caring about him, about his state of mind. He would've killed him. Maybe the violence had started because he was defending my honour, but it became something else.

"It's okay. I'm okay," I reassure him, clutching his hand, and pressing his palm against my cheek. His skin on mine seems to register deep within and I see recognition flicker within his eyes that change from bleak, to wild, to fearful, as he realises what he's done.

"Kid, I..."

"Shh, shh. It'll be okay, but we need to get back to the basement, okay?" I move to turn away, to lead us out of the alley and head to safety, but his hand slips into my hair as he tugs me close until I'm flat against his body.

"I saw red..."

"I know. We can talk about this later. We need to go."

His hold tightens. "He groped you like you were a piece of meat. How fucking dare he touch you like that."

"It's okay, Dax. He was high. It's done. It's over."

His fingers curl in my hair, tugging on the strands as his jaw tenses and his arm wraps around my back, trapping me against his body. "You're ours, Kid. Ours," he growls and something in his eyes gives me pause.

Possession. He's always been protective of me, but this is different. This is more.

"Dax...?" I question as he shifts me in his hold, his legs parting. I slot between them, a perfect fit.

"I want to kiss you," he grinds out, as though saying those words are a combination of pain and relief.

"You want to kiss me?" I parrot back, my voice quiet, a whisper.

He leans down, pulling me tighter against his body. "I'm going to kiss you, Kid." And this time my response is swallowed by his lips and nose crashing against mine.

"Ow," I pull back, rubbing at my nose and laughing a little.

"Shit, sorry," he cups my face with both hands now, pressing a sweet kiss against the tip of my nose. It's cute and sexy and I don't know what to do next. Words trip out of my mouth before I can stop them.

"Don't apologise. It's me, I don't... I haven't... *Fuck.*"

"What?" he asks, frowning.

"I haven't kissed anyone before," I say in a whoosh of breath, partly worried about the fact we're still standing here and not running, and partly ashamed of my lack of kissing skills and experience. I'm *well* aware that I'm lagging behind when it comes to this kind of stuff but by the time I was interested in kissing anyone, the only people I wanted to kiss happened to be my best friends and they've never showed me the slightest bit of interest until now.

"What, *never?*"

"I've been hanging out with you guys for the past couple years. I don't really get the chance to hook up with anyone." *I don't want to.*

"Good." He grinds out, then bites down on his lip. He smiles a little sheepishly, and my heart lifts as some of the darkness dissolves from his gaze. "Then that'll make me your first kiss, right?"

"You really want to kiss me...?"

"Are you kidding? Of course, I want to." He brushes blood-streaked fingertips against my cheek with shaking hands. Nerves steal my voice and all I can do is look at him helplessly. "Tip your head to the side, Kid," he says, his tone gravelly, deep, as though something is lodged in his throat.

I do as he asks, tipping my head to the side, trying not to think too much about the mechanics of a kiss or whether I'll mess this moment up. This time when Dax leans in to kiss me, our noses don't crash together, but my heart? That crashes and thrashes like a piston inside my ribcage, reminding me I'm still here, still alive and not caught up in one of my fantasies I've been indulging in over these past few months.

His mouth feathers against mine, hesitant at first, uncertain, but even that light touch is enough to make my knees quake. I'm aware of everything. His heaving chest, his firm body pressed against mine, the tremor of his hands clasping my face. I curl my fingers into the material of his t-shirt not sure if I'm pulling him closer, or hanging on for dear life. My skin tingles and my breath hitches as his tongue sweeps across my lower lip. He groans, one hand sliding into my hair as the other drops to my side, wrapping around my lower back. His fingers flex and just for a moment he hesitates, his mouth parted as though he's deciding whether he should step over the invisible line that exists between me and him.

"Kiss me, Dax. Please, just kiss me." I don't mean for it to come out breathless, but I can't help it. I feel lightheaded as it is. Swallowing my nervousness I close the minute gap between us and press my lips against his. I want this. I'm done waiting. My fantasies aren't enough anymore. This was the last thing I thought would happen tonight, but now that it is I don't want anything to get in the way.

Dax grunts, his fingers tightening in my hair and tugging on the strands as his tongue bypasses my lips, searching, cautious and oh so fucking gentle. For all his violence, Dax kisses with a softness that makes me want to clamber up his large frame and wrap myself around him. Instinctively, I press my crotch against him wanting to relieve the building sensation I feel between my legs. He's hard and I stop grinding, not sure what to do. I have no experience dealing with this and I'm well aware that the movement of my body is making him react this way. A rumbling kind of noise vibrates through his chest and rather than breaking off the kiss, Dax slides both his hands over my arse, squeezing tighter and just like that, I forget that this is my first kiss. I forget we're in an alleyway running from his violence.

My body melts into him as though we were always meant to be this way and my hands find their way up and under his shirt, loving the way his skin feels against the palms of my hand. Tasting the remnants of whisky on his tongue, I revel in the feel of him. Emotions catapult inside my chest like a pinball in one of those arcade games we love to play, ricocheting against my internal organs. My heart beats faster, my stomach fills with a million butterflies, my lungs desperately claw for air as I forget to breath and just dive headfirst into the moment more than willing to drown.

They say your first kiss is unforgettable, that no matter who it's with, it will be ingrained in your soul forevermore. Good, bad, indifferent, it doesn't matter. This kiss is one for the memory banks. It marks me, making a notch in my heart that I will treasure forever. This kiss is perfect.

We lean into each other, me on my tip-toes, held upright in his strong arms. Dax crowding over me, making me feel both small and big all at the same time. When we part, all heaving chests, and whispered thoughts, I smile up at him, pressing my hand over the thrashing beat of his heart.

"You're my dark angel, Dax, do you know that?

"I am?"

"Yeah, you are." He smiles, and it's so beautiful that for a moment I can't speak.

"Will you always protect me like that?"

"Always, Kid."

Capturing his hand in mine we run down the alleyway, unaware that our kiss and whispered promises were witnessed by another.

CHAPTER TEN

Present Day

JUST LIKE THE night of my first kiss, my heart pounds in my chest trying to search for a way out of this situation. Back then Dax would always come to my aid, whether I wanted it or not. Perhaps it was because he understood the kind of home I came from, perhaps it was because he could reclaim some of his own power by protecting me. Either way, he was always the one who came to my rescue first. That's what makes this so hard. I never wanted to battle against any of my Breakers, and especially not Dax who gave me my first kiss and allowed my heart to blossom with love.

"Braaap, braaap. Here comes the big man himself. It's TEARDROP DAAAAXXX!" Little Dynamite calls over the mic.

My eyes snap open, zeroing in on Dax as he strolls onto the

dance floor, bare chested, powerful, and oozing a dangerous kind of sex appeal that makes my mouth go dry and my knees, god-fucking-damnit, weak. His slacks are low on his hips, showing off his prominent v-muscle. He was always built and the biggest of the guys both in height and width. That hasn't changed. His biceps are as large as my thighs, his shoulders broad, his chest muscles defined, and his abs ripped. Somehow he's developed into a beast of a man that has all the thirsty bitches in the crowd cawing over him. I don't blame them. There's no denying his physical prowess, but his physique isn't what gives me pause.

It's the artwork tattooed onto every inch of skin he has on show.

The only part of his body left uncovered is his face and head. Dax's whole upper body and torso, from the slow slung waistband of his tracksuit bottoms, up his arms and neck are covered in beautifully detailed tattoos. It's too dark to get a good look at the smaller ones, but there's no mistaking the fallen angel on the centre of Dax's chest with dark black wings that spread out across his pecs and up across his shoulders and upper arms. I know I'm staring, but I can't help it.

Here's *my* dark angel.

None of the others knew I called him that. It was just something between us and now he has a piece of our love tattooed eternally onto his chest. Blinking back the tears threatening to pour from my eyes, I grit my jaw.

God fucking damn it. This is emotional warfare.

Forcing myself to focus, and as is customary in battles, I keep my gaze fixed firmly on Dax, hoping I'm not giving anything away. It's a good opportunity to check each other out as we circle the dance floor trying to psyche the other out. Dax locks his gaze with mine. His face is void of any emotion, but that isn't what cuts me the most. It's the betrayal I see swimming within the murky depths of his eye.

Well, fuck him.

Fuck. Them. All.

I wasn't the one who broke us first. I wasn't the one who decided that dance wasn't enough, that *I* wasn't enough. This is utter horseshit.

I'm the first one to make my move.

I zone out. It's something I do when I'm at my most vulnerable. I look into myself and find my strength in the one thing that has got me through life, *dance*. I allow movement to take over my body because it's never been the music that drives me, it's always been the dance.

Freestyling for me is as easy and as natural as breathing.

This is *my* battlefield, and I don't fucking lose.

Without even thinking, I form a series of hip-hop moves that are timed perfectly with the beat of the song. I pop and lock, drop and spin. Vaguely, I can hear the crowd go wild, but it's as though I'm underwater. They're muffled, distant. I make shapes with my body, twisting my arms up and around my head so it looks like I'm double jointed, when in fact, I'm just well versed in this kind of dance and know how to move my body just the right way. With sweat pouring down my back and strands of hair sticking to my cheeks, I throw a front flip, landing in front of Dax. I jerk my chin, looking directly into his eyes, knowing exactly what he sees in mine: challenge and blind fury.

Sound rushes back in as the crowd loses it around me. Even Little Dynamite bigs me up, impressed with my moves, but none of that matters. None of it. Instead of cursing me out like is customary in these battles, like I expect, Dax leans over and brushes his lips against my cheek. A sweet kiss that hurts me more than I can explain.

"Dax," I mutter. Forgetting we're in a club full of people, my hand lifts automatically to his chest. He captures my wrist, folding his fingers over the exact same spot Xeno had gripped me earlier and squeezes tightly, his whole demeanour changing.

"You lost the right to touch me like that three years ago. Next time you try, I won't be so lenient," he snarls, then rips himself away from me and eviscerates my heart with his dance moves.

Dax was always the least confident dancer of us all but watching him now, that's changed. He's stunning, articulate with his movements. Watching a big guy move the way he does seems like an impossible feat and yet he's as light on his feet as I am.

Like the rest of us, Dax danced hip-hop because it was a cool thing to do, but unlike the other guys, contemporary dance was his first love, just like mine. We bonded over the fluidity of the dance and the way it allowed us both to express our inner turmoil. It suited us both. Seeing Dax move now, interspersing hip-hop with contemporary has me hurting in a way I never dreamed possible. He circles me, using up the whole space, and just like a predator closing in on its prey, he stalks me with perfect poise and a rage that has me cowering. Dax is articulate with his pain, with every movement, each one telling our story so succinctly that you'd have to be stupid not to understand what he's saying.

When he lands a perfect leap into the air and finishes with

happy feet, a signature move in hip-hop and one we all used to love as a crew, I crumble. Dax knows where to slide the knife in and twist, and even though my face is empty of emotion, just like his is, we both know that he's crossed the other invisible line we drew all those years ago.

Without saying a goddamn word, Dax's pretty much told everyone our story. The crowd might not be able to completely understand it, but I can, and it hurts that he's revealed who we were so publicly to everyone here.

Dax steps towards me, sweat beading on his shaved head and rolling down his temple. He jerks his chin, waiting for me to fight back. I back away, my chest heaving as I shake my head. Turning towards Little Dynamite, I slide my hand across my throat indicating that I've conceded the win. I'm in way too much of an emotional state to even consider continuing. Dax was a better dancer. Everyone knows it, including me.

Tonight we battled, and I lost.

"Yo, arseholes, we have a new winner of the singles battle! Teardrop Dax has torn up the dance floor, laid down the gauntlet, and handed Pen her tight little arse."

The crowd loses their shit, but I don't care if I've been beaten. I just want to get the fuck out of here and as far away from the Breakers as possible. I move to walk away, but Dax grasps my elbow.

"Not this time, Kid," he growls as I snap my head around to look at him.

For a fraction of a second his gaze meets mine and his eyes flare with pain, before he snatches his hand away and strides off across the dance floor towards Zayn, Xeno and York who've appeared from the shadows like spectres in the night. Zayn chucks Dax a t-shirt and he swiftly pulls it on before the four of them melt into the crowd, leaving a clear message to me and everyone in the club.

I'm no longer part of their crew. I'm no longer their Pen.

But I knew that anyway.

CHAPTER ELEVEN

Present Day

FOR THE REST of the weekend I avoid Clancy.

I'd remained tight lipped about what went down at Rocks Friday night despite all her questions in the cab on the way home. She was sweet, kind, and said she wouldn't judge me no matter what I told her. In the end, when I refused to open up, she took a hint and backed off. At least until the following morning.

The girl is nothing if not persistent.

Admittedly, I feel sorry for her. She has knocked on my door religiously each morning, noon and night over the past two days and whilst I haven't answered the door, I have sat with my back pressed up against it and listened to her chatting to me incessantly about all sorts of shit with the aim of getting me to open the door to my room and to my heart. I know she has unanswered questions about the Breakers and my relationship with them, but that's not something I'm willing or able to discuss.

Besides, it's really not her fault that I'm a social pariah at the best of times, throw in four blasts from the past and I clam up. What can I say? I've got issues; issues in the form of the Breakers who are intent on hurting me even more than they already have. I even called into work sick on Saturday because I didn't want to risk seeing the Breakers again. That's something I never do because God knows I need the money. Cowardly, perhaps, but I don't give a shit right now. I need time to recalibrate and to figure out what the hell I'm going to do. Besides, I'm used to surviving on thin air.

One thing I do know for sure is that they should never have come back. They should've stuck to their promise and stayed the fuck away. At the time, that promise had hurt like a bitch, but now... God, I can't deal with this.

To make matters a thousand times worse, of course David found out what happened at Rocks and has been chasing my arse all weekend trying to get me to respond to his calls. *Screw that.* I can't deal with him right now. Thank fuck he's half-way around the world in Mexico.

I don't talk to my brother willingly. He's just a psychotic arsehole that I need out of my life for good. Trouble is, we had an agreement and if he thinks I'm going to renege, he'll make sure to follow through on the threat he made. I *can't* risk that, so I will have to speak to him eventually. Nausea rises up my throat and I gag on the bile that spills from my mouth and hits the white pan of the toilet, colouring it a fluorescent yellow.

"You'll only get away from him when you're dead... or he

is," I whisper to my reflection in the bathroom mirror after I rinse my mouth with water and spit it down the sink.

Sighing heavily, I rake a hand through my hair and stare at myself. I look tired. Dark circles rim my eyes, and my skin is paler than usual. I've not slept well worrying about everything. My past has haunted my dreams and my present doesn't seem so hopeful anymore. I can't even think about the future because whatever path I come up with, they all lead to the same destination.

Forcing all those thoughts away and needing to somehow wash away my past, I turn on the shower and wait a minute for it to heat up before stepping under the spray. The hot water scolds my skin, turning it a dusky pink all over. I've always enjoyed the heat, it helps to ease the tenseness in my muscles after hours of dancing, or in this case, hours of avoiding my new friend. That's if she's still a friend.

I've probably fucked that up now too.

Right now, it's seven am. My first official day at the academy starts in just under an hour. On Saturday, Madame Tuillard's personal assistant sent an email asking that her most promising dancers meet her in Studio Two on the first floor at eight am sharp. Attached to the email was my timetable packed with back-to-back dance classes that will start officially next week. This week students will have some taster sessions, but it will be more like a Freshers week at university designed to help everyone bond, make friends and let off steam before the real work starts.

Because I chose contemporary as my specialism, just under fifty percent of the lessons are centred around my chosen dance, but I also have other lessons covering most forms of dance, including tap, ballet, street and latin. I'd wanted to feel excited when I received the email, but instead of feeling happy that I've finally got to start this next chapter in my life, something I've been working towards for years now, I'm feeling anxious.

Fucking Breakers.

Why come back now?

That's a question I'm not sure I'll ever get a straight answer to.

Drying quickly, I pull on my black dance pants, green tank-top and matching muscle-vest, and shove on my trainers. I'm not a showy dancer. I don't dress up to impress, besides, I don't have the money to afford top of the range dance gear, so what I'm wearing will have to do. Combing through my wet hair, I put it up in a French plait, fold up a bandana and wrap it around my head then go and make myself a cup of coffee. It's the cheap, bitter kind, and without any milk or sugar to sweeten it up, pretty disgusting, actually. I drink it anyway because this *is* my breakfast.

Making a mental note to head out at some point to grab some supplies, I ignore the rumble of my stomach and snatch up my gym bag, heading out. Apart from the muffled sound of someone talking on a phone in one of the studio flats and a shower turning on in another, the hallway is quiet. Thank God. I'll be better prepared to face Clancy and the other students who'll be my neighbours for the next year once I've let off some steam and danced my stress away.

A couple minutes later, I'm pushing open the door to Studio Two, grateful to find that it's empty. In fact the whole academy is peaceful and quiet.

Sunlight pours through the windows situated above the

length of mirrors that run along the wall opposite. Dust motes float in the air, dancing away when I step further into the room and shut the door behind me. This studio is slightly smaller than the one I auditioned in, but other than that, much the same. It has oak wooden floors that are covered in scuff marks from the many students that have danced in this room before me. At one end of the studio is a table that has a sound system with speakers sitting on top of it and at the other, a wall of hooks to hang bags and clothing out of the way.

Placing my gym bag on the floor, and kicking off my trainers, I start to warm up using Pilates and yoga moves. Ten minutes later my muscles are sufficiently stretched, and I feel loose enough to dance. Snatching up my mobile from my bag, I flick through until I find *Work Song* by Hozier, then head over to the speakers, plug it in using the leads left out for that purpose, and press repeat so the song plays on a loop.

Moving to the centre of the room, I look at my reflection in the mirror and nod, giving myself a mental slap before pulling my bandana over my eyes and securing it tightly.

Taking away one of my senses allows me to emerge myself wholly in the dance. I have to concentrate on the music and my movement. If I make a mistake I could crash into the wall and injure myself, knowing that allows me to hone my skills.

Drawing in a deep breath, I wait for Hozier's haunting voice to filter out across the room. The moment his voice sounds, I let all the stress go and focus on moving my body instead. There's an honesty in his words, that and the beat that underpins this song matches my mood this morning. Holding my right arm out to my side, I snap my fingers to the beat, bending my right knee inward before twisting around and ducking low, sweeping my hand across the wooden floor. I feel the gritty dust particles on my fingertips, and draw in the scent of polished wood and lemon air-freshener.

On the next beat, I clasp my hands behind my head then sweep them down over my chest and kick my leg out behind me in a position similar to an arabesque. I may not know all the steps to ballet, but I've picked up enough over the years from YouTube videos and tutorials to get a good measure of it. Much of what I've learnt is self-taught and the rest, just instinct. My steps are free-flowing but measured, and a direct representation of what I'm feeling this morning. Being here at the academy is freeing, and yet my past is like a prison I can't escape.

I'm trapped.

Dipping and twirling, I float across the wooden boards and let the emotion take over, drawing on every last drop. Still blind-folded and engrossed in what I'm doing, I don't notice another presence in the studio until firm hands grasp my upper arms from behind.

I still, my chest heaving. Sweat slides down my back, and I know from the heat I feel rising off my body that I've been dancing for a lot longer than I'd planned.

"Fuck, sorry," I mumble, trying to lift my hand up to remove my blindfold.

Whoever it is prevents me by sliding their hands down my arms and pressing my wrists against my hip. I can feel their body flat against mine, all hard muscle and height. Definitely a guy then. Cool minty breath flutters over my cheek as I turn my head to the side, tipping my head back slightly. The top of my head, brushes something hard... his chin perhaps?

"You should let me go," I warn, because this is creepy as

fuck and I'm not unskilled in fighting off predators. I might be small, but I'm scrappy. I've learnt the hard way.

He releases my left hand, cupping it briefly before using his finger to write the word *no* across my palm. I snatch my hand away, reaching for my bandana, but he grabs my forearm, lets my other hand go and flips me around to face him. Grasping both my wrists with one hand, he presses the other into my lower back and pulls me flush against him.

"You think I won't fight back?" I growl, shaking with anger. It's my first fucking day and already some arsehole is trying to molest me.

"Dance," the stranger grunts, his fingers flexing on my lower back. My skin pricks, but not in the way I expect. It's as though my body recognises the person before I'm even able to figure out who it is.

The voice is muffled, hoarse but there's something in it that makes me pause. It's familiar, and yet it isn't. I don't knee him in the balls. I remain still, my heart a caged animal in my chest. Willing myself to calm down, I realise that whoever this is, they won't have much time to do any harm given how long I've been dancing. The other students will be here soon anyway.

"I'm not a puppet. I don't dance on command."

"Dance with me!" he growls. There's something in his tone that has an edge of desperation to it. Like whoever the fuck this is needs this moment more than oxygen.

Desperate to touch me, hold me, dance with me.

Me.

My stomach churns because deep down I know that it must be one of the Breakers, there's no other explanation. I should push him away, but I don't. Curiosity and a desperate need to feel wanted again overrides every other emotion. "Okay," I whisper in agreement, needing to know who it is.

If I could feel with my hands, I'd be able to get a better mental image, but it's difficult to tell just by his body pressed against mine. From his height and width it could be any one of them. His voice is different too, purposely so and the peppermint smell from his mint is overpowering any scent that might be familiar. The only way to know for sure is to do as he asks, and dance.

Work Song is still playing on a loop and I tip my head back slightly, waiting for him to take the lead. Still grasping both my wrists in one large hand, I'm lowered slowly backwards, my torso bending in an arch as his other hand supports my lower back. For a beat, I'm held in his arms. He could let me go, and I'd fall flat on my arse. He doesn't. I lean into the hold, dropping my head back and arching my neck, trusting him in the moment. I'm rewarded when he frees my hands as he folds over me, supporting my back. His breath is warm against the slick skin of my upper chest. As he guides me back up, I automatically reach out, grasping hold of his shoulders to steady myself, my heart hiccups at the touch, at the prickle of my skin and that very real need to fall into his hold.

"Why?" I ask. How can a single word have so many layers, and so many answers?

Of course he doesn't reply, instead he steps into me, his left leg moving to the outside of my right. His inner thigh brushing against my outer thigh. The air vibrates with tension, mine, his. He's not relaxed any more than I am. It's like we're both holding our breaths. One false move and this tentative truce is over. All I know is that this kind of dance rules out York and Zayn. Neither were interested in dancing intimately like this, not that they weren't intimate, because they were, just in different ways.

This has to be either Xeno or Dax, but that doesn't make sense. Why would either of them be here? I could reach up and remove my bandana to know for sure, but something stops me. Perhaps it's the way his other leg slides between mine, the thickness of his thigh pressing against my core and taking my breath away, or perhaps it's my need to reconnect with a memory of my past. Either way, I remain blind.

Gently, achingly slowly, he bends his knees and locks my thigh between his, swaying his hips from side to side, encouraging me to do the same. The movement is sensual, sexual, and full of promises I don't understand. I can't help but follow his lead, the dancer in me catching on before I can even comprehend what's happening. Something inside begins to uncurl as strong hands smooth up the sides of my torso, the top of his arms lifting up mine so that they're locked in place, horizontal to my shoulders, my fingers still gripping onto him. When the flat of his hand slides around my back, a single thumb pressing into my spine possessively, I know immediately who I'm dancing with.

This is *bachata*.

"Xeno?" I whisper.

CHAPTER TWELVE

Present Day

THE SECOND HIS name leaves my lips, his steps falter.

"Xeno?" I repeat.

He lets me go as cold air rushes in, cooling my heated skin. Ripping off my bandana, I watch as Xeno walks away from me all taut shoulders and curled fists. He switches off Hozier and unhooks my mobile from the speaker system. For a moment, he stands still, drawing in deep breaths, then walks back towards me and drops the offending item in my hand as if it's scolded him.

"That never happened," he growls.

Yet again, words evade me. It's been three years and there are many, many things I want to say, to ask, but the chasm between us prevents me from saying anything at all. I look up at him, caught in the power of his gaze. Emotion sits in the hard line of his lips, the frown darkening his eyes with heavy brows and the muscle ticking like a time-bomb in his jaw.

Thump, thump, thump goes my stupid heart. It took me years to rebuild it and now it's about to self-detonate because of one stupid dance. Xeno never asked me to partner him in bachata when we were kids. It was a sore point that hurt every time he chose another girl. Not that I ever told him that.

"That never happened. Got it?!" He towers over me, trying to intimidate me.

Tell that to my body, my soul, I want to respond because both have been set alight from his touch. Goddamn it. "Xeno, why are you back? Why are you here?" is what I asked instead.

His gaze scrapes over every inch of me until I'm raw from his scrutiny. I force myself to breathe, to straighten my spine, to not let him get to me like I know he wants to. Burrowing deep, I force my body to obey. He can't know how affected I am by him.

"Tell me..." I repeat.

Beyond the studio I can hear voices, cutting our one-sided conversation short.

Xeno gives me one last glare before stepping past me and ripping the door open. He comes face to face with Madame Tuillard who smiles broadly at him.

"Ah, Mr Tyson, I see you've introduced yourself to Pen, one of our most promising students this year," she says, flicking her gaze to me.

Mr Tyson? If he's a student here, why is she referring to him so formally? The confusion must be clear on my face because Madame Tuillard steps into the room and explains.

"Mr Tyson is a new dance teacher here at the academy, he'll

be teaching bachata, a dance that you may or may not be familiar with. If you've picked Latin, then he'll be teaching you too."

"He's a *teacher*?" My mouth drops open. I can't help but gape at Xeno who meets my gaze with a blank look, as though we're no more than strangers and he hasn't just pressed his body intimately against mine or stolen a kiss Friday night at Rocks in front of a whole club full of people. Behind Madame Tuillard, Clancy, Tiffany, a petite girl with long, black hair and a guy I don't recognise, step into the studio.

"Yes. Mr Tyson is our youngest teacher at the academy. He is also one of the most gifted."

Fuck. Fuck. Fuck.

I can feel the blood drain from my face and despite the shitty way I've treated her this past weekend, Clancy comes to my side and takes her hand in mine, squeezing it gently. "Breathe, Pen. Just breathe," she whispers.

Clancy might not know our history, but she isn't a fool and knows something is going on especially after Friday night's battle. She's a good person and I've been such a bitch. I don't deserve her friendship.

"Girl, did you shack up with *Mr Hot Dance Teacher* over the weekend? Is that why you ignored me, too busy shagging?" she asks in a low voice. "I wouldn't blame you in the slightest." A giggle escapes her lips and I nudge her with my elbow.

"No..." That single word is about all I can manage right now.

Madame Tuillard glides into the centre of the studio, oblivious to the rising tension. Out of the corner of my eye, I can see

Bitchface Tiffany eying Xeno up. Clancy clocks it too and groans.

"Uh oh, Tiffany has set her eyes on your... *man? Friend?*" Clancy questions, trying to wrap her head around our non-existent relationship. Xeno might have kissed me Friday night but that was more about asserting his power than anything else. There was no emotion behind it unless you include the very obvious anger.

"He's not my man or my friend," I correct her. I don't know what he is... Actually, I do. My fucking *dance teacher.*

Xeno glances at Tiffany and nods, casting a cursory look over her. That acknowledgement, and smidgen of interest, is enough for jealousy to wrap around my throat and squeeze tight. Xeno *never* gives his attention to the opposite sex unless he's interested. Tiffany is beautiful, even if she is a stuck-up bitch, so I get it even if I don't like it. Plus, she must be able to dance, which is really fucking annoying. I scowl, and Tiffany must feel my gaze because she turns to me and gives me her best resting bitch face.

"Don't engage, Pen. I've learnt the hard way," Clancy warns me, but I don't give a fuck. She's not my stepsister and if she looks at me like that again she'll know about it.

"Mr Tyson," Madame Tuillard suddenly says, drawing our attention back to her once more.

"Xeno," he corrects her.

"Ah, yes, I forget you don't like to be addressed so formally. Xeno, why don't you stick around. You can introduce yourself to all my dancers when the remaining two decide to turn up." Madame Tuillard says, looking at her wristwatch and tutting.

"They'd better hurry. I'm not averse to rescinding my invitation."

"There's no need for that, Madame Tuillard."

My head snaps around as York walks into the studio, Zayn following closely behind him. They briefly nod at Xeno who keeps his face neutral.

No. Fuck, no!

I half expect Dax to follow, but he doesn't. I don't know if I'm relieved or not by that fact.

"Oh, shit!" Clancy mutters, taking the words right from my lips. This can't be happening. "Looks like Zayn got in after all..." her voice trails off as she takes in my expression. I can't even acknowledge her. I want to be sick.

"Good of you to turn up," Madame Tuillard states, unimpressed. "Lateness will not be tolerated. Whilst you're attending my school, you follow my rules." She folds her arms gracefully across her chest, glaring at them both. "I don't care who you are or what circles you move around in. All of that is left behind the second you walk into my studio. Understand?"

"Circles they move around in?" Clancy repeats under her breath. Yeah, I picked up on that too but now is not the time to start discussing just what circles she's referring too. I know exactly what she means, but I'm curious as to why Madame Tuillard does.

"That applies to everyone. Whatever baggage you have gets left at the door. I don't care what happens outside the studio, but the minute you enter, you're here to dance and dance only."

I can't even look at the Breakers to see whether they're nodding in agreement like everyone else seems to be doing, because I'm too busy fighting my emotions and trying not to throw up.

Madame Tuillard starts to pace up and down in front of the mirrors, continuing her tirade. "If I ask you to meet me at eight am, I expect you to be here on the dot. If it's five am, then get here for that time and not one second after. No excuses. There are a thousand dancers willing to take your place, just like that," she says, snapping her fingers. "This might be the settling-in week, but that doesn't mean to say you can ignore my instructions. This is your one and only warning. Each of you were personally selected by me because I saw something in you worth my time. Don't make me regret my decision."

By the look on Zayn's face, he's about to say something wholly inappropriate to the principal of this school. Fortunately for him, York interrupts.

"It was my fault. I delayed us this morning. It won't happen again. Apologies," he says, fixing his icy-blue eyes on Madame Tuillard.

Always the mother hen. Always bailing his friends out of trouble with polite words and respect. No one would ever believe what he's truly capable of when pushed too far, when backed into a corner. He's loyal to a fault and more dangerous than he appears.

Madame Tuillard purses her lips and nods. "Apology accepted. Let's get started. Bags at the back, then find a space. Xeno, I'd appreciate your input."

Xeno nods, flicking an angry glare at York and Zayn that is missed by the other students who are busy dumping their bags and finding a spot in the room. I'm currently at the back of the studio as far away from the Breakers as I can get. Next to me is the only guy I haven't already met. He's tall and slim, wearing a loose t-shirt and leggings. Definitely a ballerina given his attire. He glances at me and grins.

"Hey," he says.

"Hey." I try and smile back, but it comes out more of a grimace.

"Clancy would you step forward please," Madame Tuillard asks, waving her forward.

Clancy gives me a wide-eyed look then moves to the front of the class, her cheeks flushing a little as everyone watches her with varying shades of interest. Bitchface keeps a neutral face, but if you look close enough there's daggers in her gaze that are unmistakable. Clancy lifts her chin, ignoring her. Good girl.

"I want you all to introduce yourself. Give us a little of your dance history, your choice of specialism and anything else you think might be interesting. You'll start, Clancy," Madame Tuillard insists.

Clancy smiles broadly, her awesome personality shining through. "My name's Clancy. My specialism is tap. Gregory Hines is my idol. The man was a genius. I've been dancing since I was five, and starred in Annie the Musical when I was thirteen, starting out as the understudy and then taking the lead about six months in."

"So you can sing as well as tap dance?" York asks her, a note of respect in his voice that makes my mouth go dry.

"Yep." She grins.

On the other side of the room Tiffany scoffs, muttering some nasty comment under her breath that she covers with a cough when Madame Tuillard glares at her, unimpressed.

"Thank you, Clancy. Tiffany, you're next."

Tiffany moves gracefully towards the spot Clancy just left and turns to face us, a pretty smile on her perfect face. It doesn't cover the fact that she's a bitch though.

"My name's Tiffany," she begins, stopping when I cover the word bitch with a well-placed cough. The look Tiffany gives me is murderous and I raise an eyebrow, winking at her. Don't dish it out, if you can't take it back, *bitch*.

I meet Clancy's gaze in the mirror, her grin is huge, but she quickly smothers her smile when Madame Tuillard lets out a long, frustrated sigh.

"Clearly, there's something in the air today. Need I remind you all what I said no more than ten minutes ago? Baggage is left at the door. Final warning." Madame Tuillard looks at me directly and I nod. Understanding perfectly.

I don't interrupt Tiffany again. I think I've proven my point. When she starts droning on about her illustrious dance career I can't help but wonder why she's here and not working with the Royal Ballet. I'm betting there's far more to her story than she's letting on. I make a mental note to ask Clancy about it later.

One by one, Madame Tuillard calls everyone up. The ballet dude who was standing next to me is called River. Hippy parents apparently. He took up dance when he was three and had way too much energy that needed to be funnelled into something that would keep him interested. His mum chose ballet much to his dad's disgust. But River loved it and so here he is.

Following River is the dark-haired girl. Turns out her name's Sophie. She moved to London with her family after her father got a new job. Her specialisms are street dance and hip-hop. Other than that she's tight-lipped and if my instincts are right, there's more to her than what she presents to the world. Not that I really give a shit. We've all got secrets. She can keep hers, and I'll keep mine.

After her, Zayn and York both give bullshit stories that are about as far away from the truth as you can get. I wonder why they're lying, and a thread of worry skirts my veins. Nothing good ever comes from lies. I should know.

Eventually it's my turn.

"Last but not least, Pen," Madame Tuillard says, waving me forward.

I bite down on the groan that wants to escape and weave through the group, avoiding all eye contact with the three Breakers before me. I can feel Xeno's stare drilling into the side of my face.

"My name's Pen. I grew up on a council estate in Hackney, not far from here. I danced to escape. Growing up was... difficult." I swallow hard, my throat constricting. Clancy gives me an encouraging smile and I grit my teeth, forcing myself to continue. "I learned to dance by watching YouTube tutorials. I didn't go to any dance schools like *you* did," I say, making a point to look at Zayn and York, acknowledging their lies. "Dancing is the only time I ever feel safe. Happy. Free, I guess..."

My voice trails off and Madame Tuillard smiles. "Thank you, Pen, for sharing."

"I haven't finished," I say.

She nods. "Apologies, please continue."

Gathering courage I look at Zayn, meeting his steely gaze. "I met someone who introduced me to his dance crew. We grew up together. We were friends. My love of dance grew in their company. They made me believe I could do anything. The truth is..." My gaze flicks to York, who has his game face on. I can't look at Xeno without being obvious, but it doesn't matter, I know he's watching me avidly, just like the other two. Should I continue on? I wonder what would happen if I did if I told everyone here the *true* story of us. The only story that counts, apparently, despite all the years of friendship I shared with the Breakers leading up to that point. You see it all boils down to one night, one decision, and one devastating consequence that separates who we were to what we are now. Would Xeno try and stop me if I told the real truth? Would York persist in pretending he doesn't know me? Would Zayn still look at me like he hates me? Will Dax suddenly storm into this studio too?

"The truth...?" Xeno asks, his voice steady with warning.

Flicking my gaze to a spot at the back of the studio, I take a deep breath. "The truth is, I realised that the only person I could rely on was myself. These friends I once had may have given me confidence, a family I never had, but it's always been dance that has taught me to be brave, to want *more*. Dance changed my life because it gave me hope when everyone else let me down, including them. That's my story, for what it's worth."

Heading back to my spot at the back of the class, I ignore Xeno's gaze and the piercing reflection of Zayn and York as they stare at me in the mirror.

Friday night they laid down the gauntlet with their emotional warfare. Today I've struck back with an emotional bomb of my own. If they think they can walk in here and fuck this up for me after everything they did, they can think again. I will not let them ruin my chance of making something of my life. I refuse to let them hurt me again. Screw them and their games. They might be some bullshit gangsters with a secret agenda, but this is my chance at a future, and I will not let them ruin it. Judging by the look on their faces, the truth hurts. Though, this isn't the first time the truth has caused pain, and I doubt it will be the last.

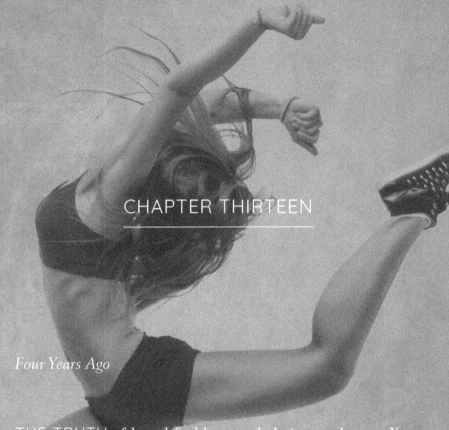

CHAPTER THIRTEEN

Four Years Ago

THE TRUTH of how I feel burns a hole in my chest as Xeno escorts his latest girlfriend, Dee, out of the basement. I can hear her complaining about the fact that I get to stay behind and hang out when she doesn't. It's past one in the morning, and for the last half-hour she's been putting off leaving, desperate to get to stay and encroach on my time with *my* Breakers.

Girlfriends are a pain in my arse.

Over the course of our friendship, they've all had a girlfriend at one point or the other. They never last long, mainly because the guys get bored easily or the girls start moaning about their friendship with me. On the other hand, I've never had a boyfriend, unless you count all four of them. Which, of course, I don't.

"Come on, Xeno," Dee whines from beyond the closed door. "Let me stay, I'll make it worth your while."

He doesn't respond with words, and it goes suspiciously quiet. A few moans later it's clear how he's got her to shut the hell up. I try not to throw up in my mouth.

"You alright, Titch?" York asks me. He pins me with his gaze, and I try not to give anything away, but given the way he's watching me, it appears that it's already too late for that.

He always seems to know when I'm down, and whilst most of the time I love that he's so attentive, tonight I wish he'd leave me the fuck alone. I've had to endure Xeno and Dee playing tonsil tennis all night and it's driving me crazy. When Zayn copped off with her friend, it took everything in me not to throw a hissy fit. Thankfully, York and Dax kept me company. So I got through the torture, *just*.

"Titch?" he prompts, leaning forward and resting his elbows on his knees, giving me his undivided attention.

"I'm just dandy," I lie, waving him off and wishing I didn't feel like my heart has been carved out of my chest and trodden on. It's not Xeno or Zayn's fault, in their minds we're best friends, just like the rest of the Breakers. Except that isn't strictly true because firstly, Dax and I shared a kiss a couple weeks ago and secondly, I've been in love with them all for months now.

"Well, I think you need a drink for putting up with Xeno's side piece all night. In fact you need a medal, but I haven't got one of those. Will vodka and Cola do?" he asks me with a wide grin, blinding me with his handsome face. God, when he did he get so good-looking?

"Yeah, I think it will." It might take the edge off the jealousy

I feel and dampen my raging hormones a bit. Nodding, he heads over to the fridge to fix me a drink.

On the floor, Zayn is sprawled out flat on his back smoking a joint. The heavy scent of weed lifts into the air, floating around the space. I'm getting high from the second-hand smoke. He turns to his side, the whites of his eyes pink from all the Mary-J in his system. As he moves his t-shirt creeps up showing me a flash of tan, muscled skin and a trail of dark hair that disappears beneath the waistband of his jeans.

"Guess Xeno's busy *tickling her pickle*." He laughs at his own joke for much longer than necessary.

"Sounds like it," I agree, rolling my eyes to cover my scowl.

"I wonder if her little friend Chastity would hook up with me again if I asked nicely?" he muses.

"I imagine *Destiny* would love it, if you remembered her name right, that is."

Zayn looks at me wide-eyed, then bursts out laughing, too high to notice the jealousy in my voice. "Fuck me, I meant Destiny! She had a great arse though, that I *do* remember."

Blowing out a breath, I almost tell York to hurry the fuck up with the drink. Loving these boys and having to put up with their hands on every other girl in Hackney, bar me, is harder than I thought.

"Shut the fuck up, Zayn," Dax says, eyeing me up from the other side of the room. He strolls over, all height and muscles and steps over Zayn who is too out of it to even notice the anger in his tone. Tonight, he's wearing baggy shorts paired with a graphic t-shirt and hoodie which, as usual, is pulled up over his head. Dax looks more like a skater dude than a badass dancer.

"Can I sit?" he asks me.

"Of course," I respond, feeling weirded out by the formality.

He plonks himself on the sofa next to me and for a while doesn't say anything, but I can feel his gaze on my face as I pull at a piece of string hanging from my t-shirt and try to block out the muffled moans coming from the other side of the basement door.

York returns with my drink, handing it to me before laying out on the floor next to Zayn and taking the joint from him. I watch as his pink lips wrap around the blunt and he inhales slowly. His gaze flicks between me and Dax, an unreadable expression on his face. We all kind of sit in silence trying to ignore the fact Xeno is most likely fucking Dee just beyond the closed door. I gulp down half of my drink, grateful for the fact York has given me a double. Hopefully the alcohol will start kicking in soon.

"You alright?" Dax eventually asks.

"I'd be better if I didn't have to listen to Xeno and Dee fucking in the hallway..."

Without meaning to, I heave out a sigh and press my eyes shut at the sudden tears that form. Dax wraps his arm around my shoulder and pulls me in close, surprising me with his sudden affection and his words.

"No matter who comes and goes, you're *ours*, Kid. Don't forget it," he says loudly enough for Zayn and York to hear. He seems just as pissed off as I am.

To be fair, usually they're all so careful around me. Making sure I don't feel uncomfortable about the girls they're seeing and reassuring me that I'm still their number one priority. For the most part, they treat me with respect and kindness. Tonight, however, it's felt like Xeno's been rubbing my face in it with Dee, and Zayn has been too high to filter the words coming out of his mouth or curb his behaviour around the girls. There's been a couple times I've wanted to leave, but either Dax or York has stopped me, managing to persuade me to stay.

"Yeah, I guess," I mumble, my words catching in my throat.

Dax bends closer and whispers in my ear. "Actually, screw them if they don't see what they have right in front of them. You're *my* lucky coin, Pen. I'll always take care of you."

My heart kind of does a summersault in my chest at his protective words and I sink into his side, wanting more than anything to wrap my arms around his waist but knowing if I do, I won't be able to hide my true feelings towards him. We haven't mentioned the kiss since it happened. We haven't kissed again either and it's not because I don't want to, because I do.

I really, really do.

I've thought of nothing else.

Actually, that's a lie. I've been thinking about the others daily, wondering what it would feel like if they were to kiss me too. I'm a greedy, thirsty bitch, and my heads been all over the place because of it.

"Dax..." I respond, pulling back to meet his gaze, the last thing I want is to get between them all. We should never have crossed that line. I've been so careful not to show my true feelings, to keep everything under wraps until that night when he almost killed a man for my honour. No one has ever stuck up for me like that before. I've always had to fight my own battles.

"It's okay, Kid. I get it." He looks away from me, but I see the tenseness in his jaw and the flicker of pain in his eyes. There's so much left unsaid between us and I know I should be braver than I am and talk to him. I just can't do that now with everyone watching.

"You don't understand," I say, trying to make him see that it isn't him. It's me. I'm the one who has fallen for all of her best friends. I'm the one who's in the wrong.

Ever since I walked in on Xeno dancing in the basement with his ex-girlfriend a few months ago, I've not been the same. Jealousy plagues me daily, and not just with Xeno. If any of my Breakers looks at a girl, let alone makes one their girlfriend it takes everything in me not to rage at the world.

They're mine.

Except they're not, not really, not in that way. We're friends. We're the best of friends and I just happen to be in love with all of them.

Twenty minutes after he left, Xeno returns with flushed cheeks and a smug look on his face that he settles on me the second he walks into the room. I down the last of my drink and heave a sigh. What is it with him tonight?

"I need the toilet," I mumble, pulling out of Dax's hold and entering the bathroom. I really should go home instead of crashing here like I do most weekends. Mum doesn't care where I am, and if it wasn't for Lena worrying about me, I would always stay out. Deciding that it's best I head off, I push open the door to find Dax and Xeno toe-to-toe, York trying to break them up and Zayn shaking his head as though he's hallucinating and not actually witnessing his best friends going at it.

"You know exactly what I'm talking about, arsehole!" Dax growls, pressing his finger into Xeno's chest.

"Do that again, motherfucker, and I'll knock you out!" Xeno explodes, shoving Dax with both hands.

I don't think. I act.

Rushing forward I get in between them both. I might be small, but I won't let that stop me. They might have tussled over the years I've known them, but I've never seen them like this with each other. Not ever.

"Get out of the way, Tiny," Xeno growls, not taking his eyes off Dax.

"No. I won't. You two need to calm the fuck down!"

"Fuck, guys. Lay off each other, alright?" York intercedes, trying and failing to get them to stop.

"Fuck you too, York. Acting like you don't fucking know!"

"Know what?" Zayn pipes up, getting to his feet. He's still high, but this seems to be sobering him up fast.

"Listen, we can talk about this," York insists, a look passing between him and Dax. "We're friends. We're a team, a crew. Don't do this..."

But Xeno doesn't listen, he shoves me to the side and punches Dax. I fall sideways, smacking my head against the corner of the upturned wooden crate that we use as a coffee table.

"Fuck! Is she okay? I didn't mean to hurt her..." I hear Xeno say before I pass out.

☘

I GROAN, my eyelids fluttering open as my vision blurs with colours and shapes. A sharp pain lances through my skull and I reach upwards automatically, only to find someone else's hand already pressed against the spot that hurts. Blinking back the tears that spring to my eyes, I try and focus. Eventually, the colours and shapes form into a familiar person.

"She's awake," Dax says gently, looking down at me in relief. He's cupping my face with his free hand and stroking his thumb over my cheekbone. I try to sit up, but he shakes his head. "Not yet, you need to be still for a bit longer."

"Bloody fuck, my head hurts," I grumble, heeding his warning.

Dax chuckles at my response, but his smile quickly falls as he leans closer, serious now. For a moment I think he's going to kiss me as his eyes soften with his touch. Then Zayn peers over his shoulder and he sits back suddenly, his fingers pressing against the bump on my head a little harder than he intended.

"Ow," I whimper, my head pounding in time with my heart.

"Shit, sorry," he mutters, pulling his hands away as guilt lacerates his face.

"Fuck me, Pen, you scared us all to death," Zayn says, blowing out a long breath. His night-time eyes rove over every inch of my face as he takes me in. There's something in the depths of them that makes me feel all warm inside. Heat creeps up my neck at his attention. At both of their attention. "You've been out almost an hour." He's no longer high, and there's a seriousness to his gaze that has me swallowing hard.

"I'll get you some painkillers. I always carry some in my rucksack," Dax explains, indicating for Zayn to take his place, and moves away abruptly. I try to turn and look at him, but it hurts too much to move.

"Thanks," I murmur, blinking back the pain that's like a knife pressed into my skull. "What happened?"

"You cracked your head on the crate. Knocked you clean

out. You've got a small cut and a lump, but it's not deep enough to need stitches. York did some first aid and patched you up whilst you were sleeping," Zayn explains.

"How did I manage..."

Then I wince as it all comes back to me in a rush. Xeno pushed me out of the way so he could punch Dax. They were fighting. My eyes widen and a sick feeling churns in my stomach.

"Yeah, Dax and Xeno were at each other's throats. York's taken Xeno for a walk to calm him down. I've never seen him so upset."

"Because of his fight with Dax?"

"No, because he hurt you. The guy's cut up about it. The second you hit the deck, they pulled their heads out of their arses and stopped fighting."

"I can hear you, you know," Dax grumbles from the other side of the room.

"I know, dickwad," Zayn retorts.

"Why were they fighting anyway?" I ask quietly, though deep down inside I think I know the answer already.

"Over you," a familiar voice states.

Zayn gives me a look before leaning over and pressing a gentle kiss against my forehead. The imprint of his kiss remains warm against my skin long after he's pulled away. When he moves out of my line of sight, I see York and Xeno in the doorway. Xeno looks grim and York relieved.

"We came back as soon as Dax texted us you'd woken up. How're you doing, Titch?" York asks me.

"Like I've had a bang on the head." I pull a face, then wince, then laugh.

"Fuck," Xeno mutters under his breath. "I'm so sorry, Pen." When he uses my name, I know he's serious. He looks pale, haunted.

"That's Tiny to you," I murmur, forgiving him in an instant. He didn't mean to hurt me, I know that. We all do.

Dax hands me the painkillers and after I've rested for another ten minutes, I finally feel okay enough to sit up. The pain in my head is a dull throb but manageable. Drawing on a long sigh, I fold my hands together in my lap and look at each of my Breakers in turn, feeling exhausted but determined. "I think we need to talk," I say gently.

York grins, giving me a warm smile "Thank fuck. It's time the air was cleared."

"I agree," Zayn says, looking at me in such a way that makes my skin heat.

Xeno catches my eye. "Yeah, we do need to talk. It's time for the truth."

"The truth," Dax repeats, nodding tightly.

CHAPTER FOURTEEN

Present Day

"SO, are you going to tell me what the deal is?" Clancy asks me as we sit together in the dining hall later that same week.

It's lunchtime and the place is heaving with dancers, stuffing their faces after a hectic morning of meeting their new teachers and getting more acquainted with each other.

I look at my bottle of water and my green apple and wish that I could spare a few quid on some of the delicious foods available. Being poor fucking sucks sometimes. But I've got to look on the bright side. As long as I'm here, I can deal with an empty stomach.

"Come on, spill," Clancy insists, dragging my attention away from the wraps and salads, and back to her.

"It's a long story..." I hesitate, not really wanting to divulge my history with the Breakers but knowing she won't drop it unless I give her something.

"We've got an hour to kill before the final lesson this afternoon..." She smiles impishly, pulling a face.

"What, only one more *meet the teacher* session left to endure today?" I roll my eyes. I get why they need this week for everyone to settle in, but I'm not five and I just want to get on with it.

"Yep, that's it for now. On Monday we can officially get back to checking out the competition... *and* the hotties," she replies, wagging her eyebrows.

"No hotties for me."

Clancy crinkles her nose, and chews on her lip. "Not even..."

"Especially not them," I cut in, knowing exactly who she's referring to.

"You are coming to Pink Albatross tonight, aren't you? The whole cohort's going. I'm planning on getting drunk and having some fun," she asks, changing tactics.

"Nope, I've got to work. Sorry." Though I'm not really that sorry. I wouldn't be able to afford the entrance fee to the club anyway, or any of the drinks for that matter. Who in their right mind spends ten quid on a cocktail anyway?

"Boo! Can't you call in sick?"

"Did that last Saturday night. I'll be out of a job if I do that again anytime soon..."

Clancy chews on her lip. "Do you still get off at midnight?"

"Yes, but..." I start to protest, but she cuts in.

"That settles it then. I'll come to Rocks with you and then we can head over to the Pink Albatross. I might even text Leo, see if he's available to hook up..." she muses, tapping her chin with her finger. "Then again, I might just keep my options open. Plenty of dancers in the club, and all that."

"Wait, no... I was just going to head back home after my shift."

"Absolutely not. Anyone who's anyone goes to the Pink Albatross the first Friday of the new term. It's tradition apparently."

"Clancy, I really appreciate your friendship, I do, but I *can't* go." I look down at my measly bottle of water and half-eaten apple as my stomach growls, giving me away better than any words could.

Clancy's eyes widen, then her cheeks flush a little red. "I'm sorry, I didn't even think."

"It's alright. I don't plan on being a pauper all my life. That's why being here is so important to me. I need to make something of myself. I'll do anything to make that happen."

Clancy smiles, giving my hand a squeeze. "You *are* already something. You're an amazing dancer and if there's anyone who'll have a career in dance when this year is up, it's you."

"I'd like to believe that's true," I reply, choked up by her compliment.

"You know what," Clancy continues, oblivious to my inner turmoil, "Despite how Tiffany likes to present herself, my parents aren't loaded. We're not poor either but we did fall just under the threshold, enabling my father to apply for the scholarship for both of us. Despite that, my parents send me and Tiffany an allowance every week. What I'm getting at in a roundabout way is that I've got enough to pay your entry into the club too..."

"No," I cut her off. "I don't want to owe you."

"I don't *want* the money back, Pen. I really want you to come because it's tradition, because you're my friend and because I don't want you to miss out. Besides, Tiffany is going too, and she'll do everything to try and ruin my night if I don't have back-up. I could use a friend."

For the first time ever, Clancy drops the smiles she wears so beautifully and shows me her real face. Beneath the optimism is a girl with insecurities no thanks to her evil stepsister. I understand only too well what it feels like to live with someone who takes pleasure in making you feel unloved. How can I deny her now? Besides, I've always wanted to see what the Pink Albatross was like inside.

"Okay..." I say, hoping I don't regret this.

"Okay, you'll come?"

"Yeah, I'll come."

Clancy squeals and reaches across the table to hug me. "We are going to have so much fun!"

"Let's not get too carried away..." I grin, but my smile fades when I see Zayn and York stroll into the dining hall with Tiffany and Sophie. Great, that's all I need. Clancy follows my gaze, then stands abruptly.

"Come on, let's get out of here," she says overly cheery. "For the next hour, it's just you and me, babe! We can discuss what we're gonna wear tonight and you can spill your beans about those hotties that have got everyone in such a tizz. I'm a good listener, I promise."

"Sounds like a plan. I need to pick up some supplies anyway."

Making a quick exit, Clancy and I head out. Ten minutes

later, we're sitting on a park bench watching some toddlers and their mums have a picnic on the green. On the way, Clancy insisted on buying me a latte and a bun after she bought the same for herself in the coffee shop opposite the park. I try not to inhale the bun in one mouthful, and take measured bites instead, so it doesn't look like I'm as hungry as I actually am.

"So, you were going to tell me about your... *friends?*" She screws up her face, not sure what to call them. I don't know what to call them either. Actually, that's a lie. I know exactly what I want to call them. Arseholes. They're arseholes. Coming back here and fucking me with like this. This was always my dream, attending Stardom Academy. They *knew* that.

"We used to be." I sigh heavily, and force myself to take a sip of the sweet coffee before continuing. Clancy remains quiet, probably realising how close I am to clamming up. "What I said in the dance studio was all true."

"You mean about the crew you danced with..." Her voice trails off when realisation dawns. "Oh, *they* were your crew. Zayn, Xeno..."

"York and Dax. Yes."

"Fuck me. You lucky cow," she exclaims, her eyes gleaming. The swear words sound funny coming out of her mouth. She's kind of posh. Well, maybe not posh, she's just more well-spoken than I am. Which isn't all that hard, I suppose.

"I *was* lucky to have them as friends."

"Was...?"

"Yeah, was." I sigh heavily. "Something happened three years ago. Something big. I can't talk about it."

"Because you don't trust me?" she asks, cocking her head to the side. She doesn't look hurt, just trying to understand.

"No, I think I can trust you. It's just... It's complicated. Actually, that's not the exact truth. It's dangerous. I *can't* tell you. It's better that way."

"Fuck. Are they gangsters or something? I mean they look the part, but I thought that was just their thing. You know, badass dancers with tats and mean scowls, all mysterious and broody and sexy as fuck. Gets all the ladies hot under the collar, if you know what I mean?"

I raise an eyebrow, but concede her point. "Yeah, I know exactly what you mean. They look the part because that's exactly what they are, gangsters."

Clancy grins, her pretty white teeth gleaming in the sunlight. "Holy shit, girl. So what the fuck are they doing at Stardom Academy? I mean, I'm happy I get to ogle them and all, but..." I give her a look, and she holds up her hands. "I solemnly swear I won't touch any of them with a bargepole, *promise!* Chicks over dicks, right?"

I'm more relieved than I let on. Clancy is definitely a keeper. "I don't know why they're here, honestly."

"I bet they want you back in their gang. Are you living a double life too? Is my new best friend a gangster's moll?"

I can't help but laugh, but it comes out sounding a little strangled. "We're not in the States, Clancy. This is London, we don't have gangster molls."

"Shame." She grins at me, but her smile drops when I remain quiet.

"So, let me get this straight. You were in their gang as kids," she begins but I cut her off.

"No, their *dance* crew. I was never in any gang."

"Okay, so you were in their dance crew. Something heavy

went down which you can't tell me about because you might have to kill me if you do..." she smiles again, but it drops when I wince.

"I would never hurt you... not intentionally anyway," I add, trying to make her understand what I'm mixed up in without having to spell it out.

"Okaaaay, fuck. I think I'm getting a picture here. Right. So, now they're back and Xeno is a motherfucking bachata teacher at the academy. So fucking hot by the way." I grimace, pushing away the memory of his possessive thumb pressing into my back that first morning. "Zayn is a hip-hop genius and York is a fricking tap-dancing gangster," she continues excitedly. "What about the big, tatted dude you battled against at Rocks? I haven't seen him at the academy."

"Dax? I'm not sure." My hands curl around my Styrofoam cup to stop them from shaking. Clancy notices and gives my arm a squeeze. "I swear to you Pen, you can trust me."

I shake my head, blowing out a breath. "I've said too much already."

"Okay, I get it. See no evil, hear no evil, speak no evil, right? So, what are you going to do now?"

I think of that night three years ago and the deal I made. Swallowing the nausea rising up my throat, I take another sip of my coffee. "Stay out of the Breakers way and hope to fuck they get bored of all the mind games and leave me the hell alone."

"You think that's going to work?" she asks.

"It has too."

"And if it doesn't?"

"Then I'll have to figure out something else."

CHAPTER FIFTEEN

Present Day

BY THE END of the afternoon, I'm exhausted. Physically and emotionally.

After the shock of coming face to face with the Breakers on Monday morning, I'd blocked them out by putting all my energy into my taster lessons. Like a sponge, I absorbed all the new steps and different techniques, all the while thinking how I can incorporate them into my own routines. I barely gave anyone my attention and didn't cross paths with the Breakers again as I got settled in, though I hear about them often enough. Already they're fast becoming the talk of the academy. Girls huddle together in the hallways chatting about the 'tattooed hip-hop guy' who dances with such aggression that it makes them weak-kneed or the 'broody Bachata teacher' who makes their knickers wet with his sultry moves. I even heard one girl say that York could tap with such lightning speed that the vibrations coming up through the floorboards made her come. Every time I hear their names on these thirsty bitches' lips I want to throat punch someone, or run. Neither of which are helpful. Instead, I tune everything out. Most of the time anyway.

"That's it, class. You're dismissed," Sebastian, my ballet teacher, says. My feet are sore from dancing barefoot. I don't have any ballet slippers, and the blisters on the balls of my feet remind me that I'm ill-equipped for such a prestigious academy. Gathering up my stuff, I pull on my socks and trainers, and hobble towards the exit trying not to wince with every step. I need to lance them, have a bath, and wrap them up if I've got any hope of getting through my shift tonight, let alone my date with Clancy at the Pink Albatross.

"Wait," Sebastian says, motioning for me to come over. Drawing on my last reserves of energy, I do as he asks and try not to make a fool of myself and faint. It's been a long week of little food, none of which has contained enough sustenance to keep my energy levels up. Noodles, cereal, and copious cups of coffee don't exactly provide a healthy balanced diet. I know I need to figure something out so that I can afford to buy better food, but the thought of working any more nights at Rocks, especially since the Breakers are back on the scene, is putting me off asking for more shifts.

"Everything okay?" I ask.

"You haven't trained in ballet before, have you?" He cocks his head to the side, narrowing his eyes at me.

"Not unless you count YouTube."

"And yet, you're better than half the dancers in this class..." There's a faint smile around his lips at my very obvious shock.

"I am?"

"Yes, you are. Ever thought of a career in ballet, Pen?"

"No!" I blurt out. He winces. "Sorry, that was rude. I mean, it's not really my kind of dance. I prefer contemporary..."

"The foundation of which is based in ballet."

"Yes, but..."

"But?" he cocks his head to the side.

"I'm not really that type."

"I didn't realise that ballet had a *type*." He laughs to show me that he isn't offended, when honestly, he probably should be. I wasn't being complimentary.

"I guess I feel more comfortable dancing what I know."

"With whom you know, don't you mean?" he cocks a brow, and his hip.

I look around the room, at the perfect dancers with their perfect hair and perfect clothes. All of them, both male and female are poised and graceful. Beside them I feel inadequate, no matter how well I can dance. The divide between the rich and the poor isn't so obvious to me in the other disciplines at the academy like it is with ballet. It makes me feel uncomfortable.

"Yes, I suppose so," I admit.

"You're quite judgmental, aren't you?"

"I don't mean to be. Comes with the territory."

"The territory?"

He seems genuinely interested in my response, but I wait until the last student leaves before explaining. "I grew up on a council estate..."

"And?"

"And we were judged all the time. I guess it's hard not to do that back."

"Can I let you in on a little secret?"

"Sure," I shrug, ignoring the rumble of my stomach and the pain on the balls of my feet.

"I'm gay, mixed race, and grew up in a poor working-class family in the Midlands. My dad was a Jamaican immigrant, my mother a hardworking cleaner. We had nothing when I grew up and believe me, I was called all the names under the sun. I didn't fit in with any group, until I found dance. Ballet, specifically. I won a scholarship to the Royal Ballet School in Richmond Park when I was thirteen."

"Good for you," I mutter.

"Don't get me wrong. It was hard at first, I had to prove myself over and over..."

"Because you were poor, and they were rich?"

He shakes his head. "No, because they were better dancers than me. At least in the beginning."

"And your point is?"

"My point is, that you should never close the door on a gift just because you don't think you fit the mould. Don't ever define yourself by what you *believe* people see. Open yourself up to possibilities because you're talented enough to do anything. Okay?"

I frown, mulling over his words. That's easier said than done when you're so used to being ridiculed for your passion by the people who are supposed to love and support you the most.

"But I don't have rich parents who pay twenty thousand a year to secure my place here."

"What has that got to do with anything?"

"It means that I'm already judged."

"Does it?

"Of course it does," I respond. "I'm a scholarship student."

Sebastian sighs. "Maybe you're right, maybe it does. Then again, isn't that the point because *you've* already judged half the students here because they're *rich*," he says, finger quoting the word. "You've not bothered to look past that to see what really counts. Rich or poor, every student is here because they love to dance. It really is as simple as that."

"I wish it was," I mutter, knowing that isn't the case for all the students. Some are just here to fuck with me. Speaking of which... I swallow a groan.

"Seb, I need to borrow your studio. Tuillard has a cleaning crew in mine. She's obsessed with polishing these damn wooden floors," Xeno says, as he strolls into the room. He doesn't acknowledge me, choosing to concentrate his attention on my ballet teacher who is currently flushing pink beneath his tan skin. Is there no one immune to Xeno's good looks?

"Sure thing, Xeno. You're always welcome to get sweaty in my studio. I'll see you next week, Pen," he says, giving me a squeeze on the arm before winking at Xeno. The flirty bastard. I make my move to leave, trying not to wince with every painful step. How the hell I'm going to get through tonight is beyond me, but right now that's the least of my worries. I need out.

"You. Stay." Xeno orders, pulling me up sharp.

If Sebastian heard, he doesn't acknowledge it. He simply leaves, closing the door to the studio behind him.

"I need to go," I respond, hobbling as quickly as I can to the door. Xeno gets there before me and flips the lock, leaning against the door for good measure.

"Where were you yesterday? You didn't turn up for your introduction to my class," he asks, fixing his gaze on me.

"You have no right to ask me anything, Xeno. Why the hell are you here, huh?"

"I asked first."

"I'm going to ask for a transfer to another discipline. I don't want you to teach me a damn thing."

He nods, scoffing. "Running again. You're good at that."

"I don't have time for this. Are you going to let me pass or do I need to kick you in the balls?"

"You could try," he grins, challenge in his eyes. "Is the feisty Tiny still in there, or did she fuck off as well? When the going gets tough, the tough gets going? Ain't that how the lyrics go?"

"I *didn't* run. It wasn't me who fucking left," I shout back, shaking. Xeno makes a snorting noise, disgust making him ugly. Still, he blocks the damn way out. If he hates me so much, why does he insist on standing in my way?

"Xeno." I grit my teeth, forcing my anger down. Forcing every emotion rising up within me away. I need to leave. I need to go. I can't do this. I *can't*. The longer I'm in his company the harder it is for me to convince myself I hate him. I've missed him so fucking much. So, so much.

"You owe me a truth, Pen."

"I don't owe you jack shit." *Please, please, just let me go,* I want to beg but I don't. He can't know how scared I am that he's here, that the Breakers are back. So I turn to the one emotion I can rely on, anger. I dig deep, funnelling it. "Just get the fuck out of my way. I don't want to speak to you, see you, fucking dance with you. *Any* of you. I will not let you ruin this for me. I've worked too damn hard."

Xeno barks out a laugh and pushes off the door, crowding me until we're chin to chest. He opens his mouth to say something, but a knock at the door prevents him. He steps back and twists on his feet, unlocking the door then yanking it open. On the other side is Tiffany, of all fucking people.

"What's *she* doing here?" she has the cheek to ask, her lip curling back over her pretty, white teeth.

"I was just leaving," I retort, trying to muscle past Xeno who grabs my upper arm, forcing me to remain. Tiffany looks between his grip on my arm and my face, her eyes narrowing. I can see the jealousy flare in her eyes.

"No, you're staying. Take a seat, Pen," Xeno says calmly, letting my arm go. He turns to Tiffany and gives her his best megawatt saved-for-sex-only smile. She melts, for fuck's sake. Any minute now she'll strip naked and offer herself up as tribute with me still in the goddamn room.

"Tiffany, put the music on. Track seventeen," Xeno orders, handing her his mobile and ignoring her lascivious gaze.

"Of course." She takes it from him, her fingertips lingering on his skin for a lot longer than is comfortable or necessary. Does she not let up?

"Staying for what, exactly?" I hiss the second she's moved away.

"You missed my introductory class. You need to catch up. Tiffany here has volunteered to help me out."

Yeah, I bet she has. "I told you, I'm taking *a different* class." I fold my arms across my chest, trying not to let him rile me up further.

"And I'm telling you, you're not. Not if you want to remain at this academy, *Pen*." He spits my name out like it's poison. I flinch.

"You can't do that..." I mutter, my throat drying.

Xeno steps close, and leans down to whisper in my ear so that Tiffany can't hear what's being said. "Yes. I can. D-Neath owes me a few favours. How do you think I got this job, Pen? You might have impressed Tuillard, but he's the money man here, and despite what she thinks, what *he* says, goes."

"So Zayn and York got in here on the back of a dirty favour... *figures*," I respond unkindly. The fact is, I know both of them are talented enough to get a scholarship on their own merits, but this makes more sense. Especially given what Madame Tuillard intimated Monday morning when she introduced us all to each other.

"Always so self-righteous..." he glares at me, his nostrils flaring.

"You chose that life. Not me."

"We *chose* it? You really are fucking dense."

"I wouldn't get too close, Xeno, you might catch something from the dirty little street rat," Tiffany pipes up. Her jealous words don't hurt me, but Xeno's lack of response does. Once upon a time he would've jumped to my defence. So much for leaving baggage at the door. He pulls back, not giving anything away. So I take my frustration out on Tiffany who is clearly using this time to perfect her nasty barbs.

"Fuck you, Tiffany-I've-Got-A-Silver-Spoon-Stuck-Up-My-Arse. You walk around like you own the damn place but like me you got into the academy on a *scholarship*. You're no better off than I am. So that silver spoon ain't so shiny from where I'm standing. In fact it's covered in shit."

She snorts, making sure to look me up and down. "Maybe so, but some of us have *class* and that can't be bought. You're nothing but a skank. I've no idea what Clancy sees in you, then again she's not much better."

"Refer to me like that again, *bitch*, and I'll knock you out!"

Tiffany laughs. "Go ahead. I'll be more than happy to watch your scrawny arse kicked out of this school."

"ENOUGH!" Xeno shouts, making Tiffany jump.

A little bit of fear flashes in her gaze followed by a whole dose of lust. I've got her cards marked. Girls like her love the notoriety of fucking with a gangster. They don't really give a shit about the person beneath the outer shell so long as they look good hanging off their arm and reap the benefits such a position affords. It was never like that for me.

Never.

They were *always* my Breakers first before they became well-known for that name for an entirely different reason. I hated what they became. The moment our dance crew turned into a gang it was the beginning of the end. My heart aches for the loss of what we had. Some days it hurts so much I can barely breathe. But they became everything we'd once hated, and as a result they broke my heart. I won't let them do that again. Whatever they're here for, I want no part of it. None.

"I'm going," I mutter. One last attempt at asserting my defiance.

"Sit down, Pen. Watch!" Xeno demands, nodding to Tiffany who flips a switch on the surround sound system, turning on the music. She's smiling like a cat that's got the cream as he strides towards her.

Knowing I really have no choice given his threat, I hobble over to the row of seats lined up against the wall, and sit. In the middle of the dance studio, Xeno places Tiffany's hands on his shoulder, positioning her arms so that they're locked into place, then holds onto her ribcage, his thumbs resting just below the curve of her non-existent tits. She grins at him, but he just nods, before sliding his legs between her graceful ones.

"You are staying in my class, Pen, and when this is over, you're giving up that truth you owe me. Understand?" he says, locking eyes with me over Tiffany's shoulder.

I'm not sure whether he means when *this* specific kind of torment is over, or something else entirely, either way I catch his meaning as he dances with Tiffany in a way that has my blood boiling and my heart aching. Reminding me, once again, of that time when I finally spilled my feelings in the basement of number fifteen Jackson Street. That was one truth I wished I could take back because it was the beginning of the end for us. Less than six months after I admitted my feelings to the Breakers, they left me for good.

CHAPTER SIXTEEN

Four Years Ago

FOLDING my hands in my lap, I wait for my Breakers to settle down around me. My head is still pounding from earlier, but at least I'm conscious now. York is sitting next to Xeno on the sofa opposite and Zayn is on the floor, his knees pulled up to his chest. Over the other side of the room Dax is leaning against the wall, separate from us all. I don't like it.

"Dax, come here," I say, my cheeks heating, feeling shy all of a sudden. God, this is going to be hard.

"Sit down, Dax. I ain't gonna throw another punch," Xeno mutters.

"You wouldn't get another chance," Dax grumbles back, and for a moment I worry it's all going to blow up again. Xeno might be the leader of this crew, but everyone knows Dax is the best fighter. Whenever we've got into scraps with other dance crews, it's always Dax who heads up the fight. Over the past year, he's gotten a bit of a name for himself. He's known as *Teardrop Dax* because fighting him will only end with his opponent in tears. Dax never cries, no matter how hurt he gets. Never. He's tough.

And yet, I know the truth. He's a kid beaten down by his abusive home life. Of all the Breakers, I worry for him the most. He holds *everything* inside. The only time he ever expresses himself is when he dances, living up to his name in a different way. There have been plenty of times where I've had to hold back the tears when watching him dance. Sometimes it's impossible and I cry for him when he can't do the same for himself, though I hold it in until I get home so no one can see.

"Please, don't fight anymore..." I reach for the sore spot on my head absentmindedly, but it's enough to remind them all what happened earlier and they both fall silent. Dax sits down, but he doesn't reach for me. The distance between us feels significant. I hate it.

Sighing, I worry my lip, pulling at a piece of loose skin with my teeth. The metallic taste of blood makes me reach up and wipe my mouth with the sleeve of my jumper.

"You had something you wanted to say?" York gently prompts me. He gives me an encouraging smile and my heart flutters.

Swallowing hard, I nod, keeping my gaze fixed on him. "I don't know how."

"Just say it, Pen. Whatever it is, just say it," Zayn says, frowning now.

"Dax and I..." I choke out the words, feeling my skin flush with heat and my heart hammer so painfully that I think there's a real chance that I'll pass out. I can feel it battering with bloody fists against the inside of my ribcage, so violent I almost choke.

"Dax and you, *what?*" Zayn asks. His black eyes spark dangerously, and the atmosphere suddenly becomes a thousand times more intense.

I can't breathe. My throat feels like it's closing up. Jesus, what was I thinking? I keep looking between my Breakers. I'm so scared I'll lose them. How am I going to tell them that I kissed Dax let alone have feelings for all four of them? This isn't how normal people behave. I'm sixteen, still a virgin and the first person I kissed was Dax for crying out loud. I don't know how to do this. I'm not like the other girls, all sexy and sure of themselves.

York clears his throat. "Would it help if I told them..."

I look at him with wide eyes. He knows. Oh God, he knows. I'm so shocked that my mouth pops open, then slams shut. "I... erm... *shit.*"

"I kissed Pen. I kissed her, okay?" Dax butts in, growling. He's angry. Why is he angry?

"You did WHAT?!" Zayn stands, his fists curled.

"Sit down, Zayn," Xeno snaps.

"This is what you were fighting about?" Zayn glares at Xeno, swiping a hand through his hair before turning his attention on Dax. "You copped-off with Pen. What the fuck, man?"

Dax grunts and I can feel his anger growing. If I don't say something soon this is going to blow up again.

"I kissed Dax too. It wasn't one-sided," I admit.

Zayn snaps his head around to stare at me, his mouth pressed into a hard line. "When?" he asks.

"A few weeks ago. The night Dax beat the shit out of that bloke who tried it on with me at Rocks. It just happened."

"Yeah, whilst we were all inside the club, Dax was putting it on Tiny in the alleyway out back," Xeno adds, his face a dark scowl.

Dax shifts forward in his seat. I hold my hand out. "No! It wasn't like that." Swallowing the sick feeling in my stomach, I shift closer to Dax and rest my hand on his arm. He tenses, then relaxes a little as I shuffle closer. "It wasn't like that," I persist.

"What was it like then?" Zayn drops back to the floor, his shoulders slumping.

"I *wanted* him to kiss me. I liked it," I whisper.

Dax's head snaps around, his eyes flashing with something I don't understand. Relief maybe, hope, even. "You did?"

"I did," I admit.

He reaches for me, cupping my cheek in his large palm. "I've wanted to kiss you for a long time, Kid."

My heart clunks against my ribcage at his words and the feel of his thumb running across my cheek. I lean into his hold. "I had no idea..."

"Fuck's sake," Xeno swears under his breath, breaking up this intimate moment between Dax and me. "So you're an item now, is that it?"

"No... It's not like that," I say. Dax removes his hand, his jaw gritting once more. He stiffens when I squeeze his arm, willing him to understand.

"Then what is it? Jesus, Tiny, you need to fucking tell us. Are you into Dax or not?" Xeno presses, glaring at me. That angry muscle ticking away in his jaw.

"I am, but..."

"But what, Titch? Come on, you can tell us. We're friends, remember?" It's York this time, he's watching me carefully. His voice is soft, supportive. God, I love him. I love them all, and that's the fucking problem.

"That's just it. We're friends. One kiss with Dax and you're tearing each other apart."

"*I* have no issue with you and Dax being together, if that's what you're worried about," York responds, though something in the depths of his eyes tells me that isn't completely true. "These two will just have to suck it up."

"But I *am* worried, York, because this isn't just about the kiss. It's about you too."

"Me?" York points to his chest, surprised.

"Yes. You, Xeno," I say, flicking my gaze to meet his grass-green stare that right now is drilling a hole in my chest like he's trying to make a path for my heart to escape and fall into his hands. "Zayn too."

"What are you getting at?" Zayn asks, cocking his head to the side.

"I'm sorry if this is going to make everything awkward, and I'll understand if you don't want me in the crew anymore. It's just..."

"Kid, just say it," Dax mutters as he places his hand over mine and squeezes.

"It's just... *fuck's sake*," I mutter, angry at myself for being such a coward. Lifting my head up, I force the words out. "I want to kiss all of you too, and I don't know what to do about that." My confession comes out in a rush of air that has me sinking into the sofa as though I've run a marathon.

"Fuck me," Zayn grumbles, scraping a hand over his face.

Dax blows out a breath, Xeno jumps up to his feet and stalks over to the fridge. I watch him pour himself a generous shot of vodka then knock it back. When I look at York, he's grinning. Great, just fucking great. I should've kept quiet.

"Well, that's thrown an interesting twist to the situation," he says, shaking his head with mirth.

"It's not funny, York," I retort, my cheeks heating. Dax squeezes my hand, his thumb rubbing over my knuckles. That gentle touch makes my heart flutter and something low down tighten. I squirm a little, trying to ease the feeling.

"So let me get this straight. You kissed Dax a few weeks ago and liked it, and now you want to kiss all of us too...?" Zayn asks, cocking his head to the side. There's no sarcasm in his tone, just an openness that I've come to appreciate from him.

"Yes, no. I mean. I've thought about it. A lot. I realise that makes me a shitty person." I turn to Dax. "It doesn't mean that I like you any less..." I mumble.

"I understand, Kid," he replies, but I don't think he does. Our eyes meet, and for a moment it's just the two of us in the room. Despite the hoodie pulled up over his head, I can see beneath his armour and all I want to do is climb into his lap and kiss all the pain away.

"No, you don't."

"It doesn't make you a bad person, Titch. We're your friends. You should be able to tell us these things. The thing is..." York pauses, his smile dropping now as I drag my gaze away from Dax and face him. "Kissing Dax has changed things."

I drop my head. "I know. I don't want you all to fall out.

You've never fought like that before," I say to Xeno's back because he's still facing the damn wall, refusing to look at me.

"I'm sorry I've messed this all up." Pulling my hand free from Dax's, I stand, ignoring the biting sting of tears and the room swimming around me because I still feel woozy from the bang to my head. "I'm an idiot. You're my friends and I love you all so much..." The words come out strangled because I mean them. *Really* mean them.

"You love us? As friends, you mean?" York asks gently. I focus on him, because I can feel the atmosphere change again and I'm shivering with... *everything*. My head thumps and this weird spot on my chest hurts. I rub at it absentmindedly with the flat of my hand.

"Yes, as friends..." *Fuck, Pen just say it.* "But more than that. It drives me crazy when you're with other girls. I don't like it. Most of the time I want to throat punch them." I laugh, but it comes out sounding hollow. "I kissed Dax because I wanted to. It felt so right. It really, really did," I say, looking over my shoulder at him. "I want to kiss him some more, but then..."

"Then?" York asks softly.

"I feel the same about you," I admit, staring at York. He swallows hard. Some of the easiness in his smile fading. I drag my gaze away and look at Zayn who seems more than a little shocked by my admission. "And you too, Zayn. I hate it when you flirt with other girls." Finally I settle my gaze on Xeno, who's turned around to face me now. "I wished it was me you were kissing earlier, Xeno." He doesn't say anything, and I can't get a good read on him to figure out what he's thinking either. "Now you know. I'm sorry for fucking things up. I'm sorry, okay? I'll go."

"No. Stay." Xeno suddenly growls, scowling at me just like that first day when I turned up with York two years ago. He strides towards us. "We sort this out now."

"You're angry," I state.

"Tell her, Xeno. Tell her the real reason why you hit me, why you're so angry," Dax demands.

"Because you were getting on my fucking nerves!" he retorts.

"Bullshit. There's more to it than that."

"Fuck you, Dax," Xeno mutters, gritting his jaw.

"I'm going. This was a bad idea." Angry tears brim in my eyes and I'm furious at myself for fucking this all up. I don't regret kissing Dax but maybe I wished I'd thought about the consequences of kissing him before I crossed that line.

"Don't do that, Pen." Zayn rushes to his feet, reaching for me. He places his finger under my chin, and lifts it so that I look up at him. My heart stops beating when his night-time eyes flash with interest, as though he's seeing me clearly for the first time.

Dax stands behind me, stepping close. He wraps his arms around my waist from behind and rests his chin on the top of my head. Without saying anything, he's making a point. That he'll always have my back. That I can count on him. No matter what. Zayn's nostrils flare, but he doesn't move away. In fact, he steps closer. Out of the corner of my eye I can see Xeno grit his teeth. York stands, placing his hand on Xeno's shoulder all the while looking at me. He's not smiling this time, but I recognise that look, it's the same one he gives to the girls he's interested in. What's happening here?

"You said you wanted to kiss us all, is that right, Pen?" Zayn asks.

"Yes."

"Okay then."

"Zayn!" Xeno grinds out, but I'm oblivious to anything else as Zayn steps closer, cups my face in his hands and presses his lips against my own without hesitation, like he's been waiting to do this for some time.

At first I'm too shocked to react, but when Dax brushes his lips against my ear, whispering that it's okay, my mouth parts and allows Zayn's tongue to slip inside, stroking mine softly, tentatively. A moan releases and I know I should be embarrassed, but I'm not. I wanted this.

I *want* this.

My hands reach up and clutch Zayn's t-shirt, my fists scrunching the material up in my hands. The kiss goes from gentle and searching to desperate and hungry, and even though a tiny voice is trying to remind me where I am and who is watching, an even bigger one is yelling at me to just go with it. When Zayn's dick hardens and he pulls back, looking sheepish, I realise that this isn't just two friends experimenting, this is so much more than that.

"Fuck, Pen," he mutters, his cheeks are flushed, and his eyes are wide.

My hands fly up to my lips and press against them. They feel swollen and tender, just like all the words lodged in my throat.

"You fucking prick," Xeno snarls at Zayn who shrugs, grinning stupidly.

Ignoring Xeno and giving my hand a gentle squeeze before letting it go, Zayn motions to York, a question in his gaze. York, for the first time ever, is lost for words.

Xeno whirls around to face him, "Don't you fucking dare!"

But York looks past Xeno and directly to me. "Do you still want to kiss me, Titch?"

Do I? I'm still reeling from Zayn's kiss. From the truth being out there in the open. It's freeing but scary as hell. I don't want them to think I'm a slut. "I... erm... Is this okay? I mean... I'm not, you know... You don't think I'm a..." *Slut*, I think, unable to say the word out loud.

"Titch, you're our girl. *Ours*. We'd never think bad of you. If it helps, I really, *really* want to kiss you. Besides, the third time's a charm, right?" He cocks his head to the side, and I try and blank out the almost deranged look on Xeno's face. He looks like he wants to rip York's head off but then also, kinda like he wants to kiss me too... I don't know. I'm never really certain where Xeno's concerned.

"Well, Titch? I can wait, if that's what you want..." he voice trails off, and I see the disappointment clear as day.

"No!" I blurt out. He flinches, but I shake my head. "I mean no, I don't want you to wait. I want you to kiss me, York."

He grins suddenly. "Are you ready for the best fucking kiss of your life?"

Behind me Dax chuckles, and Zayn scoffs.

"You motherfucker," Xeno snarls, but he doesn't try to stop him.

York squeezes Xeno's shoulder. "Sorry man, but our girl needs me and I'm not going to deny her." Stepping close, York looks at Dax over my head. "I like you a lot Dax, but would you mind...?"

Dax chuckles. "Sure thing," he says, releasing me from his hold and stepping back.

My cheeks flame as I tip back my head and stare up at York. The overhead light catches his white-blonde hair and pale skin and for a moment I swear he fucking sparkles. Then again, that might just be the bang to my head.

"From the second I saw you wet and shivering in the rain, I knew we were done for. It's taken these muppets two years to figure out the same thing," he says, resting his hands on my hips and gently pulling me close to him. "Also, you're gorgeous and you don't even realise it."

"What?" I mumble, my brain has frozen up and is unable to articulate anything right now. This is so surreal.

"You're Titch to me," he says, brushing his lips against my forehead. "Tiny to Xeno, Pen to Zayn and Kid to Dax. Don't you see? We've already claimed you as our own, even if that's harder for some of us to admit. Why do you think all the girls we've brought back have such an issue with you? It's because they know what you mean to us."

"Always so fucking insightful," Xeno growls, but York just smiles.

"Oh," is all I can manage to say. This was not what I was expecting. "Are you saying..."

York leans down, the tip of his nose brushing against the bridge of mine. "Yes, Titch, I'm saying we *all* like you. I'm going to kiss you now, okay?"

"Okay," I mutter, the word ripped from my lips as his pillowy mouth presses against mine. He holds me close against his body and my toes curl inside my trainers as his tongue parts my lips. Stars sparkle behind my eyelids as my body breaks out in goosebumps. I reach up and pull at his hair, tugging him closer. He chuckles into my mouth, smiling and kissing me with a talented tongue that soothes as well as taunts. By the time he's finished, I'm giddy.

"Xeno?" I question when York eventually steps away.

We all take a collective breath as Xeno looks beyond me to the rest of the Breakers. "You bunch of goddamn arseholes," he grinds out. Then his gaze focuses on me.

"I'm not going to kiss you, Tiny. Not because I don't want to, but because someone has to keep their head tonight, and I guess that someone is going to be me." He presses his mouth into a hard line, thinking for a moment. Then he wipes his hand over his face and focuses his attention back onto me. "What I'm about to say might upset you, but I have to do this..."

"Do what?" York asks before I can.

"Tiny, you have to choose."

"Choose?" I repeat.

"Yes, stay as we are, a dance crew, *friends* and that's it, or..."

My throat closes over. "Or?"

"Or pick one of us and walk away from the crew for good. No more dancing together. *Ever.*"

"Xeno, man, you can't make her do that," Dax grinds out, understanding implicitly what I was trying to explain with my fumbling words.

"She *has* to choose, it's the only way. Whatever choice Tiny makes we have to agree to it. No questions. No going back," Xeno continues.

My mouth goes dry. "I don't know if I can do that..." I whisper.

Didn't he hear what I said? I love them all, and yet, I also love to dance... with them. *All* of them. If I pick one of the Breakers as my boyfriend, then I'm no longer a part of this dance crew and all the happiness it brings me will be gone. If I choose the dance crew, then I'll never have any of them the way I want and will be miserable watching them all with other girls. Either way, I'm fucked.

"You've got no choice. You've got until your seventeenth birthday, the night of the crew battles at Rocks, to figure it out. Spend time with each of us. Make your decision."

"Why then?" I ask, looking helplessly between them all.

"Because whoever you do choose will want more than just a kiss, Pen, and I sure as fuck won't allow any of these arseholes to sleep with you until it's legal to do so." Xeno grabs his coat from the sofa and pulls it on, not even considering that I might choose the Breakers dance crew over one of them.

"The legal age to have sex is sixteen, Xeno. Not to mention that's both a dickish and possessive thing to say," York says.

"I don't give a fuck. None of you arseholes are fucking Pen until she's made her choice," he growls back. "Come on, I'm walking you home. We're done here tonight."

I don't have time to say goodbye, let alone fully comprehend what Xeno just said, as he grasps my hand and pulls me out of the basement. Part of me is shocked at his outburst. How dare he decide when I choose to give myself to somebody. This is not the nineteen bloody fifties and I'm not his property. On the other hand, that fierce kind of protectiveness has me feeling all warm inside. It's a strange combination.

By the time we reach my flat, I'm coiled so tightly with anxiety that I can barely look at Xeno. He's been quiet the whole way home, and I've not been able to say a word. When we step into the dimly lit entrance to my building, he pushes my back against the brick wall, shoving his thigh between my legs and pressing it against the spot that's been throbbing all night long. With his forearms resting either side of my head, he boxes me in. His breathing is harsh, his chest expanding and contracting as he presses his forehead against mine. My stomach ties up in knots at the look on his face, like he's fighting something within.

"I'm taking myself out of the equation, Tiny. You and me, it can't happen."

"But..." I'm unable to articulate my feelings around the sob lodged in my throat. "Why?" I manage to squeeze out.

He refuses to answer, instead he brushes his lips over the bump on my head, his lips lingering over the spot. "I'm sorry."

Acting braver than I feel, I capture his cheek in my palm. "We could have it all... the crew *and* each other," I whisper, wanting to believe that so much. Wanting to believe in my heart that love will conquer all and we don't have to live bound by ties that society and religion place on us.

"No, Tiny, we can't. Our world just doesn't work that way," he replies, his voice catching as he pushes off the wall and walks away, taking a piece of my heart with him.

CHAPTER SEVENTEEN

Present Day

"YOU READY YET, PEN?" Clancy calls over the music playing in the ladies' room.

I've just finished my shift at Rocks and am changing into something more appropriate to wear to the Pink Albatross before we head over there. My feet still hurt like a bitch, but the painkillers combined with two shots of vodka have helped to numb the pain enough for me to get through the rest of the evening. Unlocking the cubicle door, I step up to the mirror and dump my bag on the counter, thankful for my heeled, Doc Martin style, ankle boots. Clancy tried to offer up a pair of ridiculously uncomfortable heels like the one she's wearing. These boots were my compromise.

"Whoa, Pen, you look fucking hot!" Clancy exclaims. Her

cheeks are flush from too much alcohol, but she looks pretty damn awesome herself. I look at her in the mirror, at the dark streak of kohl eyeliner bringing out the pretty colour of her eyes. Her lips are a bright red, perfectly off-setting her emerald, boob tube dress. She, of course, is wearing stilettos as red as her lipstick. How she's going to dance in those monstrosities is beyond me.

"Cheers, you don't look too bad yourself. Dressing for anyone in particular?" I ask her, knowing full well that she's on the pull tonight. Clancy is fun and flirty and goes after what she wants, not giving a shit about what anyone might think. I admire that. I'm not sure I'll ever be free to hook up with a boy again, let alone love someone. It's better all round that I don't.

"Nope. Just for me." She grins, rummaging around in her make-up. "Ah-ha! Here it is," she exclaims, holding up what looks suspiciously like purple lipstick. She points to my face. "Can I?

"I don't wear makeup."

"You don't need to either, but this lippy will look rockin' with that outfit and a little bit of kohl liner will have those eyes poppin' too. Those leather shorts look so much better on you than they ever did on me."

"*Rockin'* and *poppin'*..." I laugh. "You're drunk."

"I'm merry," she protests. "And don't change the subject." She steps closer, armed with the purple lipstick as one of the regulars of Rocks, Desiree I think, steps into the toilet.

"Looking good, babe," she says, giving me a once-over as she passes. "You know if you ever want to swing the other way..."

"Cheers," I sing-song, biting down a laugh as she winks at me.

"See, fucking H.O.T!"

"Okay, okay, you're right," I concede.

This isn't my usual choice of outfit, but fuck it, I kinda like the loose purple tank with my black lace bra peeping out from between the material, matched with Clancy's leather shorts, fishnet tights and chunky heeled ankle boots, admittedly I look good. Besides, it's not every day I get to go to the very exclusive Pink Albatross nightclub, and I may as well dress up for it. I'm not going there to pick up anyone. This is about me feeling good about myself for once, not about anything else.

"Can I?" Clancy grins, her eyes twinkling as she holds the lipstick aloft.

"Fine," I agree, popping my mouth open slightly so she can run the lipstick over my lips. When she's done I copy her as she presses her own lips together and makes a popping sound.

"Now close your eyes," she orders.

A couple seconds later I can feel her soft breaths flutter against my face as she lines my eyes with black kohl, smudging it a little with her finger. Reaching up, she unties my hair, and drags her fingers through it until it looks a little dishevelled but in a sexy way. "Perfect! There you go, Little Miss Hottie."

I look in the mirror and grin. "Not bad, not bad at all." It's the first time I've actually felt sexy. It's a good feeling.

Clancy grabs her mobile and snaps a selfie of us, uploading it onto Instagram, then grabs my hand and drags me out of the toilet. "Let's fucking do this!" she shouts over the din.

Twenty minutes later, we're climbing out of the Uber cab and striding towards the entrance of the Pink Albatross. There's a queue that wraps right around the building, but Clancy ignores it. "Follow my lead," she says, jutting her chest out and plastering a sexy smile on her face. If I wasn't straight, I'd totally sleep with her.

We sail past the queue and walk right up to the bouncer. Clancy gives him a megawatt smile and crooks her finger at his scowling face. He leans down and she cups her hand around his ear. When he pulls back, he nods, running his eyes over her sexy body then unhooks the rope and steps to one side.

"No charge for these ladies," he says to the woman taking payment at the door. She waves us through with a roll of her eyes.

"Cloakroom is just further along. No coats allowed in the club," she mutters, pointing down the corridor.

"Thanks!" Clancy grins, giggling behind her hand.

"What the fuck did you say to him?" I ask her as we move down the dimly lit corridor that's lined on both sides with mirrors and head towards the throbbing sound of music. Pink fluorescent lights run along the tops of the walls in strips, casting us both in a pink glow.

"I just complimented his hair, that's all..." she shrugs, winking.

"Clancy, he didn't have any hair!"

She bursts out laughing and just shakes her head. "Don't sweat it. We got in free, didn't we? Now we can use the money we would've spent getting into the club on drinks! It's a win-win." She grabs my coat from me and hands it to the cloakroom assistant along with hers. "You best not have offered yourself up for payment, Clancy," I warn, not feeling comfortable with that idea at all.

She rolls her eyes. "Chill, I just said that we're D-Neath's latest protégées."

"What? We're not... And why would the bouncer let us in for that reason anyway?"

"A little dicky-bird told me that this is D-Neath's nightclub. He owns it, Pen. Besides, we kind of are his protégées by extension. Everyone knows that he's the money man behind Stardom Academy."

"You're not the first person to tell me that," I mutter, wondering why I'm the last person to know anything.

"Come on, stop stressing," Clancy cajoles, nudging me with her shoulder. "Why don't we grab a cocktail and check the place out, yeah?"

A couple of minutes later we're standing at the bar sipping on our margaritas, watching the crowd on the dance floor. Behind the bar is a mirrored wall which runs the whole length of the club, making it appear larger than it is. Around the edge of the dance floor are half a dozen private booths with purple, velvet curtains wrapped around them, giving privacy to the people sitting within and an extra layer of exclusivity to an already exclusive club. Each booth has a bouncer standing in front of it, blocking our view of the occupants. I can see faint candlelight coming from each booth, and the shadowy figures of the VIP's sitting within them, but that's about it. The place is smaller than Rocks and is lit with soft lights in pinks, purples, and reds, giving it a more sensual vibe. Hanging above the dance floor is a jewelled chandelier in rainbow coloured crystal that captures the light and throws it back out across the space.

Beneath the chandelier are faces I recognise from the academy, including Tiffany who is dressed to kill. She's wearing a fitted black dress that sits just below her arse and shows off her lithe figure. Right now she's dancing with someone I vaguely recognise from my contemporary dance class, and even though he seems to be attentive, she looks bored, her gaze constantly wondering over to one of the booths.

"Your sister's here," I point out.

"Stepsister," she reminds me, picking up her cocktail and taking a long drink as she eyes up the crowd. "She's had a stick up her arse all day and has been shittier than usual."

"Really? I wonder why." I smirk, remembering our confrontation in the studio earlier.

Clancy looks at me wide-eyed. "What happened? Spill!"

"We exchanged a few words earlier. She called me a 'street rat' and a 'skank' in front of Xeno."

"She did what?! That bitch!"

I wave away Clancy's anger. "Don't sweat it. I really don't give a fuck what *she* thinks of me."

Clancy frowns. "Wait, there's more, isn't there?"

"Yeah, there's more..." I pick up the straw in my drink and start swirling the liquid around and around before finally fessing up. "Xeno cornered me after my ballet lesson today. He asked Sebastian if he could borrow his studio and said that I needed to stay to catch up with what I missed yesterday."

"Wait, you were alone with Xeno? You didn't go to your bachata lesson? You never said."

"I was planning on switching it out for something else but Xeno had other ideas."

"Meaning?" she insists, narrowing her eyes.

"He pretty much blackmailed me into attending his classes."

"Blackmailed you?"

"Yeah, he basically said he could get me chucked out of the academy if I don't attend his stupid fucking lessons. He said that Tuillard might be the principal, heading up the school, but it's D-Neath that is the money man and what *he* says goes. Xeno and D-Neath are..."

"Friends?"

"I'm not sure, but Xeno said D-Neath owed him a few favours. How do you think he got the job?"

"Jesus."

"Yeah, then to make matters worse, Xeno proceeded to show me what I'd missed in his lessons using *Tiffany* as his partner, knowing full well that would hurt me the most. All the talk around the academy is right, he pretty much fucked her with his clothes on."

"Oh, man. Low blow."

"Yeah, my sentiments exactly. In all the years we were friends, Xeno never once asked me to partner him in bachata. Never..." Swallowing down the hurt, I plaster on a smile. "Anyway, what the fuck does it matter now. I'll go to his stupid classes and take whatever shit he throws at me. I'm past caring. He can only hurt me if I let him, right?"

"Atta girl!" Clancy beams, waving over the barman and requesting another round of drinks.

We both watch as he reaches up for an array of bottles filled with coloured liqueur and gets to work. After he passes us our cocktails Clancy points to one of the booths.

"Do you think D-Neath and Madame Tuillard are in one of those?" she asks, taking a large gulp of her drink before smacking her lips together, savouring the taste.

"If they are, they're probably fucking... Apparently, there's no limits to where they fuck or who might be listening when they do."

Clancy's eyes widen with mirth. "Oh, my God. You experienced that too? I thought I was the only one. I was scarred by it."

"Yep. I'm one hundred percent positive D-Neath was going down on Tuillard whilst she was on the phone offering me a spot at the academy."

"Dirty fuckers..." Clancy places her middle and pointer finger against her lips in a v then pokes out her tongue between them, wiggling it and making moaning noises. We both burst out laughing, and continue to giggle as the barman slides us both another cocktail each. I haven't even finished my current one and am already feeling half-cut what with the vodka shots I downed earlier.

"Oh, no, we didn't order these," I say, slapping at Clancy's hand as she continues to mimic oral sex. She ignores me and is even more provocative. The barman grins at her before answering me.

"These are compliments of the gentleman over there," he says, pointing to a figure at the other end of the bar who currently has his back to us. He's too far away and in shadow for me to get a good look, plus I'm going cross-eyed with all the booze.

Clancy peers around the long row of people, following my gaze. "I wonder if he's a looker?" she asks, almost absently, then winks at the barman and tells him to thank the gentleman for his generosity before handing me one of the cocktails.

When she starts sucking on the straw like it's a dick and she's thirsty as fuck, I bark out another deep belly laugh. "Clancy, you're being extra tonight."

She winks. *"Told* you we'd pull."

"You've pulled. I'm here to soak up the atmosphere and dance now that my feet have finally stopped throbbing."

"That'd be the alcohol numbing the pain..."

"No shit." My head is already starting to swim, and whilst I can take a drink like the best of them, I know my limits, and make a mental note to drink water or Cola after I finish this cocktail, painful feet or not.

"Next time wrap your feet up, Pen. You're not going to get through the year if you don't look after those pretty little tootsies of yours. Dancers feet are ugly motherfuckers at the best of times, don't make them any worse"

"I hear you."

"Right, drink up, and let's dance. Our admirer can come get us if he wants us..." Clancy suddenly blurts out, knocking back the rest of her cocktail.

"Correction, he can come get *you.* I'm not hooking up with anyone."

Rolling my eyes, I pick up the glass and swallow a mouthful of the sweet, tangy concoction that tastes suspiciously of Amaretto Sour and Bourbon.

"You don't like it? I'll finish it for you then," Clancy remarks, misinterpreting my reaction to the taste and snatching the glass from me, downing it.

"Actually it was my favourite drink once..." I mutter, my words lost beneath the thumping music as I look towards the end of the bar to try and catch another glimpse of the person who'd bought them for us. But he's gone.

"Hmm, yum." Clancy grins, sashaying onto the dance floor, leaving me with the bitter aftertaste of a night I'd rather forget.

CHAPTER EIGHTEEN

Three Years Ago

"TITCH! You made it. I was about to come get you. How did you get away?" York asks as he pulls me into a hug and wraps his arms around me in the dim light of the hallway leading down into the basement.

"Mum eventually passed out on the sofa at nine and Lena is staying over at a friend's house," I explain, wrapping my arms around his waist and allowing myself a moment to relax into his hold.

"I'm so fucking glad you're here. New Year's Eve wouldn't be the same without you, Titch." York presses a soft kiss against the top of my head, then cups my face in his hands, looking at me intently. "Three months to go," he whispers.

"Don't remind me."

My heart hurts.

There's no other way to describe the way I feel. It's like a constant ache in my chest that not even sleep can heal. I don't want to decide. I don't want to choose. I can't.

Just like Xeno suggested, I've spent time with all of the Breakers individually and it's only made the decision harder. I've even spent time alone with Xeno even though he already made it clear that he was taking himself out of the running. Not that this is a race or a competition. Not one I want to be a part of anyway.

Thing is, when we're together I catch Xeno looking at me when he thinks I don't notice. Since the night I confessed how I felt about them all, he hasn't brought anyone back to the basement. Then again, that doesn't mean shit. Since I've known him, he's never been without a girl. Perhaps he just spends time with them elsewhere.

"You know whoever, *whatever* you choose, you're still my Titch, okay?" York says, trying to ease the hurt that's so obviously etched on my face.

I nod my head, unable to answer him. For the last couple of months I've been trying to figure out what to do, falling more in love with them all. We're all so close, and at times I can even imagine us being happy together as a family in some big house somewhere far away from here. I know it's a pipe-dream, but I can't help but hold onto the hope that someday we'll all be together, number fifteen Jackson Street and all the trouble it harbours just above our heads, a distant memory.

"It's hard..." I mumble, not able to express myself in the way I want. I did that before, and look where we've ended up. Lately, I've kept my thoughts and feelings to myself. It's better that way. Although, that's not so easy around York. He can read me like an open book.

"I know." York nods, pulling me tighter against his chest. Pressing my nose against the dip in his neck, I breathe him in, drawing in his expensive scent. It makes me feel lightheaded. I'm not sure how he affords to buy CK One. I don't ask. It's not my business, but I love it. That scent will forever remind me of him.

"It's quiet in the house. Where is everyone?" I ask, pulling back and trying to regain control of my emotions and my need to run my nose against his skin.

"Out. According to Zayn, Jeb's taken over Tiger, a club in the city. The whole gang is there. We're currently on guard duty," he explains, chewing on the inside of his cheek.

I frown. "Since when have you guys ever been on guard duty? Isn't that for actual members of the gang?"

"Jeb's called in a favour."

"A favour?" I groan internally, worry leaking into my blood-stream. "Isn't that where it always starts?"

"We've gotten to use this basement for years hassle-free and he's left us alone. It's just one night. Don't worry yourself about it." York brushes my fear away, but I know him. He's worried, I can tell.

"York..."

"It's okay, Titch. Seriously."

For a long time, the Skins plotting world domination above our heads never affected us. In the basement below them we could dance and muck around, we could sit and talk and be friends without any outside influences affecting us. Even my mum's constant verbal and physical abuse seems like a distant memory when I'm with my Breakers. I can even cope with a world where David exists so long as I have them by my side. They hate him as much as I do. Despite the fact that he's officially one of the Skins, he spends very little time at Jackson Street because he's been given the responsibility of overseeing Jeb's drugs ring in the south side of the river. He's set up with a flat, a car and money to pay for women who let him unleash his violence on them daily. I've heard rumours about some of the things he's done that make me sick, and whilst I feel for those women, I'm only glad that I'm no longer in his line of sight.

Over the past few years, it's been all too easy to forget the dangers that surround us but lately the walls have been closing in and Jeb has been asking for more and more *favours* from the guys. Tonight isn't the first time he's cashed in. It's been small things, nothing the average Joe would consider dangerous, but every time they agree to help it makes me feel like Jeb's just getting them warmed up for more sinister stuff. I've noticed all four of them withdrawing from me. There's been a few occasions where they've stopped talking when I've entered the basement. It doesn't take a genius to know that they're hiding something from me.

"Come on, Titch, it's New Year's Eve. Let's celebrate, yeah? Everything else can wait," York cajoles, sensing my reluctance to enter the basement. It's not just because of Jeb's request. I'm not really in the mood for socialising with their extensive group of friends. I want to be selfish and have them all to myself.

"Okay," I respond, plastering on a fake smile that York instantly dissolves with a soft kiss.

"Don't put a show on for me, Titch. I see you," he says

gently, before clasping my hand and pulling me into the basement.

The moment I step into the room, my mouth drops open in shock. The room is lit up with fairy lights that hang from every corner and tea lights dotted around the room, making the space magical, but that isn't the most incredible thing. Graffitied across the back wall is a beautiful mural of four boys who look suspiciously like my guys holding up the word Breakers. Sitting with her legs crossed on top of the word is me, or at least a version of me. She's flicking a bronze coin in the air, a penny to be exact.

"Oh my God, who did this?"

"Surprise," Zayn grins, pulling me in for a hug, his excitement rubbing off on me. "Do you like it?"

"Like it, I love it!" I respond, grinning stupidly. He plants a swift kiss on my lips then moves out of the way so that Dax can step in and draw me into his arms.

"Happy Christmas, Pen," he mumbles against my hair, shyly.

"Christmas was a week ago, and I've been here in between then and now," I laugh, looking up at him.

"Yeah, but we couldn't get Asia over until today to do it," Dax explains, a sheepish look on his face.

"Shut up! You know Asia?"

"Dax knows her friend Eastern, but Asia was more than happy to do this for a few quid," York explains.

"Wow. I don't know what to say..." I shake my head in wonder, walking over to the wall and running my hand along the mural. No one has ever done anything like this for me before. It's amazing. So, so special. A lump forms in my throat and I push it down.

"Why am I sitting up there and not standing with you guys?" I ask, turning around to face them all. The three of them are all looking at me intently and my insides melt. It feels like this is more than just a mural, more than a thoughtful Christmas present.

This feels like a promise.

"Because you are our girl, Pen. There isn't anyone else who deserves that position," York explains.

"Does this mean that you've managed to persuade Xeno to change his mind? I don't have to choose?" I ask, hopeful.

Dax casts a look at York, then presses his lips into a hard line. My heart sinks, my shoulders slumping. Of course not.

"We're working on it, Pen, but he's a stubborn dickhead," Zayn admits.

Part of me wonders why they don't just tell him to go screw himself, but I realise it's the same reason why I don't do the same thing.

Respect.

Friendship.

Love.

We're a family. We care about each other and going against Xeno would almost certainly mean that we'd lose him. None of us can afford that. He's the person who holds all of us together. He might be possessive, bordering on bullish, but that's because he's a protective leader who has had to make hard decisions for the rest of us. We don't do anything unless he approves it. We didn't enter any dance battles until he said we could. For a long time I thought it was because he didn't think we were good enough. I realise now it's because he didn't want us in Rocks before we could handle what went on there. The drugs, the gangs, the fights both on and off the dance floor. We were kids. We're still kids, and yet when I look at my Breakers, I know that they're on the cusp of manhood.

I just wish that somehow we could figure out how to be together without any of the heartache that we're hurtling towards at breakneck speed. It feels like one of those horror movies Xeno loves to watch. We all know there is going to be death and destruction, but no one ever thinks to jump off the train, or in the case of those movies, *not* go in the basement. I glance around me and stifle a nervous laugh. Ironic, really, given where I'm standing.

Choosing the dance crew would mean that I'd keep their friendship but never be able to be intimate with any of them. I'd have to watch them move on and find other girls to love. But if I choose just one, then I lose the rest of them and my place in the dance crew forever, not to mention forfeit the competition and take away their chance of winning five grand.

How can I possibly decide like that? I've gone over and over it again and again in my head. I've written lists. I've talked myself into a corner, and backed myself out again. The truth is, each of them are special in their own way.

Zayn is open, willing to explain things that the others find embarrassing or difficult. He's always there when I need him and has become my rock. When we're not together, he's always a text message away. Since I've admitted how I feel he's not so much looked at another girl. He's steady, reliable and the personification of *home*, a place I never really had until now.

York is sensitive to my needs, always watching out for me,

always one step ahead. He's kind, sympathetic and comforting in a way I've never experienced before. He's the first to know when I'm sad or down and the first one to make me smile with his quirky wit and charm.

Dax understands me in a way the others don't because, like me, he's a kid beaten down by his parents. We have a deep understanding of each other that's bound in bruises and barbs. His protective nature and the way he looks out for me, makes me feel safe.

Then there's Xeno...

Xeno makes my heart beat erratically, and my body reacts instinctively. He pushes my buttons and fires me up in a way that's infuriating, but at the same time invigorating. I'm still a little uncertain around him, not because I'm afraid of him, but because there's a chemistry between us that makes me yearn for his touch and ache for his kiss.

But being the true leader that he is, Xeno's kept his promise and hasn't tried to kiss me or be anything other than a friend. I'm beginning to understand that he's a man of his word. Once he makes a decision he sticks to it, and expects nothing less from the others too. The thing is, I'm no closer to knowing what to do. Xeno left me with an impossible decision. One I've been agonising over. To make matters a thousand times worse, the night I have to choose falls on my seventeenth birthday, which is the same night we're battling for the crew title and five thousand pounds. There's so much at stake.

"What the fuck is that?"

I snap my eyes to Xeno who's walking into the basement with a scowl that seems to permanently scar his face these days.

He's holding two plastic carrier bags filled with alcohol. I can hear the bottles clinking against one another.

"Pen's Christmas present," Zayn responds. There's a note of warning in his voice and I don't know how to feel about the fact he wasn't in on the surprise.

Xeno must hear the caution in Zayn's voice because he simply nods, looking at me. "It's good."

"I'll take those," York steps in, removing the bags from Xeno's hands and busying himself with setting them on the side table. "Nice selection, man. Did you raid your mum's liqueur cabinet?"

"Something like that. Reckon you could mix up some cocktails?" he shoots back.

"I thought you'd never ask." York grins, stacking five plastic cups on the table ready to fill with whatever concoction he comes up with.

"Is that wise?" Zayn asks, jerking his thumb over his shoulder as we sit down. He pulls out a bag of weed and proceeds to roll a joint.

"Probably not," Dax chuckles.

Xeno's gaze flicks to the mural on the wall behind us. "Asia's work?"

"She came earlier today. The girl's insanely talented," Zayn explains, a little in awe.

"How's Eastern doing?"

Dax locks eyes with Xeno. "As good as any of us are. Asia's a good influence, but sometimes even that's not enough."

I don't miss the look they share, and a deep sense of foreboding fills my stomach. Xeno grits his jaw but doesn't respond, and the atmosphere becomes tense. It's been like that a lot lately and I can't help but feel they're keeping secrets from me. I don't like it one bit.

"Is something..." I start, but York cuts me off with a plastic cup of whatever he's mixed up.

"Here, Titch, give this a taste," he says, grinning broadly.

Taking the proffered drink, I sniff the liquid. It's a weird orange colour. "Is this going to put me in the hospital?" I ask, only half-joking. York has a habit of overshooting the shot measurements.

"Nah, but it will make you merry, and tonight we're all about that, right?" he glares at Xeno, who looks away, a muscle ticking in his jaw.

The bad feeling I sense between my Breakers disappears the more we drink. By the time midnight rolls around, I'm feeling the effects of the alcohol and am more than a little unsteady on my feet. When I get up to go to the toilet, my head swims and the ground undulates like an ocean would under the hull of a ship.

"Oh, shit. That drink is goooood. I want another Amaretto Sour, Yorky baby," I sing-song, stumbling past York and shoving my plastic cup in his hand.

Out of nowhere, Dax reaches for me, hauling me upright. "I think you've had enough, Kid."

"Nah, I'm just getting started," I respond, wrapping my arms around his waist and pressing a sloppy kiss against his chest. He chuckles, resting his hands on my shoulders. When I look up at him, he has two heads.

"There's two of you, Dax."

"York, man, how many shots did you put in her drink? She's out of it," Zayn says, stepping up close. He's frowning, and I reach for his face, pressing my finger into the groove between his eyebrows. Then burst out laughing as I actually poke him in the eye, my aim totally off.

"Ow, fuck, Pen." He reaches up and cups the offended eye. "You need some water."

"Shush, Zayn, I'm fine," I wave him off and my knees buckle, only causing me to laugh harder.

Dax holds me against him tighter and I kind of make a groaning sound, not because my head is spinning, but because I like the way he smells, all masculine and clean. It kind of does something to me, and the heat that sits low in my belly all the time these days, ignites.

"Hmm, I wanna lick you," I mutter, standing on my tiptoes and pressing my lips against his collarbone. My tongue snakes out of my mouth and along his skin, his taste exploding on my tongue. "You're delicious."

"Kid, don't do that," Dax grumbles, though he doesn't let me go. I take that as a good sign and lick him some more, scraping my teeth against his skin for good measure.

"I could eat you," I continue, alcohol loosening my inhibitions as I kiss my way across his collarbone, tugging at the material of his low V-neck t-shirt so that I can get better access.

"Oh, fuck," he groans, the sound reverberating through his chest into mine. "Stop, Kid. You don't know what you're doing..."

His voice trails off when I bite him. Hard. Something just as hard, presses against my stomach.

"That's enough!"

Xeno steps into my peripheral vision and suddenly I'm no longer being held up by Dax, but by him. The anger in his tone is enough to make me sober up a little. When a cup of water is thrust into my hand by a concerned looking Zayn, I take it.

"Drink," he orders, a flash of worry and... *heat*, in his gaze. I drink the water offered and this time York hands me another plastic cup, taking the empty one from me.

"Sorry, Titch. I should've gone easy on the Amaretto," he says, pulling a face.

"I need to pee," I mumble, suddenly aware of how all four of my Breakers are staring at me like I'm something they need to unravel... literally.

Oh shit.

"You need me to help?" Xeno, of all people, asks.

"Err, no. I can piss on my own, thank you very much," I respond, wincing at how that sounds.

Xeno lets me go and I flush with embarrassment, shuffling off to the toilet. When I close the door, locking it behind me, I lean my head back against the wood. Was I just *licking* Dax?

Oh. My. Fuck.

I stumble towards the toilet and relieve myself, then wash my hands and face with water. It helps to sober me up a little. Truth be known, I haven't had that much to drink, I'm just not used to it. Feeling a little more in control of my body, I unlock the door to the bathroom and head back into the basement stopping short when I see we have guests.

"Well, well, well. If it isn't my slutty little sister. Hello, Penelope, having fun?"

CHAPTER NINETEEN

Present Day

PUSHING THAT MEMORY ASIDE, I follow Clancy into the centre of the dance floor, trying not to let the remnants of that night ruin this one. Any and all thoughts of my brother, David, are unwelcome. I don't want to think about him.

"Come on girl, we need to dance off some of that alcohol," Clancy grins, weaving her way through the crowd.

We pass Tiffany, who gives us both her signature glare. I smile sweetly, then raise my middle finger. If she starts on me tonight I'm not sure I'll be able to hold back. Anger writhes in my stomach. I'm angry at Tiffany for being such a bitch for no better reason than she has an ugly heart. I'm angry at my brother for still having a hold over me no matter how many miles away he is. I'm angry at Jeb for taking away my Breakers in the first place. I'm angry at myself, for letting him. But more than all of that, I'm angry at the Breakers for walking away, for believing what they were told the night our friendship was so cruelly severed. New Year's Eve might've ended up a shit-show, but my seventeenth birthday tops it all.

"Tiffany is on form tonight," Clancy announces, laughing as she gives her sister the middle finger too.

"Forget about her," I say, dragging Clancy further into the crowd and feeling the need to work off all the memories and the stress of the past few days.

An hour later, my feet have decided to remind me that alcohol as a pain reliever only works if you keep actually drinking, so I tap Clancy on the shoulder and point to the ladies' room. She nods, giving me a thumbs up and steps back into the hold of a cute blue-haired guy who I recognise from the academy. He gives me a smile and then returns his attention back to Clancy, who is now grinding her arse against his crotch to *I Like It* by Cardi B. A wicked grin pulls up her lips as she bends over, the flat of his hand against the small of her back. I grin, she's such a lush and I love her for it.

Making my way through the crowd, I follow the signs to the toilet then sigh, even in the most exclusive clubs there's always a queue for the ladies room. Of course, like always, the male toilet has none.

"Fuck it," I mutter, shoving open the door and striding to one of the cubicles.

"Hey, wrong place, beautiful," a dude pissing into a urinal remarks as I stride past him.

"Don't mind me," I respond, flashing him a toothy grin as I open a cubicle and lock it behind me.

Quickly relieving myself, I flush the toilet then close the lid

and sit. Pulling off my shoes, I wince. Even though the throbbing's back, my feet are still wrapped up well, which is good. I
make a mental note to make sure I clean them up the minute I
get home. Pulling my shoes back on, I open the door and wash
my hands, relieved to find that the bloke has left. Reaching into
my back pocket, I pull out some painkillers and knock them
back quickly, washing them down with a mouthful of water
from the tap.

"A pretty girl like you really shouldn't be using the men's
toilets. You never know who you might meet." Straightening up,
I turn around slowly. It's the guy from earlier. My gaze flicks to
the door and he laughs. "Don't worry, love, I ain't gonna touch
you."

"You wouldn't get a chance," I respond. It's been a long time
since I've had to fight anyone, but old habits die hard, and when
you've been in enough scraps over the years like I have, then it's
not all that difficult to get back into that frame of mind. A quick
kick to the balls followed up with a kidney punch usually does
the trick even on a stacked guy like this.

"Feisty, I can see why he likes you." He opens the door indicating for me to leave.

"Who likes me?" I ask, my hackles rising.

"Come with me and you'll find out."

"And if I refuse?"

The guy grins, his teeth white against his ebony skin. "It's
your funeral, or perhaps it's your friend's...? Be a shame for that
pretty little redhead to end up at the bottom of the River
Thames."

He's smiling like he's just made the funniest joke, but the

threat is serious enough. I recognise a psychopath when I see one. My older brother was a good teacher.

"What's your name?" I ask, as I follow him down the hallway and back into the main section of the club. The music is pumping, and I catch a glimpse of Clancy kissing the guy she was grinding against when I left her. The temperature of the club has ramped up with all the bodies and the dancing, and my skin breaks out in a sheen of sweat, though not just because of the heat.

"You know how this works. We've never met. *Inside,*" he demands, not bothering to hide the threatening gaze he aims at Clancy. The bouncer standing in front of the entrance to the booth unclips the gold rope. I slide inside, blinking my eyes as they adjust to the low lighting and come face to face with the leader of the Skins.

"Hello, pretty, it's been a while," Jeb smirks, his perfect teeth glinting in the candlelight. Around his neck are four layers of thick gold chains that are probably worth twenty thousand pounds each. He's every part the gangster with his expensive clothes and his tattooed fingers wrapped in gold rings. I look up from his finger tapping against the side of the crystal tumbler glass he's holding, and to his face. Beneath each eye are three teardrops tattooed into his dark Mediterranean skin. There's only the slightest resemblance to Zayn, which I'm grateful for. I hate that they're related.

"Jeb," I respond tightly, my skin crawling the second his lascivious eyes glide over every inch of me, despite whoever is on their knees beneath the table sucking him off. The slurping noises make me want to gag.

"Looking good, sweetheart," he exclaims appreciatively.

"What do you want, Jeb?" I ask, trying to keep my fear at bay and the alcohol in my stomach.

I'm treading on dangerous ground, I know that, but I can't seem to help myself. This man and his stupid fucking crew of degenerates took my Breakers from me. Zayn always believed that Jeb would look out for him, that he'd never force him into becoming a member of the Skins, but I'd known right from the moment he told me they were related that it was only a matter of time. Blood or not, everyone is just a commodity to Jeb, only worth something if he can use them to his advantage. Just like me.

"Just checking in on my investments," he says with a wry smile.

"Oh, yeah?"

"Yeah." He smiles lazily, then shudders as the person beneath the table chokes a little on his cock. "That's it, suck me good, motherfucker," he grinds out.

I bite down on this inside of my cheek to prevent myself from saying something that will get me killed. Between us on the table is a pistol, pointing in my direction. I glance at it before forcing myself to hold his gaze. Jeb loves fear. He thrives off of it, but I refuse to show him mine. I've seen first-hand what he's capable of when the mood takes him. The problem with Jeb is that he'd surely fire a bullet in your head for being weak just as quickly if you were to disrespect him. He likes attitude, just not too much of it. Over the last three years, I've learnt how to walk the tightrope where he's concerned. Fortunately for me, I don't see him often enough to have to put it to the test. The last time we crossed paths was about six months ago when he dropped into Rocks one night unexpectedly. We'd talked and he'd reminded me of the deal I made with him the night of my seventeenth birthday. Like I could ever forget. That deal is a ball and chain wrapped tightly around my neck. One I'll never be able to shake as long as both he and David are still breathing.

"I hear you lost a battle to Dax last week. Funny, I thought you were the most talented dancer of all the Breakers?" he asks, having great concentration for someone who's getting his dick sucked-off beneath the table.

"No, that'd be Zayn and I'm *not* a Breaker," I say carefully. Nerves jangle inside my chest, but I force it away, gritting my teeth.

"Of course, my nephew, the hip-hop genius... It's a crying shame he doesn't put as much effort into his work for me as he does with dance. I've had to remind him far too often where his bread's buttered. He's a stubborn bastard though, and tough as shit. Takes after me, I guess," Jeb says, fondly. Though the smile he displays does not meet his eyes. Like my brother, family means nothing to him because he's incapable of either empathy or love.

My skin prickles. "What do you mean, *remind him?*"

Jeb smiles maliciously. "They're not your Breakers anymore, so why do you even give a fuck?"

"I don't," I mutter, even though I have a hard time believing myself.

The cruel laugh that follows inches like a spider crawling up my spine, scattering goosebumps over my skin. He doesn't believe me either. "They left you behind, remember? Those boys really couldn't have given two shits about you if they believed the story you spun. What does it feel like, having them back? Bet that was a nice surprise?"

Gritting my teeth, I force my face into a blank slate. "I really *don't* give a shit."

His hand disappears beneath the table and for a minute I have to suffer the sound of his cock being deep throated. Why won't he come already?

"So, you like my club?"

"*Your* club?"

"Come on, girl. D-Neath might have his name on the deeds, but I own this place just like all the other businesses in the area."

Of course he does, extortion is one of the long lists of crimes Jeb is involved in. I have no choice but to work for Jeb at Rocks, but socialising somewhere he actually hangs out is something I need to avoid at all costs. This is the first and last time I'll be coming to the Pink Albatross.

"It's been a while since we last talked," he eventually says like I'm some long-lost friend and not a member of his staff that he pays to keep quiet or a girl he has trapped in a god awful situation. "Business is booming. I've been kept busy."

"I'm glad for you," I respond, sarcasm dripping from every word.

This dirtbag has laid claim to the remains of the HH crew after the King was murdered just over a year ago. Jeb has taken the King's place in the criminal hierarchy given his only surviving heir, Monk, is in prison. Jeb was always an opportunist prick. Looks like he's branching out. Rumour has it that Asia and a few guys from Oceanside Academy got away and are living their best life somewhere far, far away from here. Good. I'm glad someone got out of this shit-stain of a life we live. It gives me hope.

"Spoke to David recently, Penelope?" he asks, changing the subject and shattering that hope as surely as Jeb's fist could break my face if he felt the urge to hit me. I wouldn't put it past him. I flinch, both at the mention of my brother and the fact he uses my full name just like David always does because he knows how much I hate it.

"No."

"Next time he calls, answer. I need his head in the game and not thinking about his pretty little sister... Ah, fuck!" he exclaims, his eyes snapping shut and his jaw going slack as he comes suddenly and violently. I've never been more grateful for someone's orgasm as I am right now, another minute listening to the noises of Jeb getting a blowjob and I would've hurled. I keep my face blank as the girl who's been on her knees beneath the table reveals herself. She's boyish to look at despite her short, skin-tight dress. With a spiky blonde pixie cut, square jaw, flat chest and tattoos covering her arms she's androgynous, hinting at Jeb's preferred sexual tastes. Without warning, he grabs the girl by the back of her neck and slams her face against the table. I jump at the sudden brutality, but the girl doesn't make a sound.

"A word of advice, if you're lucky enough to suck my cock another time then make sure you pay attention to my balls as well as my dick. I pay you to get me off, not test my fucking patience. Got it?" He lets her go, and she wipes at her eye, swiping away at the tear I see glistening on her lashes. The poor girl didn't stand a chance. It's a miracle she got him off at all.

"I'm sorry," she mutters.

"See yourself out, Charlie," he says, not bothering to hide

the fact that he's already bored of her company. She slides out of the booth, not meeting my eyes.

"As I was saying, speak to your brother. He's volatile when he's angry and I need him to keep his cool whilst he's dealing with my business in Mexico."

"Fine," I say, hating that I'm taking orders from this prick again. Not that I ever really stopped. Once Jeb owns you, there's no getting away from him.

Jeb shifts towards me, looking me up and down. "I understand that David's not happy about the Breakers being back, but I really don't give a shit. He'll have to suck it the fuck up. I'm the leader of the Skins, not him, and they're here on business for *me*. You might want to remind him of that fact, and do whatever you need to do to reassure him, so he doesn't come back here and fuck up my plans."

"Why don't you tell him yourself?" I retort, more afraid of my brother's response than Jeb's. Jeb might kill me for my insolence with a gunshot between the eyes, but David will take great pleasure in killing me slowly. I try not to shiver at the thought.

With lightning speed, Jeb grabs my jaw and squeezes it tight, his fingernails biting into my skin, a reminder of who he is and what he's capable of. "Because, I asked *you*. Don't forget who I am, and who I *own*, Penelope."

I nod my head, my throat constricting. "I haven't forgotten."

He nods, seemingly satisfied enough with my response to let me go. I don't rub at the pain in my jaw. I refuse to give him the satisfaction that he hurt me.

"And another thing, don't get too comfortable with the

Breakers being back. Like I said, they're here doing business for me and don't need any distractions."

"Business that involves Stardom Academy?" I question, knowing I'm taking a risk by asking, but doing it anyway.

"Business that has fuck all to do with you. Stay out of it, Penelope. Understand?"

"Yes," I mutter, waiting for permission to leave, because you can't just get up and go where Jeb is concerned. No one does anything without his say so. Not unless you want to end up as fish food somewhere in the English Channel.

"Hmm..." His gaze roves over me again and I have to suffer the sting of his interest. My skin prickles and my stomach churns. I swallow down the bile burning my throat as an evil smile carves across his face. "Such a beautiful girl, even without all that makeup you have on tonight. No wonder the Breakers lost their heads over you," he muses.

Balling my hands beneath the table, I bite down on all the things I wish I could say. I've never felt beautiful thanks to my mum and brother, so being called beautiful by a man I despise makes my skin go cold. My gaze flicks to the glass tumbler. I imagine smashing it against the table and using a shard of broken glass to slash his throat. Then I remember the gun and my itching fingers still.

Jeb's dark eyes flash with amusement like he knows exactly what I'm thinking. "That fire in your eyes is going to get you in serious trouble one of these days," he muses, then picks up his mobile phone from the table when it pings with a message. Not looking up from his phone, he dismisses me. "You can go. Talk to your brother."

Pausing at the entrance to the booth, I remember that I

haven't thanked him for the drinks he bought Clancy and I earlier, and even though it makes me sick to my stomach thanking him for anything, I do so anyway. "Thank you for the cocktails."

He cocks his head to the side and smiles darkly. "You and I both know that I don't buy anyone a drink unless I want something in return, and despite your beauty, you're not really my style."

"But who then...?" I mumble, smarting at the look he gives me.

"I don't know nor care, you shouldn't either if you know what's good for you," he says, lifting his eyes to meet mine. "Do you need reminding of what happens if you don't follow the rules?

I swallow hard, understanding the threat well enough. "No. I don't need reminding."

"Good, and Penelope..."

"Yes?"

He reaches into his jacket, pulling out a wad of notes clipped together with a silver bar and chucks it across the table at me. There's got to be at least a grand there. "Buy yourself a cocktail dress. Make sure it's short and tight."

"What for?" I murmur, my throat tightening as I pick up the money with trembling hands.

"Isn't it obvious? I need you to look pretty. Be ready next Friday night at eight and bring an overnight bag." With that he dismisses me with a flick of his hand, just like the prostitute who was sucking his cock a few minutes ago.

CHAPTER TWENTY

Present Day

BY THE TIME I've got a very inebriated Clancy into bed, it's past three in the morning. My feet are killing me, so I decide to take a bath. Knocking back a glass of water and some painkillers both for my feet and the inevitable hangover I'm going to have when I wake up, I strip and lower myself into the water. Letting out a deep sigh, I close my eyes, refusing to think about what Jeb has in store for me next week or the inevitable conversation with my brother. Sometimes burying your head in the sand is the only way to get through life, but for now I'm going to allow the water to soothe my aching feet and my worries.

Half an hour passes as I decompress. By the time I haul myself out of the bath, my fingers and toes are wrinkled enough to rival an eighty-year-old's skin. Drying myself off, I pull on my vest and shorts then grab my phone from the vanity. It vibrates in my hand, and when I look down at the screen I can see it's Lena.

"Lena, is everything alright?" I ask, snatching up the phone and already thinking the worst.

"Hey, Pen! How's school?"

"Lena, it's three in the morning, why aren't you asleep?" I hear giggling in the background and Lena shushing someone.

"Mum let me have a sleepover. Laura and Simone are here."

"Jesus, Lena, has no one told you that calling someone at this time in the morning is usually saved for emergencies only. I about had a heart attack," I laugh, shaking my head.

"Sorry, but I just had to call you. We've just watched 28 Days Later. That film is *fucked up!*" she exclaims, a nervous laugh lifting in the air. I recognise that laugh, it's the one she reserves for when she's really scared but is trying to pretend she isn't.

"Lena, was that wise? The last time you watched a horror movie you spent the week sleeping in bed with me," I remind her, flicking the call to loudspeaker and resting my phone on the vanity whilst I comb out my tangled hair.

"I was twelve then," she responds, the bravado back in her voice. "I'm old enough now not to be a cry baby. Anyway, have you seen the movie? Those fuckers can run."

"Yeah, I've seen the movie," I smile, remembering the night Xeno made me sit down and watch it after York forced him to watch Swing Time, another black and white movie featuring his favourite dancer Fred Astaire. "Try watching it in a dark and dingy basement."

"A dingy basement, why would I... Anyway," she continues,

not bothering to finish her sentence. "I swear, Pen, you won't see me for dust if this shit were to go down."

"You wouldn't see anyone, we'd all be dead within the hour," I say, darkly. I mean, come on, London and zombie apocalypse? No one would survive that shit.

"Oh, shut up, Pen. You'd just need to call your Breakers and they'd get us out of trouble no problem. They'd sling us on the back of their motorbikes and save the day."

I scoff, brushing out the last of my tangles and plaiting my hair. "I don't think so. That ship has long since sailed, or should I say those motorbikes burnt rubber a long time ago."

"Oh, I dunno..." More giggles ensue, and I roll my eyes. "I reckon they'd do anything for you."

Sighing, I shake my head even though she can't see me. Lena always loved the boys and on the rare occasion we'd bump into them outside of the basement, she would go all silly and shy. I kept my relationship with them on the downlow, but sometimes we'd cross paths when I was walking Lena to school and she would harass them with loads of questions. She especially liked their motorbikes, the ones they suddenly started riding around on about a few months before things went to hell.

"Is there a particular reason you called?" I ask her, trying to change the subject.

"I miss you, that's all. How's it all going anyway?"

"It's going... great," I eventually say, not wanting to bring up the subject of the Breakers. I'll never hear the end of it. "I've met some nice people. There's a girl called Clancy, she's an amazing tap dancer..."

"Ah, that's good, I'm glad you have a friend... Are you eating enough?" she asks me, her motherly vibes coming out. I grimace,

I should be the one worrying about her, not the other way around.

"Yeah, I'm good," I lie.

"Pen..." she warns, knowing me well enough to recognise the change in pitch indicating I'm not telling her everything. I sigh heavily.

"It's fine. I've got enough to get me by, and I'll get my wages in a couple weeks. Stop stressing."

"I could grab some shit from the cupboards and bring it to you. Mum won't notice. I do most of the cooking anyway."

"No, Lena. Seriously, it's cool. We've got a canteen here and I get lunch free anyway." Another lie, but this time she doesn't seem to notice, thankfully.

"Well, that's alright then..."

"Everything alright at home with mum?" I ask, feeling anxious at the thought.

"Yeah. It's cool actually. She's chilled out so much since..."

"Since I left?"

"I'm sorry, Pen. I didn't think."

"It's okay. I'm okay. I'm glad it's better at home now."

"Sooooo, any hotties there you want to tell me about? I mean all those sexy dancers and all," she asks, changing the subject. I hear her friends giggling in the background. Teenagers. You've got to love them.

"No! And even if there were, I wouldn't be discussing them with you." I can practically see the roll of her eyes as she huffs down the phone.

"You're no fun."

"I'm not talking about my love life with my little sister. It's not happening."

"What love life, Pen? You've not been on a date with anyone since the Breakers left."

"That's not true..."

"Urgh, you're such a bad liar. You're still so hung up on them. You should move on, it's not healthy."

"I *have* moved on, just like the Breakers did. So, you know, it is what it is."

"Tell me you at least slept with one of *them*..."

I hear more giggling and roll my eyes. "Goodnight, Lena. Say hello to Laura and Simone for me and make sure you go to bed soon, okay? Bye!"

"Pen...!"

I end the call, not willing to continue a conversation with my baby sister about my love life or lack thereof at three am in the sodding morning. Neither am I willing to go there regarding the Breakers, or the fact that I lost my virginity to a wannabe, arsehole gangster who was about as good in bed as he was at dancing. Shit, basically. It was six months after the Breakers left and I was low. I thought sex would help. It didn't. It didn't help the poor guy either. Jeb saw to it that he didn't fuck another girl again for quite some time. Ten broken bones tend to curb a person's ability to fuck and I've lived with the guilt ever since.

Puffing out my cheeks, I flick off the bathroom light and pad towards my bed, more than ready to collapse and sleep for twenty-four hours. It's pitch black thanks to my blackout curtains, so I have to hold my hands out in front of me and try not to walk into anything. When I feel the rug beneath my feet, I know my bed's just to my left. Scooting around the edge I sit down, feeling beyond exhausted. It's been a long arse day. A long week, in fact. Yawning, I curl up on my side and close my eyes, only for them to snap open half a second later.

"What the fuck?!" I screech, launching upwards and blindly reaching for the wall.

My hand eventually slams on the light switch, flooding the room in stark white light. Blinking through the dark spots, I turn on my intruder, my body shaking with adrenaline. Lying on my bed topless and barefoot, wearing just a pair of sweatpants, is York.

What. The. Actual. Fuck.

"Get the hell out of my room!" I scream, my eyes snapping up from the tattoo of an old oak tree climbing up his pale chiselled abs and pecs, its roots reaching below the waistband of his sweatpants.

"Hey, Pen," he responds with a raised eyebrow. His icy-blue eyes glinting with challenge.

"GET OUT!"

He smirks, rising slowly into a sitting position against the wall, his legs stretched out across *my fucking bed*. "Sounds like little Lena's grown-up into someone just as feisty as you."

"Keep her the fuck out of this and get the hell out of my room!" I repeat, not giving a shit that I'm screaming loud enough to wake up the whole damn floor. In fact, I *want* everyone to wake up. Maybe someone will come save me from this new level of hell.

"I wouldn't bother, Pen. They're either all out cold from booze, or otherwise *engaged*... just like Zayn and Tiffany."

"They're sleeping together?" I screech, forgetting that I don't care. Forgetting that I have no right to feel angry or betrayed or hurt anymore. Doesn't make it any easier to swallow though.

York cocks his head to the side, his white-blonde hair falling over his face. He swipes it away and I can't help but notice the prominent veins in his hand and forearms and the tree branches winding down his upper arms. I swallow hard, forcing myself to look away and concentrate my attention on the middle of his forehead instead. A nice, *safe*, area to stare at.

"Would it bother you if they *were* fucking?" he asks.

I want to scream, yes, yes it would, but of course I don't because, frankly, I don't want to acknowledge those feelings, especially not in front of him. "I don't give a shit. You need to leave. Now."

York smirks, then raises his thumb to his mouth, running the pad over his bottom lip. "You forget, *Pen*, I can read you like a fucking book. So, do you want to tell me why you looked like you'd seen a ghost after your little chat with Jeb tonight? I thought you were tight?"

"We're fine," I mumble, not willing to meet his eyes.

"Didn't seem that way to me. Odd, no, given your *relationship*."

"I don't know what you're talking about. We're fine," I fumble, taking a couple of steps backwards, needing the support of the wall before my knees fucking give way.

"I was at the club, Pen. I saw everything." *He was at the club?*

"Your Jeb's bitch, why don't you ask *him*?" I spit back. The best form of defence is offence, right? Besides, it's not as if he doesn't know the whole sorry story, well at least part of it. He was there that night too.

York stands, striding over to me. "I'm no one's *bitch*," he snaps, looking more the bloodthirsty vampire now than he ever did when we were young. He's so pale, his skin's almost luminescent, tiny blue veins run beneath the surface entwining with the oak tree's branches and roots. Close up, I can see the intricate detail of the bark, it's branches are thick and heavy with leaves, some are leaden with rain drops that drip to the ground.

"I belong to no one, *Pen*." *Unlike you*. He doesn't say those words, but I know that's what he's implying.

I flinch, as though he's slapped me.

I want him to call me Titch. I wish I didn't, but I do. Goddamn him. Goddamn all of them.

Swallowing hard, I drag my gaze away from his tattoo and look up into the eyes of the boy who could, once upon a time, look right into my soul and know exactly how I was feeling. He steps close, his forearms pressing against the wall as he cages me in.

"I don't belong to anyone..." he repeats, and I have the sudden urge to capture his cheek in my palm, to feel the dark blonde stubble that grows there scratch against my skin.

"Except the Breakers. You belong to them," I whisper back, the crack in my voice giving me away. I grit my jaw, refusing to look away from the ice in his gaze. It's sharp, jagged, cold... and yet, I can feel the heat from his body like he has a fire raging just beneath his skin, waiting to break through the last layers of the ice in his eyes.

He leans in close, his lips a hairsbreadth from mine. "You did once too," he mutters, his forehead pressing against mine. My chest heaves. I'm so fucking close to lifting my chin, to pressing my lips against his. It would be so easy to fall back into his arms. To let him really see the truths that lie beneath this thin mask I wear.

"That was a long time ago," I say instead, pushing down the cold dread I always feel when I'm reminded why our friendship was so spectacularly destroyed and why it needs to remain that way.

"What are you hiding, Pen?" he mutters, almost to himself.

"Please, just leave." I duck out of his arms, sliding away from him and backing up to the opposite side of the room. He turns slowly, his eyes glinting. He watches me for what seems like an eternity and I feel naked, bare beneath his penetrating gaze. Every ounce of strength I have is used to stiffen my spine, to shut down.

"Why didn't you trust us, huh? *Why*, Pen?" He asks, but I can tell by the look on his face that was an internal thought he wasn't supposed to say out loud.

"Trust?" I bark out a laugh, hating the brittle sound. "You became one of *them*. How could I?"

"And yet you..." he shakes his head, laughing just as coldly. He opens and closes his mouth, as though warring with himself. I see a flicker of the old York, the one who wouldn't hesitate to take me in his arms and hold me close in comfort. "You know what, Pen, this was a fucking mistake," he sneers, his eyes frosting over once more.

I watch him leave, every step away from me chipping away at my heart. When he gets to my front door, he turns and any kind of emotion he may have let filter through is gone.

"Did you like the drink by the way?" he asks, his hand curled around the door knob so tightly I can see the white of his knuckles.

"That was *you?*"

"Can't an old friend buy you a drink?"

"We're not friends anymore, York," I whisper.

His fist pounds against the door frame. Once, twice, three times, my heart slamming in time with the sound. "I fucking know that, *Pen.*"

Then without another word, he yanks open the door and storms out of my flat leaving me breathless and heartbroken all over again. It isn't until much later, as the rising sun filters through the cracks in the curtains, that I realise the significance of his tattoo.

It looks exactly like the tree I stood beneath that night we first met.

CHAPTER TWENTY-ONE

Three Years Ago

I LOOK DOWN at my phone and the text from an unknown number.

The Breakers vs Dante's Crew. Midnight. Abney Park Cemetery.

I've no idea who sent it, but it doesn't take a genius to work out what this is all about. Dax almost beat Frederico to death at Rocks because of me. This is a score being settled, and I have to put a stop to it.

What's the saying? *Violence, begets violence.*

Well, this ends now. I mean, I don't often agree with God, mostly I think he's some fucking cranky old dude who likes to mess with us all, but he's got a point with this one. Then again, didn't the Old Testament also say, '*an eye for an eye*'? Maybe

God was in a gang after all, because these arseholes use that as an excuse to fuck each other up all the damn time.

Either way, this bullshit needs to stop. I can't let the boys I love throw away their future for me. Violence is just a vicious cycle that has no end and I *hate* it. Yeah, I might've gotten into fights over the years but only ever in defence, nothing more. This is premeditated bullshit to prove which crew has the biggest balls and you can bet your arse Jeb has approved it. The thing is, these days knives and fucking guns are more likely to be used as weapons than good old fashioned fists. They could get seriously hurt, or *worse*.

Well, not tonight. No fucking way.

The air is frigid as I climb the fence surrounding Abney Park Cemetery. Pulling my hoodie up over my head, I jog towards the derelict church situated in the centre of the cemetery, warm puffs of air leaving my mouth in clouds of white. It's a huge place, with loads of crumbly old headstones covered in faded wording and green ivy glistening with frost. There are a few crypts with creepy looking angels staring down from above just waiting to come alive and scare the shit out of me. The place is dark, eerie, and full of ghosts. This is Xeno's kind of place. If he wasn't into dance and gangs, then the guy would be a horror movie director. He fucking loves all this scary shit.

Despite the full moon, I still need my phone's flashlight to guide me through the overgrown graveyard. To be fair, it's the perfect place to hold a fight. No one would be crazy enough to enter here at night. Well, except maybe for a bunch of teenagers with scores to settle and violence bubbling in their blood.

I pick up my pace, hearing a commotion already, but it's only twenty to midnight. Surely no one's here already? I wanted to get here early so that I could step in before the fight started. Stop it in its tracks. Looks like I'm already too late.

"Well, well, well, motherfucking Teardrop Dax beaten and bruised. You ain't so clever now are ya?" Frederico roars as I creep around the headstones approaching the crowd of people who are hooting and bellowing at the scene before them. Dax is standing in front of the rundown church, bleeding from a split on his eyebrow and lip. His teeth are bared as two boys hold his arms behind his back. I watch as Frederico rears back and slams his fist into Dax's cheek. The sound of knuckles cracking against Dax's cheekbone forces a cry out of my mouth and a white-hot kind of anger that gives me tunnel vision.

This isn't a fair fight.

This is revenge and whoever the fucker was that sent me the text message wanted me to witness it. I don't know how they managed to lure Dax here on his own but I'm not going to watch the shit get beat out of him. Firing off a quick text to the Breakers, telling them where I am and what's going on, I pick up a beer bottle that has been left on one of the graves, and sneak around the crowd to the far side of the church to a copse of trees that give me cover. When Frederico punches Dax again the crowd's frenzied bellowing covers the sound of me breaking the glass bottle, leaving just the neck and a jagged edge.

I grip it tightly in my hand, biding my time.

"You think you could get away with what you did to me, huh? Think again, motherfucker," Frederico snarls. "By the time I'm through with you you're gonna be nothing but a vegetable."

Dax lifts his head and smiles, baring blood-covered teeth. "Fuck you, cunt. You hit like a pussy."

Frederico tips his head back and laughs, then launches himself into the air before slamming his fist on Dax's cheek, the force of the blow forcing him to his knees.

When Dax's head drops between his shoulders, blood covering his face, rage takes over.

Fuck this bastard and his crew. Fuck them. This is my dark angel. My fucking heart, and they're *hurting* him.

I came here to prevent a fight, but it's too late for that now.

Now I'm going to end it. Violence begets violence. Yeah, it fucking does.

"Get your fucking hands off him!" I scream, running full speed towards Frederico. Dax's head snaps up, droplets of blood splattering the stony ground as Frederico twists on his feet.

He lifts his hands to protect his face as I slash at him, catching the back of one hand. He roars in pain as the jagged glass slices through his skin.

"YOU FUCKING BITCH!" he roars.

I turn to face him, holding the broken bottle out in front of me. "Let him go you cowardly piece of shit. Three on fucking one. You're nothing but a dick. I should've let Dax kill you when he had the chance."

Frederico laughs, narrowing his eyes at me. "You really are feisty, aren't you? A perfect little side-piece. She fights, she dances, and she gets gangbanged on the daily. Sure you don't wanna join my crew? I'll make it worth your while."

The crowd laughs, and Dax tries to break free from the boys' hold, but one of them elbows him in the side of the head and he's knocked out by the force.

"You wanker!" I scream, as the boys holding Dax drop him to the floor unceremoniously and step towards me, cracking their knuckles. Dax is sprawled across the floor and I want nothing more than to go to him, but if I do then we're both dead. I need to fight, or hold them off long enough until the Breakers get here.

"Stay the fuck away from me!" I shout, backing up the stairs of the church and lunging at the three boys as they creep closer to me. All three of them look deranged, and it's clear from the size of their pupils that they're fucking high too.

"Now, now, Pen. We just wanna see what all the fuss is about," Frederico says, his salacious gaze roving over me.

"You get any closer and I'll cut your fucking throat!" I shout, ready and willing to do just that, but I miss a step behind me and stumble backwards, dropping the broken bottle. It rolls away down the steps and out of reach as my arse hits the hard stone with a painful thud.

I scramble for it, but Frederico and his two goons lunge for me, getting to me first. His two minions grab my arms and I kick out, catching Frederico's jaw with my foot but my aim isn't true, and it doesn't do enough damage. With my arms trapped above me, Frederico straddles my hips, pinning me to the floor.

"Yeah, baby!" he shouts out, fist bumping the air as the crowd reacts. I feel their violence as though it's an untameable beast slicing at my defences with sharpened claws. It permeates the air, making my heart pound and fear tightening around my neck like a snake asphyxiating its prey.

"You'd do anything for the Breakers, wouldn't you?"

"Yeah, I would," I retort through gritted teeth as I twist my torso, trying to throw him off me. "I'd do *anything* for the ones I love." Leaning over, Frederico, presses his mouth against my ear.

"Are you sure they're really worth it?"

"I know they are!"

He laughs. "You really have no idea about what they've been doing in Jeb's name, do you, Pen? You're so fucking gullible."

"Fuck you!" I scream back, thrashing beneath him.

"It would make your skin crawl," he continues, taunting me. "Those motorbikes they drive were bought with *blood money*, Pen. You think just because they dance they're incapable of hurting someone. You really don't know them very well at all, but I can help enlighten you. Join Dante's Crew and you'll have my protection, for life."

"No! I'd rather die than join your crew," I spit.

"Shame," he smirks. "I guess fucking you will have to do then."

I scream loudly, fighting with every last scrap of anger as I buck and twist, thrusting my hips upwards in an attempt to dislodge him. This was all a fucking setup to get me here. He wanted me that night at Rocks, but Dax made a fool of him and served him his arse. Now he intends on taking me to prove a fucking point. The fucking rapist.

"Try it and see what happens," I snarl back.

Frederico raises his hand and slaps me hard against my check. "I'm going to enjoy this!" he retorts, unbuckling his trousers. He's too caught up in his actions to notice that the crowd behind him has quietened. I stop struggling when I see Xeno towering over him, holding onto the jagged bottle I'd broken earlier.

"Get off our girl, you dirty piece of shit," he growls, bringing down the broken bottle and sliding it across Frederico's cheek.

Blood spurts from the wound. A bright red arc that splatters across the concrete steps not far from my head.

Frederico's scream is drowned out by Xeno's roar as he hauls him backwards off me.

The two guys who were pinning my arms down, let go and launch themselves upwards. Only to back off when a gunshot is fired into the air.

My head snaps around and I see both Zayn and York holding a gun each. Zayn points one at the boys who were holding me down, and York points the other at the crowd.

Fuck.

Scrambling to my feet, I run towards Dax and drop onto my knees beside him. I check his pulse and press my ear to his mouth, he's still breathing. Yanking at his body, I turn him over onto his back so I can check his injuries.

"Dax? Dax! Can you hear me?" I say, cupping his face. "Dax!"

Dax groans, his eyelids fluttering open as he lifts his hand to his head. "Kid!" he immediately says the second consciousness seeps back in. Worry and rage making his voice thick with emotion.

"Shh, I'm okay," I say, reassuring him. Beside us Xeno is fighting Frederico, and I try to block out the sound of skin splitting and bones breaking. "Can you sit up? We need to get you out of here."

"We?" he grumbles, letting me help him into a seated position.

"The guys are here. They're dealing with Frederico and his goons."

Dax nods, then groans.

In the distance, I can hear the familiar sound of the cops closing in, their sirens piercing the cold night air but it's gunfire that has the rest of Dante's Crew scattering like leaves in the wind. My head snaps around, momentarily relieved that York had just fired another bullet into the air and not into the crowd.

"Come on, big guy, we gotta go," he says, striding over to us now that he no longer has a bunch of feral kids to keep under control. Dax grumbles but he lets us help him to his feet.

"Come on," I scream at Xeno who's still fighting Frederico, and Zayn who's still got his gun trained on the two very scared looking boys. They don't look all that tough now. "We need to go!"

Zayn drops the gun to his side and the two boys run, leaving Frederico behind. So much for mates.

Xeno grips the arsehole by the throat and snarls in his face. "You touch our girl again and you're dead. You come near the Skin's patch selling drugs, you're dead. You come to Rocks, you're dead. Don't fuck with us again, you motherfucking piece of shit, because next time I won't purposefully miss. We are the Breakers and you *know* we'll break your fucking necks."

Frederico nods once, all the bravado from a moment ago, gone. He clutches his face, blood pouring through the gaps of his fingers. His other arm hangs loosely at his side, broken and useless.

"Come on!" I yell, spotting flashlights moving in the distance.

They don't need to be told a third time.

We run.

When we reach their motorbikes parked on the far side of the cemetery, they start laughing, slamming each other on the back in mirth. Congratulating each other on the *win*. When Xeno turns to look at me, noticing that I'm not laughing along-side them, he tips his head to the side and scowls.

"He got what he deserved, Tiny. Just like the rest of the bastards who fuck with what's ours."

It's only then that I consider Frederico's words, do I really know the Breakers after all?

CHAPTER TWENTY-TWO

Present Day

"CLANCY TELLS ME YOU'RE UNWELL," Madame Tuillard says, cocking her head as I enter her studio a minute past eight am on Monday morning. She hates lateness, that was made perfectly clear last week. Clancy, being a really good friend, covered for me. I owe her one.

"Just a little under the weather. I'm good now," I explain biting down the nausea I feel. Since my *chat* with Jeb, my altercation with York and serious lack of sustenance, I've genuinely been feeling sick all weekend. I texted my brother this morning explaining that I'd tried to call him, and ask that he call back, then promptly threw up, hence the lateness.

I'm really *not* looking forward to that one-sided conversation.

"Sit, I'm feeling generous this morning," she responds with a wave of her hand.

Avoiding eye contact with Zayn and York who are both openly staring at me, I move towards the back of the studio to where Clancy's sitting. She gives me a look and squeezes my hand when I sit down.

"You good?" she whispers.

"Thanks, Clancy," I respond, avoiding her question. I'm not good. I'm far from good, but I put a lid on my emotions and give her a reassuring smile. "I ate something that disagreed with me, that's all." She frowns, but doesn't press, knowing as well as I do that the scarce amount of food I actually have in my flat is about as likely to make me sick as drinking water would.

"So, ladies and gentlemen, you've settled in and met all your teachers, now it's time for the hard work to begin," Madame Tuillard says, cutting my conversation with Clancy short. As usual she's perfectly turned out. Her slim figure is encased in a leotard and leggings ensemble with leg warmers and ballet slippers. For a forty-year old she's pretty fit. "There has been some animosity between a few of you which I'd like to address now." She looks between Clancy, Tiffany, and I, but interestingly also Zayn and York. "Over the next year you'll all be spending a great deal of time with each other and whilst I don't expect you to be friends, I do need you to at least be respectful of each other if this is going to work. There is no competition, only cohesion, when you're in the studio together."

"If what's going to work?" Tiffany pipes up, her lascivious gaze sliding over to Zayn who is sitting nearest to her. I bite down on my lip, willing myself not to react.

"I haven't just given you a flat here so that you can take

advantage of the studio space outside of the school day. I do have an ulterior motive, one which will be beneficial to you all."

"What's that?" York questions. By the tone of his voice he's as surprised as the rest of us.

"You've been chosen to headline an end of year dance production that will be televised before the great British public. It's going to be quite spectacular." Madame Tuillard smiles. "Over the coming months, I will be bringing in all the best teachers and choreographers from around the world. You were all picked for your abilities to shine in each of your specialisms... There will be a single, duo, trio, quartet, as well as a group dance with all of you as the finale."

"What the fuck?" Zayn exclaims, cutting her off and earning a glare from York.

"Is there a problem?" Madam Tuillard asks, narrowing her eyes at them.

"None whatsoever." York smiles. Madame Tuillard nods, turning her attention to Clancy who is grinning broadly.

"This is amazing, thank you!"

I chew on my cheek, zoning out for a moment as Madame Tuillard goes into more detail about the show and her ideas. Sophie, the girl who I know least, catches my gaze then leans over and whispers something in Tiffany's ear. They both look at me with calculating gazes. Great, that's all I need, another enemy. Tiffany has clearly aligned herself with the only other girl in this group. I look away, not in the mood. They've no idea about the inner turmoil I feel. Being at the same school as the Breakers is one thing, but dancing with two of the four again, quite another. Not to mention the potential repercussions from David.

"This is a huge deal for Stardom Academy, so I want your full commitment. They'll be no slacking off. Understood?"

"Understood," we respond.

A knock on the studio door interrupts Madame Tuillard. "Ah, perfect timing! Come on in." The door to the studio opens and in walks Xeno followed by D-Neath and...

"*Dax?*" I whisper. He strolls into the room wearing tracksuit bottoms and a white, V-neck t-shirt that showcases his tattoos and sheer size.

"Whoa!" I hear Clancy say. We exchange looks and I'm pretty sure my shock is clearly scrawled across my face. Swallowing hard, I force my face into a neutral state.

Madame Tuillard greets D-Neath with a kiss on each cheek, nodding to Xeno and Dax before turning back to face us all. I feel Xeno's gaze burning a hole in my face, but I refuse to look at him or Dax.

"Duncan and I decided that another dancer was required to even up the numbers and enable us to pair you off easier when it comes to the duets. I'd like you all to meet Dax."

Clancy shuffles closer to me, her hand sliding over mine as she grips it.

Fuck. Fuck. Fuck.

"If you haven't figured it out by now, Xeno will be overseeing the rehearsals," D-Neath explains, pitching in. "We can trust him to make sure shit gets done."

Xeno crosses his arms and jerks his chin in response. Our eyes meet, and I see a flash of challenge in them. This is bullshit. Utter bullshit.

"You eight are the best of the best. You are the dancers

we've chosen to represent Stardom Academy in this show,"
Madame Tuillard explains.

"But he isn't even a student," I blurt out, pointing at Dax.

Slowly his gaze meets mine. There's zero emotion in them.
None. "I was late enrolling. Shit to do," he says, by way of explanation. Everyone seems to accept the bullshit, bar Clancy and
me, though neither of us are stupid enough to question it
further.

"Well, I'm *sure* glad you're here," Sophie, the one girl in this
group I've not spoken to yet, says.

My head whips around to glare at her but she's too busy ogling
Dax to notice me murdering her with my gaze. She can fuck right
off. A sense of ownership rips through me and I want to launch
myself at her. He may not be mine anymore but that doesn't mean
to say I want him, or any of the Breakers, to be anyone else's either.

"Okay, well. We'll leave you in the capable hands of Xeno.
Tuillard and I have work to be getting on with," D-Neath says,
wrapping his arm around Madame Tuillard's back and
escorting her from the room. We all know what kind of *work*
he's referring to.

The minute they've gone. Xeno strides to the centre of the
room. "Up," he demands.

We all climb to our feet, though I make sure that I'm the last
one to stand. I'm not going to make this easy for him, the fucker.
"I'm pairing you off first," he continues, pointing to York then
Clancy. "You two are our tap experts. Get acquainted."

Clancy flicks her gaze at me, biting her lip. I give her a little
nod of my head, telling her I'm okay with this, even when I'm
not. She walks over to his side, and he grins down at her, giving

her a smile that used to only be reserved for me. My stomach flips. He doesn't acknowledge me, or the fact he was in my room half-naked the other night.

Xeno moves around us. I watch as he taps Tiffany's shoulder, then River's. Neither look happy to be paired up, but if this is going the way I think then it's obvious they've been put together because they're the ballet experts. Tiffany gives Xeno a death glare, and River blows out a breath. Poor guy.

"You're my ballet duo," Xeno confirms, leaving four of us.

Zayn looks as though he's about to explode whereas Dax isn't giving anything away. I already know how this is going to go. It's obvious to me. Dax was the one who kissed me first, he was the one who stepped across the invisible barrier between me and the rest of the Breakers, the line that kept us securely in the friend zone. Even though I loved all of them, even though I kissed Zayn and York too, Dax has never really adhered to Xeno's rules completely and because of that, he'll pair me with Zayn.

"Sophie, you're paired up with Zayn. Dax with Pen."

"What?!" I splutter, unable to keep my surprise contained.

Zayn snatches his head around, glaring at Xeno who strides past all of us, gritting his jaw. Dax doesn't even flinch, he doesn't acknowledge my surprise or even glance my way. Clancy has her mouth wide open in shock. I just shake my head at her, begging her with my eyes not to make it obvious that there's an issue even though I've just done exactly that with my little outburst.

"Zayn and Sophie are well matched in hip-hop. They have the same aggression and skill," Xeno says, by way of explanation.

Sophie grins, her silky black hair falling over her shoulder as she moves towards Zayn. On the way past she winks at me and I almost reach out and slap the smile off her face. She smiles at Zayn who gives her a cursory glance then looks away, locking his jaw tight and folding his arms across his chest.

"Despite his size," Xeno continues, "Dax is a talented contemporary dancer. He missed orientation week because he was otherwise engaged. I can assure you, you're well suited." Xeno flat out ignores the tension and begins flipping through his music list on his mobile. Hooking it up to the sound system, he turns to face us all, unbothered by the bomb he's just detonated, but I'm not. My legs seem to move of their own accord as I stumble backwards.

I can't dance with Dax.

I can't be here in this place with *any* of them.

I can't do this.

I'm a fool to ever think I could make something of myself.

I'm a stupid, naïve, fool.

"Find a spot in the studio and get acquainted with your partner. By the end of the session I expect you to have the basis of an idea down for the duets. Only one duet will be selected to showcase on the big night. So I suggest you make it good. You've got plenty of time to practice."

"Fuck this," I mutter.

Twisting on my feet, I head towards the studio door and yank it open, striding from the room. I can hear Tiffany's cackle following me out. *Bitch*. Really, what the fuck is her problem?

"Pen!" Clancy calls from behind me, but I ignore both her and Xeno who tells her to get back into the dance studio.

"Let her run," Xeno says, making a kind of scoffing noise as he shuts the door.

Pushing into the ladies changing room, I head immediately for one of the stools and empty my stomach of what's left of my non-existent breakfast, hacking up bile and the bitter taste of coffee. Even though I really want to cry, I refuse to let the tears fall.

Why are they doing this to me? David will fly back here and will follow through on the threat he made all those years ago if he thinks I'm getting close to them again. It doesn't matter that I don't want them here. It doesn't matter that they clearly don't care for me anymore. David will see what he wants to see, and we'll all be screwed. I don't even think Jeb could stop David if he really wanted to hurt me or anyone else I love, for that matter.

Who am I trying to kid?

Jeb has *no* affection for me. He sent the Breakers here on some kind of fucked up gangster mission knowing the deal I made with him and my brother. I'm just another pawn in his game. Collateral fucking damage.

If the Breakers don't leave me alone, then I'll just have to be the one to walk away. *Again.*

No! I mentally berate myself.

Why should I be the one to turn my back on the future I've worked so hard for my whole damn life? *They* chose crime. *They* chose Jeb and the Skins over me. They started *all* of this. I might have turned my back on them that night but not for the reason they believe. They obviously didn't think much of me if they bought into the lie and that, more than anything, hurts the most. They didn't even try to find out why I did what I did.

They just walked.

Maybe all those years of friendship meant nothing after all, given it was so damn easy for them to let me go. It doesn't matter now, we can never get back what we lost because the truth is, we were over long before that night. They broke my heart the second they became Jeb's bitches, and the Breakers I knew became the Breakers for an entirely different reason.

"This is horse shit!" I shout, bashing my fist against the cubicle wall. I will not be forced out of Stardom Academy. I'll just have to convince my brother of what I already know; that what I had with the Breakers is dead and buried. Gone.

"Pen..."

I stiffen as the door to my cubicle pushes open and Dax stands in the space, his huge frame making me feel claustrophobic all of a sudden. It's not fair that he's so beautiful in that deep, damaged kind of way. There's still a huge part of me that longs for him and the way he always made me feel so protected. I push it aside. There's no space for that in my heart anymore.

"Move!" I demand, not bothering to wait for him to step out of my way as I shove at his firm chest and squeeze between the slim gap he makes. I can't be in a confined space with him and his muscles and that dark angel tattoo I see peeking out of the top of his vest, taunting me with past memories and promises we'd once whispered to each other in the alleyway behind Rocks nightclub when we were kids.

"Pen..." he starts again, and I cringe at the fact he doesn't refer to me by the pet name I used to love even when I always pretended that it infuriated me. "...You need to get back to the studio."

His voice is a low rumble that penetrates my skin and I hate myself for the way it makes me feel.

Hot. Needy. *Sad.* So fucking sad.

I turn on him, fury making me brave, my angry words punctuated with my finger jabbing at his chest. "You need to fuck off out of the academy, out of my life! You, Zayn, York, Xeno. Whatever bullshit you're up to on Jeb's behalf needs to fucking stop. I won't let you all ruin what I've worked so hard for! I won't!"

"We can't do that, Pen," he says.

"You can't or you *won't*, Dax? There's a big fucking difference."

He sighs and for the briefest of moments I see real, deep pain flicker in his gaze. "We won't."

"Well, fuck you. Fuck all of you," I seethe.

"We didn't start this, Pen." If I'm not mistaken I can even hear the hurt in his voice, but it's shoved down when his voice turns icy. "You need to get back into the studio. If you don't Tuillard will replace you, so suck it up, Pen, because the Breakers ain't going anywhere."

"Didn't start this? Don't make me laugh. You did when you became Jeb's minions, Dax. This is *bullshit*," I repeat, waving my hand in the air in frustration.

"Maybe so, but your problems are no longer mine. Fucking deal with it," Dax retorts angrily. He gives me one last lingering look before twisting on his feet and storming out of the bathroom, leaving me reeling.

CHAPTER TWENTY-THREE

Three Years Ago

"WHAT THE FUCK happened to you, Kid?" Dax asks. "You're shivering."

"I'm fine, just leave it, okay?" I mutter turning my back on him and striding away. Pulling my hood up over my head, I keep walking, determined to be left alone. I've gone through enough tonight. Behind me, I hear the engine of his motorbike rev and in seconds he's cruising beside me. It's late, well past midnight, and rather than being tucked up in bed, or in the basement with the Breakers, I'm walking the streets trying to clear my head. Fat chance of that with Dax following me.

"Pen! Stop!" Dax growls, swerving his motorbike across my path. He kicks down the footrest and switches the engine off, tugging his helmet free. "We've been looking for you all damn night, Kid. You're avoiding us."

"I needed a break... just let it go, okay?" I try to step around him, and the brand new motorbike given to him on the back of shady dealings with Jeb and the Skins. The truth is, I *have* been avoiding them. Ever since that night in the cemetery, I've ignored their calls and made excuses about not being able to meet up with them. Apart from the one occasion I bumped into Zayn while walking Lena to school last week, they've not been all that hard to avoid since they're all so busy being one of the Skins and breaking bones in Jeb's name.

"No, I won't let it go. *We* won't. You can tell me what the fuck is up right now, or I'll just follow you around all night. No skin off my nose," he warns.

"Why do you have to be so stubborn, huh? This ain't your problem to fix, it's mine." I glare at him, gritting my jaw to try and prevent all my truths from spilling free. I'm hurt, sad, angry, so fucking angry. I'm also terrified and that keeps my lips sealed shut.

"That's where you're wrong kid. Your problems *are* my problems. They always will be, I swear it."

"Please just leave me alone," I say, my voice cracking. I just want *my* Breakers back. The kids who danced with me, laughed with me, comforted, and protected me. Those boys are slowly fading, being replaced instead with men who'll do anything Jeb asks.

"Is it your mum? Did she hurt you again?" he asks, ignoring me completely.

I shake my head furiously. It would be so much easier if it was her. Dax steps closer, reaching for me cautiously like he knows I'm close to laying into him. He understands how I'm feeling. Of all of the Breakers, he fucking gets it. I hate that. I hate that he knows where my pain comes from because he's suffered the same way I have.

"Who then?" His fingers find my shoulders, and the bruises covered by my jumper. I let out a yelp. "Who did this to you, Kid?" he asks, releasing his hold on my arms, and cupping my face instead, forcing me to look up at him. He doesn't need me to answer, because the person tormenting me pulls up alongside us in his car.

"Get your hands off my sister, motherfucker," David snarls through the open window of his Audi. The sleek black exterior and alloy wheels bought with blood money and violence are nothing but a reminder of what and who he is, a fucking twisted psycho who loves to hurt *me*. Dax instantly reacts, automatically pushing me behind him. I reach for his arm, squeezing tightly.

"Please don't," I murmur.

Ignoring me, Dax draws himself up to his full height. David might have a few years on him, but Dax is as tall as my brother and as broad. He also has a name for himself now, cemented by the very real violence he can unleash at the behest of Jeb. Just like the other Breakers, Dax is a fighter, a violent one at that. So when I see hesitation in David's eyes I know that it's warranted, even if my brother chooses to ignore his own sense of self-preservation. They'd be equally matched in a fist fight, but my brother has never, ever, played by the rules. He'd pull out a weapon in a second.

"You stay the fuck away from Pen," Dax growls, ignoring my pleas. He wants to protect me, except right now I just need him to leave because my brother isn't someone he can mess with and live to tell the tale. David fights dirty.

"Or what, Breaker? You'll snap one of *my* bones?" David laughs cruelly, his finger tapping against the window frame as his gaze flicks between me and Dax.

"No, I'll fucking *kill* you."

David starts laughing loudly, the sound reverberating around the quiet street. "Need I fucking remind you that it's the Skins before whores?"

"Pen is not a whore, you piece of shit, and I have no affiliation to you."

"Full of fucking bravado aren't you, Dax? Just like the other little boys you hang around with. Jeb's protection won't last long, *mate,* so don't threaten me if you know what's good for you."

The door to David's car cracks open and Dax readies himself for the fight, but the sound of motorbikes approaching gives David pause. I snap my head around to see three familiar motorbikes roaring down the street. The rest of my Breakers are here and my stomach bottoms out. I want to yell at them to turn around and go, but fear keeps my voice quiet and my throat constricted. As they pull up, Xeno climbs off his motorbike first, yanking off his helmet. His hair is dishevelled and his face a mask of rage. David scoffs, looking at Xeno with a sneer.

"You, little sister, need to find some new friends."

"Fuck you, David!" I seethe, suddenly finding my voice. The second his gaze meets mine I know I've made a grave mistake. I've learnt the hard way that defiance only ever fuels the monster that rules him.

"I would've thought that by now you'd learn some respect, Penelope. Looks like you've still got a lot to learn," he says with a wide smile that only makes his threat that much worse.

"Get the fuck out of here!" Xeno growls, stepping towards him.

"See you soon, Penelope." David laughs, slamming his car door. He hits the gas, speeding off into the night.

A breath of air whooshes out of me and my knees buckle just as Xeno reaches my side. He hauls me upright against his chest, pressing a surprising kiss against my hair. I've never been more relieved to smell burning rubber than I do at this point.

"I'm not going to ask if you're okay because I can tell that you're not," Xeno says, concern edging his voice with a violence of its own. "Take her back to my place. I'll be there soon," Xeno drops his arm from around my shoulder and Dax takes me gently into his arms, nodding tightly.

"Not the basement?" Zayn asks, looking between us all. He reaches for my hand, taking it gently. It's a simple gesture, one of solidarity and friendship. He doesn't need to tell me he cares. I already know, and yet, why does it feel so different now?

Xeno shakes his head. "No, not the basement. Not anymore."

York steps close, lifting my chin, his icy-blue eyes full of ire. "That fucking bastard," he growls, anger seeping out of every pore as he takes a good look at me. Beneath the anger is pity and for some reason that makes me feel so much worse. I don't want to be pitied. I don't want to feel so fucking helpless. I don't want to be afraid anymore. York frowns, reading me, understanding what I can't even begin to articulate right now.

"York, go with Dax. You know where to find the spare key. Mum and Dad are away for a while, so there'll be no questions," Xeno says, before turning to Zayn. "Come with me, we need to speak with Jeb."

Zayn nods once, presses a kiss against my cheek, then follows Xeno. They both climb back onto their motorbikes, and I watch as they pull on their helmets and speed off down the street.

"Hop on, Kid," Dax says, guiding me to his bike. I stall, not wanting to be anywhere near an object bought for him by the man who rules the boys I love and who also turns a blind eye where my brother's concerned. I've no idea how many people the Breakers have hurt, or the women David's beaten, but I'm betting it's a lot.

Sensing my unease, York reaches for me, tipping my chin up to meet his gaze. "It's just a short ride to Xeno's, we need to get you somewhere warm. You're freezing, Titch."

"Okay," I mutter, too exhausted to argue. I climb on behind Dax, and put on the spare helmet York gives me, hoping I can still trust these boys.

"Drive safe, Dax. No wheelies, got it?" York warns.

Dax revs the bike, kicking back the footrest. "What do you take me for, man? I've got precious cargo right here," he retorts, sliding the vizor closed and turning the bike away.

Half an hour later, I'm sitting on Xeno's bed, wearing his t-shirt and a pair of his jogging bottoms after showering and changing clothes. My hair is still a wet, tangled mess, but I couldn't find a comb to brush it out and decided that I don't really care all that much about what I look like. There's nothing I can do to hide the ugly bruises blooming on my skin, so what's the point? I gently pull up the sleeve of my t-shirt and press against the purple bruise on my upper arm, trying and failing to stop the cry of pain releasing from my lips.

David has always taken pleasure in hurting me, but this

attack was particularly violent. It's as though he's been saving up his rage to unleash on me, his favourite punching bag.

"I've got some Arnica gel for your bruises. Dax said it helps," York explains, entering the room as I quickly pull down the sleeve of my t-shirt. "I've also made you a cup of tea and a sandwich."

"Thanks," I mumble as he places the tray on the side table and sits down on the bed beside me. I hold my hand out for the gel, but York picks it up, unscrews the cap and squirts some onto the tip of his fingers. I look at him warily.

"I promise I'll be gentle," he says softly.

I nod, beyond exhausted at this point. He shuffles closer, his fingers pressing lightly against my bruised skin. "He really deserves to fucking die," York mutters.

Any response I have is swallowed up, buried beneath bitterness and pain. I want to point out that York is part of the same crew my brother belongs to. That he lives by the same rules. What had my brother said? *Skins before whores?* Is this how it's going to be from now on? My brother gets to beat the shit out of me for kicks and my Breakers have to stand back and watch because of some stupid gang rule? They rescued Dax and I from Dante's Crew and meted out their punishment, but I have to take David's abuse because he's one of them?

I suck a pained breath through my teeth as York begins to rub in the gel. He works quietly, diligently, not stopping as Dax enters the room and makes himself comfortable on the other side of me. It's just as well Xeno has a large double bed as the three of us wouldn't be able to fit otherwise.

"Are there any more bruises, Titch?" York asks.

"Yes," I whisper.

"Want to show me where?"

"On my back, my stomach, and chest." Behind me Dax growls, and out of the corner of my eye I can see his fist clenching around the duvet, his knuckles turning white. I hold out my hand for the tube of gel. "I'll do them."

For a moment it falls silent, but when Dax shifts behind me, drawing in a jagged breath as his fingers reach for the hem of my t-shirt, my heart pounds for an entirely different reason. "Dax, what are you...?"

"Do you trust us, Kid?" he asks so quietly that I almost think that I've misheard him. The question is, do I trust them? I want to. I want to believe that they're still the boys I love, but I the seed of doubt has been planted. I've heard the rumours. I've seen the evidence of their affiliation and their violence. Yet, right now, they're just York and Dax, two boys I love, and if I can't trust in that, what can I trust in?

"Yes," I say simply, hoping my instincts are right.

CHAPTER TWENTY-FOUR

Present Day

AFTER TWO DAYS of dance lessons that I should've enjoyed, but didn't, I head towards Madame Tuillard's studio for more rehearsals. It's past five pm and I've just hoovered down a cheese sandwich and an apple to appease my growling stomach. It's the first thing I've eaten all day. Breakfast consisted of coffee and thin air. Lunch was no different, and I'm still feeling light-headed, my modest meal barely sustaining me. I'm running on empty and a little jittery from all the coffee I've consumed but I push on knowing that I can't fuck this up. Monday might have been torture being paired up with Dax, but I've got to get over my shock at the Breakers returning if I'm going to survive the year here. Suck it the fuck up, basically.

Swigging down water to appease my still growling stomach, I jog along the corridor on the third floor, already late. My phone vibrates against my arse, and I yank it out of my back pocket. The second my eyes land on the caller ID, my quick meal decides it wants to break free from my stomach. Swallowing hard, I push open the nearest door into Studio Five and am relieved to find it empty. I don't need any witnesses to this conversation.

"Hello, Penelope," the voice from my nightmares says.

"David," I respond, making my voice sound strong even when the rest of me is shaking. My legs give way and I slide down the wall, landing on my arse.

"How are you?"

I almost laugh at the question, at the normality of it, as though he really is just a relative concerned for my well-being. I know better, but I humour him anyway. "Fine, and you?"

"Oh, you know, keeping busy with work. Business is booming, Penelope. Perhaps one day I'll bring you over to Mexico and show just how well I'm doing."

Over my dead body. Slamming my lips shut on those words, I choose not to respond. My silence is deafening. David laughs, the sound affecting me the same way as nails scraping down a blackboard would.

"I hear that the Breakers are back. You know what that means, don't you?"

"It's not what you think. I have no control over what they do, or Jeb does, for that matter," I blurt out quickly, panic rising. Surely he can't blame me for something his leader has set up. It's not as if any of this is in my control. David laughs again and the sound sends me hurtling back to that night that I wish I could change with every cell of my being.

"Oh, I don't know. I think you like the fact they've returned.

You never were as happy as when you were with them. Such a slutty little girl, aren't you?"

"It's not like that. It *wasn't* like that. They were my friends and now they're not. You got what you wanted, David. Why can't you just leave me the fuck alone!" I shout, anger overriding the fear I feel.

The line remains silent for a moment and all I can hear is the rushing and pulsing of blood in my ear. David would often fall silent before the rage took over. I wait for it to come. The inevitable tidal wave of destruction.

"Except I *don't* have what I want, Penelope," he responds, deadly calm. If it weren't for the fact I know it's impossible, I would almost believe that he could reach down the phone and throttle me right now. His words are laced with violence that reaches me across miles and miles of ocean. Will I never be far enough away from him?

"David, please. They're not my friends. They're not anything to me anymore. They won't ever be anything to me again. You got what you wanted. I *hate* them," I force out, putting all my hate for David into that one sentence and hoping he believes me, because I certainly don't.

"Let's see, shall we? Let's see just how much you hate them, how far you're willing to go to prove to me that I can trust you to keep your promises."

"What do you mean?" My voice is shaking now, and I hate that I can't hide my fear from him.

"Remember the deal we made. One false move and I'm cashing in, Penelope."

"Please, you can't. I've done everything you've asked. What else can I do?"

"That's rich. You're nothing but a lying *bitch*."

"I don't understand..."

"I know *everything*, Penelope. You must think I'm fucking stupid. I *know* that I wasn't the only one you made a deal with that night!" He's shouting now, the precarious hold on his temper gone.

"I don't know what you're talking about..." I fumble, my body trembling.

"Don't fuck with me, Penelope. I'm not an idiot. You think I'm a fool. I'm here in Mexico because I *wanted* to be here, not because you made a deal with Jeb to send me away. He's not as powerful as he thinks he is."

"David, I..." *Shit, shit, shit, shit, shit. He can't know. How can he know? I was so careful.*

"Don't try and fucking deny it, Penelope. It'll only be worse for you if you do."

My stomach rolls over and there's nothing I can do to stop myself from retching. My quick meal spills out over the floor beside me, a steamy pile of sick that ruins the perfectly polished wood. He knows what I did. He knows about the deal I made with Jeb. Why am I even still alive? All those thoughts ricochet inside my head as he continues on ranting.

"Three years might have passed. You might think you've gotten away from me, but my reach is far and wide. I can get to you *all* with one fucking word! You'd be wise not to under-estimate me again. *I* still own you and don't you fucking forget it."

"David, I *swear* to you, I'm not involved with the Break-ers..." I swipe at my mouth with the back of my hand, swal-lowing the bitter aftertaste of my scared seventeen year old self's poor decisions. I was a fool to ever believe I could outsmart my brother.

"But here's the thing, Penelope. You're going to be."

"What?!" I snap. "I don't understand."

"Jeb is up to something and I don't fucking like it. I'm the reason his business is booming, and the motherfucker thinks he can leave me out of the loop? No. No fucking way. So you, dear little sister, are going to do something for me."

I can't even question what that something is, because little black dots start to spot in front of my eyes. Any minute now I'm going to pass out.

"Penelope, you fucking better still be there..."

"I'm here," I croak, blinking my eyes rapidly and willing myself not to faint. It would be so easy to allow the darkness to take over, to let the silence pull me under so I don't have to listen to him anymore, but I breathe in deeply through my nose, forcing myself to do as he asks.

"Good. Listen to me very carefully. You're going to befriend the Breakers once more. You're going to make them fall in love with you again, and you're going to find out every last secret Jeb is keeping from me. Then when the time is right, *we* are going to destroy them once and for all. I will stick to my side of the deal, so long as you stick to yours."

If I could throw up again, I would, except there's nothing left inside of me. "David, I don't know how... They don't..." *They don't even like me...*

"I don't give a fuck how you do it. Just get me the information I want or pay the fucking price. I'll be calling for regular updates." With that, he clicks off the call and I'm left with the deafening sound of my heart breaking all over again.

CHAPTER TWENTY-FIVE

Present Day

"NICE OF YOU TO TURN UP," Xeno growls as I step into the studio almost an hour late. Everyone's eyes fix on me, but I avoid looking at any of them. Truth be known, I debated whether to turn up at all, but with David's threat ringing in my ears and self-preservation kicking in, I cleaned up the mess in the studio as best I could with paper towels from the ladies room, then dried my eyes and hauled arse.

"It won't happen again," I respond, gritting my teeth. I really don't need Xeno's attitude on top of everything else that's happened today. He gives me a dark look, a frown pulling together his brows, but doesn't grill me further.

"Pen's been feeling rubbish all week," Clancy interjects, doing her best to stick up for me. I give her a half-hearted smile, grateful for her, but knowing it won't make a difference. I'm fucking this up and she shouldn't have to cover for me.

"Urgh, what a piss poor excuse. *Some* of us take this seriously and don't go out every night getting pissed." Tiffany smirks, running her gaze over me like I'm a piece of shit on her shoe. I don't even have the energy to argue or to defend myself. Screw her anyway. She's insignificant when all is said and done.

"We *haven't* been getting pissed every night," Clancy retorts, giving Tiffany a scathing look. "And even if we had, what the fuck has it got to do with you?"

"*Everything*, actually. This show can make or break us as dancers. If you're not willing to put the time and effort in, then it's going to reflect badly on everyone, and I for one don't need *her* to mess it up for the rest of us," Tiffany responds, giving me a haughty glare.

"Oh, shut up, Tiffany. You've been fucking a different guy every night this past week going by the sounds coming from your room. So don't pretend you've not been burning the midnight oil getting your rocks off," River accuses, flashing me a wink. Bless him.

"That's none of your business," she fumbles, her cheeks flushing as she glances over at Zayn. Urgh, I don't need to guess who one of her *guests* was.

"I don't know why you're looking at me, *Princess*," Zayn sneers, looking her up and down. "You really need to choose your fuck-buddies wisely, the guy who was brave enough to dip his dick in your pussy last night sounded like a rhino being shot."

Clancy barks out a laugh then covers her mouth with her

hand. So Zayn hasn't slept with her then? I glance at York who raises an eyebrow and shrugs. Fucking arsehole.

"Fuck off, Zayn," Tiffany retorts, her cheeks flushing with embarrassment as she grabs her bag and strides from the room.

"Well, I'm outta here. See you bitches later," Sophie says to us all before squeezing Zayn's arm. "We did good today."

If she expects a compliment back, she doesn't get one. Despite everything that's gone down today, I allow myself a small smile at his indifference and ignore her glare as she strides past.

"Well, I'm out too. Catch you later." River strides across the studio, stopping to give my arm a squeeze.

"Thanks," I mutter. He stuck up for me when he didn't have to, and I'm grateful. It's been a long time since anyone's had my back like him and Clancy.

"Hey, I might have to dance with her, but I sure as fuck don't have to listen to her bullshit. Hope you feel better soon, Pen." With that he walks out of the studio leaving me with the Breakers and Clancy who immediately comes to my side. She's about to say something when Xeno interrupts her.

"We're done here tonight. Good work, Clancy. You can go. Dax, I need you to stay behind. I want to talk to you and Pen."

Clancy pulls a face, her eyes asking a thousand questions that I'm not able to answer right now, or ever, actually. "Pen?" she questions.

"It's alright. I've got this," I say.

"Sure?"

I plaster a reassuring smile on my face. "I'm sure."

York and Zayn make no attempt to follow Clancy, and

when Dax steps behind me locking the studio door, I ready myself for the inevitable storm. This is the first time I've been alone with all four of them since they've returned. I'm not going to lie, there have been many occasions I've thought about this moment over the years, how I'd behave, what I'd say if confronted with them all again. I've held onto bitterness and anger for so long, using it to stop myself from feeling the guilt about the part I played in our demise. I resented them for joining the Skins and I held onto that fact when I obliterated our friendship, using it to assuage my own guilt over the years. When they left without a backward glance, it only made me believe that what we had was never real in the first place. Three years is a long time to hold onto that kind of disappointment and pain.

Xeno parks his arse on the edge of the table he's standing in front of and motions for me to enter the room. "Let's see what we're working with. Dance," he orders, all business-like and emotionless.

Zayn, York, and Dax make themselves comfortable as they all watch me walk into the centre of the studio upon shaky legs that I force to be steady. When I catch a glimpse of my reflection in the mirror, I'm shocked at just how appalling I look. Talking to David and carrying the weight of his threat has turned me into a person I don't recognise. But instead of crumbling, I use that to fuel my fire, lighting the tinder of hate for my brother into a raging inferno. I need an outlet for it, and as usual it's dance.

"Music?" Xeno questions, cocking his head to the side as he watches me. His grass-green eyes fixed entirely on my face as though he's trying to read me the same way York was always capable of doing so well.

"She doesn't need any music," Zayn intercedes, watching me closely. There's no malice in his words, just a deep understanding of who I am that makes me want to launch myself into his arms. It feels like an olive branch, and yet the scowl that follows tells me it's just an observation, a fact, nothing more.

Regardless, he's right. I don't need any music. My soul just wants the outlet of dance. I can feel myself humming with restlessness, at my need to drive away the demons that chase me with something that has always soothed me whenever I'm overwhelmed with emotion. Both the good and the bad. I'm well aware that I'm about to open myself up in a very personal way but honestly, I'm past caring. I've walked the tightrope of my emotions so carefully these past three years that the Breakers return, and my brother's and Jeb's threats, have well and truly off-balanced me. I'm free falling with no idea who to trust or what the fuck I should do.

With my resolve waning, I look between each of my Breakers before finally resting my gaze on Xeno. "You wanted my truth. Well, here it is."

My anger reveals itself first as I launch into a tirade of steps, storming over the floor with heavy feet and angry jerks of my body. My fist punches the air as I twist and turn, jerking my body roughly to the slamming, staccato beat of my heart. I pop and lock, drop and spin, my rage flooding every inch of me as I push upwards onto the balls of my feet and flip forward, launching my body off the ground and landing with a violence that penetrates the air.

Every ounce of anger bleeds from my soul and into my

steps. I make impossible shapes with my body as rage implodes, detonating inside my chest and making me fearless. All those years I spent learning the hardest hip-hop tricks and never quite coming up to scratch seems to fall in place now as I shred my fear with every head spin and flare of my legs. With every flip and thrust I own my anger, and lay bare my truth.

Drawing in ragged breaths I turn and focus my gaze on Zayn, the boy who found me in the playground and decided I was worth knowing. Without uttering a word, he approaches me, jerking his chin. I take the bait, more than willing to battle. I watch him with sweat beading on my brow as he responds to my steps with a rage of his own, vaguely aware that Xeno has stepped forward to break this up, only to be prevented by Dax's thick forearm holding him back.

Zayn moves around me, jerking his body in movements that surpass any kind of hip-hop step I recognise. He rips off his t-shirt, shredding himself for no other reason than to take my fucking breath away. I've seen the tattoos on his arms, but across his chest is another kind of tattoo, except these are raised scars that cut horizontally across his pecs. Scars that weren't there the last time I saw him with his top off three years ago.

"What happened to you?" I mutter, stumbling back as he comes at me in a series of vicious steps before dropping into a corkscrew, only to rear back up, his nostrils flaring. Standing before me, our noses almost touching, all I can do is stare into his night-time eyes. They used to give me comfort, their black pools somewhere I could find peace. Not today. Today they're a black hole ready to drag me under.

"Zayn..."

His lip curls up. "Don't," he warns, before dropping to the floor and performing an air-flare.

I watch in awe as his legs windmill, his feet inches from my face. I have no choice to move away or get hit. The power and the strength to perform with such skill shouldn't be underestimated. Zayn only makes it look easy because he's an incredible dancer.

Hip-hop is inherently aggressive, but what he's sharing with me now is painful to watch because this isn't about the dance, this is about *us*, about *me*. I'm not the only one telling my truth today. When he finally comes to a standstill, both of our chests heaving, I narrow my eyes and launch myself into a backflip, my feet only inches from his body as I slice through the air. Six feet apart and both of us glaring at the other, York steps in front of Zayn. He cocks his head to the side and for the first time since he's been back he lets me see what he's been holding inside.

Anguish.

"My turn..." he snarls.

Those two words slash at my resolve to remain strong and I flinch as he begins to move. The sound of his feet slamming against the wooden floor, a percussive kind of anger that makes me want to cover my ears, close my eyes, and curl up in a ball. Instead, I stand tall, taking the beating with every last ounce of strength I have. York's feet move with lightning speed as I try and absorb the tap steps that are so familiar and yet, so alien. I can barely keep up as he slams his feet onto the wooden floor so quickly that my eyes tear up from the sheer weight of his truth.

He's furious, so fucking mad, and I reel from the emotion he displays.

The one person who was always so kind to me, who understood me even when I failed to understand myself, rips into me with every step. All I can do is watch and wait for him to tire himself out. On the surface tap appears to be such a cheerful dance, teamed with Jazz music and the light, fluffy black and white movies York so loved to watch as a kid, it often brings happiness and joy, but it's origins come from something more tribal. Seeped in black history of repression and slavery, tap has a darker, more sinister edge. Today, his moves are percussive, well-timed, and varying in tempo, but every single one of them angry. Every time his feet hit the floor I flinch as though he's struck me.

Feeling raw with emotion at his pain. I try to match his movements, making my own feet light in an attempt to draw out the boy I knew with a wobbly smile and pain etched around my eyes. "York..." I plead.

His feet suddenly still at the sound of my voice, and he lifts his eyes from my feet to meet mine. With a heaving chest, he speaks a thousand words without saying anything at all.

My heart plummets.

Twisting on his feet, he strides to the edge of the room and sits, clasping his head in his hands as he stares at the floor, refusing to meet my gaze.

I mirror him.

Gripping my head, I sway from side to side, my body rocking on my feet. Around me, the room is charged with a pungent kind of electricity that barbs the air with unspoken words. Three long years of distance separate who we were to who we are now, that and the terrible decisions of that one night. To each other they're still the Breakers, I can sense their deep-seated loyalty to one another, but me? I'm someone to be wary of, to hold at arm's length. Someone that's separate from the cohesion they still share, an outsider looking in.

Someone to hate.

Shaking with adrenaline, I push on, the anger making way for hopelessness. Stretching my arm wide and lifting my right leg out whilst holding all my weight on my toes, I form my body into an arabesque. It's not perfect, far from it, and my feet still throb from the recent torture I put them through, but I push through, wanting to express myself in the lighter more graceful movements of contemporary dance. Right now, I need the soothing fluidity.

This is where I'm most comfortable. This is where healing comes from, at least for me.

With featherlight movements, arched feet, and soft hands, I glide around the studio, twisting, turning, soaring with long-held emotion. After a while, the Breakers here in this room with me now fall away, and the boys I loved return, their ghosts dancing alongside me. Over the years, my loneliness has conjured them up like this. It's the only way I've got through their absence.

When I feel warm hands at my waist and I'm lifted into the air, I know it's the real-life Dax and not some figment of my imagination dancing with me now. Dax lowers me to my feet, his arm encircling my waist, his fingers digging into my side as he takes my free hand and pushes my body away from him. I twist outwards, only to be pulled back and lifted again. It's instinctual, how we dance together, and when he holds me against his chest, his heart beating into the smouldering heat of my back, tears finally prick my eyes.

"You destroyed us. That ain't something we can let go," he grinds out before folding himself over my body, not giving me a chance to defend myself. Smoothing his palm down my thigh and encouraging my leg to slide out beneath his extended leg, I feel the hot rash of heat and the familiar shiver run up my spine at being close to him again. He mirrors me, movement for movement, not once letting me go until all I am is an extension of him.

The physical contact has me quaking, my heart racing and my core clenching with an ache I don't think I'll ever be able to soothe. We move fluidly, and to an unsuspecting audience it would look as though we were two people in love, dancing for enjoyment, but I know different. The tightness of his grip, the harshness of his breath and the trembling of his body, not to mention his harsh words, tell me his anger is just a whisper away. Dax has never once hurt me, not physically anyway, but he wants me to feel his pain, to hurt me the way he believes I've hurt him. When he lets me go abruptly and storms away with clenched fists, I know I'm right.

Panting and with sweat sliding over every inch of my skin, I remain standing in the centre of the room, my emotions all over the place. For three years I've tried to forget about the Breakers. I've blamed them so I didn't have to blame myself. I've tried to hate them, so I didn't miss them, but when all is said and done, the only person I truly hate is myself.

I loved them.

I *still* love them, and if I do what David asks, I'm going to destroy them once and for all. Can I really be that person? Can I make the Breakers love me again only to betray that love so cruelly? Can I survive hurting them all over again? The truth is, it doesn't matter either way because the consequences of not doing as David asks are too horrific to even contemplate.

Drawing on the remains of my strength, I look at each of my Breakers in turn trying to decide how to wade through this volatile situation. In the end, I opt for a version of the truth, the only version I'm able to share right now.

"I didn't play you. I made a choice," I say, trying to explain, but it sounds weak even to my own ears.

"You made the wrong fucking choice, Pen," Xeno spits, his self-righteousness getting my hackles up. How dare he? Has he forgotten the choice he'd forced upon *me*? At least I had a valid reason for doing what I did, unlike him.

"Are you fucking kidding me, Xeno? *You* were the one who wanted me to choose, who gave me a fucking ultimatum because I was stupid enough to fall in love with you all. It was an impossible decision," I yell back, my fists clenching and unclenching at my side.

"I was trying to do the right thing!" he booms, his fist slamming onto the studio wall. Zayn, York, and Dax all snatch their heads around, looking at Xeno in shock. His outburst was clearly something they hadn't expected. Not that I give a shit. I laugh hysterically in the face of his reasoning.

"The right thing! What, you mean like joining the Skins was?"

When he doesn't answer, when he *won't* answer, I just shake my head. Grief claws at me, threatening to shred me open until I'm nothing but a mess of skin, bone, and muscle.

I'm trembling all over as they watch me unravel before them. I've never felt so fucking open, so raw. It doesn't matter how much I ache, how far I need to swim through the river of pain separating us, because it's too late. It's too fucking late.

Remembering what David had said and what I'm supposed

to do now, my shoulders drop, my energy and self-righteousness dissolving, leaving me boneless. I look at each of my Breakers in turn because they're still mine even though I'm not theirs.

"I'm sorry," I say, meaning it.

I'm sorry for the past, I'm sorry for the present and the gulf between us all and I'm sorry for what's to come. I'm sorry for that most of all.

My apology is met with stony silence.

With as much self-preservation as I can muster, I walk towards the studio door holding onto what's left of my tattered heart. I won't cry because we've surpassed tears at this point, they're useless. Tears never saved me from my brother's wrath and they never brought my Breakers back no matter how many I've shed over the last three years. Ironic then that once I finally stopped crying for their loss, they returned. My hand lands on the door handle, stilling when I hear angry footsteps approaching.

"Where the fuck do you think you're going?" Xeno asks, his voice dark, ominous with threat.

Drawing on my last ounce of strength, I turn and face him.

"Why does it matter? This is what I do, isn't it? I run." I ask, feeling suddenly cold, all the internal fire I felt doused in sweat that slides over every inch of my skin.

For a beat we just stare at each other, and even though I can tell he wants me to, I refuse to look away. I'm unable to read him any better now than I could back when we were friends. Perhaps that's a good thing.

When he doesn't answer my question, when none of them make a move to approach me and bridge the divide between us, I raise my chin, draw on my last reserves of energy and yank open the door, David's threat a dark cloud looming over me.

As I walk away, only one thought echoes in my head: how the hell am I going to make them love me again? More importantly, how am I supposed to live with myself if I fail, because it isn't my life I'm desperate to protect, but Lena's.

CHAPTER TWENTY-SIX

Three Years Ago

DAX'S FINGERS ARE WARM, that's what I notice first. The second thing I notice is that they're trembling. "Lift your arms up, Kid," Dax instructs, his calm voice certain even though his hands aren't.

I can't see his expression, and maybe that's just as well. I might lose my nerve if I looked into his eyes, I might tell him to leave me be, so I can lick my wounds and sleep.

Instead, I'm brave and allow Dax to remove my t-shirt.

"Jesus fucking Christ," York mutters, his gaze fixed on my chest area, flickering between my bra covered boobs to the bruises that blossom across my skin. When his gaze finally lifts to meet mine, York is looking at me with a mixture of anger and desire. A strange combination that I'm not sure how to handle.

"That motherfucking, psycho bastard," Dax growls behind

me, his fingers are gentle as they push my hair forward over my shoulder so he can get a better look at the damage caused by my brother's violent hand. "The next time he comes near you, I'm going to fucking kill him."

My cheeks heat in shame but also in arousal. I have no business feeling turned on, especially after the beating I endured, but the desire in York's gaze and protectiveness in Dax's voice makes me feel loved in a way I haven't really felt before.

Silently, York hands Dax the Arnica gel and he begins to rub it into the bruises on my back. When he's finished he passes the tube back to York, his hand dropping to my hip as he rests it there. The heat from his palm has my heart battering against my ribcage as the tension in the room expands like a bubble about to burst. It's a comforting touch, but I can tell by the way the pad of his thumb circles over my skin that there's more to it than that.

"Here, lean back on me, Kid. Let York deal with the other bruises," Dax instructs, his voice a low grumble as his breath flutters against the bare skin of my shoulder.

I don't question him. I shift on the bed so that I'm laying back against Dax's chest, my legs stretched out between his. My head rests against his upper chest and I turn my cheek to the side wanting to hear the solid beat of his heart. It pounds against my cheek. Thump, thump, thump.

Shutting my eyes, I let York deal with the bruises on my front and even though my cheeks flame as his fingers graze the skin underneath my bra covered tit, I don't move or tell him to stop. His touch is gentle, kind, and tears clog my throat.

"Look at you, Kid," Dax exclaims, his chest heaving, his breaths matching those of York's.

"Why didn't you say something sooner, Titch? Why didn't you tell us what that piece of shit was doing to you?" York asks. I can hear the hurt in his voice, and I blink back the tears that I've been holding in all night as I look at him. He's resting his hand on my thigh, staring at me intently. My hands are clenched together in my lap, and goosebumps rise across my skin as Dax's fingers slide up and down my arms, comforting me.

"Because it wouldn't have made a difference if I had. You're one of them now, York. What did David say, *Skins before whores?*"

"You're *not* a whore," Dax grinds out angrily.

"How long has he been hurting you like this?" York asks, trying to hide the shame that creeps into his voice, but I hear it, see it written all over his face. Out of the four, he was always the most adamant that joining the Skins was the last thing he'd ever do, and yet here we are.

I blink back the tears, not wanting to give David any more power over me. Tonight is the last time I shed any tears for that bastard. "For as long as I can remember..."

"Fuck, Titch."

"When he moved away, it got better. He only comes back to see mum occasionally. I avoid being home when he visits. I thought he'd finished with tormenting me. I guess I was wrong," I explain, unable to keep the bitterness from my voice.

"Yet, you came to Jackson Street all these years knowing he was just a floor above us. Why put yourself in danger like that?"

"Because I trusted that I would be safe with you all. That you'd never let him hurt me," I admit, realising how foolish that sounds now. How could they protect me when I never told them how bad things were?

"Like he did that night we met?"

I'm silent for a long time.

"Titch?" York prompts gently.

"That night was the first time he let go of his restraint. I'd been hit by him before then, but it was only ever a punch here, a slap there. My mum turned a blind eye to it. In her own twisted mind, I think she thought if he had me to use as an outlet for his rage, he'd steer clear of Lena. She loves *her*," I say bitterly, then feel immediately guilty, because I love my little sister too and I would do anything for her to not suffer the same pain I do.

"Your mum needs to be shot," Dax says darkly. I can't disagree with him there. I've thought about killing both her and David over the years, but then that would leave Lena on her own, and I can't have that. So I endured for Lena. Besides, thinking about murdering someone is one thing, actually going through with it, something else altogether.

"So that night...?" York, asks softly. I don't know whether he realises he's doing it, but his hand is rubbing up and down my thigh in time to Dax's movements. Their touch makes heat pool between my legs and a rash of heat bloom over my skin.

"That night we first met; David came home drunk after partying with the Skins. I knew the second he came in that I was in trouble. Mum watched him walk into the living room with this cold kind of dread. She looked at me for a couple of seconds and I honestly believed she would stop him this time. She didn't. She got up from the sofa, walked silently down the hall, grabbed Lena and locked them both in her bedroom." My lip wobbles, but I bite down hard on it, blinking back the furious tears.

"She *let* him beat you?" York grinds out through gritted teeth.

"Yes."

"What happened then, Kid," Dax mutters, his lips finding my hair and pressing a kiss there. His mouth lingers, and I feel the expanse of his breath as he breathes in deep, as though he's drawing in my scent to keep him steady.

"He was out of it. High on alcohol and a cocktail of drugs... I tried to get out of his way, to leave, but he was big, and I was so small..." Choking down the rising sickness of that memory, I grit my teeth, willing myself to go on. "I knew if I fought, he'd make it worse. I let him hit me, and then when he stumbled and fell, passing out on the living room floor, I grabbed my shit and ran."

"Why did you come to Jackson Street, Titch?"

"Because I literally had nowhere else to go. Zayn was the first person who looked at me like I was *something* rather than nothing. Looking back now, I know it was stupid... Maybe it was the punches to my head affecting my decision-making skills." I laugh bitterly, the sound coming out as a mixture between a sob and a croak. "Then I found you four. Complete strangers who didn't question what had happened, who just knew I needed help. That meant, that *means* everything to me..."

"And this time, why did he beat you, Kid?"

"Because on New Year's Eve he witnessed my happiness and that's something David doesn't allow me to feel for very long."

"Fuck, Kid," Dax exclaims, the shake in his voice evidence of his sadness for me and hate for David.

York swipes at his eyes, and I'm sure I see tears glistening on his lashes. "Come 'ere," he says, holding his arms open.

I sit up, shuffling forward and curl up against his chest, wrapping my arms around his back. Pressing my nose against his shirt, I breathe him in and try to rid myself of the memory of David's scent. Dax shifts behind me until I'm enclosed between them both, their body heat and comforting hands holding me close.

I'm not sure when it changes from comfort to something far more intense, but before I can really think about what I'm doing, my lips find the crook of York's neck and I kiss him there. A groan releases from his throat as my tongue flickers against his skin, his musky, manly taste exploding in my mouth.

"Titch...?" he questions, his voice wavering as he pulls back slightly, holding on to my shoulders. Behind me Dax shifts slightly, his hands gripping my hips above the material of the jogging bottoms I'm wearing.

"Please, don't push me away," I say gently, one hand covering Dax's at my hip, the other resting on York's chest, my fingers curling into his top.

"What are you asking for, Kid?" Dax asks carefully, the rumble of his voice seeping through his chest into my back as his lips whisper against my ear.

Swallowing down my fear of rejection, I decide to be brave. "To be loved," I murmur.

Until this moment I didn't realise how much I craved human affection. Used to being pushed away, beaten, belittled, and denied, I never once sought out any form of affection. Until now. All I know is that right here, right now, I need to be loved. I need to know what it feels like. I need to wash away the hurt and replace it with something else, otherwise I'll go insane.

Dax's fingers tighten over my hips as York's eyes flash with the desire he's been keeping a lid on. I can tell he's fighting with himself, that he thinks he'll be taking advantage of me in a vulnerable moment, but he's really not. I want this. I want to forget my brother. I want to forget the Skins. I want to embrace these boys here and now. There's a kind of desperation in how I feel, like they're slipping away from me. It feels inevitable somehow.

"I want you to kiss me, York. I want to pretend for just one moment that I'm loved."

Dax reaches up around me, his thick forearm flat against my chest as he grasps my chin gently in his fingers and urges my face to the side. I shift in his hold so I can look up at him. The pad of his thumb runs over my bottom lip as we stare at each other.

"See, here's the thing, Kid. We don't need to pretend... *I* don't need to pretend."

My heart hiccups in my chest at his words, my own response dissolving on my tongue as he leans down and kisses me, obliterating any rational thought with his plush lips as he shows just how much he cares for me. Dax has never expressed himself well with words, so to hear his honesty is a gift that brings me so much joy.

"Oh, fuck," I hear York mutter as Dax adjusts me in his arms so that I'm lying across his lap.

Cupping the back of my head, Dax kisses me long and hard. I can feel his dick pressing against my hip and it both thrills me and scares me at the same time. When I reach up, clutching at him, my small hands running over his shoulders and neck, Dax breaks the kiss and rips off his t-shirt.

"Feel this, Kid. This is what you do to me. Do you understand?" he asks, reaching for my hand and placing it onto the centre of his chest. I can feel his heart slamming beneath his skin just like mine is now. Two hearts that have experienced what it feels like to be broken only to beat again for someone special. "Do you understand, Kid?" he repeats.

"Yes," I whisper.

Dax nods then lowers his mouth back to mine and kisses me until I forget David's fists and cruel words, until I forget my mum's years of indifference and abuse. If a soul had a taste, it would be found in his kiss. In *this* kiss. Dax, my dark angel, my protector, my forever.

When he lowers his hand, smoothing over my collarbone and resting his palm at the base of my throat, my beating heart reacts, slamming against my ribcage wanting to break free and offer itself up to him. He pulls back, a small smile making his face less serious.

"Kid, I need to stop." His voice is gravelly, pained almost.

"Why?" I ask, fully aware my chest is heaving, and York is watching us both, his own breathing matching the weight of ours.

"Well, for one, York here is desperate to kiss you and two, my dick is getting way over excited right about now..." He laughs at his own honesty and my cheeks flood with heat. Scooping me up gently, Dax hands me to York, laying me across his lap. "I need to go sort myself out," Dax says, moving to climb off the bed.

"Don't go," I whisper.

"What?" he responds, snapping his head around to look at me.

"I said, don't go. If your dick needs attention, then give it some," I say, feeling brave.

Honestly, I don't know what's come over me, but any kind of awkwardness I thought I'd feel is gone in the heat of the moment.

I want Dax to touch himself.

I want to *watch* him touch himself.

I want to be touched.

Curiosity and a burning desire to blot any last lingering thought of David out of my head makes me brave. Sitting forward, I unhook my bra refusing to feel embarrassed. My tits are small, no more than a handful, but given the way Dax and York are eye-fucking them, they really don't care. I want to get them off. I want to get myself off and I've watched enough porn to have some idea how this works. I think.

"Oh my fuck," York whispers.

The only sound I hear coming from Dax is his fly unzipping. I turn to look at him, at his hooded eyes, broad chest and then, the shaft of his cock as he releases it from the confines of his jeans and boxer shorts. He's big, scarily so, and I find myself wondering how something so large could fit inside another person.

"Don't stop on my account," Dax growls, his large hand fisting his cock as he leans back against the headboard. The head of his dick is a deep pink, almost angry looking. I swallow hard.

"You've done it now, Titch," York mutters, his own pale cheeks blushing furiously. I know my Breakers are close, but I doubt very much they've seen each other's cocks up close and personal like this. I almost giggle at the absurdity of the situation. Nerves flutter in my stomach but I push them away. I've been fantasising about a situation like this for months now. If that makes me the slut David accuses me off regularly, then so fucking be it.

I don't care, I love these boys. If Zayn and Xeno were here too I can't say that I'd act any differently, though I suspect Xeno would refuse to partake given his promise to me. In fact, I'm betting he'd try and break it up.

Resting his fingers against the side of my face and drawing me out of my thoughts to look at him, York smiles down at me, his white-blonde hair tickling my brow as he leans close. "You've thought about this a lot, haven't you?" he asks, reading me expertly.

I nod, catching my lip between my teeth. York stares at me, looking between my eyes and my mouth that has now parted on an exhale of air. I really want him to kiss me, touch me.

"I want to touch you," he says, speaking my thoughts out loud. We've always had some weird kind of synergy, York and I. It's never been more apparent than right now.

"So, touch me," I urge him, allowing my legs to drop open, wanting him to touch my clit. I know what it feels like to come from my own hand, but by someone else's, never.

York's tongue sweeps across his lower lip, making it glisten in the low light. They're pink against his pale skin and oh so kissable.

"Jesus fucking Christ, York. Kiss her, or I will," Dax grinds out.

York doesn't need to be told twice. His mouth slams down on mine, his tongue darting out and parting my lips. I groan then gasp as York's scorching fingers slide over my chest and circle my nipple before cupping my breast gently, lighting me up from the inside out. I squirm beneath his hand, arching my back, telling him without breaking the kiss that I want him to keep touching me this way. Next to us Dax groans, the sound of his fist jerking his cock an aphrodisiac like nothing else. My knickers are wet with desire and I squirm in York's hold, undulating my hips, needing to feel something between my thighs, loving this strange new feeling that I could very well become addicted to.

"Touch her, York," Dax orders, and my heart nearly jumps out of my chest at the sheer desperation in his voice.

York smiles against my mouth. "Xeno is going to fucking kill us if he finds out."

Despite myself, I stiffen. I'd promised Xeno I'd make a decision about the boys. Being here with both of them is stretching his suggestion of spending *time together* to the limit. There's only a month to go and I'm still no better off knowing what I'm going to do.

"Fuck Xeno and his restraint. The guys a goddamn martyr."

"What about Zayn?" I mutter.

"Zayn isn't here, but if he were, you can bet your arse he'd be fucking your pussy with his tongue by now," Dax growls, sending my heat levels spiking.

York laughs, sliding his hand lower, kissing me. He doesn't disagree, and the thought of Zayn's tongue lapping at my pussy has me groaning against York's mouth. I've never experienced it before but from what I can gather, if done well, it's a pleasant experience. If feeling this turned on from a kiss on my lips can make me feel this needy then I've no idea what a kiss to my *pussy* would feel like, but I can imagine.

"You'd like that wouldn't you, Titch?" York asks between kisses.

I don't bother to answer, he knows me well enough to know that I would. Feeling adored like this is what gives me something to fight for after being starved of love and affection for so long. Loving the Breakers is my greatest sin according to David, but fuck him. If feeling like this, this *loved,* is a sin, then I will walk into the gates of Hell willingly. He can take his sanctimonious bullshit and fuck right off. That man is no saint. He's the devil incarnate.

York pulls at my bottom lip gently with his teeth and I groan into his mouth, loving the way he tastes so sweet, like he's been sucking on a hard candy. His tongue strokes mine, exploring my mouth, and when I suck on it, the sound he makes is music to my ears. Breaking free from the kiss, York watches my expression as his hand reaches the waistband of my joggers. He hesitates and I can't have that.

"Touch me," I whisper, covering his hand with my own and urging it lower.

"Fuck," Dax pants beside us.

When I glance over at him, his cock is gripped in his hands, the head glistening with his arousal. I watch as he spits, lubing his dick with his own saliva. My thighs clench and my heart thunders at how fucking erotic that is.

It's strange, I should be feeling shy, but I'm not. This feels right somehow, and it makes me feel good knowing that Dax is as turned on by me as I am by him.

"Titch, I'm gonna touch you now," York says, his voice low, guttural, and when his fingers slide beneath my knickers, I snap my head back around to look at him. With pure concentration on his face, York lowers his mouth to mine once more just as his finger parts the lips of my pussy and slides over my clit. The sensation is overwhelming and my hips jerk at the touch. When he swirls the pad of his finger in circles over the tiny bud, I can't help but moan, my head tipping back.

"You're so wet," he groans, his hot mouth closing over my nipple as he strokes me.

Pressing my eyes closed, I lose myself in the moment and just enjoy the feeling of York kissing and stroking me. Moving my hips instinctively I rock against York's hand. Low down in my stomach, a familiar sensation builds, making me feel coiled tight like I'm about to freefall from the top of a cliff. Up and up I go, sensation climbing and growing with every swirl of York's thumb and kiss of his soft lips. Heat expands between my legs as I grow wetter and wetter.

"Let me touch you, York," I pant, wanting him to feel what I feel, needing him to know I'm not selfish, that I can pleasure him the same way he's pleasuring me.

He nods, shifting me in his hold so that I'm laying across the bed between the two of them. Reaching back between my legs, he swipes with his fingers, gathering my own arousal then pops open his fly and shoves his jeans and boxers low, slicking his dick with my wetness. I pant, my cheeks flushing at the sinfulness of such an act. Cupping him, I feel his velvety smoothness covered by my desire and something desperate unleashes within me. I let out a little moan, and his fingers find their way back between my legs, slipping and sliding expertly across my sensitive flesh.

Unlike some other girl's my age, I've never touched a dick before, but when Dax shifts closer on his knees I decide that I may as well go all out and pleasure them both. Gently, I wrap my hands around the bottom of their shafts, both feel enormous in my small hands as they jerk at my touch.

"Holy fucking shit!" Dax grinds out. I peek over at him. He looks almost in pain with his eyes squeezed shut and his mouth slack. I'm not sure what to do next. I mean I know what I should do, but fear of doing it wrong makes me hesitate.

"Slide your fist up and down, Titch. Keep that same kind of pressure," York says, guiding me in a voice I don't recognise. It's low, deep, and filled with passion.

I do as he asks, and when Dax leans over and kisses me, the tight coil in my stomach intensifies further as more heat and wetness blooms beneath York's deft fingers.

Instinct takes over.

I pump my fists up and down, revelling in the silky warmth of their cocks and the power I feel holding them both in the palm of my hands. Their pleasure is mine to give, and mine to receive. I feel wanton, delirious with lust and love.

York replaces Dax's mouth, his kiss hot, urgent, and when Dax's mouth closes around my nipple, that tightness within me unravels like a spinning top, sending an explosion of sensation ricocheting out from my core. York pulls back and I catch a glimpse of his satisfied smile before my eyes roll back in my head and my hands drop to the side as waves of splintering pleasure wash over me. I swear to God, fireworks go off behind my eyeballs. If this is what an orgasm feels like then no wonder guys jack off all the time. I want to do it all over again.

"Oh. My. Fuck," Dax grinds out as I come down from my orgasm. He shudders and jerks, quickly pulling up his boxer shorts to capture the cum shooting out of his cock. York follows shortly afterwards and like Dax he captures his cum in his underwear.

When they both finally come down from their orgasmic high, York fastens his jeans, looking sheepish. "Thank fuck we didn't get any jizz on the covers, Xeno would've lost his fucking mind."

"Yeah, though I kinda wish we had..." Dax pulls a face, reminding me that his boxers must be just as wet as my knickers are. "Do you think Xeno will notice if I borrow some boxer shorts?"

We all start laughing and despite the bruises that cover my body, I no longer feel any pain.

These boys, my Breakers, they're *my* forever. No matter what.

CHAPTER TWENTY-SEVEN

Present Day

"GOOD LUCK," Clancy says, squeezing my hand as I hover in the hallway outside studio nine, wishing I was taking krumping lessons with her instead of bachata lessons under Xeno's tutelage.

"I'm going to need a lot more than luck," I mutter, knowing that this lesson is going to be a special kind of torture.

Since my phone call with David, I've been trying to figure out how to keep Lena safe. I even considered running away with her, but both David and Jeb's reach is too far, and they'd catch up with us eventually. Running isn't an option, it never was, and neither is begging Madame Tuillard to switch my classes, not if I'm going to keep my sister safe. There is no alternative but to make the Breakers love me again, or at least trust me enough to tell me what Jeb's up to so that I can feed the information back to David. Whilst I'm not foolish enough to believe that will happen at the drop of a hat, I know that our friendship was once built on our mutual love of dance. It's the only logical place to start.

Giving Clancy a quick hug and forcing aside the gut-wrenching feeling in my stomach at what I must do, I head inside the studio. The space is already filled with students, mostly girls, all of whom are starry-eyed over Xeno. Right now an attractive blonde girl is talking to him. She keeps touching his arm and laughing at what he's saying. I hold back my sudden urge to go storming over there and yank her backwards by her hair, instead I hang up my gym bag and find an empty spot in the room and start warming up like the rest of the students.

After a couple of minutes, Xeno looks at his watch, and indicates for the blonde to join the rest of us. She saunters off, but not before squeezing his forearm and sashaying away sexily. I roll my eyes, gritting my jaw to prevent myself from saying something I shouldn't.

"You know, you really don't stand a chance, *street rat.*"

I bark out a laugh, looking over my shoulder at Tiffany. She's like a fucking wasp buzzing around my head, irritating the fuck out of me, and waiting for the perfect moment to inject me with her venom.

"And I suppose *you* do? I'm not sure that pretty blonde thinks the same, not to mention every other female in this school *and* a few of the men. Just face it, Tiffany, the competition's steep, so why don't you just give up and go back to fucking rando's you pick up in clubs."

Tiffany's scowl deepens, her mouth popping open, but Xeno coughs to get our attention, preventing her from coming back with a suitably cutting remark. I look at him in the afternoon sunlight as it filters through the windows. He's doused in a glow that makes his black hair chocolate and his tawny skin golden, a mythical god with angry eyes and a defined jaw that's sharp enough to cut glass. Just like every other girl here, I imagine running my finger against the stubbled edge and losing blood just for the pleasure. Xeno's always had the ability to make me bleed. My heart hasn't stopped dripping blood since that night he refused to kiss me and asked me to choose. I wonder if he's ever regretted that decision.

"Last week was just the taster session. Today, we're going to get into the nuts and bolts of the dance. You're all here because you love bachata. It intrigues you, right?"

The class murmurs in agreement but I smirk, unable to keep my derision in. Yeah, right. The majority of the people are here because they want to fuck Xeno. He's everything you could possibly want; fit, beautiful to look at, an expert in his speciality, and edged in danger. I'm betting most of the girls in here are already fucking wet.

"This week I want you paired up, because this isn't a dance that can easily be taught without a partner. Steps can be learnt individually, but the feeling of this dance, it's *truth*, comes in the arms of another. The connection between dance partners is as important as the steps. More so." He looks at me again, and for a split second I swear he's trying to tell me something.

"Did you hear that, street rat, the connection is more important. Xeno chose *me* to dance with him last week. Tell me that doesn't mean something," Tiffany snarls under her breath.

I flinch, not wanting to give credence to her words, but

knowing from experience that she's probably right. Xeno never chose me as his partner.

Never.

Except last week when he'd held me against his body and pressed his thumb in the middle of my back. It hadn't lasted long, but the connection I'd felt, the charge between us had been electric. He'd have to be dead not to notice.

Maybe *that's* the problem... He notices. He's *always* noticed. I remember those words he said to me back when I was fifteen, the night I admitted my feelings to the Breakers.

"I'm not going to kiss you, Tiny. Not because I don't want to, but because someone has to keep their head tonight, and I guess that someone is going to be me."

No matter the circumstance when we were kids, he never stepped over the boundary he drew between us, never acting on any feelings because of some deep sense of responsibility that I've never really understood. Yet last week he kissed me at Rocks in front of the whole damn nightclub, knowing my situation with Jeb. He kissed me understanding that it would get back to his boss, back to *David*. The question is why?

"You can't deny it can you? You saw how we danced together," Tiffany continues, her words making tiny cuts in my armour, scarring me, no matter how much I wish they didn't.

"You're deluded," I growl.

"He practically fucked me. You can look at him like all you wanna do is ride his cock, *street rat,* but we all know that someone like him would never choose someone like you," she growls into my ear.

Without knowing it, Tiffany has hit a nerve and I react.

Stepping backwards I slam my heel onto her foot. "Fuck you, Tiffany."

"Ow! You bitch!" she yells, lifting her foot and hopping on one leg. Good. I hope I've broken a few toes.

"Oops," I respond, lifting my hand to cover my mouth in mock horror. "I'm *so* sorry, it was an accident."

"You fucking liar!"

Xeno strides over and looks between us. He grinds his teeth together on the cusp of doing something that could get him fired. He's pissed. Well, what does he expect? It's bad enough I have to put up with Tiffany making a claim on him, let alone the rest of the fucking academy. A girl can only take so much. I've been telling myself for years I hate him, but I've only been lying to myself. I still feel that throat squeezing kind of possession when it comes to Xeno. I want to do bad things to anyone who steps near him. I want him to do bad things to me. Swallowing the bitter stones in my throat, I try to put a lid on my feelings.

Dropping to the floor in front of Tiffany, I watch as he wraps his hands around her ankle and gently presses his thumbs over her foot. "Wiggle your toes," he says.

Tiffany does as he asks, giving me a satisfied smile the whole time. Fucking bitch.

Xeno stands, addressing Tiffany. "I don't think anything's broken, but you might want to sit this lesson out."

"I'm not sure I can walk on it right now," Tiffany wheedles, milking this for all its worth. I should've stomped harder. Next time.

"Pen, pair up with Niall," he states, wrapping an arm around Tiffany's waist and helping her over to the front of the studio. The smile she shoots over her shoulder at me makes my blood boil. I'm about two steps away from losing my head. If it wasn't for Niall distracting me, I might have.

"You're not going to stand on my foot if I piss you off, are you?" Niall asks, only half-joking.

"It was an accident," I respond with a shrug.

He looks at me warily with pretty cornflower blue eyes and dimples in both cheeks that I would've found cute if I wasn't completely distracted by the fact that Xeno has yet again cast me aside in favour of another girl, just like he always did when we were kids. The pretty blonde who was flirting with him earlier is now up the front of the class standing next to him, looking smug as fuck. Me and Tiffany aren't the only ones scowling now.

"As I mentioned last week, bachata has a basic four step timing," Xeno begins, motioning for the pretty blonde to come closer. He doesn't hold her close like he did with me that morning in the dance studio, or like he did with Tiffany the other day. Instead he holds her hands in the open dance position with their bodies arm's length apart.

"Like this, one, two, three, tap. Five, six, seven, tap. It can be danced in the open position as we're doing now," he explains, keeping space between himself and the blonde as they continue to showcase the steps. "Or in the closed position, like this." Xeno draws the blonde against his chest, placing his thigh between hers, holding her right hand in his whilst his other hand rests on the middle of her back.

I watch with fascination at the way his hips sway and the muscles in his arm tense and release with every step. There's a fierce concentration on his face, as he guides his partner in a sensual, slow dance, that not only brings a flush to my cheeks, but to everyone else's in the studio. God, this dance is so beautiful. *He's* beautiful.

"Fuck sake," I mutter, drawing attention from Niall who frowns. I ignore him. I don't need to explain my reaction to anyone, let alone someone I've only just met.

"Over the years the dance has evolved, mixing in tango and salsa steps but never letting go of its origins," Xeno continues, still moving with the blonde. "The music is just as important as the dance, and often tells the dramatic story of love..." Xeno steps to the side, moving his partner so that her back is to the class now. He catches my eye just at the point he pulls her tighter against his chest, and drops her backwards, "And heartbreak."

The blonde giggles as he sweeps her back up and drags his gaze from mine, schooling his features into an emotionless state.

BY THE TIME the class finishes, I'm about ready to murder a bitch. The blonde, Saskia, has well and truly thrown herself at Xeno and I swear to fuck there's a damp patch blooming in the crotch of her strawberry red leggings. In fact, there's a distinct smell of arousal mixed with sweat and pheromones as though all the women in the room and a couple of the blokes have wet underwear too.

It pisses me the fuck off.

Especially since Xeno made his way around the studio and danced with every single one of the girls during the lesson bar me. *Never* fucking me.

Anger bubbles dangerously inside like a volcano ready to

spew lava and hot rocks. I know I should be figuring out ways to get back into the Breakers good graces again, but right now all I can think about is giving Xeno a piece of my mind.

Shoving my sweatshirt into my gym bag and growling at Niall when he says goodbye, I plonk myself onto the bench at the back of the class and wait for the thirsty bitches to leave. Tiffany and Saskia are the last to go, both of them lingering to get Xeno's attention. It gives me a great sense of satisfaction when he ignores their attempts at flirting. Eventually they get the picture and leave but not before throwing daggers my way.

"The class is over," Xeno says, not bothering to even look up.

There's a tautness around his shoulders and stiffness in the way he moves, but still he refuses to engage further which is ironic given he forced me to attend this class. When he pulls off his t-shirt, wiping away at the sweat on his face before spraying some deodorant under his arms. It's such a simple, every day act, but it reminds me so much of those blissful few days I spent at his house when we were kids after that awful confrontation with David. Spending time with the Breakers and playing happy family, even if it was only for a short time, was one of my happiest memories, actually. Not that I ever told him that.

Perhaps now's the time.

"Xeno..." I begin, losing some of the anger on the back of those sweet memories.

"What do you want, Pen?" he growls, grabbing a clean, black t-shirt from his gym bag and pulling it on over his head. I bite down on my lip at his sheer masculinity. He's broad-shouldered, not as wide as Dax but bigger than York and Zayn, and has a slim waist with strong arms. When I look at his reflection in the mirror, my mouth dries at his defined six pack and beautiful v-muscle.

"What do you want, Pen?" he repeats.

I flick my gaze upwards. *I want you to dance with me. I want you to forgive me. I want you to fucking fight for me...* That's what I want to say. Instead, I ask him something else.

"Do you remember that time when I stayed at your house?"

Spinning on his feet so he faces me, he narrows his eyes. I ignore the harshness of his stare, and the sharp glint in his emerald orbs, reminding me of the broken bottle he'd once used to cut a kid who wronged him. "Where's this going?"

"Stop answering every question with another question. Do you remember or not?" I repeat.

"Yes, of course I fucking remember." He swings his bag up onto his shoulder and strides towards the door. I rush forward, getting there before he does, kicking it shut and blocking his way. If he can do it, then why the fuck can't I?

"It was one of the happiest times of my life..."

"What's the point of all this?" he asks, running his gaze up and down my length, feigning boredom when really I see the restless, baying beast just beneath the surface. When we were kids that beast would come out in a number of ways, aggression when dancing, sarcasm in a serious conversation, humour to disguise desire, withdrawal when everything got too much. I wonder, if pushed, what it would look like now.

"What *is* the point?" I muse out loud, laughing a little. "Christ, I don't know Xeno. I suppose I was trying to work out who the man is that stands before me now. I'm trying to work out if the boy I loved is still there within him."

"Well, I can help you with that. That boy is fucking *gone*."

He hunches over, nostrils flaring like a bull ready to impale its tormentor. I nod, wishing he'd just let out his anger in dance like the others did. Except that's never been Xeno's style. There's always been something that holds him back from really sharing himself with me.

"Why are you here, Xeno?" I wish he would just tell me the truth and save us both the heartache.

Tell me what David wants to know. Tell me so I can keep Lena safe.

For a moment I actually consider being truthful, completely truthful, then I'm reminded that Jeb would kill me and Lena for it before David could even get his hands on me. So I swallow down my truths and push a little harder.

"Why are you here, Xeno?" I repeat.

He scoffs, shaking his head. "I thought I made that clear at Rocks."

"So you want to punish me, is that it?"

"That would imply that I actually give a shit about you. That any of us do."

"Yet, you're all *here* at Stardom Academy. Every night I wonder if I'm going to find another one of you lying on my bed waiting to fucking pounce."

"What are you talking about?"

"York broke into my flat last Friday, just to fucking mess with me..."

"He did *what?*" Xeno snaps, but I don't explain further, he can go ask York himself.

"You've *coerced* me into attending these bachata lessons," I continue. "Today I've had to endure watching you dance with every fucking girl bar me, just like when we were kids. You *forced* me to battle Dax knowing what that would do to me, and then paired me up with him just to dig the fucking knife in. You *kissed* me at Rocks knowing that would get back to Jeb.

Why, if not to punish me?"

"I told you, we're here to reclaim what's *ours*..." he answers automatically, as though that vague, bullshit response is enough of an explanation.

"Reclaim what's yours?" I push, cocking my head to the side as I rest my hand on his chest. Could he mean me? Or is that just wishful, desperate thinking on my part? Xeno stiffens at my touch, but he doesn't step away. In fact, he steps closer, crowding me. His gym bag drops to the floor as he lifts his hands and slams them against the door on either side of my head.

"Oh, I see. You think we're back to reclaim *you*, Pen." He barks out a laugh. "Don't flatter yourself. I didn't want you back when we were kids, and I sure as fuck don't want you now." Shadows flitter across his face in his attempt to dissolve our memories into charcoal and dust, but like a phoenix rising from the ashes, I remind him of the fire that was always there between us.

"Bullshit! I have a good memory, Xeno. I remember what you'd said to me. I remember how you looked at me when you didn't think I noticed. I remember the jealousy in your eyes when York, Zayn and Dax kissed me. I'm not a fool. You loved me too. Maybe not now, but back then you did."

"Back then I told you what you wanted to hear because you were my friend, because I felt sorry for you, nothing more."

"And now?" I ask, humouring him because I know that's crap.

"Now," he leans over, pressing his lips against my ear. "You mean shit to me."

"That kiss told me otherwise," I retort, grinding my teeth and swallowing the bitter taste of rejection and the sharp shards of his hate.

"That kiss was a fucking warning, Pen."

"A warning?"

"Yes, a warning," he hisses, sending my blood boiling.

"Kissing me was a bad fucking idea. You of all people should know that."

"Oh, you think Jeb didn't know?" Tipping his head back, Xeno laughs cruelly. "He's the one who ordered me to do it."

"What? *Why?*"

"It was a *test*, Pen." He slams his mouth shut, yanking back his hands, and stepping away from me.

"A test?" I press, stepping into his space, not letting him off so easily.

Xeno scrapes a hand over his face, schooling his features into a mask. "This conversation is over. Get the fuck out of my way."

He's shaking now, visibly trembling, and I don't understand it at all. Not one for letting anything go and throwing caution to the wind, I line my body up against his. "What test, Xeno?" I ask, tipping my head back to look up at him.

For a moment he just stares down at me, and all I see is conflict burning brightly in his green orbs. When his hands come up to grip my face in his palms, a cool kind of calm seems to wash over him, like the current of a salt water lake caressing a stone on its banks.

"I was the only one who never kissed you. Never crossed the fucking line. Jeb believes it was because I cared too much."

"He was right..."

"No, he was wrong. Just like you are now."

"That's *bullshit*. Tell yourself what you need to if it makes you feel any better, but I know how you felt about me. How you *still* feel about me. It's so obvious now."

"You're delusional." He glares at me, his fingers gripping my face harshly. "I kissed you because you mean *nothing* to me. To prove to Jeb that I don't give a shit. Kiss you, don't kiss you. Mess with you, don't mess with you. We're here for one thing and one thing only and it has fuck all to do with you! You can fight me on it all you like, but it won't change the fact that you're insignificant, Pen."

"So insignificant that you threatened to kill Frederico if he came near me again when we were kids? So insignificant that when you caught Zayn and me making out on your bed when we were younger you watched us both with fucking *love* and lust in your eyes? So insignificant that you couldn't keep your hands off me in the dance studio last week? So insignificant that you're full of rage right now? Stop lying to yourself."

"Frederico was a thorn in the Skin's side and was dealt with accordingly, it really had shit all to do with you. There might've been lust in my eyes when I watched you and Zayn, but it was the equivalent of watching a porno. I was a *boy* and it was a good show. As for dancing with you last week, it was nothing more than me fucking with your head..."

"And the anger? If you really don't give a shit about me, why so goddamn angry?"

"*I'm full of rage* because you're in my damn way."

He lets me go with a shove and a well of anger rises up within me because I *know*. I know he's lying. You don't get to love someone as long as I have and not know when they're lying to you. What's that saying: *he doth protest too much*? Right now Xeno is full of shit. He fucking reeks of it. Reaching for him as he tries to sidestep around me, my fingers curl into his t-shirt, scrunching the material in my hands.

"I don't believe you."

"Believe what you like, Pen. You could offer yourself up to Zayn, York and Dax, and I wouldn't give a shit," he snaps, a cruel smile carving across his face.

"Be careful what you wish for, Xeno," I warn, before slamming my lips against his and kissing him with all the hurt, anger, hate, lust, and love I can muster. This is me fighting back. This is me showing him what he missed out on when we were kids, and what the other Breakers experienced when he was too fucking stubborn to do the same.

He steps back, trying to pull away, but I chase him, grasping the back of his head and forcing my kiss on him, forcing my tongue inside his mouth. Just like he did to me at Rocks, I'm stealing a kiss now. I don't care if he wants it or not. I don't care if he's disgusted, pissed off, indifferent, angry. He needs to know that I'm not to be fucked with. I refuse to let him pretend that I meant nothing, that I mean nothing now.

I *refuse*.

When his lips finally respond, when his arms wrap around my back and his fingers dig painfully into my hips as he clings on tightly, like he never, ever wants to let me go, I break the kiss even though it's the last thing I want to do. Releasing him, I step back, my lips as bruised as my heart.

"Maybe you should have accepted what I was offering back when we were kids. *Maybe* if you had kissed me like the others did then none of this would've happened."

I realise how stupid that sounds, that I'm suggesting we'd all be together now if only he'd given in and kissed me, but it's always felt like he was the missing link. That if he'd allowed himself to fall like the others had before it was too late, then we wouldn't be where we are now. That together we could've dealt with my brother and Jeb, somehow.

"A kiss wouldn't have changed a thing. *This* kiss doesn't change a damn thing. You're still..."

"Don't! Don't ever say that what we shared was insignificant," I cut in, refusing to let him say that damn word one more time. "Because one day, Xeno, you're going to kiss me with *love* and when that day comes, we'll both be fucked and there won't be a damn thing I can do about it."

Turning on my feet, I storm out of the studio, leaving him with the one truth I want to run from. This isn't going to end well for the Breakers or for me, but I have no fucking choice. Lena's life is under threat and I won't allow her to be David's next victim. I won't.

CHAPTER TWENTY-EIGHT

Three Years Ago

"HEY, PEN. YOU AWAKE?" Zayn asks me as he pops his head around Xeno's bedroom door, looking ruffled from sleep.

I yawn, peering at him from beneath the duvet that smells so deliciously of Xeno. I've spent all day in bed wrapped up in his scent of spiced musk. Now I feel rested and calm. By the looks of it, Zayn has been sleeping all day too.

"Where is everyone? What time is it?" I ask. Wondering at what point Dax and York left me to sleep after our encounter. My cheeks heat and my skin flushes at the memory of York's hand between my legs and both their cocks in my hands.

"It's five in the afternoon. York had to go home before his mum called the cops, and Dax is out getting us some pizza."

"Five? Fuck, I've slept for like twelve hours or something."

"Yeah. You needed the rest," Zayn says, stepping into the room.

"I..."

My words are lost as he saunters over to the bed, topless, with just his jeans hanging low on his hips. A smattering of dark hair covers his pec and a line of softer hair runs downwards from his belly button, disappearing beneath the waistband of his jeans. Zayn is older than me by almost a year, and just like the rest of my Breakers he's already a man even though his age would suggest otherwise.

"What's up, Pen?" he grins at me, his night-time eyes sparkling with mirth and something a little darker as I sit up, the duvet revealing my bruises and my bra covered tits. "Fucking Christ." His mirth disappears as he looks at the damage caused by David's fists.

Sighing, I give him a tumultuous smile. "They don't hurt so much now," I lie. They still hurt like a bitch, but I don't want his pity and I see so much of it in his eyes right now.

"York told us what he's been doing to you, Pen. I'm so sorry..." His voice trails off as he pulls back the covers and climbs into bed next to me.

"Why are you sorry? You didn't do this," I respond quietly as he shuffles close to me, pulling me into his arms. I rest my cheek against his chest, my fingers reaching for the dark hair growing across his skin. Breathing in, I draw in his familiar scent of honeyed bread and weed.

"Because he hurt you. Because I feel fucking helpless to do anything to stop it. Because... because I *love* you, Pen," he admits, his arms circling me, holding me close. Zayn has always been honest with me, and his honesty now is the biggest gift I could ask for. It means everything.

Shifting in his hold, I sit up, straddling him. My hair falls over my shoulders, the ends tickling his chest as I lean forward and press my forehead against his. "I love you too." It feels so easy to say those precious words. I like the way they make me feel, and I like the happiness that lights up Zayn's face when I say them back.

"We tried talking to Jeb about David..." he suddenly blurts out, his fingers caressing my spine.

"And?"

"And he didn't want to listen." Zayn breathes out a long sigh, shaking his head. "I'm sorry, Pen."

I nod, and I know he isn't just apologising for not being able to persuade Jeb to do something about my brother. He's apologising for everything else too. He's apologising for the fact they're part of the Skins crew. He's apologising for the fact that they've bad done things to earn expensive motorbikes, that the rumours about them are true.

My Breakers break bones.

But like last night, I don't want to think about David, about Jeb or the Skins, about who these boys will eventually turn into. I want to live in the now and hang onto our friendship because it's the only good thing in my life besides Lena.

Zayn rests his head back on the wall and looks up at me, watching me carefully as I inch closer. My fingers trace his lips as I stare into his onyx eyes, loving the way his dark orbs drink me in.

"What are you doing, Pen?" he asks, a rueful smile playing

about his lips as my fingers lower, tracing the length of his neck and feathering across his collarbone.

"What does it look like I'm doing?" I whisper, leaning closer to him and brushing my lips against his forehead.

"I didn't say I love you to get you into bed…"

"You're already in bed, Zayn."

"You know what I mean. This isn't about that," he says, looking up at me.

"I know, but this is what people in love do, right? They kiss, they make each other feel good." Memories of York and Dax filter back in, and I react, rocking my hips against his dick that is growing between us.

"Pen, I'm not sure…"

"I want to do this. I want to kiss you, Zayn. I'm not a feeble, weak thing. I bear the evidence of my strength right here," I say, pointing to my bruises. "David hurt me, and I want to erase every bruise, every punch, every bad word, every snide comment from my skin and my heart. I want you to help me to do that."

I'm fully aware that in the early hours of this morning I professed the same to York and Dax, but I don't feel guilty about it. They all know how I feel, and aside from Xeno, they've not pushed me away despite knowing I love them all. This is how I want to heal.

For the first time, dance isn't enough.

"Then I will make sure every last memory of that bastard hurting you is replaced with ones of love," he responds fiercely, grasping the back of my head and slanting his lips over mine. His mouth parts on a sigh as his hands find my hips and dip beneath the waistband of Xeno's joggers that I'm still wearing, minus my knickers. I took them off after they left, feeling uncomfortable in the soaked material.

"Pen!" He mutters against my mouth, shocked at my bare arse that his hands are so firmly clutching now.

"Zayn!" I mock, smiling as I rock my hips and slide my tongue between his parted lips, searching for his words of love, wanting to taste them, swallow them, needing them to satiate the hunger and appease the starvation I've endured for so fucking long. Yesterday, I didn't know what to expect, what might happen, but now York and Dax have shown me the way, I know what I want and it might be more than just a kiss.

With one hand firmly grabbing my arse, his other finds its way to my bra strap and with deft fingers, has unhooked it. It's actually quite impressive how he manages to do that so easily, though I suppose he's had plenty of practice. I push that thought away, not wanting to think about how many girls he kissed and touched before me. My bra slides off my shoulders as our tongues, lips and teeth, search, soothe and bite.

Our kisses become more and more intense as his fingers find my breasts and his thumb rolls over my nipple, teasing me and sending bolts of sensation right to my core. I react, pressing myself against the length of his cock, thick beneath his jeans. With a slick pussy and a full heart, I reach between us, my nails trailing down his chest and abs, desperate to hold him in my palm.

"I knew I should've fucking come upstairs myself," a dark voice says from the doorway.

We break apart, panting, and my cheeks flush a deep pink. I almost reach up to cover my bare breasts, but think better of it. Tipping up my chin, I look at Xeno defiantly. I won't be made to feel ashamed. I appreciate him letting me stay here, I really do, but I won't stop loving these boys just because he says so. The thing is, when I meet his gaze, I don't see anger or disappointment. I see something else. Desire.

Hot, molten, raging desire.

He's turned on. I'm sure of it.

"Xeno... I love her," Zayn says calmly. He's firm, sure of himself in the moment, and he doesn't let me go. In fact he pulls me tighter against him, resting his lips against my collarbone and running his tongue over the mound of my breast.

"I know," Xeno bites out, shutting the door behind him.

With my head turned to the side, I watch Xeno as he leans against the door, his hands stuffed into his pockets, staring at us both.

"You gonna stand there?" Zayn asks. I note the missing but implied word, *just*.

"Yeah, I am." Xeno's is acting stubborn even though his eyes are dark and full of glittering promises, like jewels locked away in a glass cage. He gives me glimpses of the riches he could bestow if only he would let himself.

Zayn shakes his head. "Why torture yourself, man?" he asks before grasping my face in his large palms and gives me a kiss to rival all other kisses. His tongue swirls and dips, his teeth nip and bite, his lips soothe and caress. It's a hot, messy, glorious kiss that burns me white-hot and turns me inside out. When Zayn's mouth closes over my nipple and his fingers slide between my legs, I turn my head to Xeno and let out a low moan. Heat builds within me, around us. Emotions swirling in the torrid air, conjured up by our love and our lust.

Through the haze, I can see Xeno push off against the door,

his body rocking on his feet as though he's fighting every instinct to come and join us. Our eyes lock and he drags a hand through his hair, a frown marring his beautiful face.

"Xeno," I mouth, but the sound is ripped from my lips when Zayn presses his thumb against my clit and I orgasm, my eyes falling shut and my chest heaving.

When I finally open my eyes, blinking back the stars, Xeno is gone.

↯

THE NEXT MORNING it's just Xeno and me in the house. The rest of the Breakers are coming back later in the afternoon and we're going to have a movie night, making the most of our time together before I have to go back home tomorrow. Right now, Xeno's sitting at the kitchen table, drinking a cup of coffee.

"Hey," I say, giving him a wave and then mentally kicking myself for being so awkward. I've changed back into my own clothes and I've got the ones of his I borrowed folded up in my hands with my dirty underwear tucked between the folds. "Could I use your washing machine? I need to wash your clothes."

He glances at me, his gaze moving between my face and his joggers and back again. "Sure, laundry detergents under the sink," he indicates, jerking his chin towards the cupboard before returning his attention back to his phone. I see red spots heat beneath his tan skin, and feel my own flush at the memory of what happened last night. I came on Zayn's hand and all over Xeno's favourite pair of jogging pants.

This isn't awkward, much.

"Did you speak to your mum?" I ask, picking a fairly neutral subject to try and ease the growing tension in the room whilst I throw the clothes into the washing machine and switch it on.

"Yeah, they're back the day after tomorrow. I'm going to have to make sure this place is tidied up before then. Mum'll blow a gasket if she sees the mess."

"I'll help tidy up. It's the least I can do after you've let me stay. I really appreciate it, Xeno. It means a lot to me."

"Sure," he mumbles, returning his attention to the mobile phone and whatever he's so engrossed in watching on it. Feeling like I need to clear the air, I pull up next to him and peer over his shoulder. He's watching a dance battle on his phone. A couple of the guys are doing insane flips, jumping over each other, and wiping the floor with their opponents.

"Impressive," I comment. It would take a lot of skill and strength to do what they're doing and not face-plant onto the floor or collide. "It looks tricky."

"We could totally ace this move. I'll show it to Zayn later..." he replies, flicking the screen upwards and placing his phone face down on the table. He sits stiffly beside me as silence descends. I feel more awkward than ever around him.

"We're still doing it... the competition, I mean?" I ask him, surprised, honestly.

"Of course we are. Why do you think we wouldn't be?"

"You've been busy..." I point out.

"And you've been avoiding us," he retorts. "I guess that makes us equal."

I don't respond because I can feel the beginnings of an argument forming, and I really, really don't want to fight. So we sit in silence until I can't deal with it anymore.

"Are we okay?" I ask eventually, worrying my lip like I tend to do when I'm anxious.

"Why wouldn't we be?" he answers way too quickly for my liking.

"Because you're acting weird, because you're looking at everything in this room bar me." *And because I feel like I'm losing you.*

At that he shifts in his seat so that our knees bang together, and the heat of his gaze is fixed firmly on my face. "Is that better?"

"Not really," I mutter, wishing I hadn't said anything.

"You didn't seem to mind me staring last night."

Puffing out my cheeks, I decide to grow some lady balls. "You're right, I didn't. But that was different. You looked at me like you wanted me. Now you're looking at me like you don't know who I am. I'm still me. I'm still, Pen and I love Zayn."

"So is it him? Is he the one you're going to choose?"

"You're still adamant about that, after everything that's happened?" My voice is sharp. It angers me that he's still so determined to break us apart. I'm not any nearer to knowing what I want. If anything, being intimate with York, Dax and Zayn has made this harder.

He puffs out his cheeks, then blows out a steady breath. "I never change my mind about anything once it's made up."

"What, never?" I ask, placing my hand over his, my heart battering like a piston against my rib cage.

"Never."

"Have you ever considered the possibility that I won't have to choose, that they might choose me?" I whisper, feeling both hope at the possibility and agony at the thought.

Xeno meets my gaze and I see the truth in them. He has thought about it. He's thought about it a lot. Xeno opens his mouth to respond, but slams it shut when his phone starts ringing. Snatching it up, he strides from the kitchen. By the time he returns, the moment of honesty is gone and neither of us bring up the subject again.

CHAPTER TWENTY-NINE

Present Day

"AGAIN!" Zayn snaps, striding across the studio in front of us.

He's sweating, tiny beads of water forming on his forehead as he waits for us to drag our tired-arse bodies up off the floor. The arsehole has given us just five minutes to rest after two hours of dancing nonstop. Picked by Xeno as the choreographer for the group dance, Zayn has taken it upon himself to act as a tyrant whilst Xeno watches from the side lines.

We've been learning the steps for our group dance for almost two hours without a break and there's not one of us who doesn't look like they're about to collapse. I'm strong and fit, but this is fucking ridiculous. It's Friday afternoon and tonight I have to get ready for Jeb and whatever the fuck he has planned. I need this like a hole in the head.

"What the fuck's got his goat?" River grumbles, casting a look at Clancy who shrugs.

"I've no idea. It's not as if the show is any time soon. Maybe he needs to let off some steam. I could totally help him out in that department," Sophie pipes up, butting into our conversation.

She can fuck right off in her skimpy dance outfit that shows of her tight figure and six pack.

"Never going to happen," I respond, glaring at her over my shoulder.

She tips her head back and cackles, drawing everyone's attention. I want to fucking scream that he was *mine* first. That he loved *me* first. I also want to fucking scratch her eyes out.

"Right, that's enough!" Xeno gets up from the bench and saunters over, flicking me a dark look.

"I'm not finished," Zayn grunts.

"Yeah, you are," Xeno retorts, handing Zayn a bottle of water which he snatches out of his hand. I watch him unscrew the bottle top and down the whole thing. "It's the weekend. Get some rest. We'll start up rehearsals again next week. In the meantime, try not to fucking kill each other." Xeno looks directly at me and I roll my eyes.

What the fuck ever.

Everyone disperses, gathering up their stuff. Clancy drops down on the bench, her creamy cheeks pink with exertion. She blows a strand of curly orange hair out of her eyes.

"Fuck, that was brutal. Was he always such a goddamn tyrant?" she asks, taking a deep glug of water from her bottle.

I give her a look that says, not here. No one bar Clancy and the Breakers actually know that we were old friends and I'd like to keep it that way.

"Sorry," she mutters.

"I gotta run," I say. Grabbing my bag and swinging it over my shoulder.

"You working tonight?" she asks.

"Yeah..." It's not a lie per se, but I don't want her to come to Rocks and find me not there.

She grimaces. "You don't mind if I give it a miss, do you? Only I got my period and I'm bloated as fuck."

"Of course I don't mind. We'll catch up Sunday," I say, trying to hide the relief I feel.

"You not around tomorrow?"

"No, I'm going home to see my little sister." Another lie. They seem to slip so effortlessly from my mouth today.

"Okay, cool. Catch you Sunday."

"Yeah, Sunday," I mutter, heading out of the studio, just as my phone starts vibrating in my bag. I snatch it up and answer. "Yes?"

"Penelope, that's no way to greet me, now is it?"

Shit. It's Jeb. That'll teach me not to check the caller ID before answering. I push through the door leading into the flight of stairs that leads up to the flats.

"Hey, sorry. Just got out of a rehearsal," I explain, forcing myself to be polite.

"Are you ready for tonight? Did you spend my money wisely?"

"Uh-huh. I got a cocktail dress like you asked. There's money left over, I'll bring it later."

"Keep it," he says.

"No. That's okay..."

"I said, *keep it*, Penelope."

Gritting my teeth, I bite back the response I want to say, and smile into the mouthpiece. For the most part I can convince myself that I'm just an employee of Jeb's and nothing more, but on occasions like this I can't hide the fact that I'm his property just like the rest of the Skins are. "Sure."

"Good. I'll send a car to pick you up from Rocks at eight. Don't be late."

"I won't be."

He clicks off and I jam my phone into my bag and take the stairs two at a time. I've got a couple hours to sort my head out and to make myself look presentable. I just wish there's a pill I could take to make me forget what's to come, because whatever Jeb has planned, it won't be good.

$$\textit{\textbf{Ł}}$$

FEELING uncomfortable and out of my comfort zone, I stand a little further along from the entrance of Rocks trying to avoid the occasional glances from Tommy, the bouncer. He's in his late thirties, built, and covered head to toe in tattoos, but despite his reputation, is a good guy. At least he's always been nice to me. I can't say the same for the countless number of people he's manhandled out of the club over the years and given a beating when the need arises.

Fortunately for me, there are only a few eager beavers lining up and Tommy ushers them through without so much as a glance. All of them were under sixteen, let alone eighteen.

Pulling at the hem of my off-the-shoulder, figure hugging,

mid-thigh, black, cocktail dress, I wait for my lift to arrive. My hair is styled in soft waves that took me over an hour to perfect. Add to that a dash of mascara and cherry-red lipstick and pair it with killer, red, stiletto heels and I look nothing short of slutty. I'm the perfect dolly-bird, and I fucking hate it.

Eight o'clock on the dot, a black limousine with tinted windows and shiny silver hubcaps pulls up. Jeb couldn't be anymore ostentatious if he tried. Internally I roll my eyes, externally I plaster on a fake smile and steel myself for the evening ahead, wondering whether this is the time I'll pay off my debt and will be free to live.

The back passenger door opens, and picking up my overnight bag, I slide into the limousine as ladylike as I can, given my restrictive outfit. Expecting to see Jeb sitting next to the mini fridge, I'm shocked to come face-to-face with Zayn.

"What are you doing here?" I blurt out, pulling the door shut behind me. I place my overnight bag on the floor, trying to hide the surprise in my voice as I slide along the seat

"Jeb is otherwise engaged. He's going to meet us at the venue. I'm your... *chaperone*," Zayn replies, his eyes roving over my outfit. I see a flicker of surprise followed swiftly by disgust and I try not to react. Screw him. He doesn't know why I'm doing this.

Clasped between his middle finger and thumb is a crystal glass filled a quarter of a way up with a deep amber liquid. He lifts it to his lips and takes a mouthful leaving a bead of liquid on his bottom lip. I watch with a pounding heart as his tongue snakes out between his lips, licking at the droplet in such a way that my skin warms.

"I see your tastes have changed," I comment, unable to help myself.

Zayn was always a beer drinker and a Mary-J smoker, avoiding the hard liqueur that Xeno and Dax used to indulge in. He was also a jean, t-shirt and trainer wearing hip-hop dancer too, but right now he looks every inch the gangster with his perfectly fitted black suit and stark white shirt, unbuttoned to reveal the smattering of chest hair I used to love so much.

"Drink?" he asks me, ignoring my comment and looking at me with dark eyes that swallow me up. There's a cool kind of calm about him and when he checks his gold Rolex watch on his wrist for the time, I realise this is a side to him I've never seen before. Zayn was never this closed-off, this guarded.

I swallow hard. I can deal with Zayn as an angrier version of the kid I used to know charging around a dance studio, but this, not so much. His mannerisms are more like his uncle than I'd like. In fact, they're build is horrifyingly similar now that I think about it. I don't want to see Zayn as a younger version of Jeb, but the way he's looking at me now is testing my ability to ignore the fact they're related.

"I'll have whatever you're having," I respond tightly.

He raises a brow, but doesn't question it. Knocking back the remains of his drink, Zayn deposits the glass on the tray with the decanter and pours me a generous shot into a clean glass.

"Here," he says, placing the glass on a small side table that's nearer to him than me before leaning back and watching me approach from his spot on the leather seat opposite.

Manoeuvring in a moving vehicle isn't easy at the best of times, but in the outfit I'm wearing, almost impossible. But, just like the bad-bitch that I am, I do it without face-planting on the floor at his feet, and fold myself elegantly into the seat that runs perpendicular to his. I'm itching to pull the hem of my dress down, but that would signify that I'm not as comfortable or as confident as I'm making out to be. So, I don't.

"Nice outfit," he muses coldly, his gaze sliding up from my curved foot to my knee and the expanse of my thigh.

"I could say the same for you," I retort back, flinching at the way he studies me. Sipping on my drink, brandy as it turns out, I wait for Zayn to speak up. When he doesn't, I fill the silence with my own question.

"What are you up to Zayn? What has Jeb got you involved in now?"

Zayn chuckles darkly, meeting my gaze with his cold stare. "Wouldn't you like to know."

"Not really, just making conversation," I lie.

Again.

Deciding to go for a different tactic, I twist my body to face him. He mirrors me and I get a whiff of his delicious smelling cologne with its spicy top notes and zesty undertones, a luscious combination. I fight everything not to let my eyelids droop and breathe him in deeply. "Do you know where we're going tonight?"

"Yeah."

"And?" I press, feeling decidedly unnerved by the silent, almost calculating way he's looking at me.

"You'll see when we get there." He taps on the blackout divider behind his head and it slides open to reveal the driver. "How long?" he asks.

"Five minutes, Scar," the driver responds.

"Scar?" I question.

"That's right. I've got a few of them." He shrugs, like that's no big deal.

"How? What happened to you?" I ask, remembering very clearly the jagged scars across his pecs that he bared in the dance studio a few days ago. He scowls, his eyes darkening to a black so bottomless that I wince.

"That is none of your damn business."

For a moment, the air between us is fraught with the burden of our past hurts and I have an impulsive need to lean across the divide and press my fingers against the ridge of one the scars I see peeping out from beneath the open collar of his shirt. He looks down at where I'm staring, and his inked fingers come up and fix the button, hiding the scars once more. It's only then that I notice a fresh tattoo on his inner wrist. I gasp at what I see.

"Zayn, is that a...?" I stare, reaching for his arm and tugging it towards me, forgetting the fact that we're not friends and I can't just grab him like this. "...A penny?"

My fingers pull back the sleeve of his shirt and suit jacket enough to get a good look at the tattoo on his wrist. It wasn't there earlier today. He must've had this done between the end of our practice session in the studio and now. My heart squeezes painfully, and I look at him in confusion. "Why do you have this tattooed on your wrist?" His jaw muscle ticks, and I can hear his teeth grinding over one another as he looks at my finger gently moving over the gold one pound coin tattooed there. "Zayn?"

His eyes snap up to meet mine, and I'm shocked by the anguish I see there. "To remind me."

"Remind you of what?"

"The price you pay for love," he says bitterly.

CHAPTER THIRTY

Three Years Ago

"WE WON! Holy fucking shit, we won!" I scream, ripping off my red mask and throwing myself into Zayn's arms, laughing with joy. It bubbles up and out of my chest, mixed up with pride and a huge sense of achievement. *We did it. We actually did it.*

Zayn lifts me off the floor and spins me around and around until we're both dizzy with happiness. By the time he puts me down, he too has lost his mask we all wore as part of our performance. White for the boys, red for me. A nice prop that the crowd went crazy for. Team that up with Zayn's insane choreography and *X Gon' Give It To Ya* by DMX and there was no fucking contest.

"You were *insane*, Pen!" he says, fist bumping me, then pulling me in for a hug.

"So were you!" My face splits into such a wide grin that my

muscles already hurt from overuse. I've never been this happy. Not *ever.*

We. Killed. It.

Just like old times, we've spent hours perfecting the routine this last month. Since the whole cemetery thing and that night my brother decided to beat the shit out of me, Jeb's backed off and has given us some space. Maybe whatever Xeno and Zayn had said to Jeb that night sunk in. All I know is that they've been spending all their spare time with me this last month and not with the Skins, so things have calmed down a lot.

I've never been more relieved about anything in my life. It's my birthday, we've just won the battle and the Breakers I know and love, are back.

The roar of the crowd and the excitement in the air is nothing compared to how I feel as Dax steals me from Zayn's arms and plants a hot kiss against my lips. He engulfs me with his body, wrapping me up in a sweaty hug.

"We aced this, Kid," he says. Happiness, a tonic we both need so desperately.

I chuckle as I'm hauled out of his arms and into York's who hugs me close and plants a kiss on the top of my head. "Titch, you were fucking outstanding. Do you know that?"

"We all were. That trick you and Xeno did. Fuck, it was like you were flying, York!" I laugh, joining in with his *happy feet* as the crowd around us starts piling onto the dance floor to congratulate us on our win. The opposing crew make their way over and give us all begrudging handshakes. "Where's Xeno?" I ask, looking for him in the thickening crowd.

"I dunno. He disappeared the second the announcement was made," Dax responds, a frown marring his happiness.

"I'll find him," I say brightly, pushing through the crowd before they can stop me. Casting a look over my shoulder, I laugh as they're engulfed by well wishes. All I want is for Xeno to share in our success, he was incredible and danced with a kind of freedom I've never really seen before. He executed all the steps with precision and a fierce determination. Something fucking magical happened tonight and I need to tell him that.

Spotting him across the far side of the dance floor talking to one of the organisers, I make my way over to him, stopping periodically to speak to people congratulating me on our win. When I feel a firm grip around my upper arm, I turn around expecting to find another enthusiastic clubber only to come face to face with David. My next fucking breath gets snatched from my lungs and I feel all the blood drain from my face.

"Hello, little sister. Quite a show you put on tonight," he says. His voice is cold, and he has a dangerous smile on his face. One I recognise only too well.

"What are you doing here?" I stutter, his presence having the desired effect.

Despite the heat of the club, my sweaty skin turns cold. Ice fucking cold. The last time I saw him was the night my Breakers had seen him off and he'd driven away with the smell of burnt rubber and threats in the air. That was almost two months ago.

"Did you enjoy it?" I ask, stalling for time. *Still* by Dr Dre and Snoop Dog starts to play and the crowd, already hyped by the show we just put on, start getting down, completely oblivious to my predicament. David laughs, gripping my arm so tight I know it's going to leave a bruise. I grind my teeth against the pain.

"No. I didn't," he snarls, hauling me against his side and pulling me through the crowd.

"Wait. I need to collect my prize winnings. You can have it, all of it. I don't want it. I got it for mum, but I'm sure she'd want you to have it," I lie.

David barks out another laugh, manhandling me through the crowd. "You never were a particularly good liar."

"David, *please...*"

"You are coming with me quietly, otherwise I will make this night so much worse for you, Penelope." His features turn even more monstrous and fear makes me compliant.

"David, can we talk about this..." I begin, a feeble attempt at trying to appease the monster inside of him. His silver cross glints in the club's flashing lights and I want to yank it from his neck and shove it down his throat so he can choke on his belief that he's doing all of this to save my fucking soul. But I know the truth. Religion is his excuse to mete out punishment in the Lord's fucking name. It's *bullshit*. He's the devil incarnate. A psychopath. An abuser. There's nothing saintly about him and no cross wrapped around his neck will ever absolve him of his fucking sins. Fuck, I wish I was tougher when it comes to him, but I'm not. He scares the shit out of me.

"Yeah, we're gonna talk, Penelope. Somewhere private." He looks down at me, his brown eyes the same shade as my own. It makes me feel sick that I might resemble him in any way.

"Why don't we get a drink at the bar?" I suggest, not wanting to be alone with him any-fucking-where. *Where the hell are my boys?*

Keeping me close to his side and his grip bone-crunchingly

tight, David laughs. "Nice try, but you ain't getting away from me. Besides, your boys are otherwise engaged."

"What do you mean?" I ask, as I walk stiffly beside him to the VIP area of the club I've never been to before now. I've heard the rumours about what goes down behind those solid, black doors and I don't want any part of it. I come to Rocks to dance. That's it.

"They're Skins and they've got business to attend to, giving us plenty of time to *talk*."

The bouncer nods at David and holds open the door to the portion of the club used for shady deals and fuck knows what else. Stepping into a dimly lit room that smells of weed, alcohol and sex, David walks me over to an empty booth in the corner of the room. I can hear moaning noises and the distinct sound of people fucking. Elsewhere people are playing cards, betting with money and lives, most likely. I don't look around too much, instead, I keep my gaze fixed ahead of me and pray for a fucking miracle.

"Sit down, Penelope," David barks, watching me with soulless eyes as I slide into the seat opposite him. Shivers wrack my body and I try desperately to keep a lid on them. He feeds off my fear, he always has

"What do you want, David?" I ask, schooling my features and tucking my shaking hands beneath my thighs. I still bear the bruises from his last beating. They may no longer mark my skin, but the scars of his abuse run far, far deeper than what you see on the surface.

"I told you not to go near the Breakers again the last time we spoke. I warned you, Penelope, but you wouldn't listen, would you?"

"We're friends, nothing more," I lie, hoping to fuck my face doesn't betray me. "We're just dancing. They're your crew members. I thought you'd approve of our friendship."

"APPROVE?!" he roars, slamming his fist on the table and making me jump. "You do not belong to them, Penelope. You're *my* flesh and blood. You're fucking *mine!*"

"I'm your *sister*, David, not your property, you twisted fuck!" I bite back, unable to help myself. That feisty part of me is still holding onto the hope that one day I'll be strong enough to end him. I really should've known better.

Before I even know what's happened, David has launched at me over the table and slammed his fist into the side of my head, just behind my hairline. The force of his punch knocks me sideways against the leather seat, my ears ringing. Stars form behind my closed eyelids and for a moment I think I'm going to pass out. With a panicked heart and tears springing from my eyes, I force myself upright, swiping at my face furiously.

"Now look what you made me do," he remarks, sitting back in his seat and watching me with narrowed eyes as I blink away my double-vision and shake out the ringing in my head.

"What do you want, David?" I ask, quieter this time, because I know what he wants and this time ignoring his threats isn't going to work.

"Your friendship with the Breakers ends tonight. You don't see them again. You don't speak to them. You don't fucking *think* of them," he snarls, his pitch black hair falling into his eyes.

"David, please..." Begging has never, ever, got him to change his mind, but I do it anyway.

"You've been sneaking around under my nose all this

fucking time making a fool out of me, and I will not allow it, Penelope. Understand?!"

"No, I don't understand. I don't understand why you hate me so much. What did I ever do to you?" I ask.

For years I've wanted to know why I was the butt of all his hate. Why I was his punching bag. We both grew up with a shitty mother and whilst that brought me and Lena closer, it never did the same for David and me. I wonder whether something terrible happened to him before I was born. Whether our mother or father did something to scar him so badly that he's never gotten over it and it's twisted him into this monster I see before me now.

He cocks his head to the side. "You think I do this because I hate you?" Something softens in his gaze but instead of making me feel better, my fear turns sickly, it grows nails and claws churning up my stomach.

Oh God no. Please no.

"I don't hate you, Penelope." He reaches across the table and grabs my hand, his fingers trailing over my knuckles whilst his other hand fingers the cross at his neck. "I love you."

But this isn't a brotherly-sisterly kind of love. The way he's looking at me is something far, far worse.

"No!" I snap my hand away from his and push back into my seat. "You're sick."

The softness evaporates, replaced instead with a menacing glare. "The only one who is sick is you, with your slutty ways, tempting me. Making me think sinful thoughts. You deserve to be punished, you filthy little whore."

My skin pales as I realise how much worse growing up with

David could've been if he'd given in to his own sick desires. David's fist slams against the table, making me jump.

"Tonight you dump the Breakers. You cut them out of your life for good because if you don't..."

"If I don't..." I swallow the bile burning my throat and blink back the tears.

"If you don't, I will wrap my hands around Lena's pretty little neck and squeeze until she can't breathe again."

This time the bile I've been holding in catapults itself from my body and I throw up all over the floor and seat, barely missing myself and the table. David laughs and slides out of the booth.

"Catch you later, Penelope," he says, before sauntering off and leaving me to clean up the mess.

❦

STUMBLING out of the booth and blindly looking for the ladies room, I push through a door just off the side of the bar and into a dark corridor beyond. I'm sobbing now, smothering my hand over my mouth as I try to stifle the sound. This isn't the place to be weak. Most of the people lurking in this area will spit me up and chew me out given half the chance. I need to splash my face with water and get the fuck home back to Lena. I need to know she's okay. If I tell mum what David's threatened to do, maybe she'll *do* something. For all her faults, of which she has many, she loves Lena.

Another round of nausea rises up my throat and burns my tongue threatening to spill out onto the floor, so I push open the nearest door hoping I've stumbled across the toilet.

"What the fuck?!" a voice roars.

Oh, my God. Oh, my God. Oh, my God.

Before me, Jeb, the leader of the fucking Skins, is standing with his pants pushed down to his ankles whilst a guy on his knees deep throats him. A guy. A fucking man.

Holy fucking shit.

I'm dead.

I'm fucking dead. Not metaphorically. *Actually.*

Jeb is straight as a die, or so everyone believes. So if he's back here getting his cock sucked behind closed doors then this is a *secret*, something he doesn't want anyone to see, let alone me. I'm so fucking dead.

Two things happen at once. I promptly throw up again with the stress of my brother's threat, barely missing the guy on his knees, and Jeb lunges for me, his dick slipping from the guy's mouth.

I run.

Blind fear fuels me and I skid on my own vomit, grabbing the wall to keep steady before legging it down the corridor.

I don't get far.

A thick arm folds around my waist, hauling me backwards. "Now, now, pretty girl. Where the fuck do you think you're going?"

"I didn't see anything... I-I was lost. I-I'm sorry, I'll clear up the mess," I rattle out, my tongue a loose, word-spewing, mess.

"Let's have a chat, shall we?" Jeb says. His voice is a low, threatening growl in my ear.

I consider fighting back. That thought lasts all of a second when I realise that Jeb will sooner put a bullet in my head than let me even raise a fist to him, or run again. The only thing I can do now is exactly what he asks and hope that somehow he doesn't decide to kill me.

Letting out a whoosh of breath, I allow Jeb to drag me into one of the other rooms along the corridor. Inside is a medium sized office with a large mahogany table, along the back wall are six TV's, all recording footage of the club. A large man is sitting with his back to us, busy watching his mobile phone, his head-phones plugged into his ears, laughing raucously. He isn't looking at the screens and he definitely isn't paying attention to his environment given we've just walked in without him notic-ing. Jeb deposits me on a seat in the corner of the room then steps up behind the man, picks up his gun that he'd left so care-lessly on the table and places it against his temple.

The man freezes.

I stop breathing.

Jeb yanks out the man's headphones and leans over, pressing his mouth against his ear. "You're fired," he snarls, then pulls the fucking trigger.

Blood, brain, and bone burst out of the side of the man's head, splattering the wall opposite, leaving nothing but a gaping mess.

My mouth opens in a silent scream. Inside my head the sound is blood-curdling.

Tonight, I'm going to die.

CHAPTER THIRTY-ONE

Present Day

THE LIMO PULLS UP outside a large, gated site that from the outside looks little more than an industrial estate, but given the heavy duty security and the rows and rows of expensive cars already parked inside, appearances aren't as they seem.

"Where are we?" I ask Zayn, who's been broody and silent for the last five minutes.

Ignoring my question, he taps on the glass divider between him and the driver. "Pull up around back, Grim is meeting us there."

"Sure thing, Scar," the driver agrees before the glass divider slides back in place.

"Grim?" I question. The name is vaguely familiar, but I can't quite place it.

"She's the owner of this fight club and well respected. Don't piss her off," Zane responds, leaning over and opening a hidden draw beneath the seat.

"Why would I piss her off..." I begin, only to lose my train of thought when I notice what he has in his hands, a red mask. The exact same one I wore when we were kids.

"Why have you got that?" I ask as Zayn places the mask in my lap. I've not seen this for three goddamn years, and it brings back way too many memories, most of them unhappy given the way the night went. My gaze snaps up to meet his.

"You're going to need to wear that."

"Where did you find it?" I ask him. Has he kept hold of it all this time? More importantly, why is he asking me to put it on now? What the fuck is going on?

"Put it on," he repeats.

"Why?" I croak, my voice quivering with past memories, many that he has no knowledge of.

"Put the damn mask on, Pen," he orders darkly, pulling out another mask from the draw. This one isn't made of plastic like mine, but is a full head mask, with a space cut out for the eyes and mouth. It resembles a balaclava but looks like it's made out of some kind of thin, silky material. He pulls it over his face, adjusting it until it sits exactly right. Then he grabs a pair of leather gloves, pulling them on too.

"Are we about to rob a bank or something?" I joke.

"Not today, no," he responds dryly, and I can't tell if he's joking or not.

When I'm too shocked to do anything but stare at him, Zayn shifts towards me, grabs the mask from my lap and secures it over my face, making sure the strap is pulled tight around my head. His gloved covered fingers gently run over the length of my hair, adjusting the strands so that they fall over my cleavage. It's a surprisingly gentle act, but not as surprising as the words he whispers into my ear next.

"For what it's worth, I'm sorry too," he mutters, his breath a warm caress against my cheek.

I should be relieved by his words, but something about the tone of his voice and the finality of his apology makes me nervous.

For just a second, he leans his head against the side of mine and I can feel the heat of his body through his clothes. It takes everything in me not to throw my arms around him and forget we're no longer friends. Instead, I reach for his hand, my fingers brushing against his. I expect him to pull away. Instead, he captures my fingers within his grasp and squeezes them gently, the pad of his thumb running over my knuckles.

"Pen..." he starts, staring into my eyes, searching for something. His onyx eyes bleed with unanswered questions, muddying our past and the friendship we once shared.

"I've missed you, Zayn," I whisper, hoping he hears the sincerity in my voice and sees the truth of that statement in my gaze. It's a truth that I can no longer hold in. I've missed him so fucking much. Maybe it's stupid to admit how I feel. Maybe I'm reading into this silent conversation way more than I should be. Maybe I'm just a fool, but I can't seem to help myself.

"Fuck, Pen," he mutters, and just like that the animosity I've felt between us falls away and we're left with a momentary stalemate. Right at this moment, we're just two old friends who aren't sure how to move forward with all the bad blood between us, but maybe, just maybe, are willing to try. Then the car stops moving and the bubble around us bursts.

"We've run out of time. Fuck!" he exclaims. His eyes are wild, fearful.

"What is it?" I question, feeding off his fear.

"Follow my lead. Do not question my actions and for fuck sake don't call me Zayn," he says quickly.

"What do you mean don't call you...?" but the door to the limo is pulled open and he jerks away from me, leaving my question unanswered and a sick feeling in my stomach.

With no other choice but to follow him, I step out of the limo. Outside the air is surprisingly cool for a September evening, and I wish, not for the first time, that I'd chosen something far less revealing to wear. Keeping on Jeb's good side is essential though, so I follow the rules like I always have because all I care about is keeping David the fuck where he is.

Before me, an attractive woman greets us. She has long dark hair shaved off on one side, and left long and loose on the other. It tumbles over her right shoulder in a mess of waves. From behind her black, jewelled masquerade mask, she gives me a once over, noting my attire and immediately dismissing me. I know what she thinks. I'm arm candy, nothing more. That riles me up more than I'd care to admit, but my pride has to take a backseat. If this is what I need to do to keep Lena safe, then so be it.

"Good evening, Mr Bernard. It's my pleasure to welcome you here tonight," she says, holding her hand out to shake. Zayn takes it, nodding briefly.

This woman, Grim I'm assuming, isn't wearing a revealing dress like me. She's got tight leather pants on and a sheer red shirt showing off a black lace bra, paired with chunky black biker boots and a really fucking impressive rose tattoo that winds up the side of her neck. Next to her is a huge bear of a man who has his gaze fixed solely on Zayn as though he's the biggest threat around here. He isn't wearing a mask, and I get the distinct impression he doesn't give a flying fuck who sees him. He's here to protect Grim, that much is obvious.

"This is Beast. He's my partner and will not hesitate to end anyone who he deems a threat to me or our club."

"Understood," Zayn responds.

"Good. Let's get you seated," she says, twisting on her feet and striding towards the huge warehouse, Beast keeping pace alongside her. When he reaches over and lays his hand on her lower back, his fingers tracing the mound of her arse, I realise that he's more than just a business partner, because a woman like her isn't going to allow just anyone to put their hands on her uninvited. She might be a foot smaller than him and slight against his large frame, but it's clear who holds all the power and it isn't the six foot seven, man-beast with the same name.

"The fight is due to start in ten minutes. We have your table ready. Your crew has already arrived," Grim says.

"Good," Zayn responds, his voice sounding off, weird, as we step into the warehouse and into a caged area that is made private by large black curtains encircling the space.

"Mr Bernard, Grim's club has strict rules. No weapons. I need to search you," Beast says, stepping towards Zayn who promptly holds his arms out to the side and spreads his legs. He's patted down swiftly, and when Beast is satisfied Zayn's not carrying a weapon, he steps back and nods at Grim before turning his attention to me and arching an eyebrow.

"Don't even think about it," Grim snarls, shooting me a

warning look even though I'm just standing here and not encouraging any kind of interaction in the slightest.

"She could be hiding something," Beast says, holding back a smirk that makes his lips twitch.

"Unless she's got a weapon stuffed up her coochie, then she's good," Grim snaps, giving Beast a look that could slay the toughest of men.

It doesn't seem to bother him though as he barks out a laugh and looks at Grim with the kind of love and affection that makes me feel sad and, weirdly, angry. I'm angry that someone like her, a criminal who's clearly up to shady shit, has found love. It pisses me off.

"Stuffed up my *coochie?*" I snap, unable to hide my indignation. I've not had *anything* stuffed up my coochie for three fucking years, let alone a fucking weapon. Actually, I'm fairly sure I'm a born again virgin, and my hymen has grown back for all the lack of use.

Grim shrugs, looking me up and down before turning her attention back to Zayn. "In my club there is no fighting between crews, period. Anyone starting a fight will be dealt with swiftly and *finally*. Understood?"

"Understood."

"Good, follow me."

Unlocking the wire cage door, we all pass through the curtained off area and into the main building. The space is huge and set up like some fancy nightclub with soft lighting and chandeliers hanging from the vaulted ceiling. In the centre of the warehouse is a huge fighter's cage with dark patches of dried blood splattered across the padded canvas.

Surrounding the ring in a semi-circle are tables filled with masked men and women. The tables are covered with red material and lit with flickering candles. Crystal decanters and cut-glass tumblers adorn every surface alongside bottles of Dom Perignon and fluted champagne glasses. The air reeks of a mixture of weed, cigar smoke, masculinity, and heady perfume, making it even more difficult to breathe in a mask that is all but suffocating. I remember being barely able to breathe in the damn thing before, now with my senses on high alert and my heart pumping wildly, it's even harder.

The air is thick with tension as we follow Grim towards a table situated nearest to the cage. All of the tables are filled with men dressed similarly as Zayn, in expensive suits and face masks of varying designs. Plenty of bling accompanies the tailoring as is custom with gangsters, there's enough gold here tonight to fund a small country with all the Rolex watches, chains, diamond studded earrings, gold teeth and rings. Some of the women accompanying the gangsters wear similar outfits to mine: provocative, sexy, and barely covering their tits and arse. Though I do spot others who are more demurely dressed and who ooze power. I'm betting they're not merely arm candy but gangsters in their own right.

"Jesus fucking Christ," I mutter under my breath.

Zayn reaches for my hand, grasping it in his then drops it, acutely aware that all eyes are on us. No doubt the other crews are trying to figure out who we are and which crew we belong to. The masks give a level of anonymity, yes, but I doubt it would be very hard to work out which crew is which if someone really wanted to put their mind to it. There are way too many giveaways: tattooed covered hands and necks, accents, mannerisms, all of them dead giveaways. Grim is a brave woman to hold such a gathering when rival gangs could be sitting mere feet from each other. Then again, she seems to command a certain level of respect, going by the almost friendly nods of acknowledgement as she walks past each table. That is a feat in itself given the criminal scene is predominantly run by men. Whatever she did to gain their respect must've been pretty fucking epic. Despite her attitude towards me, I begrudgingly admire her for it. Either way, the atmosphere, though tense, isn't half as volatile as it could be. Partly due to the fact that there are armed men high above circling the space on a grated walkway, and partly because people can pretend to be whoever they want behind a mask.

Speaking of which, Grim stops at a table where two other men are seated. They're both wearing the same black mask as Zayn. I feel their gaze on me as Zayn pulls out a chair. I sit, immediately recognising the two men opposite. York's piercing blue eyes and plump lips are a dead giveaway as are Xeno's green orbs that flash with derision at my outfit. They stare openly at me and my cheeks flame beneath my mask at their blatant perusal.

"The fight will start shortly. Your bets have already been noted. If you need anything, Mr Bernard, be sure to let me know," she says directly to Zayn.

"I will," Zayn retorts gruffly.

Grim nods her head at Xeno and York, completely ignoring me. "Gentleman."

I watch her leave, wondering why she's treating Zayn like he's the leader of the Skins. It makes no sense. Xeno taps the table, then leans forward suddenly and pours Zayn a double shot of the golden liquid. His hands are covered with black, leather gloves just like York. Now, I understand why. Tattoos on hands are dead giveaways to the identity of a person. They're keeping their identities closely guarded.

"Where's Dax? Jeb?" I mutter, my heart thundering and my head full of questions.

What the fuck is going on? Why am I at Grim's Fight Club with the Breakers and not Jeb? Where the hell is he? My internal question is answered a few moments later when another man dressed in a suit, wearing leather gloves and the same black head mask as the rest of the crew, sits down next to me at the table.

"Good evening, Penelope. You look beautiful. I see my money was well spent."

Opposite, Xeno slams his glass on the table.

"Jeb?" I whisper, my whole body quaking at his sudden appearance and the animosity Xeno is throwing my way. He's glaring at me with such fire and fury that I can't help but react. I could submit to my fear, to the sick feeling that something huge is about to go down. Instead, I straighten my spine and stare back at Xeno, daring him to spill the derision from his lips.

"No that'd be the man sitting to your left. I'm Zayn," Jeb responds with an evil chuckle.

On the other side of me, Zayn stiffens, but I don't get to question what the fuck is going on as the overhead lights go out and music starts pumping over the speaker system.

The second the warehouse falls into darkness, their black masks transform, lighting up with the outline of neon red skulls. My mouth falls open at the eerie, floating faces around me. Like headless spectres waiting for the moment to consume me whole and drag me into the depths of hell with them.

"Nice touch, don't you think?" Jeb says with an amused laugh.

I swallow hard. Nothing about this is *nice*.

Before me, a spotlight brightens the cage dragging my attention away from their hellish masks. I watch as Dax walks onto the canvas barefoot, wearing just a pair of black boxing shorts with the same red skull motif emblazoned across the silky material. His hands are wrapped up with tape and when he looks over at our table, Dax makes eye contact not with Jeb on my right, but Zayn on my left. A look passes between them. Then, for the briefest of moments, Dax rests his eyes on me, his scowl deepening. I'm not the only one to notice how his fists curl, how he bares his teeth and snarls.

Fuck, who is this man?

"Perhaps you've been wondering what the Breakers have been up to these past three years, hmm, Penelope?" Jeb asks, his voice low.

I snatch my head around to look at him, focusing on his eyes beneath the mask, so similar to Zayn's, yet so vastly different and lit with a red hue that makes him seem more beast than human. "I haven't," I hiss. Another lie. I've thought of nothing else.

"It turns out that these boys aren't just talented dancers, but have other gifts too. Dax is a brutal bare-knuckle fighter and performs best in the cage. My nephew can hold his own in a knife fight. York is as light on his feet in the boxing ring as he is on the stage and Xeno, well, Xeno has a special kind of talent. Don't you Xeno?" Jeb asks, a cruel laugh seeping out from behind his mask.

Xeno's eyes flare with anger and for a moment I swear he's

about to launch across the table at Jeb, but the music changes and our attention is drawn to another man who enters the cage. Well, at least the attention of the three of us on this side of the table, York and Xeno still have their backs to the cage and seem more interested in what's going on behind us than anything else. They're like coiled springs, expecting trouble, ready for it.

Ripping my attention away from them both, my heart flip-flops as a tough looking guy, matched in height and width to Dax, enters the cage. The only advantage I can spot is youth. Dax is probably at least ten years younger than the mean looking bastard. But that means shit. I've heard about these underground fight clubs. I know that the fight only ends when the opponent is knocked out or too injured to fight back. Despite everything that's happened recently. I don't want to see Dax hurt. I must give away my feelings because Jeb leans closer.

"Relax, Penelope, we both know that Dax is more than capable of winning. He's brutal when pushed."

He's right, Dax is.

CHAPTER THIRTY-TWO

Three Years Ago

"WELL, we seem to have a little issue now, don't we, pretty girl?" Jeb says as he kicks the dead man's body off the seat and places the chair in front of me, sitting down.

He's still holding the gun. It dangles from his fingers carelessly as a pool of dark red blood spreads over the wooden floor getting closer and closer to my feet. I look at him with wide-eyes, fear leaving me mute.

"You know it's a shame because I hear my nephew has taken quite a liking to you. Putting a bullet in your head won't do good things for our relationship," Jeb muses, cocking his head to the side and running his fingers over my cheek. My jaw begins to chatter, and he grips my chin tightly in his hold. "Then there's the small matter of you seeing something you shouldn't. This bastard was shot because he was supposed to be keeping an eye out and preventing someone like you from stumbling across something you have no business seeing. It's quite a predicament, don't you think? So, what should I do, huh?" He lifts the gun and places the cold, hard, metal edge against my cheek.

"P-please, don't kill me. I'll do anything..." I stutter, slamming my mouth closed as he leans forward, the gun biting into my skin. He looks into my eyes for a long, long time. His eyes are as pitch black as Zayn's, but there's no life in them. When I look into Zayn's eyes I see stars, when I look into Jeb's I see nothing but a void as black and final as death.

"Funnily enough, I believe you." Jeb suddenly jerks back, removing the gun and throwing it onto the table. I flinch, expecting it to go off. It doesn't.

"Safety's back on, pretty girl," Jeb says with a smile that's far too dark to be friendly.

"So, how are we going to play this, huh? You look like the kind of girl who can keep a secret. Can you keep a secret, Penelope? That is your name, isn't it?"

"Yes," I confirm. He can call me what the fuck he wants as long as I'm still alive to hear it.

"You keep my little indiscretions a secret and I'll let you toddle off back to the Breakers and keep my nephew happy. Provided you keep this quiet, then we're all good. I'm happy, you're happy, my nephew is happy."

"I-I can't," I stutter.

"What do you mean you *can't?*" Jeb spits out, reaching for the gun once more.

"My b-brother, he threatened to kill my little sister if I stayed friends with the Breakers. I-I have to break up with them, tonight. He's going to kill her if I don't," I sob, tears falling freely now. I swipe at them, forcing anger into my heart so that fear doesn't make me look weak.

"Did he now? Why am I not surprised?" Jeb says, lifting his foot and placing it on the dead's man's back. "Your brother is volatile and has already expressed his dislike of you hanging out with my nephew and the Breakers. I can't see the problem myself. Then again, no one quite knows what the fuck goes on in David's head at the best of times."

"I *hate* him," I seethe. No truer words were spoken and Jeb, being the kind of man he is, recognises that powerful emotion all too well. Hate fuels violence and violence fuels hate. A vicious cycle that people like Jeb thrive in.

"I can see that. Thing is, I'd offer to put a bullet in David's head myself if it wasn't for the fact that he's exceptionally good at his job. Business is booming and I owe a lot of that success to David. Of course, I'd never tell him that. So, I really need to keep him on my side. Hmm..." Jeb taps his chin, thoughtful for a moment.

"He can't hurt my sister... Please, she's just a kid. Isn't there anything you can do? Even if I walked away from the Breakers he'd still find a way to hurt her, to hurt me. I know it. I don't want to lose them, but I can't lose my sister. I can't." I'm shaking so violently now that the tip of my trainer slides into the pool of blood. I yank my foot away, holding back the puke threatening to break free from my mouth.

Jeb nods, watching me closely. "The way I see it, keeping away from the Breakers is your only option. David is a man of his word. I know that. He *will* kill your sister if you break your promise. Now, I can deal with Zayn's broken heart. All he'll need is a few women to fuck and he'd be over you, but I sure as fuck don't need a little girl's murder on my hands." He laughs raucously and I flinch. This isn't funny. None of this is fucking funny.

"Will you help me? I'll keep your secret. I swear to you I will never, ever, tell a soul about anything I saw today. I'll do whatever you want, I swear it."

Jeb nods. "Isn't it ironic. Here I was thinking that I'm going to be indebted to you and now you appear to be indebted to me. Funny how that goes."

"Please. I'll do anything," I repeat, determined to save Lena's life even if that means sacrificing my own happiness. I need to get out of this room and back home to my sister. I need to hold her and know that she's going to be safe.

"Okay, here's what we're going to do. Tonight, I'm going to secure your sister's safety and send your brother away in exchange for your silence. I've got contacts in Mexico and have been looking to widen my net. Your brother is going to run my business over there. It's a win-win on all counts."

"Thank you." I blow out a heavy breath, tears pricking my eyes.

"But, you're still going to dump the Breakers because your brother won't be any good to me if he's obsessing over you and your *friendship* with them." He rolls his eyes at the word, as though such a thing as friendship is insignificant. I suppose for a man like him, it is. "You'll have no contact with them for this moment on."

My heart fucking cracks, bleeding as heavily as the dead man on the floor, but I nod my head anyway. "Okay," I whisper, dropping my head and gritting my teeth against the flow of tears that threaten.

"But you're going to have to do something else for me too," Jeb says, inching closer. He lifts my chin with his finger, forcing me to look at him. "You're going to have to be mine."

"Yours?" I choke, shock filtering into my features.

"Yes, *mine*. Don't worry, Penelope, I don't want to fuck you, but one day I'm going to call in this debt and you're going to have to do what I ask. No fucking questions."

"What do I need to do?"

"Tonight you're going to go out there and walk away from the Breakers. Then you'll work for me here at Rocks and when the time comes, I'll call in the debt. If you fail to do what I ask, then your life and that of your sister is forfeit. Understand?"

"Yeah, I understand."

$\mathcal{E}$

BY THE TIME I make my way back into the main portion of the club with Jeb, it's nearing closing time, even though the club is still pumping. I walk alongside Jeb in a daze, feeling numb. I've gone through a gamut of emotions this evening: joy, fear, hate, desperation, resignation.

Now I feel nothing.

Self-preservation has kicked in and I've buried every thought, every memory of the last three years with the Breakers just so I can survive the night and do what I must.

We walk through the crowd, stopping periodically so that Jeb can greet members of his crew and business acquaintances. Every single one of them stare at me now with interest, noting how Jeb guides me through the crowd with his hand on my lower back. Finally we reach the booth where the

Breakers are sitting. Xeno notices me first, standing abruptly but the second his gaze meets Jeb, he stops dead in his tracks. I drop my gaze, not able to look at the fire burning in Xeno's eyes.

"Good evening, boys. I understand congratulations are in order?"

"Yeah, we won the battle," Zayn says carefully. I can hear the questions in his voice and when I glance up at him, his face is a mixture of relief and confusion. He keeps looking between Jeb and me. Next to him York is watching my face carefully, his face paling when his gaze meets mine. Dax is glaring at Jeb, his hands curled into fists on the table.

"Five grand is a nice tidy sum. I was just saying as much to Penelope here. We've had a good chat, haven't we, pretty?"

I nod my head, forcing my face into a mask. "Yeah."

"Well, I'm gonna grab us all a drink to celebrate. I'll leave you to tell them the good news," Jeb says, and I can see the delight in his eyes as he walks away knowing that I'm about to detonate a bomb on our relationship.

"What the actual fuck, Tiny?!" Xeno growls. "We've been looking for you everywhere and you've been with *Jeb*?"

"I bumped into him. He wanted to buy me a drink and I couldn't say no to the leader of the Skins. You of all people should know that," I fire back, trying to hint at the predicament I'm in without snitching. He just frowns, leaving me hanging.

"Sit down, Kid, before you fall down," Dax remarks after a moment, his tumultuous gaze resting on my face. He knows something's up and as much as I want to tell them all what's happened, I can't. *I can't.*

"Too much to drink, that's all," I say, plastering a smile on my face as I slide into the booth next to Zayn, careful to keep my distance.

"What's the good news you need to tell us about, Titch?" York's ask, his voice cautious.

"Jeb has given me a job here at the club," I respond immediately, plastering a fake smile on my face and hoping he can't read the sheer fucking terror I'm feeling beneath the mask I wear. I'm positive I have droplets of that man's blood covering my dark jeans.

"You don't seem to be happy about it." Xeno points out, narrowing his eyes at me.

"I am happy about it. I can earn some money working behind the bar for a few hours on a weekend night and then dance the rest of the time. It's a no brainer." I fall silent, stuffing my hands beneath my thighs so they can't see them trembling.

Silence descends and I worry my lip not knowing how to bring up the devastating news that we can no longer be friends. Ever. Any minute now, Jeb will return, and he'll have expected me to have done the deed. I glance over at the bar, noticing that Jeb is currently talking to one of his crew. Drawing in a shaky breath I return my attention to the Breakers.

"There's something I need to say," I begin, my voice trembling so much that I have to cough to keep it steady.

"Wait! Before you say a word, we wanted to give you this," Zayn says quickly, reaching into his pocket and pulling out a small black jewellery box, placing it on the table. "Happy Birthday, Pen. This is from *all* of us." There's a smile in his voice that matches the happiness in his eyes. My heart fucking plummets. The evening had started so well, the perfect fucking birthday, winning the battle with the boys I love. Now, the only thing I know for certain is that Lena will remain safe so long as I do what Jeb and David asked.

"What's this?" I whisper, staring at the box, knowing that whatever lies inside is going to break my heart for good.

"Open it, Titch," York says gently, leaning over the table and pushing it towards me.

With trembling hands, I reach for the box and flip open the lid. Inside is a necklace, the thin gold change holding onto the word *Breakers*. My eyes immediately swim with tears, but I blink them back. If I cry, if I give in, I might just confess everything that's transpired tonight, and my sister will die for it.

"Well, ain't that pretty," Jeb says, making me jump. I snap the lid closed on the jewellery box and grasp it in my hand as he places a tray of drinks on the table.

"So, have you told them the good news?" Jeb asks, a wicked smile on his face.

"Yeah, Pen said you offered her a job at Rocks," Xeno comments, his face unreadable.

"That's right." Jeb turns to look at me and it's clear from the sheer joy on his face that he knows I haven't dumped them yet. He hands a drink to each of us, then takes a swig of his. "So what did I interrupt?"

"We were wishing Pen a happy birthday," Zayn says cautiously.

"It's your birthday?!" Jeb exclaims, wrapping his arm around my shoulder and pulling me against his side, planting a kiss on my head. I hear Dax growl, and out of the corner of my eye see York lay his hand on Dax's arm. Xeno's nostrils flare and Zayn looks utterly lost.

"Why didn't you say so?"

Because my sicko brother was confessing his deepest desires and threatening my sister's life, and you were busy shooting the brains out of one of your employees.

"It didn't seem all that important at the time," I whisper, cringing as his fingers start stroking up and down my arm.

"Tiny?" Xeno asks, looking at me with confusion.

I want to tell him what's happened. I want to tell them all, but everything's stacked against us. David won't just kill me and my sister, he'll kill them too if I defy him. Jeb's no different. I tell the Breakers about his secret then we're all dead. That man's lifeless body is proof enough that Jeb has no qualms ending someone's life without any thought or care. He didn't even flinch.

"What, Xeno?" Jeb snaps as the tension rises. He's getting bored and I'm running out of time.

"I have a question for Pen, do you mind...?" he asks Jeb, maintaining the level of respect Jeb has come to expect from his crew members.

"Whatever..." Jeb waves his hand and leans back in his seat. He's fucking loving this, and I hate him. I hate him as much as I hate my brother for putting me in this position.

"Tiny, you remember what I asked you to do?" he says, staring at me intently, just like the others are doing.

"Yes," I whisper, still clutching the necklace in my hand. My heart thunders painfully. I know where this is going and it's killing me. Right now, part of me wishes that Jeb had shot me because this, this is too fucking hard.

"It was a mistake. You don't have to do that anymore. You can have what you want, Tiny."

There's so much hope in his eyes, in all their eyes and I can't help it, my lip starts to wobble, my eyes tearing up. I think about our friendship, about my love for them all. I think about my innocent little sister oblivious to the threat hanging over her head. I think about my brother and his sick, twisted heart. I think about the man with his brains blown out in a room not far from where we're sitting now, and I think about Jeb's threat. Knowing I have no other choice, I take a deep breath and harden my heart so I can break theirs. It's too late.

"No, we can't. I've made my choice," I say, placing the jewellery box back on the table and sliding it away from me.

"And what have you chosen, Titch?" York asks me, his voice even, steady, careful.

I press my eyes shut, forcing back the tears. "None of you. We're over."

"What?!" Zayn snaps, shock making his voice sharp, brittle, *broken*.

"You don't mean that, Kid," Dax adds. There's a crack in his voice that cuts right into my heart.

"Titch..." York begins, but I refuse to look at him.

"It's over. I'm done with you all." I swallow, hardening my features and forcing down every last ounce of emotion deep inside. "This was never going to work. At least now you get to screw as many women as you like without fear of me getting in the way." Bitterness seeps into my words, an ugly and cruel mistress.

"No!" Xeno's fist crashes against the table, making me jump. "What are you doing?"

"I'm moving on. Isn't this what you wanted?" I accuse, forcing myself to forget the fact that there's a necklace sitting on the table that tells me otherwise.

Xeno presses his mouth into a hard line, shock rendering him speechless.

"Titch, what are you saying?" York shakes his head as though trying to clear his thoughts and get a hold of the situation, of me.

Biting on my tongue, I force myself to look at him and pour all of my hate for my brother and David into this one hard stare. He needs to believe me. They all do. "I *don't* love any of you. I don't think I ever really did. Don't embarrass yourselves by chasing after me because I'm done. Understand? We. Are. Over."

All four of them flinch, but I make sure to keep my emotions locked down. I don't buckle under the weight of their obvious hurt, their shock. I refuse to acknowledge the angry tear glinting in Dax's eye or the disappointment in York and Zayn's stare, and I certainly don't entertain the deep well of pain that emits from Xeno's gaze.

"You heard her. Penelope has made her choice, haven't you, pretty girl," Jeb purrs, brushing his lips against the top of my head, before wrapping his arm around my shoulder and guiding me out of the booth. As we walk away, it feels as though every single person in the club is staring at us both. I bet they're thinking the same thing as my Breakers. I'm Jeb's now.

With a broken heart and a heavy soul I leave my Breakers behind.

I don't look back at them, and they don't follow.

CHAPTER THIRTY-THREE

Present Day

DAX WINS THE FIGHT. His opponent didn't stand a chance and is currently sprawled out on the floor with a barely recognisable face. Two men are checking him over as Dax is declared the winner and the room erupts. Some are cheering and others are clearly unhappy, slamming their fists on the table, probably losing thousands of pounds backing the wrong fighter.

"Never fucking loses," Jeb remarks, knocking back the remains of his drink with a sly smile.

It was a brutal fight, violent but swift.

Dax didn't hold back. He went in with aggression and speed and didn't stop until his opponent hit the deck ten minutes later. There's blood everywhere, darkening the already stained canvas and gathering around the guy's head as blood oozes from his mouth and nose. Dax got off lightly with a swelling cheekbone and a split eyebrow that's dripping blood, but is nowhere near as injured as the fighter out cold on the floor. The scene makes my stomach roil. The crowd loved it. I fucking hated every second. It might have been a quick fight, but it lasted an eternity for me.

Fighting to survive, to protect someone you care about is one thing. Fighting to inflict pain, to maim or kill, for *dirty* money, is something altogether different. I can't correlate the man I see before me in the cage to the boy I bonded with as kids. Yes, he always had a violent streak when pushed too far, but that was born out of necessity, never desire. Underneath all of the provoked aggression was just a kid desperate for a home that provided safety, and parents who loved him. Right now, that boy is nowhere to be found, because the man I see before me enjoyed every second of this fight. Like a caged animal, Dax paces back and forth, shaking out his arms, rolling his head on his shoulders and fucking grinning at the audience with blood-stained teeth.

Every punch he threw reminded me of the ones I endured at the hands of my brother. The sound of Dax's knuckles splitting his opponents skin, and the crack of bones breaking beneath the force of his wrath stirring up memories that I've tried so fucking hard to bury. I might not be a stranger to getting into scrapes over the years, I stuck up for myself on the street when I needed to, and fought for the ones I loved, but I never, *ever* enjoyed it.

"See, fucking brutal," Jeb whispers against my ear. I stiffen, revolted by the sheer joy in his voice and the salacious way his words caress my skin.

"I need to go to the bathroom," I suddenly say, wanting to

remove my mask, to breathe deeply and settle my nerves as anxiety and memories from that night three years ago threaten to drown me. The blood on the canvas, the glowing red of the skulls on their masks, the heady violence in the air proves too fucking much. My skin crawls, my teeth grind, and my fingers curl into fists as my nails bury into the skin of my palm, seeking pain to numb the fear. If I don't find a moment to control the crawling fingers of trauma, I'll fucking crumble. I refuse to allow myself to do that. Not here, not now.

Zayn stands, Jeb getting up with him. Xeno and York watching us both.

"I'll take her, *Sir*," Jeb says with amusement.

Zayn nods once, then sits back down. I can feel them watching us as Jeb leads me to a darkened corner of the warehouse. Pushing through a door in front of me, Jeb steps into a bathroom that is surprisingly well decorated for a warehouse in the middle of nowhere.

I rip off my face mask and breathe in deeply, sucking in a lungful of air. "What the hell is going on?" I ask Jeb, forgetting for a moment that he is in fact the leader of the Skins and not Zayn who's just acting like it.

"I thought that would be obvious," he chuckles, leaning against the vanity.

"I don't mean the fight..." I grind out.

"You need to loosen up, pretty girl. Violence is in our blood," he remarks, removing his mask and gloves and avoiding my question as he pulls out a small cellophane bag from his pocket that's filled with white powder. Jeb dips his little finger into the baggy and rubs the powder along his gums. "This is fucking good shit. Newest delivery of cocaine from your dear brother, David. How is he by the way?"

"Much the same," I say vaguely, not willing to get into a conversation about my brother. Not when I have so many questions. Nothing tonight is making any sense. Why is Zayn pretending to be Jeb when everyone's identity is hidden anyway? Grim appears to have a handle on the situation. There won't be any blood spilt tonight other than in the cage. Then again, what the fuck do I know? Anything could happen.

"You managed to calm your brother down?" Jeb asks me, drawing me out of my head.

"Yes."

"Good." Stepping close to me, Jeb pushes back a strand of sweaty hair away from my forehead. "You know I appreciate you playing along tonight..."

"Playing along?" I ask, not liking the look of glee in his eyes.

"Zayn is doing a fucking excellent job as my doppelgänger, don't you think?"

"Why though? I don't understand. Everyone's identity is hidden."

"You don't need to understand, pretty girl. You just need to put that mask back on and follow me," he says, pulling his own mask back on, the red neon flickering on the moment he pulls it over his head.

When we head back into the warehouse, Dax is no longer in the cage. Instead there are five topless women dancing provocatively to the music that's now playing out over the speakers. It's a low, sultry beat with a sensual base that vibrates up through the floor. The atmosphere has changed dramatically. It's like all that violence has bled into a different kind of passion. Debauchery unravels around us as a dense kind of heat envelopes the space. In the corners of the warehouse fires are lit in oil barrels, and from the ceiling women dressed in nothing more than lingerie are hanging from lengths of black silk, performing acrobatics that would impress me if there weren't people fucking at every table.

Everywhere I look there are women spread out across the surfaces, their masks askew, their short dresses lifted up to reveal peachy arses and glistening cunts. Some of the gangsters are feasting on their women, their tongues deep inside of them, and some are fucking their women from different angles whilst others look on, their hands firmly gripped around their cocks, jacking off. One of the female gangsters has a man on his knees in front of her, whilst he eats her out.

"It's a fucking orgy," I blurt out, cold dread covering my skin.

"No, just a damn good party," Jeb laughs, his lascivious voice making my skin crawl.

Stopping for a moment, he grips my arm, pulling me up sharp. "You know you really *did* fuck the Breakers up, Penelope."

"Don't talk to *me* about fucking the Breakers up," I snap, biting my tongue to prevent me from saying something that's going to get me killed.

"They were never quite the same after you dumped them. I didn't realise quite how special you were to them until that night," he continues.

"I didn't want to hurt them."

"But you did."

"I had no choice," I grind out, not wanting to have this conversation with *him* of all people.

He waves his hand in the air, dismissing my remark as we traverse through the tables once more. "They were always so reluctant to really let their true nature out when they were friends with you, but the moment you screwed them over they didn't hold back. They show no mercy to our enemies, and I have you to thank for that. Without you as their conscience they were set free."

"Set free?" I scoff, wanting to hurt him with words brimming on my tongue, but knowing it would be a pointless exercise. Jeb has no conscience. He doesn't give a shit. Nothing I could say would make him feel any guilt and anything I do will only give him ammunition to hurt me further. So, I hold my tongue.

"Anyway, I decided that they deserved a little RNR for all the work they've done for me over the years. When I heard Grim was throwing one of her infamous parties, I figured it'd be a good way to let them know just how much I appreciate them."

"Well, aren't you the perfect boss. Illegal fighting and live porno, just what the doctor ordered," I grind out under my breath.

Jeb laughs so loudly that he draws the attention of the gangsters sitting at the table closest to us. They're wearing white skull masks that cover only half their faces. One of them looks at me, his gaze travelling lazily up from my feet to my chest, then stopping on Jeb's tight grip on my arm. His gaze flicks up and he smiles at me. All his teeth are gold. Every single one.

Ignoring his salacious gaze, I snatch my arm out of Jeb's hold and stride towards our table on the other side of the warehouse.

He catches up with me, grasping my arm once more. "I have big, big plans for you, Penelope, and I'm willing to overlook your sassy mouth tonight. But test me, and I'll make this so much worse for you."

"I want to go home," I reply, firmly. My chest is heaving with anger and that acidic trickle of fear I always feel around Jeb. The debt I owe is a ball and chain that imprisons me, something that I won't ever be able to escape until it's paid off in full. The problem is, I still don't know the price.

"Home? You're not going anywhere tonight, Penelope. You, sweetheart, are going to put on the best show of your life," Jeb explains with an evil smile.

"My best show?"

"That's right, pretty girl. The leader of the Skins can't come to a party like this and not partake now, can he? What would everyone think, hmm? Besides, Zayn is my blood, and I owe him a gift. Tonight that gift is you."

My head snaps around to meet Jeb's gaze. "No, please," I whisper, backing away from him as realisation dawns.

"Zayn jumped at the chance to have you. Perhaps he'll fuck you out of his system for good. We'll just have to see."

"That bastard!" I seethe.

That apology in the limo was because he *knew* what was going to happen here tonight. He fucking knew and he thought that would be enough to absolve him from his guilt.

Fuck him.

How could he agree to *this*? Are the rest of the Breakers here so they can fucking watch? Is this some twisted, fucked up punishment to get back at me?

"I must say, I'm mighty curious about how this will all pan

out. I never gave my permission for the others to enjoy you. Perhaps I'll let them all have a go at fucking your sweet pussy tonight."

"Fuck you," I bite out, my voice cracking and my stupid, stupid heart shattering with the threat. Stepping away from Jeb, I ready myself to run. He tuts, wagging his finger and shaking his head, loving every second.

"Don't even think about running from *me*."

But I don't listen, I do run.

Kicking off my ridiculous heels, I sprint through the crowded space, shoving people out of the way and careening past people fucking like animals. My body thunders with adrenaline that pours inside my veins and blurs my vision. Tears prick at my eyes as the full weight of what's about to happen crashes over me.

But I'm not fast enough. No one gets away from Jeb. No one.

He moves with lightning speed and before I know it, my arms are pinned behind my back roughly as he brushes his lips against my ear.

"Consider this the first down payment of your debt, pretty girl."

THE STORY CONTINUES IN LYRICAL. Available now.

AUTHOR NOTE

So, what did you think? I hope you've recovered from the cliffy and don't hate me too much! If you enjoyed the book, please do consider leaving a review.

As always, thank you for continuing on this journey with me and my characters. Most days I'm still awed that people actually want to read what I write. So, to you, dear reader, I am indebted.

To be certain that you keep up to date with all my new releases and author news, please do come and join my Facebook group, *Queen Bea's Hive*, where I'm most active.

Once again, thanks for sticking with me. Here's to plenty more stories to come.

Love, Bea xoxo

ABOUT BEA PAIGE

Bea Paige lives a very secretive life in London... She likes red wine and Haribo sweets (preferably together) and occasionally swings around poles when the mood takes her.

Bea loves to write about love and all the different facets of such a powerful emotion. When she's not writing about love and passion, you'll find her reading about it and ugly crying.

Bea is always writing, and new ideas seem to appear at the most unlikely time, like in the shower or when driving her car.

She has lots more books planned, so be sure to subscribe to her newsletter:

beapaige.co.uk/newsletter-sign-up

ALSO BY BEA PAIGE

Grim & Beast's Duet

1 Tales You Win

#2 Heads You Lose

Their Obsession Duet (dark reverse harem)

#1 The Dancer and The Masks

#2 The Masks and The Dancer

Academy of Stardom

(friends-to-enemies-lovers reverse harem)

#1 Freestyle

#2 Lyrical

#3 Breakers

#4 Finale

Academy of Misfits

(bully/academy reverse harem)

#1 Delinquent

#2 Reject

For all up to date book releases please visit

www.beapaige.co.uk

Lightning Source UK Ltd.
Milton Keynes UK
UKHW021047210822
407563UK00003B/264

9 781915 493002